"Let me buy you

Susan's sanity came b
of the company for which she worked. Susan forgot that she could leave and get another job. She knew what it was to be an employee and to be the owner of a business.

"I think I've had enough to drink," she said. "I'm ready to go home."

"So you're going to escape my presence the way you did at the wedding?"

Her head came up to stare at him. Instead of seeing a reprimand in his eyes, she was greeted with a smile.

A devastating smile.

It churned her insides, not the way Fred had done for her, but with need and the fact that it had been a long time since she met a man with as much sexual magnetism as André Thorn. No wonder he fit the bill as a playboy.

Shirley Hailstock began her writing life as a lover of reading. She likes nothing better than to find a quiet corner where she can get lost in a book, explore new worlds and visit places she never expected to see. As an author, she can not only visit those places, but she can be the heroine of her own stories. The author of forty novels and novellas, Shirley has received numerous awards, including a National Readers' Choice Award, a Romance Writers of America's Emma Merritt Award and an *RT Book Reviews* Career Achievement Award. Shirley's books have appeared on several bestseller lists, including the *Glamour*, *Essence* and *Library Journal* lists. She is a past president of Romance Writers of America.

Books by Shirley Hailstock

Harlequin Kimani Romance

His Love Match
Someone Like You
All He Needs
Love in Logan Beach
Love in San Francisco
Love in New York

Visit the Author Profile page
at Harlequin.com for more titles.

SHIRLEY HAILSTOCK

and

JANICE SIMS

Love in New York &
Cherish My Heart

HARLEQUIN® KIMANI™ ROMANCE

ISBN-13: 978-1-335-99880-4

Love in New York & Cherish My Heart

PLEASE RECYCLE • THIS PRODUCT IS RECYCLABLE •

Recycling programs for this product may not exist in your area

This edition published by arrangement with Harlequin Books S.A.

For questions and comments about the quality of this book, please contact us at CustomerService@Harlequin.com.

Printed in U.S.A.

CONTENTS

To Glenda Howard,
who's helped me in ways even she doesn't know.

LOVE IN NEW YORK

Shirley Hailstock

Dear Reader,

We all have at least one vice. Mine is the lottery. I play it, but I don't purchase more than two tickets. Even when the jackpot is eight or nine figures, I only buy two tickets.

Have you ever wondered how your life would change if you suddenly became rich? This happens to Susan Dewhurst, forcing her to leave her home country. After several years and a new career, Susan is back in New York, where she takes a job at the House of Thorn. Running into André Thorn wasn't in the cards. And if she thought her life changed when she was in Europe, find out what she's in for when she and André are in close quarters.

I hope you enjoy this second book in the House of Thorn series.

Sincerely yours,

Shirley Hailstock

Chapter 1

Starting over was harder than Susan Dewhurst had expected it to be. After two years in Europe, returning to her home country should have been a snap.

But it wasn't.

Pushing aside the sheer curtains of her Manhattan bedroom, she took in the breathtaking skyline of the city that never sleeps. Susan wasn't a native New Yorker. She wasn't even Susan Dewhurst. Until a couple of years ago, she'd been Marcia Atherton, who had been content running her own art-and-photo-framing business. But that had all changed on a warm summer evening, when the lottery results had been displayed on the flat-screen television in her small apartment above her store.

Propelled from her seat, she'd danced around the living room, shouting at the top of her lungs, as if there was no one in the building who'd be disturbed. She'd felt like a kid who was allowing the thrill of getting her desired Christmas present to burst forward.

She was a millionaire. Even after the government had taken its tax cut, she'd walked away with over fifteen millions dollars. Her life was set, right?

Wrong.

Susan panned the skyline. From the sixteenth floor, she was too high to hear the street noise. A smile tugged at her lips, even though she remembered the reason she was in Manhattan and not in Mountainview, Montana, where she'd once had a business. Susan wouldn't say she had been happily poor. That would be an oxymoron.

A few years ago she'd had a struggling framing company. The economy had taken a lot of her business, but she had been covering the bills by constantly changing the due dates and using creative methods she hadn't learned in her finance classes, back in college. Then the fire had happened. That was the end. Even after the insurance settlement, she couldn't rebuild.

But life, or rather the lottery drawing, had saved her from bankruptcy. On the downside, all of that money had forced her to flee the country. She was back now and living in a city where she could be both rich and anonymous.

* * *

The five Thorn brothers stood next to each other, according to age, watching the white water churn behind the huge cruise ship heading out of New York Harbor. Their parents could no longer be seen on board, yet the brothers remained at the guardrail. André wondered what the others were thinking. Their parents were the anchors of the family, and they were sailing out of sight.

"What now?" David asked.

"It's all up to us," André replied. His words were braver than he felt. Doubt clenched his heart. Was he good enough to manage it alone? He had the flagship store. The entire reputation of the House of Thorn rested with him. And he had sole responsibility. In a day or two the others would leave and return to their stores. Their parents had always been there for advice, but they were officially on vacation, and he now held the keys to the largest and most successful store of the House of Thorn.

Blake clamped a hand on André's shoulder.

"We can handle it," David said. "We have to."

André looked left and right from his place at the center of the group. His two cousins, whom they thought of as brothers, stood to his left. Carter and Christian, who were twins, had come to live with them after their parents had died, and they were now going to head stores in Montana and Washington, DC. David and Blake, André's brothers, had already experienced the growing pains the Logan Beach and San

Francisco stores required. André didn't know what his challenges would be, but he planned to be vigilant about keeping track of any change in the store's status. He didn't want his parents returning in a year to find the anchor store in less stellar condition than it was when they'd left.

"You're not alone," Rose said from behind them. The five men turned, with all eyes trained on David's wife. David moved to her and slipped his arm around her waist.

"You need a plan," Ellie Thorn, Blake's wife, said. Blake mimicked David's action by slipping his arms around Ellie and kissing her on the temple.

"And you've got us," Carter said.

André raised one eyebrow. "I'm not sure that's a positive thing."

"And you two are going to have your hands full with your own stores," David said.

"We've always had our parents behind us, there to reply to or discuss any issues that came up. Now we're on our own."

"It's sink-or-swim time," David said.

"You should talk," André replied. "You have Rose to back you up."

"Yep," he agreed. "She's a wonder."

David's wife wasn't just a wonder; she was running the Logan Beach store, while David managed a community law practice. André wished he was lucky enough to find someone who could love him and be a partner in the business. But most of the women he met saw his bank account before they saw him.

Turning from the pier, André took in the huge buildings that defined New York. Despite his brother's comments, he knew he was in this alone. Sure, he had their support, but they were scattered about the country, managing their own businesses and relationships. The twins were the youngest, just out of college, and likely to need the most help. And even though the four other Thorn brothers would be there for André in case of any emergencies, the flagship store was his responsibility, and he had to make sure it still maintained its high status when his parents returned to this port, a year from now.

André was late and it was Blake's fault. The two had been talking, and André had lost track of time. After checking his watch, André took the stairs two by two. The new-employee orientation was on the mezzanine level, and he was late. The store felt different now that his parents were no longer available for impromptu discussions on store issues.

He was alone.

The weight of the store was on his shoulders. André shrugged it off as he slowly opened the door and slipped inside. He stood against the back wall. Emily Sheffield, the human-resources director, nodded to him without missing a word of her practiced speech.

“Let me introduce our store president,” Emily said a moment later.

André only needed to say hello, welcome them to the store, ask for questions—of which there were rarely any—and then leave to return to his office.

Emily called his name and extended her arm toward him, as if he was a rock star and she was the mistress of ceremony.

He came forward, to a smattering of applause, and gave his customary welcome message. Before he’d finished his first sentence, he saw *her*. He had been sure the two of them would never meet again, so what was she doing at the new-employee orientation meeting?

André hoped his presentation was as flawless as Emily’s when it came to dealing with distractions during the session. Their routine was that André would come into the room just as the meeting started. André was taken by surprise when he saw the woman who’d upended a tray of champagne glasses and covered him with the bubbly wine at a wedding a few months ago.

“Any questions?” he asked. His glance went to Emily. She was an efficient employee, and after conducting these meetings once a month for the last ten years, she’d already answered almost everything new employees would need to know.

Today was no different. There were no hands in the air. André made eye contact with the woman from the wedding. She looked directly at him, but he detected no questioning glance in her eyes. He wondered what department she was in.

"Then welcome to the House of Thorn." After he had finished his standard address, he would usually exit the room. There was always something pressing in the office that needed his attention. Taking another moment, he looked around. Emily's raised eyebrow told him she noticed that his actions were different from usual.

The two worked like a team. Emily's expression told him he'd gone off the script. He was ad-libbing, and she did not approve.

André smiled and, with a second glance at the woman, left the room. What was she doing here? Why would she need a job? She'd been wearing a Christian Siriano gown at the wedding. The classic royal blue sequined gown had showed off every curve of her body. André had noticed, and not just because he was in retail. His hands had come out when she had upended the tray, in hopes of preventing the spillage, but the worst of the champagne had soaked into his tuxedo.

The dress could have been borrowed, he thought, or even rented. After all, she hadn't offered to pay for the cleaning of the tux, as people usually did when they stained something. His parents had instilled that in him during one of his many childhood antics. Still, the way she had carried herself spoke of someone used to having a lot of money. He didn't mean that she seemed conceited or entitled, just that there was a certain aura to women like her. Then his mind came back to the orientation. If she was what he'd initially thought her to be, why would she need a job?

André was still thinking of it when he entered his office. His desk was littered with reports, letters and catalogues that required his attention. After sitting down, he accessed his personnel file and looked up employees who'd been hired within the last month. Thankfully, photos were a requirement on personnel files. He found her photo quickly and read the name under it. Susan Dewhurst worked in the furniture department and had been employed for three weeks.

André sighed. He hadn't thought of her since the incident at the wedding, yet in the conference room, he'd singled her out. He knew what that meant. Even though she had the aura of class and privilege, that didn't mean it was true. She could be just another gold digger out for a meal ticket. His mouth twisted unconsciously. Why else would someone who wore a gown that cost more than some people's annual salaries take a job in the furniture department?

Sitting back in his chair, André laced his fingers. He stared at the computer screen, but his mind saw Susan Dewhurst walking toward him in a blue sequined Christian Siriano. He knew he should leave it alone, but he wasn't that kind of man. He needed to know what her story was. But no matter how well he remembered the shape of her body in that gown, he'd keep an emotional distance. He could do that. Hadn't he been doing it since his former fiancée, Gail Collins, had ripped the rose-colored glasses from his face and showed him the real reason she wanted to be the next Mrs. Thorn?

He had recognized her, Susan thought as the meeting broke up and people began angling toward the exit doors. The conference room was tucked behind one of the departments. It had huge windows that looked out on Fifth Avenue, but the inside doors were concealed. Susan hung back from the group, not really needing to speak to anyone. She didn't want to find André Thorn on the outside. He was known for being friendly, for knowing his employees, and for remembering names and faces.

He'd looked directly into her face. And she had no doubt that he knew who she was. Though, maybe not her name. They hadn't gotten as far as exchanging names, although everyone at the wedding had been aware of the young playboy heir to the famous department stores. That he remembered with vivid clarity how she'd spilled champagne all over his suit, then escaped the wedding as if fearing a fire, was in no doubt.

"Susan?" Emily called her name.

She turned to look at the human-resources director.

"Do you have a question?"

Susan dropped her shoulders. The tension she felt remained, although outwardly she looked calm. "I'm fine," she said. "Just looking at the city."

Susan headed for the door.

"That's right," Emily said, as if remembering something. "You haven't been here long."

Susan's gesture was noncommittal. She hadn't been in the city long. She'd spent the last two years in Europe, mainly Paris, France, and Verona, Italy. Emily didn't need to know why Susan had gone to Europe or the truth of why she had returned to the United States. Protecting herself from unwanted questions had become so automatic that Susan did it without thinking.

Back in the furniture department, Susan was still on edge. She shouldn't be. She didn't need this job, but she also didn't want to be fired. Susan was now one of the rich, but her memory often reminded her of her former day-to-day existence.

She'd gone to the House of Thorn store to shop and had interviewed on a whim, never expecting to be hired and thinking that even if they made an offer, she probably wouldn't take the job. Yet everything had worked in her favor, and she was here. Her plan was to meet new people, find some friends. In the six months she'd lived in New York, all she'd done was shop, mostly at the House of Thorn, and decorate her apartment. Now she expected the store's president to personally terminate her.

By the time she had removed her name tag and dropped her access ID into her purse as she'd prepared to leave for the evening, she was still employed, and she hadn't seen André Thorn.

"Susan, it's Friday. A few of us always stop for drinks and appetizers across the street. Would you like to join us?" Dawn Reed, a short redhead who worked in her department, asked. Susan had been in the store for three weeks, and tonight was the first time she'd been invited.

In a split second, Susan decided to go. "I'd love to," she said. Her purpose in taking the job in the store was to meet people, so she shouldn't turn her back on an invitation when it appeared.

Drinks turned out to be happy hour at a little pub not far from the store. The place was packed, and as the hour progressed, more and more people poured in. Susan found herself packed into a booth, next to Fred Lang from the marketing department. Fred's subtle moves went from suggestions to innuendo to outright requests. She turned them all down.

She had to get out of the booth and possibly leave the group. She decided to go to the ladies' room, then return and give her regrets. She got up, slid past two other people, who were both jovial with drink and the vision of having two days off, and reached the edge of the bench seat. Unfortunately, Fred was directly behind her.

"Fred, I'm going to the ladies' room. You can't follow me there," Susan told him.

As she turned to find her way through the crowd, she came up short against the white-shirted chest of another man.

"Excuse me," she said, looking up. André Thorn stood in front of her.

"Well," he said. "This time there isn't a waiter carrying a tray of champagne."

"I apologized for that," she said, with anger coming to her aid. She was already annoyed with Fred and had been expecting this sword to drop all day. Because she was unprepared to have it fall when she thought she was safe, her sarcasm was stronger than she had expected it to be. "Please excuse me."

She moved to go around him, but he stepped sideways, blocking her escape.

"Let me buy you a drink."

Susan's sanity came back to her. This was the president of the company for which she worked. Susan forgot that she could leave and get another job. She knew what it was to be an employee and to be the owner of a business.

"I think I've had enough to drink," she said. "I'm ready to go home."

"So you're going to escape my presence, the way you did at the wedding?"

Her head came up to stare at him. Instead of seeing a reprimand in his eyes, she was greeted with a smile.

A devastatingly handsome smile.

It churned her insides, not the way Fred had done for her, but with need and the fact that it had been a long time since she had met a man with as much sexual magnetism as André Thorn. No wonder he fit the bill as a playboy.

"I guess I am," Susan finally said. From the corner of her eye, she saw Fred sliding out of the booth again. He had to know who André Thorn was, but if he planned to put his arm around her in front of another man, he was sadly mistaken. "Excuse me," she said and hurried away.

Susan stood in front of the bathroom mirrors. She freshened makeup that didn't need it, stalling for time. Why had she reacted to André Thorn that way? Embarrassment, she rationalized. She'd run into him at her friend Ryder's wedding. Judging from where he sat in the church, he must have known Ryder's bride, Melanie. He would. Frowning at her reflection, she chided herself for the unbidden thought. It was a total accident that she had slipped and tipped the waiter's tray filled with champagne glasses. He'd reached for her, and the comedy of flying glasses and fumbling hands and feet would have made her laugh if it had happened in a movie. But it had happened to her—to them. And there was nothing funny about it.

Too embarrassed to do anything but apologize and leave, Susan had rushed away to try to remove the splashes that had hit her dress and shoes. She hadn't returned.

Never expecting to see the unnamed man again, she had felt surprised when their eyes had connected across the orientation room, but the recognition had been instant. And now she had to return to the bar, where he was. Snapping her purse closed, she went back to her group. It was thinner, with a few people having left while she'd been in the bathroom. Fred was not one of them. He immediately stood to allow her to slide back into the bench seat.

"Please sit back down," she said. "I'm afraid I have to be leaving." The group looked at her without censure.

"Not yet," Fred said. "Just one more drink."

"I've had my limit," she lied. "And I have a lot to do tomorrow, so I need to get going." Before Fred could protest further, she picked up her sweater and said good-night.

Unfortunately, she had to pass the table where André and several other guys were sitting. From the look of several of them, they had to be related. Susan had learned something about the House of Thorn. She knew there were stores in several major cities and that André had brothers who ran those stores.

She smiled as she neared the table. André stepped out of the booth and away from the group. Susan knew it would be rude to slip past him, but she didn't want to engage in a conversation. They had nothing, except an overturned tray and a wedding, in common. Her steps slowed as she approached him.

"Don't run away yet," he said, opening his arms as if to stop her if she tried to get around him.

Susan looked him directly in the eye, but didn't say anything.

"I just want to introduce myself, since you're working at the store. André Thorn," he said.

"Susan Dewhurst," she replied. "Although, you were introduced this afternoon."

"I know all of the staff, and I wanted to personally greet you and welcome you to our family of employees."

"Thank you. I've only been here for a few weeks, but it seems like a good place to work." She glanced over her shoulder, at the booth of coworkers she'd just left. "There are a couple of other newbies at that table over there. Maybe you want to go and introduce yourself to them too. I have to run now." Susan slipped her sweater over her shoulders and smiled. "Good night, Mr. Thorn."

As she opened the door, she heard a whoop of laughter from the direction where André stood. Were they laughing at her?

"Ah-ha." Blake's hand clamped on André's shoulder. "Someone who doesn't bow to your charms. We've got to meet this Wonder Woman."

André's brothers laughed. He did too, but he didn't think it was funny. He knew his reputation within the family. They all thought he was the love-'em-and-leave-'em type. Nothing could be further from the truth. He was cautious. He knew why most women wanted to go out with him, and he wanted to be sure of a woman before he fell in love with her.

After slipping back into his seat, André sipped his

drink, forcing himself not to glance at the door where Susan had exited. He wondered about her. She'd intrigued him at the wedding, and she was a mystery to him now. He wasn't used to women running away from him. As Blake had pointed out, rarely did a woman want to avoid him. Was she acting?

He mentally shook his head. If she'd known who he was, and he was sure she had, then she'd have made contact with him long before now. He frowned. Maybe she was just shrewder than the others were. Maybe she'd taken a job at the House of Thorn to get close to him.

André shook his head. That sounded arrogant. He wasn't arrogant. He was cautious.

"André," Blake said, interrupting his thoughts. "You're not still thinking about that woman, are you?" Blake glanced toward the door. André's eyes followed, but Blake's position obstructed his view. He knew she wasn't there. It was the last place she had stood. For some reason, he felt her presence would still be there.

"Of course not." André covered his lie by taking a drink. Then he shifted toward his brothers and toasted them with his glass. While he'd given the answer Blake had expected, he continued to think about Susan. Why was it that she seemed to run in the opposite direction whenever he came near her? And why was he allowing it to matter?

The store was super busy on Saturdays. André liked to get in early. He'd review the sales reports and check the analysis on special offers and clearance items. He'd review proposals from the various departments in preparation for the Monday-morning meetings. Then, when the doors opened to customers, he'd walk through the various departments. That was the part he liked best. He'd done it since he was a boy, and he loved the store.

And it was time.

After checking the clock on his desk, André stood up. Glancing through the window, he looked at the streets below. They were teeming with people, as they always were. Day or night, there were always crowds on the street. And in one minute, they would begin pouring through the doors.

André began his morning ritual. He loved the tourists who came in and considered everything. More of them bought goods to take back to their homes than not. And they either went for the souvenirs or the really expensive items. From a young age, André had learned to pick out who bought inexpensive gold necklaces and who headed for items like handmade, soft-as-butter, designer boots. He could tell a man who shopped for his wife from the one who was there to buy his mistress an expensive piece of jewelry or a designer negligee. He could distinguish a grandmother buying for her grandchild from a mother-in-law shopping for a son-in-law or daughter-in-law she didn't like. He could also tell the one who did like their son or daughter's choice of a spouse.

He'd reached the furniture department. Naturally,

Susan came to mind. She wasn't there. He wondered if she was on the schedule for this Saturday. New employees usually got the weekend hours. He waved and smiled at several employees in the area. Since he didn't see Susan, he could only assume she had the day off.

The first customers got off the elevator and entered the department. They were a couple, and they were looking at one of the beds. Again, André wondered about Susan. Why was he obsessing over her? Why did she keep coming to the front of his mind? Was she genuine, or was she just like the others? He didn't know. With all of his knowledge about people, he couldn't tell a real relationship from one based on his bank account.

During the course of his walk, he spoke with more and more department heads and a few customers. When he got to the first floor, the place was teeming with people—mostly tourists, he assumed. They were at the perfume counters and the makeup areas, and a few looked through the glass cases in the jewelry department. The only place left to inspect was the exterior of the building. The revolving doors were swinging so rapidly, he was practically forced out onto the street. As usual, the tourists were looking in the windows, while locals rushed to take care of errands. André turned left. He would check the windows. The staff had themes for the Fifth Avenue side of the building, but along the side street, there were daily changes.

Just as he turned, he stopped short. Across the street was a woman with a camera. That in itself was not unusual. The reason he had stopped was that the woman he saw was Susan. She had a tripod set up and was taking timed shots of the building. There was so much movement on the street, she couldn't be taking photos of people.

André saw the traffic light turn green and rushed across the street with the mass of people.

"Susan," he said.

She turned. He saw her smile. Then she raised a camera that was hanging around her neck and snapped a picture.

"I didn't know you were a photographer," he said, stopping in front of her. Her eyes were clear and brown, and he took in the violet color of her lipstick, which matched her dress. Her lips called to him with an urgency so strong, he clasped his hands behind his back.

"It's something I picked up in Europe and love doing."

"So, you're taking a photo of the store?"

"I've taken several. It's really an architecturally beautiful building."

So was she, André thought, but instead of having hard edges like the building, she had soft, rounded curves. André cast his eyes toward the upper edge of the House of Thorn's New York store to keep from allowing her to see the appraisal in his eyes.

He heard a shutter open and close in succession

and knew she'd taken another picture of him. He looked at her.

"Is this how you spend your days off?"

"Mostly." She smiled. "New York is hard, though. Every picture you take is already a postcard."

"And still, photographers and tourists take their own." He glanced at the street encompassing the crowd of tourists, many looking up, mostly with cell-phone cameras, recording their own versions of stock footage. Turning back, he faced Susan just in time for her to snap another photo. "You won't find that on a postcard," André said.

Susan smiled.

André looked at her camera as she was about to raise it again. "Is that a Hasselblad?" he asked, unnecessarily. The name was written in silver lettering above the lens. André didn't know much about photography, but he recognized the expensive camera.

"It was a gift," she explained.

André's brows rose. "That must have been a very good friend." The camera looked too new to be secondhand.

"I studied photography for a while."

"You must be good at it." André wondered if she was being careful with her words. He felt there was more to this story. Who'd give her such an expensive camera? How close had she been to that person? He felt an arrow of jealousy go through him. Shifting position, he pushed it aside. She worked for him. There would be nothing between them.

"I'm afraid I have to go," she said, packing the tripod and camera into a bag. "I'm meeting someone and I don't want to be late."

He watched as she walked away, unable to stop himself from seeing what direction she went. Or from taking note of the way her body swayed as the pants she wore outlined every curve of her slim frame.

André didn't stop checking her out until she turned a corner and was out of sight. Mentally, he shook himself. He shouldn't have the thoughts for Susan that he did. He'd been able to exclude every other woman who worked in the store from his mind. But Susan was someone different. He didn't know why. But he was a red-blooded American male, and she fit the bill of a hot woman.

Lord, did she make him hot.

Chapter 2

Susan saw her coming through the lens of her camera. She'd have recognized Minette Marchand anywhere. She was the image of her father, only with a mane of dark curly hair. Jerome Marchand had once had the same color hair, but at fifty-five his hair was salt-and-pepper. He looked more like a distinguished college professor than a world-renowned photographer.

"Minette," Susan called, moving the camera from her face.

The woman who was about Susan's age smiled and walked faster toward her. "Hi," she said.

The single word brought Susan home, like so many references she hadn't heard in years did. In Europe things had been more formal—the words weren't truncated or reduced to shortened phrases.

"I'm Susan. Thank you for meeting me. I met your father in Italy, and he's told me so many things about you."

"Really?" She frowned. The expression on Minette's face froze, and she dropped her eyes to hide it. Susan knew Minette and Jerome were estranged, but Jerome loved his daughter, and Susan wasn't sure the woman knew how much.

"He's got photos of you all over his studio."

Minette took a moment and then cleared her throat. Susan wondered if an unexpected emotion had caught her unaware. "I see you're a photographer, too."

"I am." Susan smiled. She glanced at her camera. "I have your father to thank for that. He took me under his wing in Italy and taught me everything about the camera and good photographs."

"Is he a good teacher?" she asked.

"Excellent. Didn't he teach you things?"

Minette took a moment to glance up at the sky. Susan followed her gaze. A moment later, Minette looked her straight in the eye. "I haven't seen him in years."

"Do you know he's thinking about coming back?" Susan asked.

The two began to stroll toward the river. Susan occasionally lifted the camera and snapped a photo.

"He eluded to it when he wrote about you being in New York."

"How do you feel about that?" Susan asked. She saw the surprise on Minette's face. "He told me the two of you weren't on the best of terms."

"I suppose you two talked a lot."

Susan heard the disapproval in her voice. "We did, but if you're thinking I replaced you as a daughter, you couldn't be more wrong. First he was my friend, when I really needed a friend. Then he was my teacher and mentor. But he loved you, and while he's never said it to me, I think he needs you."

"He's never needed me in the past."

Susan stopped walking. "Do you really believe that?"

"If not, why did he leave me? Why did he go all the way to Italy and never reach out to me?"

"I don't know. What I do know is your father is a wonderful, compassionate man. I believe he has a reason. And I believe the two of you should talk about it when he arrives."

She sighed, as if she'd been through this before. "He'll be too busy. Whenever he does one of these shows, he has no time for anything or anyone except his photographs."

Susan smiled. "Just keep an open mind and talk honestly with him."

"I'll try," Minette said. "Now, I know you've been in the city for a long while, but I'll bet you haven't seen much of it."

She was wrong. Susan was a tourist at heart, and before getting her job at the House of Thorn, she'd visited many of the monuments and places of interest, but she didn't say that. She knew that even if she lived in this city for the rest of her life, she'd never see it all.

"I've got my camera." Susan raised it in one hand. "Let's go."

Susan sat comfortably on the sofa in her living room. The fact that Minette had walked her all over Manhattan and she could barely get up was beside the point. The curtains were open and the lights of the city helped to soothe her. A cup of tea was close to her hand, and her laptop rested on her knees. As Jerome had taught her, she reviewed the photos she'd taken that day. There were many of Minette, Rockefeller Center, the skyline from the top of the Empire State Building and other places they had visited, but time and again she returned to the photo of André.

He was smiling as he walked toward her. The photo felt so real. Susan could almost see him step out of it and speak to her. She'd had these kinds of photos before. Jerome called them wall images. As raw images, they were ready for framing. Susan smiled at the man in the picture. The sun was high and warm, and he walked east. Sunlight illuminated his features, showing the brightness of his brown eyes and the breadth of his strong shoulders.

Susan put the photo down and concentrated on the view. Moments later, André Thorn was back on her mind. Why did she keep thinking of him? She hadn't been this conscious of a man in a long while. Not with the secret she held. The only person who knew her real identity was Jerome. Susan had been careful to keep to herself and not get involved in any relationship. She couldn't trust anyone. The deluge of scam artists who had run her out of the country would return if she let her secret out.

Going back to the photo, she frowned. She wondered what it would be like to have a relationship and if this was the man she wanted to include in her life. She knew she couldn't do it, but a small fantasy wouldn't hurt anything.

André set his briefcase on the floor, next to his desk, and slipped into his chair. He didn't turn his computer on or even reach across the expanse of his clean desk to snag a pencil from its leather cup. His mind was on Susan. Was she in? He glanced at the computer but refused to go so far as to look at the store's personnel schedule. He hadn't stopped thinking about her since he had seen her on the street, in front of the store, two days ago. Seeing her holding that camera, and the fact that he had felt her words had been guarded, had disturbed him.

André didn't know why it bothered him or why she seemed to invade his thoughts. He'd gotten up in the middle of the night and looked the camera up on the internet. A long whistle had escaped him when the price had drawn his attention.

He swiveled around in the chair, facing the windows, but not noticing the light or the world outside. The lines between his eyes deepened as he wondered who'd given Susan a camera that amounted to a small mortgage? And she lived at a very expensive address. That could be the result of having several roommates, he rationalized. André had lived with roommates when he'd been in college. Although his parents were wealthy, they had wanted him to understand the reality of a budget, so as soon as he had been able to afford it, he'd moved into his own apartment. But roommates didn't explain that pricey camera.

Before he could investigate it any further, his watch poked a silent reminder against his arm. André checked the time. After standing up, he left for his usual morning walk around the building.

The bakery staff had been in for hours and they were adding pastries to the glass cases as he went by. Katie handed him a cup of coffee, as she'd done five days a week since he began working in the store. While his movements weren't strictly by the clock, the coffee was always hot and exactly the way he liked it. Thanking her with a raise of his cup, he smiled and continued on in silent friendship.

Passing through fine jewelry, shoes and handbags, André moved fluidly from department to department. There were few people working at this hour, so he didn't expect to see Susan, yet he purposely didn't go to the furniture department until he was on his way back to his office. He heard her before seeing her. Immediately his heart leaped. Not a large leap; only a tremor, but he was so unprepared for it that it felt like he'd fallen off the top of the building.

He should leave. The escalator wasn't working yet. The system worked on a timer and wouldn't kick in for another forty-five minutes. André turned just as she came out of a storage area. Her arms held several small boxes, but her hand was to her ear as she spoke into a cell phone. Her eyes opened wide when she saw him, and she lowered her voice and turned away from him.

He didn't intend to eavesdrop, but he was close enough to hear her side of the conversation. It appeared she was making a date with someone. For some reason, that didn't sit well with him.

"André," Susan said.

She slipped the phone into the pocket of the lavender jacket she wore over a pair of white pants. The expression on her face told him nothing. After a moment, a smile replaced the unreadability of her features. It affected him in ways he didn't want to describe—not even to himself.

"I heard you do a walk-around every morning," she said.

"You're here a little early yourself," he said.

She put all but one of the boxes down and walked over to him.

"I wanted to get these candles out before the store opened."

She lifted the box so he could see it better. It was

small and white and had a photo of a lit candle on the side. André could smell their scent, even through the packaging.

"There's so much traffic here these days, we don't get any time to do much other than sell."

"That's good," André said. He'd seen the numbers from the furniture department, and since Susan had joined the staff, there had been a marked improvement in revenue from that area. He couldn't give all of the credit to Susan, but she had changed things in the store, and by all accounts, she was a very likable person.

So why did André have the feeling that she was hiding behind a mask? For a moment, he thought of a possible criminal element. It wouldn't be the first time an employee had been motivated to steal. But looking into her eyes, he was sure larceny didn't fit her profile.

But what did?

At seven o'clock the elevator doors slid open. Susan lifted her foot and stopped. André stood at the back of the small cab. Immediately her heart thumped. Why did she react this way whenever she saw him? As he looked up and his light brown eyes connected with hers, she stepped into the tiny space, feeling sorry now that she'd stayed back to rearrange some of the furniture in her area. Most of the shoppers had gone and the department was quiet, so she had no choice except to be confined in the elevated room with him, for the length of a ride to the ground floor.

"How's it going?" he asked, pushing away from the back wall and standing up straight.

"I'm sure you know how sales are," she said, without any censure in her voice.

"I get reports, but how is it going for you?"

"I've been here a while now, but it's still hard to spend the entire day on my feet."

He looked down at her shoes. Susan followed his gaze.

"I'm sure you didn't work in those."

She smiled at her tennis shoes. "I left my work shoes in my locker."

"But you took the camera bag."

She adjusted the bag on her shoulder. "As you know, it's a hobby of mine."

The doors opened and they both stepped out. Susan turned toward the employee exit. It was thirty feet down the corridor and only a few steps from the subway.

She'd taken about ten steps when André called her name.

She turned back, watching as he jogged toward her.

"Are you in a hurry to leave?"

"I thought I'd get some pictures before the light changes," she said, hesitatingly. It was summer and the evening light cast a golden glow on the buildings. She didn't know what she should do. "Was there something you wanted?" she asked.

"Not really. I was going to invite you for a cup of coffee."

It was social, she thought; it had nothing to do with work. Susan had run a small business, but she knew the president of the company didn't concern himself with hiring and firing sales people.

"Are you sure you want to trust me with a hot liquid?"

He smiled and looked at the floor, before bringing his attention back to her. She smiled too.

"I'll risk it," he said.

Susan nodded. She knew it wasn't a good idea. The company's president and a salesclerk from the furniture department… The situation came to her mind, reminding her of some black-and-white movie she'd watched years ago. Still she said, "I have time."

They went to a small coffee shop across the street from the building. When André had gotten their coffees and they had sat down at a table for two, near the windows, she looked at him.

"I thought we'd go to the restaurant," she said, glancing across the street, to the store. All the Thorn stores had a four-star restaurant inside them.

"Here, I'm unavailable for interruptions."

She nodded, understanding. "I take it you're interrupted often."

"Occupational hazard," he said, but his smile took

the sting out of his words. How did you happen to come to work at Thorn's?" he asked.

"I needed something to do. I've only recently moved to the city."

He leaned forward and Susan was sorry she'd said that. It opened her up to the obvious question, and André stepped right in and asked it.

"Where did you come from?"

"I was in France for a while."

"Studying?" His brows rose.

She nodded, not really committing to a definite answer.

"Judging by how you are constantly carrying a camera case, I assume you have a lot of photos from the City of Lights."

"I do. But Paris is a lot like New York City. Every picture you take is already on a postcard."

He laughed at that and Susan took a sip of her coffee before continuing. "I love the energy of New York City, and every minute is different here. The light changes, and the scene offers an entirely different photo."

"You like it," he stated.

She nodded. "Probably as much as you like the store." She paused. "I've been told you're a workaholic. Always in the office or on the floors." She tried to turn the conversation away from her.

"Guilty," he said, and she saw the color in his face darken. "I've been in stores since I was born, practically."

Susan waited for him to go on. She knew part of the story. There was a picture book full of anecdotes and photos pertaining to the origins of the House of Thorn. But a personal account would be far different.

"My mother actually started the business, and she remains the principle stockholder."

Susan glanced at the huge building across the street. "What did she do?"

"She was a stay-at-home mom at the time. She told us she always wanted to be a master chef, and she was a good cook. I remember having some of the best meals."

"Was she experimenting on you?"

"Not exactly," André said. "She was a great cook even before we were born. She said her father taught her how to cook. When we went to school, she started out selling cakes from our kitchen. We lived in DC then."

"Is there a DC store?"

He nodded. "Eventually the business grew so large that she couldn't maintain it in the house. She rented a small store and added ice cream and cold drinks to her menu. We still have that store, and that's all it sells. The main store in DC is downtown."

Susan had seen it. When she had first returned to the US, she'd visited Washington, DC, spending a few days as a tourist and reuniting with her family in Montana.

"After a few years, my father quit his job as a retail salesman to join her. Tired of the road and being away from his family, he was ready for a change, and my mother's businesses needed help. After that, Thorn's branched out, and here we are today."

"How many stores are there?"

"Five, one for each of us."

"I thought there were only three brothers." She tripped up again, revealing that she knew something of his family.

"Technically, that's true. The other two are cousins. They came to live with us when their parents died."

"I'm sorry," Susan said. She hadn't known about the deaths.

André reached across and placed his hand on hers. "Thank you," he said.

Susan wanted to move her hand, but that would make it appear that she didn't want his touch, and the opposite was the truth. She liked the feel of his hand on hers. It had strength and confidence, and it made her feel safe. That made no sense, she told herself. She couldn't get involved with this man.

She looked at her hand.

André removed his.

Susan felt a weight lift from her, and not just from her hand. Her shoulders felt lighter, as if an invisible blanket had slid from her neck to the floor. She let out a controlled breath.

"Tell me about you. How did you come to work at Thorn's?"

The truth, she wondered, or some made-up story. She couldn't tell him the complete and honest truth.

"It wasn't my intention."

His brows rose. Susan smiled. "When I first moved here, I shopped a lot." She watched his expression change to pride. "I needed practically everything for the apartment. While looking for linens one day, I saw an ad saying you were hiring."

"So you applied and got the job," he suggested.

She was shaking her head before he could finish the sentence. "I left the store. Two days later I was back, and as I passed the customer-service area, someone mistook me for an applicant and handed me a paper to fill out."

"You did it on a whim?" André laughed.

"Almost. I knew I wanted a job. Once I had the application, I applied and I got hired." André was quiet after she had finished. "I'm sure this isn't the usual story you get from employees."

He shook his head. "Most tell me how glad they are to be working here."

"Do you believe them?"

"Some of them. Those who really need a job are grateful. Those who are here to keep food on the table until they find something different are often obvious, but I don't mind."

"You've never been one of them?" Susan posed it as a question, but she knew he'd grown up with plenty of money and had never wanted for food. Neither had she...wanted for food, that is. Her family was more middle-class—comfortable, but not able to get everything they wanted.

"I've never been hungry, yet I did work for a while on opening a fast-food restaurant."

"Really?" Surprise showed in Susan's voice.

"High school rebellion. I thought I knew it all. My parents didn't protest much. They gave me an argument, but I persevered. At least I thought I did."

"What do you mean?"

"They knew it would likely fail. It wasn't a popular hamburger joint, just a new start up with a limited menu and none of the marketing savvy of the big guys. But I had to learn that for myself."

Susan understood that. She'd put everything she'd had into her business, and she had taken pride in it, but she had learned a lot about how hard it was to maintain a business. So much could go wrong. She had also learned a lot about the dark side of human nature.

"Other than working with the public on an up-close-and-personal basis, I met people who had not had the advantages in life that I had. It made me appreciate more what my parents provided for me."

"Great lesson," she said. "Is the fact that the store is so charitable an outcome of your teenage discovery?"

"Partly. My parents said we should give back to the community, but it became more than words after my experience."

"I salute you." Susan held her nearly empty coffee cup up, and the two clinked their cups as if they were champagne flutes.

"All right, I've given you my story. What about you?"

Time to go, Susan thought. She finished the last of her coffee. It was cold, but she managed not to frown. "That'll have to wait until another time," she said. "I really have to go now."

"Pictures?" he asked.

"An appointment." She intended to be vague. She had no appointment. The truth was she didn't want to lie to André. She couldn't say why. The lies had been repeated so often that she had no problem saying them with conviction. But she didn't want to lie to him.

"Maybe we can do this again."

"Maybe." Again, she did not commit.

They both rose and Susan grabbed her camera case. It was an old one, banged up from years of use, but it was made of quality leather, and even with the nicks from overuse, it was still holding up.

They left together. "Good night," she said. "Thanks for the coffee."

"I'm glad you took the job, even if it wasn't in your plans."

"Plans change all the time," she said. Then, smiling, she turned and walked away.

André watched her. She felt it and she turned at the first corner, even though that wasn't the way to the subway. *Plans change all the time.* The words came back to her. Whose plans? Was she bending? Why hadn't she answered his question about herself? Why hadn't she just given him the passel of lies she'd told everyone, except Jerome?

And why was she even thinking about him? She worked for his company, and that alone was reason enough for her to forget everything about the House of Thorn family.

But as she walked down the steps to the subway, she knew that plan needed an alteration.

Chapter 3

Susan blew out a long breath and dropped her shoulders. She was finally alone. She couldn't think with all of the activity that went through the furniture department and the transitions to the other areas of the store. Furniture, bedding and bathroom accessories took up one entire floor. The amount of people walking back and forth kept her mind off André and their coffee the night before. So far, today she hadn't seen him. She had a clear view of the elevator, and each time the elevator door pinged, she braced for him to exit.

Coffee had been fun. André was easy to talk to. That's probably why she had stayed longer than she'd intended. She knew she needed to be careful. André had celebrity status. While the paparazzi didn't follow him night and day, he made the news several times a year. And if she made a habit of being with him outside the House of Thorn, her name—her *real* name—could make those papers, and she'd be hounded again.

Taking another breath, Susan centered her attention on the bedroom section. Pastels next to vivid reds. Susan frowned at the color combinations. There was a good amount of foot traffic, but if the arrangement was different and the colors were coordinated better, the aesthetics would cause an unconscious trigger that made people stop and think about what their own homes could look like.

She knew this was true, both from her previous framing business and from long conversations with Jerome, the photographer she had met while living in Italy. She'd accompanied him on various photo shoots, and had watched and listened as he'd explained why he combined or eliminated certain elements.

Taking another breath, Susan looked in the direction of one of the bedroom setups. The first thing was the bed, she thought. It needed to be moved to the other side of the display. She pulled the coverlets off and stood the mattress and box spring on their sides. Then she began to walk the frame to the opposite side.

"Whoa, whoa, whoa," someone shouted from behind her. She heard running feet on the wooden floor, before they reached the carpet, which then muffled the sound. She knew exactly who it was. She'd been expecting him since they'd had coffee together.

Startled, she dropped the end she was holding. It went *thunk* as it made contact with the rug. André Thorn came up beside her.

"What are you doing? We have staff to move furniture. You could get hurt."

Susan felt heat flash inside her. Being caught with her hand in the proverbial cookie jar—and by the owner of the company—was above and beyond an infraction of the rules.

"I think this bed would be happier in that display." She pointed to the place she wanted it, keeping her voice steady and calm, although it was a note or two higher than its usual pitch.

André followed her gaze. For a long moment, he said nothing. She was sure he'd tell her the designs needed approval from the department head. But instead he said, "Let me give you a hand."

After taking off his suit jacket, he hung it over the arm of a chair and moved to the front of the headboard.

"Be careful," he said. "It's heavy."

Susan's shoulders dropped in relief. Her body became cold and then hot with sweat at being caught doing something she shouldn't. Her hands felt clammy and buttery. She wiped them down her pants and lifted the foot. André did the same with his end. Together, they crossed the floor and set the frame where she wanted it. With an unspoken mutual consent, they silently replaced the box spring and mattress, and he helped her remake the bed.

"Anything else you want moved?" André asked.

She could hear the humor in his voice. It made her relax a little.

"Are you sure you want to ask that?"

He raised his brows in response to her question.

"We have to put something else back there." She indicated where they'd left an open gap in the floor plan.

"And…?"

"And I want to change that room."

"Why?" he asked.

"It will draw people into the department."

"People who stop on this floor are coming to this department."

"Not all of them," she said. "Many people go to the sheets and towels. They don't think of needing a bed, but if there is a display that catches their eye, they may stop and take a look. If they don't buy then, they might come back."

Again an eyebrow rose. "You think you can do that with a bed?"

The way he said *bed* made her pulse race. "Not only with a bed. It's the entire picture of the room that they'll see, and like a book, they'll fill in the rest."

He said nothing, but the expression on his face had her wondering what he was thinking. She wondered if his mind was seeing a couple on the bed.

Seeing *them* on the bed.

"Could you help me with one more?" Susan tried to cover her feelings with the question.

André gestured for her to lead on. She put together another room mock-up, and they stood back, looking at it.

"This is it?" He spread his hands.

Susan could see he wasn't convinced.

"Not quite," she said. "I have a few other things to do, but I won't hold you. I'm sure someone is waiting for you. And I promise I won't move any more furniture tonight." She hoped he hadn't heard the opening she'd left in her comment or the way her voice had broken when she'd suggested he was heading out to meet a woman.

"I'm waiting to see how this pans out. I want to see a bedroom that draws people in."

It wasn't the ending she'd hoped for. Susan waited a moment, then smiled.

"Just wait here." She rushed off to the bedding department and found the comforter and pillow shams she'd had her eye on for a week. After gathering it all up, she went back, barely able to see above the packages. André took some of them just before they all fell to the floor.

"Could you do me a favor?" she asked.

He nodded.

"I need some photos. Could you go to the framing department and get me three or four? Use different sizes and preferably ones with family-type photos in them."

He cocked his head, obviously trying to figure out her plan. Then he nodded and turned to go.

Susan worked diligently while he was away. She knew the framing area was at the back of the art-supply department, on the first floor. He must be having a hard time making a decision. Making use of the time, she rushed to housewares and grabbed a few things before returning to the furniture department. Moments later she heard André's footsteps. Turning, she saw him carrying several frames. Thankfully they looked to be the perfect size. Then he put them down on the new bedcovers.

The gasp came involuntarily. Susan's hand went to her mouth. "These..." She hesitated. "Aren't these your personal family photos?"

She stared at each photo, following the order in which he had laid them out on the bed. There was one of a wedding. The couple smiled in happiness at the camera. It was so real, she could almost hear the guests in the background. Instantly she wondered who the photographer was.

"It's my brother's wedding. Blake and Elliana—we call her Ellie. They were married last spring."

"They make a beautiful couple," she said, surprised to find emotion in her voice. She glanced over the others. There was a photo of three boys dressed in swimming trunks, with their arms hooked together as they stood on a beach. Pre-teens, there was only a little height difference between them. They looked about twelve, all resembling each other. "Your brothers," she stated.

"Just after that was taken, we had a sand fight."

Susan heard the pride and happiness in his voice. She knew the memory he'd shared was far more crystal clear in his mind.

"You must have had a wonderful time as a child."

"Like most kids, I guess."

This time there was an undercurrent of regret in his words.

"I can't take these," she said, beginning to gather them up. "They're too personal, and you wouldn't want anything to happen to them."

She turned and pushed the frames toward him. His hands covered the metal and glass, but they didn't take them. He held on, with his fingers wrapped around the photos and imprisoning her hands. Lightning bolts shocked her bloodstream.

"It's all right." André took the frames. "I'd like to see the room with them displayed." He laid all but one of them back on the bed.

Susan wanted to check her hands to see if they were singed. Instead she looked up at him. She didn't know what she expected to find in his face—maybe assurance or a question asking for agreement—but what she saw was touching. It flustered her. Her throat went dry and she knew she should look away, but she didn't want to. André was the first to drop his gaze.

"Why don't we try this one over here?"

He took the photo of the three boys and set it on the top of a dresser. Susan looked at the remaining frames. She picked them up and set them about the room, in places she thought would give them the best advantage. Her movements felt stilted. Susan could feel André's eyes following her around as she arranged the room. She had already been disconcerted by his appearance, but his gaze on her back made her even more nervous.

After placing the last photo, she picked up the tray she'd pinched from housewares, along with a coffee cup and saucer, and placed them at the foot of the bed. It was the last touch. She stepped back, but bumped into André's warm body. More heat went through her, even though she froze in place.

"You're right," André whispered. "People will probably be enticed here or at least stop."

His hands were still on her arms. And his voice was close enough to her ear for her to feel his breath. She hoped he couldn't feel the tremble that was going through her.

"Breakfast in bed. I could go for that."

Susan turned and stepped back, forcing herself out of his touch. "You've had breakfast in bed before." She stated it as a fact.

"Not unless I was ill."

"Well, you've got time," she quipped, trying to dislodge the images in her head. Images of them. Images that had no right to be there. "It will also help when we have real food on the tray. Something from the bakery that has a wonderful aroma."

Susan lifted her head as if she could smell the sugary air prevalent in the bakery.

"You intend to have real food on the bed?"

She could practically hear him thinking that people would want to eat the food or that the kids coming through would sneak something and make a mess in the bed.

After laughing at his discomfiture, she said, "The pastries would be in jars—sealed jars. It won't be real, but it will look real."

André looked at the room scene and had to agree it was inviting. However, the day had been long and he could just be tired.

"You know this is against company policy," André stated. "There are crews to move furniture, rules to follow and safety measures to adhere to."

Susan wanted to drop her eyes, as someone who'd been caught doing wrong usually did, but she refused to conform. If he was going to fire her, she'd take it.

"I understand," she said. After a long moment, she spoke again. "Am I fired?"

André looked as if he hadn't expected that question.

"I don't usually get involved in overseeing the store at this level. The department manager is responsible for hiring and firing personnel." He paused, looking over the room setup that Susan had rearranged. "It'll be up to Jessica Cresswell to deal with this. But my suggestion is you don't do it again without her permission."

"Of course not," Susan agreed, but crossed her fingers behind her back.

André purposely avoided the furniture department the next day. He'd done his usual morning walk through the departments, but by the time the staff began to arrive, he was back in his office. However, he wondered how Susan's *experiment* was going. By three o'clock he'd done little more than sign a few letters. It was time to talk to Jessica Cresswell.

Ten minutes later she stood in the doorway to André's office.

"You wanted to see me," Jessica said.

"Come in." André rose from his chair and walked around the desk to meet her. He offered her a chair and she sat down, while he leaned against his desk.

Jessica ran the furniture department. A fifty-seven-year-old woman, she barely crested at five feet tall. Yet she was agile. He'd seen her once turning cartwheels in the fitness center. She had a winning smile and dark brown eyes that always seemed to be happy. She'd started in the children's department fifteen years ago. For the last five years, she'd been the department head in furniture.

"I wanted to talk to you about Susan Dewhurst."

André paused, checking Jessica's expression. Her face changed—it fell a little. André tensed.

"She's certainly enthusiastic," Jessica said, with caution evident in her tone.

"In what way?"

Sighing, she leaned forward. "I was very surprised this morning to find the rearrangement she'd made in the department. Don't get me wrong. Her heart is in the right place, but she could have gotten hurt moving all that heavy furniture."

"I helped her," André admitted.

Jessica's mouth dropped open and her face showed the surprise he expected.

"I found her moving the bed and feared she might get hurt." He waited a moment for her to recover. "What did you think of the arrangement?"

Jessica swallowed. "It's not what I would have done, but it does set a mood. That was how she explained it. And the photographs were a nice touch."

André saw the knowing mischief in her eyes.

"I'd never seen them before."

He glanced at the place on his étagère where they had once sat. "Has anything sold?"

She shook her head. "But people do stop and take long looks."

Somehow that made André feel better. He knew it shouldn't, because the emotion didn't really involve the placement of dressers, beds or photographs. It had to do with Susan, with the way her hair seemed to swing when it was down. The way her waist dipped in as if waiting for his hands to curve around it.

André blinked and changed positions in his chair.

Jessica was still sitting in front of him. He hoped his face didn't reveal anything. There was nothing between him and Susan, but that didn't mean he wasn't thinking about her in the most carnal way.

"I told her to make sure she clears things with you before making any other changes."

Jessica's nod was barely visible, but André knew she felt better knowing that decisions in her department rested with her, and no one was infringing on her responsibilities.

Last night, when Susan had assured him she would comply with the rules of the store, somehow André hadn't felt there was a lot of backing behind that statement. Susan struck him as a woman who was used to getting her way, and a little thing like moving furniture wasn't going to hinder her.

"Thanks." She hesitated a moment, and André felt she had more to add. "I won't say I'm against what she did. I think it looks better than it did before. Maybe we should think more outside the box than in it."

Susan was an outside-the-box person. André agreed with that. He was just unsure if he wanted her in a box, and did he want to be in that box with her?

While André hadn't asked Jessica to keep him informed about Susan's work, her reports on the furniture department always included specifics about Susan.

André purposely avoided the seventh floor, which

housed the furniture department. He was getting too interested in the brown-eyed beauty and knew it was time to back off. Even though he'd usually date a woman before dropping all association, he'd only been present at the same wedding as her. The two had exchanged only a few words and a tray of champagne that ended up covering his jacket, shirt, and pants.

Her upsetting the tray had been an accident, so he couldn't really fault her for it, but when she had showed up in the store, something inside him had snapped. And while he knew it and acknowledged it, he could not—would not—act on it.

André got on the escalator going down. He'd skipped breakfast that morning and was in the mood for a chocolate éclair that was only available in the Thorn bakery. After pairing the pastry with a cup of coffee, he spotted Jessica waving him over. He both wanted and didn't want to go. For all intents and purposes, he owned the House of Thorn store in New York. It was prudent to know everything that went on. Yet he felt as if he was breaking a trust by listening to Jessica relate details about another employee.

"Running late today?" she asked, then indicated his coffee and pastry.

André acknowledged it with a nod as he took a seat at the table. "Skipped breakfast. And I had a taste for this." He lifted the éclair and took a significant bite.

"We sold three of the bedroom sets," she said, without his inquiring.

André stopped chewing. "Today!"

"Two yesterday, one this morning."

"That doesn't necessarily mean—"

Her head was shaking while André spoke. He stopped.

"They said it was because they felt that bedroom display spoke to them."

André had no comeback.

"And that's not all," she went on. "She's changed two more room configurations."

"She promised me she wouldn't do that."

Jessica put her hand up to stop him. "I know I was a little hesitant at first, but you have to see what she's done."

They both got up. André carried his cup and pastry, although he was no longer hungry.

The furniture department had more people browsing than André had seen in several years. Although the department had always held its own, André couldn't help doing calculations in his head. It was his nature. The department always made money, but if only 10 percent of the people who came in the department eventually bought, the sales would triple.

"Look over there." Jessica indicated a new room setup. André had focused on the customers and Susan, who appeared to be handling two of them at the current time.

The mock-ups Susan had reset were for a teen's

bedroom and a nursery. Both had people in them, opening drawers and checking out the walls, and one teen was listening to the music coming from an iPhone connected to personal speakers. From the look on the teenager's face and the enthusiasm she exhibited to her parents, she wanted that room.

Susan glanced in his direction, then looked back and smiled. André smiled too, but his eyes weren't on the newly designed rooms.

The store restaurant had both an outside entrance and one that led into the main retail floor. Susan sat, facing the outside. Minette was expected at any moment. Her father, Jerome, was coming to New York. That phone call yesterday morning had been from him, and in between the minutes Susan wasn't thinking of André, Jerome's conversation was on her mind.

The waiter brought her a drink, and Minette slid into the seat opposite Susan's.

"Is that for me?" she asked. "I've had a long day and I'm stressed."

Susan passed her the glass of white wine. She knew the day was about to get worse. "I'll have another," she told the waiter, who smiled. They ordered quickly. Apparently Minette was familiar with the restaurant. She didn't consult the menu, but told the waiter exactly what she wanted. Susan agreed to the same meal.

"What happened to make the day long?" Susan asked.

Minette took a drink and set the glass on the table. "Everything that could go wrong today went wrong." She sat up in the booth and pushed her hand through her hair. Minette was a web designer for a major media corporation. Looking up, she said, "We were offline for three hours. We couldn't keep up with the calls or the angry threats that people will unsubscribe. You'd have thought the world was ending."

Susan laughed and Minette looked at her. "You have to admit, it is kind of funny. People can't live without their connection to the internet."

After a moment, Minette laughed. "So, how was your day?" Her mood changed quickly when she saw the humor of the situation.

This was her opening. Susan could put if off and wait until after Minette had drank a second glass of wine, but she wasn't used to beating around the bush.

"Most of it was fine—much better than yours." She paused a moment, remembering her encounter with André. Forcing her thoughts back to Minette, Susan lifted her wineglass and took a sip. "I got a call from your father," she began.

Minette picked up her glass and then set it down with a *thunk*.

"How is he?" she asked, although her tone was tight.

"In perfect health," she said.

"Why did he call?"

"He's coming to New York." Susan took a long

breath, as if she was about to plunge into a swimming pool.

"When?" Minette asked. Her voice was low, barely audible.

"Three weeks. He's being honored at the Photography Society Museum of New York. They're displaying his photos and giving him a banquet. He wants you to come."

Minette slouched back against the banquette wall. "I don't know. We haven't really communicated in years."

"Maybe it's time," Susan said.

Their meals were served. Minette looked at hers, but didn't touch it. "I can't eat this," she said. She slid out of the booth and got up. "I'm sorry, but I need to think about this."

Susan twisted in her seat and stood up too. "I understand," she said. "Don't worry about anything. We'll work it out."

Minette looked at her as if she believed that she had a friend to help with her pain.

"Thanks," Minette said. "I'll call you tomorrow."

Susan reseated herself and was about to call the waiter when André appeared, standing next to the seat Minette had vacated.

"She didn't like the food," he commented.

"That wasn't it." Susan stared at the exit where Minette had gone.

"Is she all right?"

"I'm not sure." Susan stared at André for a long

time. She wanted to talk to someone. Maybe getting another opinion, a male opinion, might help her get the father and daughter back on track. Unfortunately, Susan didn't know much about the stake that had driven them apart.

"André, would you have dinner with me?"

He took a seat and raised his hands to the table, as if the question had come from the fourth dimension. Susan understood the absurdity of what she'd said.

"Sorry, I'm a little distracted. Minette didn't touch her food, but I'm sure the waiter will bring you whatever you want." She glanced at Minette's plate.

"This is fine," he said, although the waiter appeared, removed Minette's wineglass and replaced it with a glass of water for André. After acknowledging the waiter, André looked at Susan. "Do you want to go somewhere else?"

She shook her head. To prove it, she lifted her fork and took a bite of the fish on her plate. André waited. She liked that he didn't push her or prompt her to begin. He was giving her time to gather her thoughts and begin when she wanted to.

"The woman who left is Minette Marchand. I met her father in Italy and he taught me to use my camera."

André had a reaction, but Susan couldn't define it.

"So he was the one who gave you the camera?"

"I bought the camera. It was a gift to myself. Jerome gave me the camera bag."

"That's a very expensive camera."

"We're not talking about the camera."

André covered himself by taking a bite of his food.

"Minette and her father are estranged," Susan began. "I don't know much about what caused the riff. Jerome is a famous photographer."

"I recognize his name," André said.

"He has a studio full of photos of his daughter and he talks about her all the time."

"So what's the problem?" André sipped his drink.

"I just told her Jerome is coming to New York in three weeks."

"Photo show at the gallery?"

Susan's eyes opened wide. "You know about it?"

"Vaguely. Because of the store's contributions, we get invitations to a lot of events. One was lying in the camera department as I passed it a week ago. It's apparently a huge event."

"I'm sure that's why Jerome agreed to return."

"That and Minette," André supplied.

"That and Minette," Susan repeated, bobbing her head up and down.

For several moments, they ate in silence. André was the first to break the silence.

"What are you going to do?"

"I don't know. I'll tell her that I will go to the banquet for support. If she wants to leave, I'll be with her."

"You've already mentioned this to her father?"

"I have."

"Would you like some moral support?"

Susan's eyes flashed and her stomach suddenly turned over. How was she to answer that? It was a sudden and unexpected offer. And getting involved, even for an altruistic reason, with André Thorn, was not a good idea. Her brain knew that, but her heart didn't, and in this situation, it appeared her brain was overruled.

"Do you mean go with you?"

"Yes," he said. "That is if you don't already have a date."

She didn't. Since she'd been in the city, she'd had very few instances to meet men, although she'd been on a few dates that proved fruitless for a sustaining relationship.

"Well?" André prompted.

"Isn't there some unwritten rule about employee relationships?"

He laughed. "I make the rules and there's nothing of that sort. We abolished it two centuries ago."

Susan had been looking for any reason not to go with him, even if she wanted to, but the straw she grasped was skillfully removed from her reach.

"So, is it a date?" he asked.

"Not a date," she said. "I'm not ready to date the owner of the House of Thorn. We can be two people going to the same event, to support a father and daughter."

"I'll take that," he said. "But before the banquet, we should discuss how we're planning to get Minette and her father together. We can do it over dinner tomorrow night."

If that wasn't a line, Susan had never heard one. Nevertheless, she greed to have dinner with him, but only for the sake of Minette and Jerome, whom she would tell owed her *big-time*.

Chapter 4

The two women stood back, each with folded arms, as they surveyed their latest furniture setup. This time it was a dining room. The lighting was perfect, with a crystal chandelier hanging over the polished table that had been staged for the upcoming summer sale. They'd set the room up using a whimsical fantasy scene that coordinated with one of the hottest plays on Broadway.

A few people had stopped and looked at it while they had placed the elaborate centerpiece on the polished surface.

"What do you think?" Susan asked Jessica.

The head of the department looked over the room. Turning to Susan, she smiled. "I love it."

"Do you think it will draw people to it?"

"Without a doubt," Jessica whispered, glancing at the woman who was walking away, but had her head turned toward the setting.

Susan smiled. She remembered her first encounter with Jessica. The woman had suppressed her feelings about the arrangement that Susan and André had put together, but now the two had become fast friends.

"It just needs one more thing," Susan said.

"What's that?"

"I'll be right back." Susan started walking. "I need the military sale sign."

A special discount was being offered to military families who bought the dining room set. Jessica nodded and turned back for another look. Susan headed for the printing area, at the back of the store. The printers were taxed with making all of the signs for the store.

Susan was on her way back to the furniture department when she heard a familiar voice call her name.

"Marcia."

No, not her name. Not her current name, but her real name. The one that was on her original birth certificate. She hadn't answered to it in over two years. She had a new birth certificate, reflecting her new name, the one she'd legally changed it to.

The woman who had called her caught up with her. "I thought that was you. What are you doing here?"

It was Constance Malloy—Connie for short—

someone from Susan's hometown of Mountainview, Montana. What had brought her from the mountains, all the way to New York?

Stunned, all Susan said was "Connie." The single word came out so low, Susan wasn't sure she could be heard.

Connie gave her a big hug and stepped back. "I'm sure you're the last person on the planet I expected to find in New York."

"What are you doing here?" Susan asked in awe. Her voice still sounded strained.

"My daughter. You remember Penny?"

The question sounded more like a statement. Susan could hear the pride in her voice.

"Well, she starts Columbia in the fall. She's taking a summer course and getting settled in. We're here helping her get everything she needs."

That's when Susan recognized the bags with the House of Thorn logo on them in Connie's hands. Penny was of college age. Susan hadn't seen her in years. She still pictured the little girl with long braids, running up the driveway across from Susan's house when she got off the school bus.

"She's really taking to the city well. I haven't seen her so happy."

"That's wonderful," Susan said, not matching the motherly pride in Connie's voice. "Is she with you?" Susan looked over Connie's shoulder, but didn't see Penny.

"She's at an orientation and getting to know her new situation. I thought it best to give her *time*."

Connie didn't use the air quotes on the word, but it was apparent that she emphasized her understanding of a daughter's need to expand her horizons. Susan wasn't that much older than Penny, but she'd gone through the same phase. It had been a difficult parent-daughter situation, but thankfully both she and her parents had come through it successfully.

Noticing the sign in Susan's hand, Connie asked, "Do you work here?"

Susan glanced at the sign. "In the furniture department. I doubt Penny needs any of this."

Connie shook her head. "Just sheets, towels, linens." She raised and lowered her hands, showing the bags she was holding.

"I have to go, but we should get together for dinner while I'm here. I'm sure Penny would love to see you. We're staying at the Elmwood Hotel on Central Park West."

Susan nodded. She knew it.

"We'll be here until the weekend. Then Frank and I have to go back home. How about tomorrow night?"

"I'm not sure I can make it," Susan said. She liked Connie and Frank, and she'd love to see Penny again, but she felt wary. Suddenly she was homesick. She'd been that way when she had initially left Mountainview, but seeing someone from home brought all the feelings of loneliness and separation back.

"If you change your mind, we'll be having dinner

at six. The hotel has a wonderful restaurant. Hopefully we'll see you there." Connie smiled. "I'd better be off now. Good seeing you."

She hugged Susan and headed toward the escalator. Before reaching it, she turned back. "Marcia," she called. "I'll tell your mom how well the city seems to agree with you when I see her."

Susan smiled and waved as Connie stepped onto the escalator. For a moment, she just stood there, looking after her friend. Then, remembering the sign in her hand, she turned toward the dining room setup.

André stood ten feet away from her. She froze in place, although heat that was hot enough to melt marble burned through her body. How long had he been there? Did he hear Connie call her Marcia? Would it mean anything to him? At the wedding, when he'd first seen her, she had still been known as Marcia. Susan hadn't been born yet. But Marcia wasn't technically dead. Would she resurrect memories that could destroy everything Susan had built?

It was the third outfit Susan had discarded. One was too low in the front. One was too tight around her waist, and the last one, the one she had on now, felt too formal. She didn't know where they were going, and that made it harder to decide on what to wear. She didn't want her dress to look like a date outfit. She didn't want to encourage André or project that this was anything more than a meeting to discuss people she cared about.

Maybe earrings and a necklace would make it more to her liking. Susan raced to the dresser and sorted through several pairs of earrings until she found the pearl teardrops her father had given her five years ago, for her birthday. She put them through her pierced ears and added the pearl necklace with a single teardrop in the center. This made it look more formal, she thought and reached to remove the necklace when the doorbell rang.

Checking her watch, she wondered who could be at the door. She wasn't expecting anyone. She and André had agreed to meet at a restaurant in the Village. They wanted to be away from the theater crowds. After moving quickly from her bedroom to the front door, she checked the peephole, jumping back when the fish-eye lens showed a distorted image of André.

What was he doing here? she asked herself. How could he even be at her door? She'd never given him her address. Then she realized he'd have access to all personnel records.

Opening the door a crack, she said, "André, weren't we supposed to meet at the restaurant?"

"Change of plans," he said, as if there was a conspiracy in tow.

Susan opened the door farther and he came inside.

"I apologize for not communicating that I would meet you here. I brought dinner."

He held up a large shopping bag with a Chinese-food logo on the side.

"I dressed up for Chinese food?" she asked sarcastically.

"Don't you like Chinese food?" His brows raised in question.

"It's one of my favorites, but I assumed we'd be going to a restaurant. I could have made my dinner here and spoken to you on the phone."

"Well, as long as I'm here and we have food, let's talk."

What could she do? He was here, bigger than life. He was dressed in a dark suit with a bright white shirt, accented by a red-and-white-striped tie and the dark tan of his skin. Susan spread her hands in agreement. She had no other choice.

"What's in the bag?" she asked.

"I'll show you." He walked away from her then, heading toward and finding the kitchen, where he set down the bag and began unloading its contents. The apartment was large by New York standards, and the space was open, making it easy to access any of the rooms. Setting a bottle of wine on the counter, he looked at her. "Wineglasses," he said.

Susan was flustered. This was her apartment, her kitchen, yet André had walked in and taken over as if he owned the place.

"You look nice, by the way," he said, taking her anger away. "I like the shoes." His eyes looked her up and down.

Susan glanced at her feet. She wasn't wearing shoes. Quickly she padded to her bedroom and grabbed a pair of high-heeled sandals that she rarely wore. When she got back, André had two plates on the counter and was ladling fried rice onto them.

"What would you like? I bought a variety of dishes, since I didn't know what your favorite was."

She was surprised that he didn't decide for her. Susan moved to look into all of the white boxes that were now open and releasing their steam. The combination of aromas made her stomach growl. She hadn't eaten much at lunch and it was almost seven o'clock now. Together they set the table in front of the massive wall of windows. Susan pulled the wineglasses out and poured the Chardonnay before taking a seat opposite André's. He faced the windows and the skyline beyond.

"This is a beautiful apartment." André twisted around in his seat, looking at the walls and rooms of the apartment Susan called home. "I thought you might have roommates."

"No roommates," she said. "I use the second bedroom as an office/studio."

He nodded. "I forgot you're a photographer."

"Why don't we talk about Minette and Jerome?"

Susan had been around long enough to know that André's appearance here, and even his invitation to dinner, was due to an attraction. It wasn't just one-sided. She was attracted to him too. She tried to hide it, but he seemed to come by her department more often than she expected, and each time her heart did its own dance.

She hadn't expected to entertain him in her apartment. The place was spacious, but it felt smaller when he was next to her. Susan was tall for a woman, standing at nearly five feet seven inches. André was over six feet, and next to him, she felt short.

"You should tell me something about yourself."

"I'm not Minette."

"No, but you know her father. So tell me about you and… Jerome." He hesitated before saying Jerome's name.

Susan took a bite of her sweet-and-sour chicken and drank some of her wine. She knew this conversation wasn't about Jerome and her. André was fishing and she was bait.

"I spent a few years in Europe. Italy, then Paris. I met Jerome there. He's a photographer. I was a tourist. He took my picture, and I told him he couldn't use it without my permission and I wasn't giving it."

André laughed. "I can hear just the way you'd say that."

"We started to talk. I eventually gave him the permission he needed. It's that photo over there." She pointed to the wall above a table by the door.

André got up and walked over to it. "Wow," he said. "This is beautiful."

"Thank you." Jerome had snapped her picture while she had been sitting on the stone steps of the Teatro Romano di Verona. She'd been reading a book and had suddenly looked up. The light had hit her at just the right angle, and her face had held a wistful expression. It was at that moment that the camera had captured her.

Once he had resumed his seat, Susan continued her story. "When the photo arrived, I went to his studio to thank him, and I saw all the cameras and photos. I started asking questions, and eventually he handed me a camera and told me to go and take some photos. Since I already had a cell phone full of photos, I showed them to him and he said the camera he gave me was better. I tried it and several days later went back. He told me all the things that were wrong with the photos." Susan laughed at the memory. "Then he sent me out again. I think he was trying to get rid of me, but I kept coming back. Eventually I showed up with a photo that silenced him."

"It must have been good."

"Or the worst thing ever recorded."

"What did he say?" André had his elbows on the table and the wineglass in both hands.

"He said that was the best an amateur photographer could do."

André smiled.

"That's when he began training me. Later we became friends and he told me about Minette."

"What does he want you to do?"

"I'm not sure. Get her to talk to him, I guess."

"Wait a minute." André pushed back from the

table. "He's not ill, is he? Dying and wanting to reconnect with his daughter before it's too late."

"Not in the least." Susan shook her head. "He's as strong as an ox, so they say. I've seen him hanging from structures that made me cringe so he could get a good shot."

André had planted a seed in her mind. She'd been back in the States for two years. In that time something could have happened to Jerome. Why was he having a showing now? And why was it important that he see Minette? He hadn't seen her in years. Could André be right? Was Jerome ill? She had to find out.

"So, when you see your friend, what will you tell her?"

"I guess I'll have her tell me why she's reluctant to see her father, and we'll go from there."

Susan got up and carried their plates to the kitchen. She rinsed them, put them into the dishwasher and closed the containers of leftovers. When she got back, André was standing in the living room, looking out the windows. Standing next to him, she enjoyed the best part of her apartment.

"I'll never get tired of this view," she said.

"It is impressive."

André took a step closer to her. Everything within her said to move away from him. Yet Susan stood still. André's hand found hers, and their fingers entwined. Susan looked at their hands. André's was strong and solid, and she liked the feel of it against hers.

He turned her and slipped an arm around her

waist. “It’s time for me to go,” he said, leading her toward the door.

Leaving was the last thing she wanted him to do, but it was the only sane thing. Neither said a word as they walked, but Susan felt as if a universe of questions hung in the air. She searched for something to say, something to break the silence. As they reached the door, she turned to thank him. André faced her at the same time. Any words in her mind were gone. André was close, too close, kissably close.

Her eyes roamed over his face, settling on his mouth. Her throat was suddenly dry. For what felt like the space of a lifetime, Susan hung in suspense. As André’s head bowed toward hers, she found enough sanity to step back.

André cleared his throat. The moment was lost.

It had been a long night, and Susan had slept badly once she had finally fallen asleep. Why were there so many mirrors in the furniture department? They seemed to mock her by throwing her tired-looking reflection at her from every angle. After childishly sticking her tongue out at herself, she turned away.

André hadn’t kissed her, but had intended to. And she had wanted him to kiss her. The urge had been so strong, she’d come close to letting it happen. That would have been disastrous. Even if she wasn’t in hiding, getting involved with anyone at the store was not a good idea. If things didn’t work out, someone would have to leave. In Susan’s circumstance, quitting was an option, but her heart needed to be consulted on this. What if she really liked André? What if she fell in love?

André didn't exactly have the reputation for long-term relationships. And that brought her to her own feelings about relationships. She hadn't had one in a long time. There had been the framing business she'd struggled to keep afloat. She'd poured all of her time and energy into it. A casualty of that, other than the fire, had been losing Harris.

He had been her longtime friend and sometimes boyfriend. While Susan had been deciding on gold-toned frames and locking pictures of wet Paris scenes in shadow boxes, Harris had found a more reliable girlfriend. While Susan had been in Italy, he had gotten married, and from what she'd heard from her mother, a baby was due in October.

Susan wasn't in love with Harris, but she envied his finding someone who made his life whole. She wondered if that was in the cards for her.

Sighing, she glanced at one of the beds, wanting to climb in it and fall asleep. Closing her eyes, she removed the image from her mind. Feeling a presence, she opened her eyes again. Expecting to see a customer, she was disappointed to find Fred Lang near her. Replacing her disappointment with a smile, she watched him come nearer.

"Fred, what are you doing here?"

"I heard about the changes in this department and

thought we could use some of it to develop a marketing campaign."

Susan heard the words, but more so she saw the body language. She'd been avoiding Fred since that night in the bar, refusing any invitation for drinks after work. And now he was standing in front of her.

"We haven't done anything except rearrange the department," she said, downplaying the effect it was having on sales, but Fred seemed doubtful.

"Maybe," he said. "Yet the sales figures in this department are on an upward climb. Jessica asked me about showcasing the bedrooms in an upcoming campaign."

"So you're here to check it out?" Susan finished for him.

He nodded.

At that moment, Jessica appeared. Susan took a breath. "Wonderful," she said. "Here's Jessica. I'm sure she wants to work things out regarding that. I know nothing about it."

After smiling at Jessica, Susan left them only to run into André the moment she rounded a display section and was out of Fred's sight. André's arms came around her as she bumped into him. They were so close that she froze. A moment later, she tried to pull herself out of his arms, but felt resistance. She stopped and glanced up. Then she was in his arms, pressing her body to his and her mouth to his mouth. Susan didn't stop to think about kissing him. She acted as though she was pushed by her own suppressed emotions.

She could say it was lack of sleep and the fact that his almost kiss of the night before weighed so heavily on her that she had to complete the circle. His mouth was strong and sure against hers, but instead of tamping down her emotions, it ramped them up. Heat flared within her and she raised her arms toward his neck. Suddenly she heard the sound, a chime. She recognized it. The world that had started to spiral stopped on a dime. She realized where they were. People could be watching them.

She took a step back and looked around. Her head was spinning, and Susan forced herself to calm down and tried to regain control of her mind. She'd never before let herself go like she just had with André. And that had been only a brief kiss in a public place. What would it be like…? She stopped the thought.

"I have to go," she said.

"Not yet," he said, trying to stop her.

Susan remained where she was, out of his reach. She felt the heat in her face and wondered if she looked like someone who'd just been kissed and found her world rocking?

"We need to talk," André said.

"No," she contradicted. "We need to forget this ever happened."

"I don't think I'm capable of that."

People appeared, casually looking at the displays, but no one took notice of them.

"I have to help the customers," she said, trying to get him to leave.

"We *have* to talk." This time his voice emphasized his determination.

"Later," she whispered.

"I'll see you at lunch." André's statement was a command.

He left her then, and Susan went to ask if any of the customers had questions. She was amazed that her voice sounded normal, even if it was a note higher than usual. When the couple left, she checked her watch. Lunch was an hour away. Susan racked her brain, trying to think of a way to get out of lunch with André.

She could quit. The job was getting complicated anyway. It wasn't really the job. She liked it. She enjoyed the people she worked with. She even looked forward to interacting with the customers, especially the engaged couples and newlyweds who were looking to furnish their first home. But she didn't like the complications. And she was the one who had created them. She couldn't tell him who she really was. What kind of relationship began with deception?

Susan wasn't one to quit, unless circumstances were dire enough. When her business had burned down, she'd had no choice but to start something new. She wouldn't quit today, but she might start something new.

At noon she'd meet him head on.

But before that, Fred returned. This time with a full camera crew. Lights were erected quickly and efficiently, and the photographers began taking photos of the displays.

"What's going on?" she asked Jessica.

"Apparently Fred decided to put us in the ads for next week," Jessica whispered conspiratorially.

"That should be good," Susan said. "It'll bring in more sales."

"It will, but I wonder if his reasoning is sound."

"What do you mean?"

"He's never been to this department before. Mainly he advertises jewelry and fashion. In January there is the obligatory white sale."

"But now we have new displays, with brighter bedding. It will make a great ad."

Jessica nodded, but Susan could tell she was skeptical. It was nothing new for Jessica. Until something is proven, Jessica didn't accept it. Susan was glad she'd passed Jessica's test and they were now friends.

"Susan—yes, you'll do fine," Fred said, inviting her over with his extended arm. "Come over here." He waved her over.

Susan gave Jessica a questioning look and moved toward Fred. She wasn't going to get within touching distance of him. He was a little too handsy for her. And in front of the camera people and all of the gawking customers, she didn't want to cause a scene by decking him.

"The guys thought it would be good if there was a person in the picture, and I agree," Fred explained.

"Sure, where do you want me to stand?"

The look that passed between Fred and the man holding a large camera wasn't lost on her.

"I'm not getting in that bed," she said.

"But it'll make the scene so much more real," Fred said.

"Fred, I'm fully dressed and wearing a suit, no less. I won't make the scene more real."

"I'd hire someone if we had the time, but I have a deadline."

"Sorry," Susan said.

"I'll do it."

All eyes turned toward the direction in which the voice had come from. André stood there. Susan's mouth dropped open. She didn't know when Jessica had moved, but when she spoke, Susan realized she was right behind her.

"Close your mouth," she whispered.

Susan's hand immediately went to her mouth.

"That's a wonderful idea," Fred was saying, when her attention went back to him. "The photos are yours, so it really could be your bedroom."

And women would flock to get in bed with someone like André, Susan thought.

"Where do you want me?" he asked.

"It would be best if you dropped the jacket," one of the photographers said.

"And put on a robe," a female crew member said.

Susan's stomach turned somersaults. She heard the sudden intake of breath from the women surrounding the area.

Moments later André had his jacket off. One of the photographers took it and handed him a robe.

He put on the robe and pulled the cover back on the bed, a cover she had chosen and set up. His long legs slid between the sheets, one at a time, slowly, as if they were guiding her eyes as they moved.

Someone gave him directions, but Susan couldn't hear them. She was in the time warp, and the sound was a slow buzzing noise.

"Let's get you out of the shot," Jessica said and led her away.

Safely out of camera range and behind the crowd, Susan reached under her hair and wiped the sweat off the back of her neck. She tried breathing slowly, concentrating on taking air into her lungs. She hadn't been prepared for her reaction, especially after the kiss only a few minutes earlier.

Neither was she prepared later that day for all of the catcalls about André. *Did that gorgeous model come with the bed*? More than one person asked this question. She smiled congenially and said he didn't.

The department had been so busy after all the hoopla, Susan forgot about lunch. Apparently, so did André, since he had never appeared after he'd put his jacket back on and had left the department. Susan breathed a little easier, since their confrontation had been postponed. She knew it wasn't over. André wasn't the type to let things lie. But she wouldn't have to deal with it today.

After retrieving her purse and changing her shoes,

she left through the employee entrance. As usual, the streets were crowded, but the weather was comfortable. Susan decided to walk. She didn't live far from the store, and she loved weaving through the streets. New York City was so different from the small town she'd grown up in. Her trips to Paris and Italy had taught her about crowds. Those places were the same, and they were different. New York was home. At least now it was. She didn't see herself returning to the Midwest. She'd visit, but the beat of this city was home.

She pulled open the glass door to her building and slipped inside. She took two steps into the lobby and saw André. Susan stopped in her tracks.

"I suppose it's too late for lunch," he said.

"What are you doing here?" Susan blinked slowly in disbelief. In her head, she was still seeing him in that bed, with one strong arm resting on the coverlet.

"We need to talk, remember?"

"Can't it wait until tomorrow?"

"It could," he said. "But I'm already here."

Susan wasn't ready for this conversation. She needed to get her thoughts together. She needed time to think about what she wanted to say or what replies she could have to whatever it was he had to say. But it appeared she was not going to get that time. He was here. Better to do it now than to let it worry her all night.

"All right, but I'd rather not talk here." She didn't want him in her apartment. The place was too confining. And she didn't trust herself. Things could easily get out of control.

"Is there someplace close by we could go?" He looked around as if a restaurant or empty building would magically appear.

"Let's just walk."

He took her arm, and Susan felt every one of his fingers as he pushed the door open and they exited the building. For several moments, they said nothing. Silence loomed like an elephant between them. After three blocks, Susan couldn't stand it any longer.

"You wanted to talk," she said, glancing at him.

He stopped abruptly and stood in front of her. If she hadn't reacted quickly enough, she'd have walked directly into him.

"I kissed you."

Would this element of surprise from him ever change? she asked herself.

"You kissed me back," he continued.

The statement was true, but Susan couldn't speak for several seconds. When she found her voice, André eclipsed her.

"I want to do it again."

The clog in her throat returned. Emotions she didn't know existed exploded inside her. She wanted to kiss him too. Her body almost swayed toward his. A herculean effort kept her in place.

"André," she finally got out in a voice she didn't recognize. "It's not a good idea, the two of us."

"Why not?"

"You're the head of the store and I work there."

"This is the twenty-first century, not Victorian times."

Susan would have laughed if she could. "I said that wrong. I mean you're the head of the store, and a relationship between us that didn't go well would cause tense feelings between us, but it could also affect other departments in the store."

"Why would you think it wouldn't go well?"

Susan was confused. She hadn't expected their conversation to take this turn. "Because it wouldn't."

"How do you know?"

"André," she started, feeling exasperated. "You don't know me."

"I'd like to change that."

"But I know you and your history with women."

"Rumors," he said.

He could be teasing. Susan wasn't sure, but she was serious. "They're not rumors. Isn't it a fact that your last five relationships didn't go past the fourth date?"

André glanced up toward the sky. "I don't keep records."

"You should read your press…"

"My press? Where is that?"

"The internet, not to mention the store's rumor mill. You're an attractive man and people talk about you."

"You think I'm attractive?"

Susan swallowed. He would latch on to that one statement. "That's not the point."

"What is the point?"

"That you're not serious about a relationship. You don't want one. Just a pretty woman to hang on your arm."

His face changed. The blood rushing to his face darkened his skin. Susan knew she'd crossed a line. She stood up a little taller and lifted her chin a little higher. If André wanted to challenge what she'd said, he could do it to her face.

"That's what you think?"

"That's what your history says. Why should I think anything else?"

"Here's why."

Susan didn't know what André meant until he stepped closer to her and his hands cupped her face. Her heart pounded so loudly, she was sure he could hear it. She was on dangerous ground and she knew she should stop this. But she was past being able to do that. Her breath caught and held in her throat. She felt her world changing with the descent of André's face. Time slowed down. It didn't stop, but moved in lessening degrees as his mouth sought hers. She felt his breath mingle with hers, knew the heat of their bodies, as it transferred through the tiny space that separated their lips. Her eyelids adjusted downward, pushed by the weight of anticipation. She saw and felt his features blur before her. Their cheeks were nearly touching, bringing a torture that she both wanted and craved.

Susan's tongue darted out to wet her lips, which were suddenly Sahara dry. So close to André, she tasted the sweetness of his mouth. Like a narcotic elixir, it hooked her and she clamped her mouth to his, opening to him as his tongue plunged between her teeth. Moving in closer, her body aligned to his, just as their mouths clung to each other. With twisting heads, they turned left and right, balancing the kiss as if it was a choreographed dance that neither was willing to end.

Electricity crackled in the air as the essence of sex they created collided with the charges, and sound snapped to the rhythm of their movements.

Susan's mouth broke from André's, as the need for air forced her to give way. They stood together, entwined in each other's arms, her head on his shoulder. Their bodies heaved air inside. She felt his chest rising and falling in the same rapid pattern as hers rose and set against the solid strength of his. Ragged breathing crashed in her ears like the sound of a conch shell whirling the air inside her head.

Sanity slowly inched back into her brain. It didn't return completely, giving her full control, but just enough to make her wonder if André could make her feel this delirious with a kiss, what was making love going to be like?

Chapter 5

He hadn't broken any rules. At least not yet. But that kiss on the street had been closer than he'd come in years to wanting to break his own covenant of not letting his heart get involved in a relationship. This wasn't a relationship. He told himself that over and over as he walked the streets, on his way to his Fifth Avenue condo.

Then why had he kissed her? Why had he kissed her like that? Like his life had depended on it. And once his lips had touched hers, there had been no going back. There had been no stopping the intensity of the kiss or of the connection he'd felt within himself. What had caused that? He'd been in relationships before. He'd dated seriously before. Yet none of his past relationships had prepared him for the emotions that had assailed him on a public street in the heart of Manhattan.

André crossed block after block, oblivious of people on the street, not seeing the storefronts change to apartment buildings, not even noticing when he passed his own building and walked three blocks farther than necessary. After reversing his direction, he went home, entered his apartment and immediately wanted to call Susan. He needed to talk to her. It seemed there was never enough time to talk. He was different when he was with her, and even when he was only thinking of her, fantasies entered his head, and that seemed to take up a lot of time these days.

André couldn't tell her they needed to talk again. Clearly they preferred doing other things with their mouths than stringing words together. He paced his apartment, moving from window to door to kitchen to hall, then returning and completing the steps again. Half an hour later, he'd made a decision. He needed to present it to Susan. Checking the clock, he decided to wait until the next day to approach her.

He went to the furniture department, just before Susan's lunch hour, and was greeted by Jessica. She was obviously stressed. And Jessica didn't get stressed—at least she didn't let it show.

"What's going on?" André asked.

"I had to call in extra help today. It took a while, but I got two extra associates to give up their day off and come in to pick up the slack."

"Is someone ill?"

Jessica cut her eyes at him as she straightened a pillow on one of the sofas.

"Not that I know of." Her voice held a bit of sarcasm.

"Then, what happened?"

Jessica straightened her shoulders and stood up to her full height. She tilted her head to look him directly in the face. "Susan quit this morning."

"Quit!"

"This morning and without notice."

André was stunned. It took him a moment to regain the power of speech. By then Jessica was talking to herself.

"I don't understand her," she said. "It doesn't seem like her to just abandon a job, especially since she appeared to like it so much. Did she say anything to you?"

André shook his head.

Jessica did too, but hers was a gesture of confusion. "I thought I was a good judge of character, and this doesn't seem like something Susan would do. At least not without a really good reason."

André wondered if he knew the reason, but he said nothing to the department head except thank you.

"She liked you. See if you can find out if we did anything to offend her?" Jessica asked.

"I'll try," André said.

"She was the best sales associate I ever worked with."

André nodded. He knew Jessica liked Susan. Everyone who met her liked her. It was probably the reason he liked her too. But why did she quit? Her reaction had to be because of him. She'd given him reasons why they shouldn't have a relationship, and he'd replied by kissing her—by ignoring her wishes. But André hadn't been the only one involved in that kiss. Susan had been on the other side of it.

And she had been willing. He was in no doubt about that. Was that the reason? Was she attracted to him and fighting it? Why?

André didn't have to hear an answer to that question. He knew why.

Susan looked cautiously in both directions, outside her building. André must know by now that she no longer works for the House of Thorn. It had gone against her grain to call Jessica and quit over the phone, but she'd had no choice. Jessica would have asked questions Susan couldn't answer, if she'd gone in. And there was the possibility of running into André. After their last encounter, she couldn't face him again, not with the way he made her feel.

She'd lied to him. From the moment they'd met at the employee orientation, she'd kept her real identity a secret, and deception, like fraud, had no statute of limitations. It didn't matter that she had a good reason for doing it or that she hadn't expected things to progress between them. They'd begun something, but neither had reached the point of no return. Walking away was the best thing to do.

She turned left and merged with the crowds walking toward Madison Square Garden. André wasn't outside. She was both glad and sad. In the back of her mind, she had the thought that he might rush to find her as soon as the news had reached him. But she didn't want another encounter like the last time. Expecting him outside her building and not finding him there was both a joy and a sadness.

Susan lifted her head and continued walking. She was meeting Minette for an early dinner. Her apartment was becoming too small, so she was grateful that she had someplace to go. For most of the day, she'd wandered from wall to wall, finding the space cramped and small. She'd turned off her phone just in case he called.

Minette was sitting by the hostess's stand in the restaurant and stood up when she saw her coming. Her face said she could see the tension in Susan.

"Turn around," she said, taking Susan's arm and propelling her out onto the street.

"What are you doing?"

"We're going to my apartment," Minette said. "I have a bottle of wine there and you look like you need it."

"Do I look that bad?"

"Let's just say you look like there's a man who's kept you awake all night, and I don't mean for sex."

Twenty minutes later Susan had a glass of wine

in her hand and she was sitting on Minette's sofa. Unlike Susan's apartment, which had a panoramic view of the city, Minette's faced the back wall of another building. The place was tiny, but had an intimate, cozy feel to it.

"I know we haven't known each other that long, but you need someone to talk to, so tell me about him."

Susan didn't consider claiming that there was no man involved.

"I quit my job today."

"What?" Minette sat forward in the chair across from Susan. "Why?"

"I couldn't work there any longer. Things started to get complicated." Susan tried to suppress a yawn, but she couldn't. After being in André's arms and having him kiss her stupid, she had found it hard to sleep. Her bed looked like she'd been fighting with the sheets all night. And *she* looked like the sheets had won.

Minette waited for her to continue.

"The man is André Thorn."

"Thorn?" She frowned. "Didn't I meet him?"

Susan nodded.

"Is he part of the department store the House of Thorn?"

Again she nodded. "President of the store."

"What happened?"

Susan took another sip of her wine. She had to

be careful now. She didn't want to reveal the whole and complete truth, not even to Jerome's daughter.

"I'm not ready for a relationship. And..." She hesitated. "Things were progressing a little too fast."

"Do you like him?"

Susan nearly sucked in a breath. She hadn't expected that question. "That was the problem. I do like him, but I don't see a future for us."

"Why not?"

"I'm not ready for a relationship. And I don't think he is either."

"Why do you say that?"

Susan had known a little about André Thorn before she had first seen him a few months ago. She'd seen him at the wedding they'd both attended, and a friend had pointed him out. His reputation for love 'em and leave 'em was well-known. Why he'd sought Susan out after she'd spilled champagne on him was a mystery to her.

"Susan?" Minette prompted.

"A man in his position has a footprint that follows him. André's says he's not serious about relationships. At the moment, neither am I, but I know the dangers of thinking one way and having your heart do something else."

"So you left."

"I don't need that job. I'd much rather focus on my photography. I never expected to get hired anyway. I was new in New York and wanted to meet people." She hunched her shoulders. "When they offered me the job, I took it. But it's not working out, so leaving isn't a hardship."

Susan hoped she sounded honest. She believed the words, but in the back of her mind, she knew her real reason was the growing feelings she had for André. She closed her eyes for a moment, trying to stifle a yawn, but she was so tired.

"I see you're exhausted, Susan. I have a guest room. Why don't you take a nap, and when you wake we'll have a late dinner?"

"I can make it home. It's not that far." She yawned again, and her eyes watered a little. She wiped the moisture away with her fingertips.

"Humor me. Just lie down for a few moments and I'll wake you when dinner's ready."

Susan was too tired to fight. It seemed the moment she'd entered Minette's apartment, the entire night had descended on her. And the thought of a bed was too inviting. Minette helped her up and led her to the bedroom door.

"The bathroom is on the right," she said.

Susan kicked her sandals off and fell onto the bed. She was asleep the moment she wrapped the bedcover around her. When she woke it was totally dark, and for a moment she was disoriented, not remembering where she was and why the room she was in wasn't her bedroom. Her memory came back and she heard the faint sound of someone talking in the other room. After pushing her feet to the floor, she sat up, dropped her head into her hands and took a moment to push the cobwebs in her brain away.

She stood up, stepped into her shoes and opened the bedroom door. Minette was curled up on the sofa, watching television. She looked up as soon as Susan reached the end of the tiny hallway.

Minette uncurled her legs and stood up. "I tried to wake you, but you were so tired. I thought it best to let you sleep."

"What time is it?" Susan asked, looking down at her watch, but finding the room too dark and her eyes too unfocused to read the numbers.

"Midnight," Minette supplied.

Susan couldn't believe she'd slept that long. "I have to go home," she said.

"We haven't finished talking," Minette said. "And if it goes long, you can always sleep here." Minette grinned. "You must be hungry. Come on—I made things that you don't have to heat." In the kitchen, Susan was treated to a Cobb salad, fruit, cheese, wine and French bread.

"Wow, is all this for me?" Her stomach growled at the sight of food.

"I had some, and it's not often I get to cook." She used finger quotes to surround the word *cook*. "For guests," she finished.

"Really? You don't have a string of guys vying for you?"

Minette was extremely attractive. Susan couldn't imagine her spending her nights alone.

"Not at the moment. I was in a relationship, but it didn't work out."

"What happened?" Susan asked between bites. "That is, if I'm not being too nosy."

She looked away, then down at the table. "We wanted different things. I wanted to get married and he didn't."

Susan's heart hurt for her. "I'm so sorry."

Minette smiled quickly, the kind of smile that said she was hiding her own hurting heart. "I'm doing fine," she said. "This is New York. There are plenty of men out there. I'll find one who thinks like me."

It was time to change the subject. Susan didn't want to return to her own love life—or rather her loveless life.

"We'll just have to band together and find two of those guys," Minette said.

She raised her glass to Minette. They clinked a toast. Yet Susan couldn't help thinking of the glasses that tumbled together and ended up on André Thorn.

Where was Susan? André still wore the clothes he'd had on the day before. He'd walked the floor of his apartment like a father whose daughter was out on her first date, finally dropping onto the bed for a couple of hours before waking. He'd called Susan at least seven times since the sun had risen. By nine o'clock he'd made several more calls, not to mention the times he'd called her yesterday afternoon.

Maybe she was involved in an accident. André

dismissed the thought. If anything had happened, surely someone would have answered her phone. Or found out who her previous callers were. With so many calls from him, someone would have dialed his number.

So wherever Susan was, she didn't want to talk to him. But he wanted to talk to her. He wanted to know why she'd left her job. If the situation between them was the reason, he could accept that. It was what he wanted, right? André wasn't so sure anymore. He was pursuing her, not the other way around. Not the usual way he'd seen women. Maybe because she didn't look at him the way those other women had. In her eyes he saw no dollar signs. Still, he had to know if she was real or just an extremely good actress. He'd encountered those in his lifetime too.

André stopped pacing and took a shower. He called the office to let them know he wasn't coming in. His assistant's surprise at this drastic change in his routine was evident, yet he offered no explanation. He had previously accessed the office systems to find out Susan's street address.

If she wouldn't come to him, he had only one alternative.

André arrived at Susan's building just after ten o'clock. While he came from one direction, she stepped out of a taxi at the curbside. The relief that went through him was physical. While he'd rationalized that nothing had happened to her, seeing her alive and well sent a shock wave through him. He got to her as she pushed the taxi door closed. Her back was to him as he began to speak.

"Susan, where've you been? I've called you a hundred times."

She turned. The surprise on her face was frightening. André took a step back to give her room.

"What are you doing here?" she asked.

"I was concerned. Jessica told me you resigned without notice."

"I did," she said and started toward the entry door. André fell into step behind her. The building was protected and had a doorman, who quickly opened the glass entry. André acknowledged him as he passed.

At the elevator, he asked, "Did it have anything to do with our kiss?"

Her eyes stabbed him as hard as she stabbed the elevator button with her finger. The door opened.

"Yes," she said, with her voice sounding knife sharp.

André followed her into the elevator. They were going to talk. Apparently Susan thought so too, or she'd resigned herself to it. She didn't invite him into her apartment, but she didn't shut the door in his face either. After dropping her purse on a chair, she disappeared into the kitchen for a moment. André took the time to look again at the beautifully appointed room and the sweeping view of the city. Susan returned with two bottles of water. She handed him one.

"Sit," she said.

André complied, watching her take the seat where she'd dropped her purse. It was the farthest from him the room would allow, and she sat on the edge of it as if she'd need to escape quickly.

"Why did you quit?"

"I don't think the work environment was good for either of us."

"It was a kiss, Susan, not a proposal."

As soon as the words left his lips, he knew it was the wrong thing to say. He didn't want to travel that road. He wasn't looking for an engagement, and the color seemed to drain from Susan's face.

"I didn't mean that the way it sounded," he said, apologetically. "I mean you don't have to leave the store because of..." He didn't know how to continue.

"I don't think it's a good fit," she said.

"Jessica thinks the sun rises and sets on your designs."

Susan smiled at that. André knew she and the furniture-department head had clicked. Each respected the other, and each complimented the room designs. Jessica had said that if it wasn't for Susan, she'd have let things remain as they were.

"Thank Jessica for me, but I want to focus more on my photography."

"And less on me," he said. He wanted to talk about them. He wanted to know what she found objectionable.

André got up and moved closer to her. As he sat

on the edge of the coffee table, he noticed her slight movement farther back into the chair.

"I know you're wary of a relationship."

André didn't know if this was true, but he knew his own history, and he was sure that somewhere in her past there was a relationship that had gone wrong. He could tell by the look in her eyes that he'd struck home.

"I understand," he said. "The same has happened to me."

André hadn't intended to say that. He'd never told anyone about what had broken him and Gail up, what she'd said to him and how involved his heart had been. But since then he'd protected himself. At least he had until Susan had crossed his path.

"I don't want to begin a relationship with you," André said.

Susan's eyes opened a little wider. "Then what do you want?"

"There is obviously something between us." He thought of the way she felt in his arms. "I think we should at least see where it goes."

"Why?" she asked. "You already said you weren't seeking a relationship. Neither am I."

"Well, now that you no longer work for the House of Thorn, you can't have any objection to our getting to know each other better."

"That may not be something I want to pursue," she said.

André knew she was dead serious, and it irked him. “Why not?”

“We’re not from the same world.”

He looked around the smartly appointed apartment. While it had a traditional feel, the furnishings and decor were rich and upscale. The room reflected its occupant.

“It appears that we are.”

“Don’t be deceived by what you see.”

“How about we go out?” He had changed the subject.

“Now?” she asked.

“I was thinking of a date.”

She didn’t recoil, as he felt she might, yet she was shaking her head.

“I might not be elegant enough for your class of friends. I’m more of the beer-and-pretzels type.”

“You cut yourself short. I’ve seen you in action, and I know you can talk to anyone about anything.” André smiled. “I think you’ll be very comfortable at any gathering.”

“So, what do you have in mind, dinner and a movie?”

That was the usual first-date thing when he was younger, but he commanded a department store that yielded the greatest profit of any of the stores in the chain.

“Do you have anything against dinner and a movie? It will mean I get to sit in the dark with you.

And depending on the movie, you might throw yourself in my arms."

He was teasing and Susan knew it. He saw the slight smile that curved her kissable mouth.

"Trust me," he said. "I'll choose something that we can do that won't involve anything getting too complicated."

She said nothing and André took that as assent.

"Pick you up Saturday morning?"

"You won't be working?" she asked.

André shook his head. He wanted to see her, and his routine at the store was just that—a routine. If he didn't walk the floors before the store opened in the morning, no one except Jessica might notice. Susan wouldn't be there. She'd come in early, and he'd looked forward to seeing her and discovering what changes she'd made to the department. But from now on, she wouldn't be there. But he wanted to keep seeing her, needed to keep seeing her.

"What do I wear?" she asked.

André stifled the joy that jumped in his chest.

"A bicycle shop," Susan said on Saturday morning, when André took her to a place near Central Park.

"We're going riding," he said.

"How do you know I can ride?"

"Everybody knows how to ride," he answered.

Susan laughed. Of course she could ride. From the time she had been in middle school, until she had gotten her first car at seventeen, the bicycle had been her only mode of transportation around the winding roads of Mountainview, Montana.

The rental took no time, and they were off and riding. Susan was pleased that the morning traffic was light. They didn't race, but stayed close enough to talk, while negotiating the path with other cyclists.

"Jessica asked about you," he said. "She wants to know if you'll come back."

Susan didn't want to talk about the store. She had really liked working there. She had loved doing the interior designs. She had ideas for other areas of the store too, but she didn't want to get so invested in the place or its president only to find that nothing can come of it.

"I think it's best if I find something I can do as a career."

She sped away from him then. It was harder to talk and ride at the same time, and André obviously wanted to discuss a subject Susan wasn't comfortable with. When André caught up with her, he didn't speak. They road together for a while, then slowed down and pulled off the path. They parked their bikes and stood, looking over the grassy green park.

The weather was warm, and for July the humidity was low. The park was crowded with people.

"What kind of career are you looking for?" André continued as if the subject was still part of their conversation.

Susan honesty hadn't thought about it. She had

enough money, but she wasn't used to sitting around, doing nothing. When she'd been in Italy, she'd had Jerome teaching her, but she looked at that time now as a long vacation. Now she was back to the real world and she wanted to be useful. To do something she could be proud of.

"I like photography." She lifted the camera that was hanging across her body. "I thought I could do something with that."

André sat down on the grass and pulled her down with him. Susan pushed the camera to the front and lifted it.

"We have an advertising department that needs photos every week for sales. We chronicle the store windows for past and future displays."

Susan thought about that. "I've always written my own copy for my photos. I could do that, but right now I'd like to change the subject."

André's brows rose and fell. "All right. What do you want to talk about?"

"I don't know."

"How about you? I told you about my family. What about yours? Brother, sisters, parents?"

"All of the above," she said. "I have two sisters and a brother. One still lives in Mountainview."

"Mountainview?"

"Montana."

"So that's the accent I hear."

"I don't have an accent," Susan contradicted.

André laughed. "You do, but it's more continental than Midwestern."

That she liked.

"Back to the siblings," André prompted.

"I have a sister in Chicago, and my brother—he's the youngest—is in college in Massachusetts."

"My family is spread out too, but we get together frequently, and we talk online."

"We do too. I FaceTime with my parents at least once a week. They worry about me living here alone."

"Most people who don't live here worry. Even with the rep, there is a lot to like about the city."

Susan nodded. She loved it. "Mountainview is a small town. It's picturesque, settled between two mountains and relies on tourism for most of its income."

"What did you do there?"

"I ran a small business."

"What kind of business?"

"It was an art-and-photo-framing business."

"Your own photos?"

She shook her head. "This was before I went to Italy and met Jerome."

"Why did you stop doing it?" André asked.

Susan swallowed, remembering the rubble that was left of her former life. "There was a fire. The building burned to the ground with everything I had in it."

"Surely there was an insurance settlement."

She nodded. "It wasn't enough to rebuild."

"So you went to Europe and then came here?"

"Pretty much."

André had skipped over a large part of her life, but she wouldn't fill him in.

"How long were you there?"

"A couple of years. I spent one in Paris, then moved to Italy."

"You didn't like Paris?" He looked incredulous.

"I loved it, but I wanted to see some of the other countries, so I traveled around for a while, and when I got to Italy, I met Jerome and stayed awhile."

"He must be a very interesting man."

Susan's hackles went up. She understood a fishing expedition when she heard one, and André was trying to get information from her. She'd told him about Jerome, but only in relation to Minette.

"He is. I couldn't have met a better man."

"I guess after losing your framing company, you needed a lifeline."

She wondered if he understood or if he was trying to find something. She hoped it was the former.

"He'll be here soon. I talked to Minette again."

"How's she doing?"

Susan thought about her consoling influence just a few nights ago. They didn't talk about Jerome or anything related to his visit to New York or a reconciliation between father and daughter.

"She's fine. I think she's getting closer to meeting with her dad."

"That's great. I can't imagine not having a relationship with my dad," André said. "He and my mom are on an around-the-world cruise. It's strange not talking to them."

"Can't you reach them on the ship?"

"We—my brothers and I—decided to let them have their time. Unless there is a major emergency, we aren't going to call them."

"Not even to say hello?"

"That's hard to do with them moving from one place to another, and you don't know how my mother will want to see everything there is to see in the amount of time she has."

"Sounds like a wonderful family."

André smiled, letting that be his answer.

"We've rested long enough," André said, unfolding his body and standing up. "Let's get back on the trail."

Susan got on her bicycle and the two started riding again, following the path that led through the park.

"You must have caused a sensation at the store today," Susan said later, as they sipped fruit smoothies at a sidewalk café.

"Why?"

Susan laughed. "André, you're a creature of habit. You didn't go to the store today and you left early a few days ago. Believe it or not, people keep track of your movements."

"Why?"

She frowned at him. "You're the president. Everyone works for you. Believe it or not, no one wants to get caught doing something that might displease you."

"They all know me and know I'm not a vindictive person."

"Still, you head the company. You control their livelihoods."

"And what do they think of you?" he asked.

"Other than Jessica, no one thinks I even know you."

He smiled, but his next question was serious. "Is that something you'd like to keep a secret?"

Susan took her time before answering. She needed to see if he wanted to continue seeing her as much as she wanted to see him again.

"More getting to know you?" She smiled.

"If that's your wish."

"That's my wish."

Chapter 6

It didn't appear that either of them wanted the day to end. Their bicycle trip had turned into a two-hour laugh-fest lunch, and then a walk around the city. Susan had taken hundreds of photos, many of which included André. Finally, at seven o'clock, they were back at the park.

"I know we've been out all day, but it's nearly dinnertime," André said. "Do you want to stop and get something before going home?"

Susan was hungry. It had been hours since they'd last eaten, and her stomach growled at the mention of food. "I have an idea," she said. "I don't live far from here." She glanced up the street, in the direction of the Dakota. "I'll make you something to eat and we can watch the lights come on as the sun sets."

"In addition to designing bedrooms and taking world-class photos, you cook too. Marry me now."

Susan laughed, but an emotion she wasn't familiar with went through her.

Back at her apartment, Susan grabbed a couple of steaks from the freezer, defrosted them in the microwave and popped them into the broiler. While she prepared other items, André talked to her from the other room.

"Have you lived here long?"

"About eighteen months." When she'd first returned from Italy, she had rented a house in Jersey City. Since she'd spent so much time traveling to places in the city, she had then looked for a permanent place that was close to the museums and theaters.

"It's a great location. How did you find it?"

"I was lucky. I lived in New Jersey and one of my neighbors told me about it. She told me I would be pushed to the top of the waiting list if I offered cash instead of a mortgage."

"And you decorated it yourself?"

"It's all me." Glancing through the doorway, she saw André staring at the photo of her that Jerome had taken. He'd done that the first time he had been in the apartment.

"Whatever you're cooking smells good," André said. He came to the doorway and watched her.

Susan checked the steaks and then pulled dishes and glasses from the cabinets. "Make yourself useful," she said, handing him the plates. "Set the table."

Susan had strategically placed it in front of the windows. As she ate each day, she got to see the city as the sun rose, crossed the sky and set.

"Wine?" André was back and standing in the doorway. "You handed me wineglasses."

She opened the refrigerator and pulled a bottle of red wine from the door. She handed it to him, along with a corkscrew.

It had taken only forty minutes from the time they had come through the door until they were seated at the table.

"This steak is perfect," André said. "You really can cook."

Susan's fork stopped halfway to her mouth. "Was there any doubt?"

"Maybe a little." André used his fingers to show a tiny amount.

"I take it you don't cook?"

"I'm an excellent cook," he said. "My mother made sure we could all cook our own meals. In fact, when we were growing up, it was our duty to prepare dinner at least once a week. And..." He paused, using his hand, palm out, to drive his point. "We couldn't cook the same thing two weeks in a row. We also could not serve someone else's leftovers."

"She sounds like a wonderful woman."

She was also going to be impossible to compete

with. While they had still been on the street, André had mentioned marriage. He wasn't serious and she knew it, but she wondered how he could remain unattached for so long.

"Your mom sounds like she reared you and your brothers well. How is it you're still single?"

His expression changed. It was subtle but she saw it. Immediately Susan knew she'd hit a sore spot.

"I'm sorry I asked that." She tried to retract it. "It's none of my business."

André took a long sip of his wine. "There was someone once. We parted three years ago. It didn't work out."

That was all he said. Susan didn't pursue it. She searched for something to say that would restore the mood. It was obvious that André's past still affected him. Susan wondered if he was still in love with the woman who'd no doubt broken his heart.

"How about dessert?" she asked with a smile.

"You made dessert?" His smile showed he was back in the present.

"Not exactly *made*, but I have something."

She removed the dinner plates and, in moments, came back with chocolate cake and ice cream topped with caramel syrup, whipped cream, and a cherry garnish.

"That looks good enough to eat," he teased. "We mis-hired you. The bakery would have been a better place."

They ate in silence. The lights that made New

York's skyline at night available from every street vendor came out in vivid display. Susan left the lights off, and together they watched the outside display its beauty.

"It's about time for me to go," André said an hour later. "I have an early morning."

He stood up and Susan joined him.

"I had a wonderful day," she said.

"Me too. Let's do it again," he said when they reached the door.

She knew this was going to be the hardest part of the day. They'd been together since early morning, and she enjoyed his company. She enjoyed talking to him, hearing his stories and even sharing her own. She wanted him to stay, but Susan knew it was better if they parted. He didn't really know who she was.

Despite the two of them being adults, she felt like an awkward teenager. Should she let him kiss her good-night? She'd already experienced his kisses—twice. Yet she wanted him to repeat it. And she wanted more. But she was scared of the way he made her feel. Afraid of how much she wanted him.

Susan looked up. André was standing close to her. His eyes had a smoldering look in them. It made her pulse race. Neither spoke for several seconds. Time seemed to stand still, with everything moving in slow motion. She saw him reach for her. His hands touched her arms and she moved toward him. She couldn't tell when it happened, but she melted in his arms.

His mouth came down to cover hers in a hungry

embrace as her hands circled his neck, connecting at the nape as she pushed closer to him. Fires inside her leaped into being, carrying her away on an unfamiliar tide of passion. His lips moving against hers, evoked a response that was total and complete. She had been kissed before but never like this, never with this intensity, never with this heat, taking any resistance she might have away from her.

Emotions she hadn't known existed battled for dominance as he pressed her farther into the door behind her. His hands roved over her, slipping under her shirt to explore the soft flesh beneath. She moaned lowly as his fingers moved over her back, then around to brush against her nipples, which were already hard and erect.

His mouth left hers and she dragged breath into her lungs. André moved back enough for her to see him. His eyes asked permission. Susan was beyond refusal. She wanted more from him. She'd wanted it since they'd met at the new-employee orientation. If she was honest with herself, she'd known they would end up here. He wanted her and she wanted him. What could it hurt? She refused to answer that question.

Her eyes moved up to his. No words were spoken—none were needed. Her arms moved farther up his neck, seemingly with a mind of their own. His arms tightened around her waist until there was no space between them. Susan pulled his head down as she went up on her toes to meet his waiting mouth. It was hot, wet and desirable. Fire burned in her and sprang up around them as they both responded to the inciting need for each other.

With their mouths still connected, he reached down and slid his arms under her knees. He lifted her. Susan felt suspended, but safe. André carried her into her bedroom. No light illuminated the area, only the ambient light from outside. She floated on the darkness until he stopped. Slowly he let her down. Susan felt the bed give as he laid her on it. His eyes, warm and brilliant with desire, devoured her face, as if he needed to imprint it on his mind. Her eyes traced his features in the subdued light. She didn't know what she looked like, but she was sure her feelings were evident in her eyes. André kissed her, planting soft, teasing kisses on her cheeks, the hollows under her ears and her throat, touching the rapidly beating pulse before reversing the direction and returning to her mouth, which opened like a flower, allowing him to taste the sweetness inside. Slowly his hands began an exploration of her body as his passion deepened to meet hers, and he quickly undressed her.

Momentarily afraid, she whispered, "André… I…"

"Don't talk," he said, stopping her, with his voice sounding husky. "Don't talk, don't think, just feel."

His quiet voice was her undoing. She reached up to pull his mouth back to hers, hearing a low moan in his throat before restraint snapped in him. In seconds he'd discarded his clothes and pulled her back into his arms. He moved his fingers over her body as if he was reading braille, causing tiny fires to ignite along the trails his fingers traversed. She in turn unashamedly memorized every inch of his taut body, pressing her lips to his shoulders, chest and face. She trembled as his body covered hers, feeling the long length of him against her slender frame. His hands were tools of sensation, incinerating the skin along her arms, her throat, and her breasts, and quickly leaving her a mindless mass of emotion. Slowly her desire levels rose higher and higher, and André found every erotic area of her body while his tongue and hands exploited them to the point of a beautiful pain, a pain so sweet that she shuddered, arching herself closer to him.

He made love to her slowly, entering her body for the first time with such tenderness, she could hardly stand it. She murmured his name time after time, saying it with the same rhythm as the joining of their bodies. Susan moved beneath André. She didn't have a choice. The pleasure quota she needed to fill pushed her on. Her need for André drove her, and his need for pleasure seemed to rise with hers. Together they reached for more, giving and taking, climbing over hills and mountains, as they reached for the clouds and beyond. There appeared to be no end to their climb. Pleasure took them to the stars.

Susan wasn't sure if she heard her own voice or André's. Suddenly an intense pleasure slammed into her. The jolt was so strong, she couldn't remain quiet. The feeling consumed her, like waves of rapture coming one after the other. Susan let them take her. She'd never felt like this before, never been on a plane this high or felt as if she was only complete when she was with André. Feeling totally mindless, she writhed beneath the heightened rhythmic thrusting of his taut body with a blind knowledge. They soared, with her hands moving over his powerful body as she moaned incoherently into his shoulder.

His mouth covered hers again as they came to a final, shuddering climax. While they clung to each other, savoring the sweet moment as long as possible, she kissed any part of him she could reach. His arms tightened around her, gathering her closer to him. What they'd done, what they'd felt, was beautiful, the most beautiful experience she had ever known or imagined. She was overcome with the force of emotion that welled up inside her.

André was kissing her again, pushing her tousled hair away from her face, understanding her feelings as she understood his. She'd never known how powerful a man and woman could be with each other. Yet she was unsure if it happened to all couples or just between herself and André.

Finally, spent and exhausted, they lay in each other's arms. He looked at her. Susan knew her face was open, devoid of makeup and shining. Her eyes were drowsy, but she felt beautiful, felt as if she was displaying the real Susan, the woman under the mask. With her eyes, she communicated silently to him.

He gathered her closer to him and stroked her

flushed face with his hand. Her body was moist with perspiration, and her hair had to be wild against the pillow she rested on, but she'd changed. In the last few minutes, she'd become a different woman, all because of the man who stared at her with dark, hooded eyes.

Susan settled in André's arms and fell into a restful and dreamless sleep. When she woke, the sun was peeking through the base of the distant buildings. André was gone. Susan was alone. She reached for the space where André had slept. Her hand brushed against a piece of paper.

After raising herself up on her elbows, she pulled the sheet over her naked breasts and read the note.

> I couldn't wake you. You looked so pretty sleeping. I had to go to the store. One more day out of the store, and I'm sure the cavalry would storm the citadel. See you tonight.
> André

Susan smiled. Her internal furnace started to burn. She'd see him again. Hopping out of bed, with a bounce to her step and feeling that all was well with the world, she headed for the shower. She danced through the door, humming a song. Suddenly she stopped and gripped the doorjambs with her hands as if the building would fall down without her support.

What was she thinking? After their night together, she knew she wanted to see André again, but what about her lie? What about the fact that he didn't know who she really was? And what about him? He didn't do relationships. How often had she heard that?

Turning around, she saw the note he'd left her lying on the rumpled sheets. Should she try to storm that citadel?

Susan had to get out of her apartment. She mainly had to leave the bedroom, but André's impression was in all of the rooms. She saw him looking at her photo. When she faced the windows, she remembered the two of them watching the sunset and the city lights blinking on as darkness fell.

She needed to think, but thinking was the last thing she wanted to do. After taking her camera, she left the apartment and started walking. She wanted to talk to someone, but other than Minette, most of her friends worked at the House of Thorn.

Jessica came to mind. Susan needed to talk to Jessica about leaving the furniture department. It would keep her from talking about André. But it was too early.

Susan couldn't go into the store, and Jessica rarely left the building for lunch. Her only option was to meet her after she got off for the day. Checking her watch, she noted that Jessica wouldn't leave the store for another three hours. She pulled her camera out, walked toward the river, and spent time taking photos of the tour boats and New Jersey, on the other side. So many photos pictured New York from that side of the Hudson River.

Jerome had taught her to read the light, and it was beautiful today. She wondered if her life was now going to rank as "before André" and "after André." The sky seemed brighter and the colors more vivid. Did André have anything to do with her outlook, and was he going to command her attention every hour of the day?

Apparently he was, since the hours seemed to go by at the speed of an ant. But finally it was time for her to try to find Jessica. Susan had been following her for three blocks, through the rush-hour crowd. Jessica commuted from New Jersey each day. She got on the train in New Brunswick, rode it to Penn Station and then walked to the House of Thorn.

Catching up with her, Susan called her name just as Jessica reached the escalator leading down to the station's main concourse.

Jessica looked over her shoulder. A huge smile covered her face as she reversed direction and rushed toward Susan.

"I'm so glad to see you," she said. The two stepped out of the flow of traffic. "I've been meaning to call you."

"I figured you wanted to know why I left."

"I do," she admitted.

"Let me buy you a cup of coffee or something," Susan suggested.

The two walked across the street to the Hotel Pennsylvania. Once they sat down with their coffee, Jessica waited for Susan to speak.

"I'm really not a salesperson," she said.

"You're the best salesperson I've ever worked with," Jessica contradicted. "Without you the department wouldn't be doing as well as it has."

"I'm sure you can keep that going."

Jessica shifted in her chair, coming toward the edge and tucking her feet to the side. "What's the real reason? Is it André?"

Susan's eyes widened. "How did you know?"

Jessica sat back. "I've worked at Thorn's for a lot of years. I've seen women come and go. He's usually not serious about any of them."

Susan wondered if he was serious about her. She hoped so, but she couldn't be sure.

"After that breakup with his fiancée, he..." She hesitated and spoke slowly. "He didn't seem interested in another relationship. Until you."

"Me? What do you mean?"

They hadn't really done anything to cause talk, but the word that caught her off guard was *fiancée*. André had been engaged in the past. Why hadn't the rumor mill sifted that tidbit of information her way?

"The way you look at him when you don't think anyone sees. And the way he looks at you, not to mention the two of you rearranging furniture after hours."

"You make it sound like we were sleeping on those beds."

Jessica leaned forward. "Didn't you want to?" Her voice was conspiratorial.

"Absolutely not," Susan said, truthfully. The thought had never crossed her mind.

"But you do like him?"

Susan couldn't lie. She nodded, not wanting to verbalize her answer in case her voice rose higher than its normal pitch.

After a moment, she swallowed and said, "He's one of the reasons I quit. I couldn't stay there and let things get out of hand. They were heading in that direction. Also, I do want to do something other than sell furniture."

"How about design?" Jessica suggested.

Susan shook her head. "Designing furniture? I don't think so."

"Not furniture. I'm thinking store design. You have an eye for color and placement, and you understand how people's minds work, what makes them stop and look—what makes them buy."

Susan mulled over the idea in her mind. She did like putting her newly acquired skill as a designer to work. Instead of working only in furniture, she could check out the other areas of the store. With all of the holidays and special events, she could do it full-time.

"And I could use my photographer's mind to develop designs." She spoke before she had thought it through.

"Exactly," Jessica said. "I'd put a word in for you with personnel."

"Don't do that."

Jessica looked perplexed. "Why not?"

"I really have no experience designing and I can't work at the store."

Jessica's face fell. "I've seen what you've done. André would probably rubber-stamp the decision, but he's the reason you don't want to be there, isn't it?"

She nodded. She wished she could share her secret with Jessica, but she knew it was better to keep things to herself.

"Does he know how you feel?" Jessica asked.

Their lovemaking came to mind. Susan saw herself glowing in the aftermath of their joining. She could almost feel André's arms around her, the way they had been as the two had fallen asleep together. Even when she had woken to find him gone, she had been dancing on air.

"I'm not sure," she answered Jessica's question.

"Why don't you tell him how you feel?"

She couldn't. "It's complicated."

"That's what people always say, when if you just talk, you might find out it's not complicated."

Susan smiled. Jessica gave sound advice.

"It's still a little early. I think I need to spend more time and see where this goes, if it goes anywhere. I'm not sure if André is interested in a relationship or if I am."

Jessica looked confused. "He looks it."

"You can't tell just by looking."

Thoughts had been running through André's head all day. All of them involving Susan. He couldn't wait to see her after work, although he couldn't say he worked today. His body was in the House of Thorn's New York store, but his mind was a few miles away, in Susan's apartment. And now he was only a couple of blocks away.

He stopped at a traffic light and looked up. He could see her building from where he stood. Images of how she'd looked in the early morning as she'd slept were clear in his mind. He'd hated to leave, but he'd had to, and he'd needed time to clear his mind, to think about what had happened and how they'd gotten to the point of making love. The day had progressed, but he had not. He was no closer to thinking about her without emotion than he was to lassoing the moon.

The light changed and he was rushing along with the crowd. They had no definite plans, although they'd texted each other several times during the last few hours. He thought of buying her flowers and wine and bringing them to her, but changed his mind, feeling she was someone who would see his uncertainty through the sentiment. And despite how André was feeling, in the back of his mind, he still wondered if she was like the other women who'd come and gone in his life.

Dinner, he thought. She'd cooked for him yesterday. Maybe tonight they could go to a restaurant. But he'd rather spend the night in her arms.

Susan was in the lobby when he arrived. He went directly to her, with his arms outstretched. She walked into them and he felt his arousal begin. She stepped back.

"I know we didn't make any plans, but a friend told me about a Cuban jazz club that's not far from here," she said.

"Great, we can grab something to eat and go there."

André couldn't remember what they had eaten. She was easy to talk to, and he was the one who talked. He felt nervous for no reason and accorded that to why he spoke so often. He'd never been affected by a woman the way he was by Susan. After he slept with a woman, he usually became more comfortable. But with her, the opposite was true.

He told her things about his childhood, about growing up with his brothers, about his aunt and uncle dying and their sons coming to live with them. About David and Blake getting married within two years. He wanted to tell her everything—wanted her to know him.

And he wanted to know her, but as he was about to ask her a question, it was time to go to the jazz club. The music was hot and loud, making it impossible to speak normally. People danced at their seats and joined the performers by beating out rhythms on the wooden tables.

When they eventually left, the sound on the street was dull in comparison. When another couple passed between them, he caught Susan's hand and kept it in his.

"What did you think?" she asked.

"It was fun. Something I haven't done before." He laughed, knowing there were so few things he hadn't done.

"Have you ever been to any of the islands?"

"Several. We used to go there for spring break every year."

"Bypassing Fort Lauderdale?"

"So old-school," he teased. "And the pretty brown girls were on the islands."

Susan looked at him and laughed. Just being with her made him feel different. He didn't want to do anything but make her happy.

"You were lucky. I spent my spring break working."

"What did you do?"

"I laid hardwood flooring."

"You didn't," he said, feeling sure she was kidding.

"I did. It paid more than working in an office and helped me buy my first car. And, in the long run, I learned a lot about wood. When I started my framing business, that knowledge came in handy."

"Did you make your own frames?" His question was facetious.

"I did," she answered before he could tell her not to. "The first one, I tried to carve all those little intricate curves. Way too ambitious a project to begin. I tend to do that. It's a weakness."

"Who told you that?"

"My mother, my father, my sisters, Jerome—practically everyone."

They laughed.

"So, is the store an ambitious project?"

"Well, you saw what I was doing there."

André stopped and faced her. "You were doing a very good job. Jessica loved that you were innovative. She said you were the best sales associate she'd ever had."

"I know."

Even though their hands were still linked, Susan looked at the ground before returning her gaze to him. "I already told you why I couldn't stay there. No one said anything, but I know the talk had begun."

"You're not afraid of a little talk?"

"André, I'm not you. I don't crave attention."

"You think I crave attention?"

She stared at him for a moment. "Look at your record. A different pretty woman every other week, a love-'em-and-leave-'em attitude. A fourth-date rule."

"None of that is true," he said.

"We've been over this before," she said.

"What if I've changed?"

André hadn't intended to say that. He had said a lot of things to Susan that he'd never say to anyone else.

"You think you've changed?"

"I don't know," he said.

"Maybe you'll know if we get to the fourth date."

Chapter 7

Tonight was it—their fourth date. André never counted dates. It just so happened that women began getting serious about dating by then. Was it always the fourth? How did Susan know that? He knew he wasn't the type to let things go further if he knew there was no future. But what about Susan? He had changed when it came to her. He was willing to open his heart, but he still had reservations. She was such a mystery.

He knew so little about her. She didn't appear to be like the other women he'd dated, but he couldn't be sure. She lived in a luxurious apartment. Her clothes carried designer labels. She'd received a fire-insurance settlement that didn't support a rebuild of her business under Midwestern standards. So how could it support a Manhattan apartment with a panoramic view? Who was supporting her? Was she like all of the others?

Maybe the ball he'd invited her to would provide the answer one way or the other. It would be their fourth date, if someone was counting.

He was going to find out—tonight.

After picking up a brush, André put the final touches on his hair. Perfect, he thought, straightening his tie in front of the bedroom mirror. Could a person be too perfect? So far Susan had everything he was looking for in a woman. But was it real? Doubt and indecision clouded his judgement. There were so many inconsistencies in her, yet they didn't distract from her, but made him want to pursue her more. André couldn't force the voice in his head saying there was something wrong to be quiet. Was it him? Had he been closed to relationships so long that he didn't see the real thing when it was right in front of him?

What was it about her that kept him wondering? André could have her investigated, but because she had worked for him and he had no legal reason to do it, it would be an invasion of privacy. When she had been hired, the store had done a background check and had found nothing out of the ordinary. Of course, he could look her up online and find out what was public, but he still considered that an invasion. If she wanted him to know something about her, she would tell him. And if he needed to know more, he should ask.

Questions filled his mind on the way to pick her up. None of them would get answers. If he wanted to ask, he didn't know where to start. He couldn't ask her where all of the money had came from. Her salary at the store didn't support her lifestyle.

The doorman tipped his hat as André entered the building. "She said to let you go up," he said.

André nodded. He'd passed the man enough times to be recognized. The fourth date came to mind again. Was that the magic number?

His breath caught in his throat when she opened the door. Purple was her color and she wore it regally. Everything from her lipstick to her Valentino gown and jewel-encrusted Christian Louboutin shoes matched. The white sparkle of the diamond necklace and earrings added to that of her eyes. All she needed was a crown to pull off the queenly charade.

Speech deserted him. André blinked a couple of times, dispelling the image.

"Come in," she said. "I'll get my purse and then I'm ready."

Inside he watched her sensually walk across the room. The gown clung to every part of her, and he had to turn away to keep from moving to touch her.

She lifted a purple beaded bag that matched her shoes and turned back.

"Wow!" André said. Actually, the word was forced from him. "You look fantastic."

She blushed. He saw the color highlight her cheeks.

"Well, if clothes make the man, you're fully cooked." She smiled.

André's thoughts whirled. He didn't want to go anywhere. He'd rather stay exactly where they were and spend the night alone—together.

"Maybe we'd better leave," he said before he could act on the thoughts going through his head, thoughts that had him removing all that purple one inch at a time.

Heads turned when André and Susan entered the ballroom. Like the wedding where he'd first encountered Susan, this was an area where André was well-known. Many of his friends and colleagues were here, and he expected to see his brother David and his wife. But it wasn't David he saw. When they reached their table, Carter and Christian, his twin cousins, were already seated, along with their dates.

The men stood and came around to hug André.

"Hello, I'm Carter," one of them said to Susan.

She accepted his handshake, and introductions were made all around before they sat down.

"Anyone seen David and Rose yet?"

Both cousins shook their heads. "You know Rose," Christian said. "More than likely, David is still trying to pry her out of the store."

Each time they came to New York, Rose wanted to see every department of the New York store and compare it to what she was doing in the Logan Beach store.

"I'm sure they're on their way," Carter chimed in.

"What do you do, Susan?" Christian asked.

"I'm a photographer," she said.

André noticed that she didn't expound.

"Gee, you could be the model," one of the women said.

Susan smiled her thanks. André had to agree with the woman. Susan was the most beautiful woman in the room. He could tell that when they'd entered and heads had turned as they'd walked by.

"I thought photographers always had cameras hanging from their necks," Christian said.

Susan smiled as she drew her purse closer to her and clicked the catch. Then she opened to reveal the tiny camera hidden inside.

"Be careful what you do, guys," Christian's date said. "You could find yourself on Instagram."

They all laughed.

"Why don't we dance?" André said.

They left the table and went to the dance floor. The music was soft and André got to hold her close. It was exactly what he wanted to do. With Susan in his arms and the music surrounding them, he felt as if nothing could be better in his world. His eyes closed and he swayed with her, feeling the softness of her skin under his hands.

They hadn't been at the ball more than half an hour, yet he was ready to take her away, keep her for himself, learn her secrets and have her learn his. This was the fourth date, but he feared their roles were reversed. She might be the one to call things off, because he was surely the one who wanted to take things more seriously.

A commotion behind them had André turning to look. David and Rose had arrived and were being greeted by the other Thorns at the table.

"Is that your brother?" Susan asked. "I recognize him from the photos."

He took her hand, and then they left the dance floor and started toward their table. Rose saw him first.

"André," she called and rushed to hug him. David came behind her. The two brothers pumped hands.

André introduced her, and while David's reaction was a wider smile than was already on his face, Susan had the feeling he was totally surprised to see his brother with a date, or maybe just with her. They shook hands.

Rose was less formal. She was warm and happy. She looked Susan up and down without any malice in her gaze.

"That is an absolutely fabulous gown," Rose said instead of hello. "Valentino?"

Susan nodded.

"And you wear it well."

"*Regally* was my word," André said. He slipped his arm around Susan's waist and pulled her an inch closer to him.

"Where did you find it?" The awe in Rose's voice was evident.

"It was a shopping-spree treat from a couple of years ago."

André forced himself not to tighten his hand. Instead he set his teeth and held any comment that might escape inside. Valentino was not an off-the-rack brand.

"Rose, we're not spending the night cross-examining André's date on her clothes," David cautioned his wife.

Rose glanced at David, then back at Susan. "I apologize," she said. "I used to be a buyer at Thorn's before it was Thorn's."

"She's referring to the Logan Beach store," David explained. "The building was once Bach's Department Store. A lot of it was damaged by a storm. The House of Thorn bought it, and that's where I met Rose, the love of my life."

He leaned over and kissed her cheek. All eyes were on David, but André watched Susan. She smiled and turned to look at him. Usually he would pretend to be interested in something else. But he found himself unable to look away.

Their gazes went on too long. If it hadn't been for the band playing a fan favorite that snapped his attention, they'd still be looking longingly into each other's eyes.

Couples left the floor, and through the magic of electrical hydraulics and some very crafty engineers, a carpeted runaway grew out of the wall and extended across the floor. Quickly, men appeared and dressed the floor around it with flowers that matched the animated roses appearing on the walls, again through the magic of intelligent lighting.

"The show is about to begin," André whispered to Susan.

"There's a show?"

He leaned close enough to her ear that his lips nearly touched her skin. "There's always a show at these affairs."

"It's not Fashion Week," Rose spoke up. "But with this many retailers in one place, it's perfect to entertain them with future sales products."

"Future?"

"What they show today will be for sale this fall and winter."

Susan nodded as the first model stepped onto the runway and began her signature walk. She wore an open red wool coat that fanned the floor. Under it were snow-white wide-leg pants that flapped as she strutted down the runway and a shimmering gold sequin to-the-waist bandeau sweater. The coat naturally swung, but as she walked, she used a hand to efficiently flip it around, showing the gold lining.

Growing up in a family of retailers, André and his brothers had sat through more fashion shows than they could count. His mother had insisted that even though they were boys, they needed to understand that women made most of the purchases, so they needed to understand what made women buy, and they needed to know the designer names so they could talk intelligently to their clientele.

The program passed the fifteen-minute mark, but no one was checking their watches. Each outfit outdid the one before.

André leaned close to Susan and whispered, "They're right, you know."

"About what?" Susan asked, glancing his way.

"You could be up there?"

She shook her head.

"Why not? You must know you're a standout."

"Thanks, but I don't crave the limelight."

"And that's why you're dressed as if you're about to step onto the red carpet," he teased.

"I'm dressed this way because being out with a captain of industry like you calls for a certain expectation."

"So, you dressed this way for me?"

Susan gave him a Mona Lisa smile, pressed her cheek to his and turned back to the models on the runway.

The show was coming to a close. From experience, André instinctively knew that. Often they ended with a wedding gown. He expected to see a winter wedding dress, complete with fur around the neck and cuffs. But he was disappointed. The model stepped onto the carpeted runway, and heads popped up. People sat straighter in their chairs. And the exhalation of air was noted and deserved.

Tonight's final gown was an ice-blue waterfall of ruffles. The exclamation and applause from the crowd was resounding. Right when the finale of all of the models in their last outfits was expected, something unexpected happened. Two models dressed identically to the first ice-blue one joined her.

"I know what they're going to do," Susan said into André's ear.

"What?"

"Just look at the background."

André looked at the cycling points of light that swam along the walls in perfect syncopation to the soft music accompanying the models.

The three women turned in several circles, as though they intended to perform a dance. They came together, arranging themselves back to back to back. The gowns flared out as the models crouched into what appeared to be one sitting position. When they tucked their heads, the result was one large rose with three black-haired models' faces forming the center.

"Wow!" Rose exclaimed.

The crowed came to its feet, including everyone at André's table. Deafening applause reverberated through the ballroom, along with shouts of bravo.

"That was wonderful," Susan said when she was able to talk again. The applause went on for several minutes, and then the designer gave a speech.

"It wasn't what I expected," André said.

"I don't think anyone did," David agreed.

Susan had. He wondered how she'd known. That's what he asked her as they entered his apartment later that night.

"It was obvious. The model showed the huge ruffles time and again by twisting them in huge flowing circles. The walls had the flowers all over them, but they turned to blue roses when she stepped onto the runway. And when the two other models appeared, I knew they had to do something together. Otherwise they'd have been in different colors. I could see the dresses becoming rose petals."

André pulled a bottle of wine from the refrigerator and started to open it while she walked around his apartment.

"I love how you can see things that no one else can," he said, handing her a glass.

"I'm sure other people can see the same things."

"Not like you."

No one he'd encountered was like Susan. It was like finding a new world around every corner when he was with her. He'd had a plan for the night, but any thought of it had left his mind when she'd opened her door earlier tonight.

His brothers had approved, and by the long conversation she'd had with Rose, the two of them seemed to act more like sisters than people who had just met.

They sat on a large sofa that faced a modern glass fireplace that burned propane fuel. He knew lighting it would make the room more romantic, but since it was July, that wasn't an option.

Susan placed her wineglass on the coffee table and turned to him. "So," she said. "What did you think of our fourth date?"

André placed his glass next to hers. He sat back,

ran his hand along the back of the sofa and caressed her neck. Pulling her close enough to kiss, he whispered, "I think we should go on a fifth one."

Chapter 8

Susan leaned back from the short, but mind-blowing kiss. "How long have you lived here?" she asked.

"About five years. Why? Does the place look like I've just moved in?"

He looked around the apartment, probably seeing it as a stranger would.

"It's a beautiful place and I like the way you've decorated it."

"I can't take credit for that. Someone from the store did the designing."

She looked at him in surprise.

"But I picked out all the furnishings." He raised his hands in defense. "It doesn't have all the windows yours has, but I call it home."

Susan laughed. He reached for her and pulled her next to him. She rested her cheek on his shoulder as his arm held her close. They sat like that for a while, with neither speaking.

"André, I had a very good time tonight," she said. "I enjoyed meeting Rose and your brothers."

"They had good things to say about you too," he replied.

Susan turned her head to face him. He smiled at her and kissed the top of her head. His fingers threaded through her hair, undoing the expensive salon style she'd had done especially for tonight. She didn't stop him. Susan liked the way his hands felt. He looked at her hair as he undid it, following the long strands all the way to the end. He laid them along her back and then repeated the procedure.

"You know, I sat for an hour while the beautician crafted my hair in just that style?"

"She did a wonderful job," he said, as he continued to undo her work.

"So, you're the take-the-toy-apart-to-see-how-it-works type of guy?"

His hand stilled. "I would never take you apart or think of you as a toy."

The air was suddenly charged. She could almost hear the question in his mind asking if anyone had ever treated her that way before. She answered his question.

"No one has."

"Has what?"

"Ever treated me that way."

Susan felt tension leave his body, and his hands resumed their work. When her hair was totally undone, he looked into her face, but continued to finger through the strands. She saw the desire there. For a long moment, they stared into each other's eyes. She knew hers reflected the same thing.

Susan wanted to look at the floor, but her gaze was held by an invisible force to the brown pools of deepening desire in André's face. The feeling of timelessness and heat beat its message into her until her body clamored to close the short distance between his mouth and hers. She didn't know who had moved first. Suddenly they were both on the floor.

She was in his arms and he was kissing her. The heat around them intensified. She could feel the flames and almost see tongues of fire licking around them. If it was possible, the fire consuming her was even hotter. She pressed closer to him, running her fingers over his head and down his hair, to his neck. Stroking her back, he kissed her eyes, her cheeks and her chin before returning to devour the sweetness of her demanding mouth.

His hands traveled exploringly down her arms, to her breasts, which responded immediately under his expert touch. Her hands loosened the buttons on his shirt, beginning their own exploration of his chest and back. Sanity and reason were somewhere in the farthest recesses of her mind. Here there was no thought, only the mindless possession of her senses of touch, feel and taste—his touch, his feel and his taste. Her body cried out for fulfillment. She wanted him, wanted him more than she'd ever thought possible. She wanted to be his completely and fully.

A low moan escaped her as he slipped the dress from her shoulders and burned her skin with his mouth, first trailing kisses across her shoulders, to the valley between her breasts, and then upwards to her throat and ears before returning to her mouth. Without warning he wrenched away from her. After getting to his feet, he dragged her up with him. Confusion gripped her for a split second before he lifted her in his arms and headed for his bedroom.

No words were spoken—none were needed. She rested her head on his shoulder and hugged him as she floated through the dark hall. He lowered her until her feet touched the floor. Warm hands cupped her face, and his mouth covered hers. The kiss was slow, sensual and penetrating. André held her loosely, but the connection between them was as strong as steel. Susan let her thoughts drift away. Her hands circled André's waist, slipping inside his open shirt and feeling the smoothness of his skin. It was hot. He was hot.

She looked up as waves of something indescribable went through her. She wanted André now. She pulled him to her, clamped a hand around his neck and pulled his mouth to hers. He stretched out on the bed, aligning their bodies. Susan felt the impression of him. His hardness against her softness.

They fit together like pieces of the same puzzle. André moved from her mouth to shower her face with teasing kisses that developed into a desperate need for each other. Their tongues tangled and heads bobbed as they moved together, each taking and giving pleasure to the other. She pulled at his shirt and pants, while he unzipped her gown. And though it didn't fall into a rose on the floor, her body felt like a petal opening for him.

"André," she whispered. Her voice sounded low to her ears.

"Don't talk," he said, stopping her, with his voice sounding husky. His soft voice was her undoing. She reached up to pull his mouth back to hers, hearing a low moan in his throat before restraint snapped in him. His hands explored her, pulling her into him and taking her mouth while he felt the softness of her body contrasting with the solidness of his. She in turn unashamedly memorized every inch of his taut body, pressing her lips to his shoulder. She trembled as his body moved over hers. She knew this was dangerous, but she pushed the thought away.

She was afraid of her feelings. She wanted to push him away, but the sensations his hands were causing as they trailed fire along her arms, her throat and her breasts quickly left her a mindless mass of emotion. Slowly he raised her desire levels higher and higher, finding every erotic area, with his tongue and hands exploiting them to the point of an exquisite physical pain, a pain so sweet that she shuddered, arching closer to him.

The sound from Susan's throat pushed him forward as they joined in the most intimate way. It could be her first time. She murmured his name over and over, almost moved to tears by the care he took with her. It was a memory. They were making a memory. When he was gone, when André realized she was getting too close, when their fourth date was over, she would have this night.

Change came at that moment. The tenderness in André's movements intensified. Susan rushed to go with him. Her body was so hot, so ready for him to take everything she offered that she could hardly contain herself. The rapid movements of their bodies brought pleasure to her with each stroke. Yet André wasn't ready to take her over the edge. His hands slipped under her, raising her legs, and then he entered her to the hilt. He didn't seem able to control himself. Neither did Susan. She matched André one rhythmic stroke for another. Together they should be creating fire.

She had no idea why they didn't burst into flames. She wanted to touch André all over. She wanted him to touch her. Not only her body, but she wanted their minds to meld. She wanted to know him, know everything about him. She wanted to wake with him and find their nights not separated by streets and avenues. She wanted André to keep giving her pleasure, and she wanted to make sure that all of the pleasure she had to give went to him. The two merged, with their legs and arms moving faster and faster, and they dug deeper into the primeval dance.

Suddenly the world around them disappeared. Nothing existed except the two of them and the fire they created. She could see the flames, feel their burning, yet she wanted more of them. She wanted André to continue the exquisite pleasure he was giving her. And she wanted to return it. She wanted to make sure that he felt as she did, that her gift to him was special and as consuming as an explosion.

Their bodies seemed to know each other. They were in tune and each stroke brought them higher and higher toward a new universe, Susan moved faster and faster, matching André's thrusts with her own.

When she was sure she could take no more of the passion that had been unleased inside her, André took her a step higher, increasing her need for him and forcing her to shout his name to release the force inside her. Emotions vied for dominance as they thrashed about the sheets. Inside her the surge began, a swell of carnality so great and so strong that she felt it might push her over the edge. Then it did. She heard her own voice, shouting as the two of them performed the oldest dance.

The sensation of floating somewhere on an astral plane carried her high above the rumpled sheets. She took André with her. The two of them, alone in the world, *their* world, their place. This was theirs, never to be shared by anyone else.

André was kissing her again. Without words, he seemed to understand her feelings as she understood his. Until now Susan had never known how powerful love could be for a man and a woman.

Finally they both lay exhausted in each other's arms. He looked at her. Susan didn't try to cover herself. She wanted him to look at her. She wanted him to see all of her. She was his.

Did he love her? Was that what she saw in his eyes? Her heart pounded harder than it ever had. Did she want that? She did. But it wasn't possible. There was too much unknown between them. He didn't know who she really was, although most of what she had told him was the truth.

And how could any relationship survive when it was based on lies and deception?

Susan's eyes were shiny and drowsy. André gathered her to him and studied her flushed face, her body slightly moist with perspiration, her beautiful hair almost obscuring the pillow she rested on. She didn't know how gorgeous she looked. Would she always look like this after lovemaking? He knew he wanted to see that look again and again. He wanted to be the only one ever to see it.

He wanted her; he wanted to see her smile, make her laugh, feel himself moving inside her and be rewarded by this look after making love, to see it shining in her eyes. Reverently, he kissed her forehead and then contentedly fell asleep.

When he woke, she was still lying next to him. Just as before, when they had made love at her apartment, he watched her for a long while. He counted the rise and fall of her chest as she breathed. Moonlight spilled through the windows and over part of her face. Her eyelashes were resting on her cheeks. A slight smile curved her lips, and he hoped she was dreaming of him. He dreamed of her even when he was awake. The entire picture aroused him. He didn't try to tamp it down, and his body grew hard with wanting.

He played with the idea of waking her. Morning sex was a perfect way to begin the day, even if the sun was only tingeing the eastern horizon. He was still holding her, listening to her breathing, smelling the lilac scent of her shampoo and taking in the electric aroma of sex in the air. It was a signature scent, unavailable for sale and only purchasable by two unique people.

André waited, watching, but he knew as long as his body was in contact with hers, his arousal would remain engorged and ready.

A low growl in André's stomach signaled to him. Had he ever been this hungry? He couldn't remember if he had. Smiling, he attributed it to the night before—his night with Susan. He was hungry for her and for food. Their lovemaking had pushed him well past the stamina he'd thought was his maximum, but she'd proven he was stronger than he had even known.

Slipping out of bed, he left Susan sleeping. He'd wake her with breakfast, and then more lovemaking. André planned to spend the day in bed with her. Nothing else mattered. The store could take second place today. Barefoot, he padded to the living room, after closing the bedroom door so he wouldn't wake her. The sun was rising, but the room was still too dark to see details clearly. Susan's rose gown lay on the floor. It wasn't a rose, but that was how he thought of it. Picking it up, he remembered how good she had felt in it. Running his hands over the silken fabric was like caressing her. His stomach growled again.

André threw the gown over the sofa. It landed with a flap, down where the zipper was, and the designer label caught his attention. He knew labels. It was part of his occupation to know them. Rose had called it. Valentino. But there was another label.

He carried the dress to the kitchen and turned on a light. The dress had been rented. Susan didn't own this gown. Of course, he thought. How could she afford it? Memory took him back to their first meeting. She was wearing a Christian Siriano gown. That's what she was hiding. She wasn't who she pretended to be. The apartment, the camera and rented clothes. Who was bankrolling her?

Was she looking at him as a replacement?

André collected her clothes and folded them neatly. Forgetting breakfast, as he was no longer hungry, he returned to the bedroom, placed the clothes on the bottom of the bed and went into the bathroom to take a shower. He didn't try to be quiet. He wanted her awake and gone.

Susan sat up. "Good morning," she said, but he was already closing the bathroom door. After locking it, he turned on the water so he couldn't hear her.

And she couldn't hear him.

His stomach was tied in knots, and he felt like kicking himself. Why had he let her in? Why had he deviated from his normal fourth-date plan? He'd told her he had never thought of the fourth date as being when things turned, but that was exactly where it did. He could certainly tell that by the way he felt about Susan.

He'd get over her. He had gotten over women in the past. He could do it again.

Stepping under the needlelike spray of the shower, he let the water sting his skin. He took longer than usual. Normally he got in, washed, rinsed and got out. He was always on his way to the store or to some social event that was directly or tangentially connected with the store—like the one he'd attended with Susan last night. It felt like a lifetime ago now.

André reached out and turned the shower off. He couldn't stay in it for the rest of the day. His dressing room was across from the shower and he dressed quickly. Susan was no longer in the bed when he stepped into the bedroom. Her clothes were gone, but he knew she was still in the apartment. He heard her happily humming from the kitchen. And he could smell coffee brewing and bacon cooking. His hunger returned—both forms of it.

Something was wrong. Susan could tell it the moment André appeared in the kitchen. She was wearing the gown she'd had on for the fashion show and ball. André was dressed in a suit and tie. She could feel the tension. The two of them were night and day, however.

"What's wrong?" she asked. "Shouldn't I have made coffee and breakfast?"

He shook his head. She noticed he did not speak. What had happened between last night and this morning? What had she done? Or not done?

"I have to go to the office," he said.

"I see," she responded, but both of them knew she didn't. "Did something happen at the store?"

He shook his head again. "Everything there is fine."

"Then what happened here?"

It was hard to look at her in that dress. He wanted to cross the room and pull her into his arms. "The fourth date," he finally said.

Susan felt as if he'd hit her. Her entire body seemed to turn to stone. She couldn't move. A flash of heat burned her face. She knew her normal light brown color was either as pale as snow or as red as fire. She stared at him for a long moment. When she recovered, she turned the flame off under the frying pan.

"Not a problem," she said.

Susan walked past him. After picking up her shoes and purse, she left the apartment barefoot. She felt numb. By the time she got to the elevator, her numbness had changed to anger. Outside the building, she got into a taxi. The driver didn't give her a second look. In Mountainview, eyebrows would've been raised, and before she would have gotten through her front door, the entire town would have known she'd spent the night with a man.

But this was New York. And nobody cared.

Not even her doorman, who opened the door as she exited the cab and didn't show any expression as she walked through the door. She headed straight for the elevator, but before she got there, a man stood up from one of the reception chairs.

"Jerome," she screamed and ran toward him. She grasped his arms with her hands, and the two nearly toppled over. Jerome stepped back to keep them balanced. Tears sprang to her eyes and spilled down her cheeks.

Jerome pushed her back, but held on to her arms. "I'm sure there's a story about this dress and why you're arriving home at ten o'clock, in the clothes from the night before."

"There is, and maybe I'll tell you about it later."

Together, they went to the elevator while Susan apologized for forgetting he was coming to New York and staying in her guest room.

"All right," Jerome said after he'd settled in and Susan had showered and changed clothes. "What's the story? Those tears in the lobby weren't because you were so glad to see me."

Susan's hair was wet and slicked back, off her face. She took the cup of coffee Jerome had made for her and sat at the end of the sofa. Jerome knew some of what she'd done since coming to New York. He had kept in touch with her by phone and email. He knew she had gotten a job working in the furniture department of a store, but he didn't know about André.

"You must be tired. You just flew all night."

"Jet lag is less of an issue when you travel west," he reminded her. "I'll probably go to bed early, but I'll be up long before the sun. Besides, I got some sleep on the plane."

Susan stood up and went to the kitchen. The open concept of her apartment allowed them to see each other and talk. She opened the freezer door of her refrigerator, pulled out a large container of ice cream and proceeded to fill a bowl with it.

Jerome sighed when she resumed her seat. "I've seen enough scenes like this to know there's a broken heart, either in the making or completely torn apart."

Susan waited a moment, spooning ice cream into her mouth. "His name is André Thorn."

"Thorn?" Jerome's brows rose. "Thorn, as in the House of Thorn?"

"You know it?" Jerome wasn't a retail guru like André. Jerome dealt in paint and canvases. He worked with light and shadow.

"I've shopped there a time or two."

"For whom?" she teased, as a smile tinged her mouth. "Some Italian lady?"

"We're talking about you, not me." He diverted her attention back to her own problems. "What happened with André?"

"I should have known better," she said. "He had a reputation for only dating a woman three or four times."

"What?"

She hunched her shoulders. "He denies it, but his reputation is that when a woman becomes serious—"

"He breaks it off," Jerome finished for her. "And you got to date number four?"

"Last night."

"I'm sorry."

Susan knew there was nothing he could say to ease how she felt. Truthfully, she didn't know how she felt. She was still numb from his abruptness this morning. When they had made love last night, it had been life altering. Yet this morning he had become a completely different person. And she didn't know what had happened.

She hadn't given him a chance to explain, not that an explanation had seemed to be forthcoming. Had he only told her there would be a fifth date to get into bed with her? Anger swarmed inside her.

"Does he know who you are?" Jerome asked.

She shook her head. "I don't think that would make a difference. At least the money wouldn't. The deception is a different story."

"I'm sure he'd understand if you told him."

"He might, but that's not the issue between us. André isn't a man to make a commitment. He'd proven that time and again. And I was the idiot who thought he was changing for me."

"You're not an idiot."

"Do you mind if we change the subject?" she asked.

"Not at all. In fact, I have an idea. I want to see the gallery. So go get dressed, comb you hair, do your makeup and let's go. You've got fifteen minutes."

Susan didn't want to go, but after a moment she thought going out would be better than being alone with her thoughts, in the apartment.

The gallery was a beautiful white brick building that had windows everywhere. Inside, the walls were white, but the lighting could change them to any color an artist might want. While Jerome found the director, Susan walked through the rooms, admiring the arrangements.

She'd come here with Minette before the photos had been hung. Susan recognized some of the photos from her time in Verona. There were some new ones depicting places she had been when she'd lived there. She rounded a corner and was stopped when she saw two photos on the facing wall. One was of Minette as a child. See looked about ten years old. She stared directly at the camera. The light behind her made a halo of her hair.

The second photo was of her. Susan knew exactly what she'd been thinking when that photo had been snapped. She'd been sitting on the stone seats in the arena, trying to imagine gladiators and lions. Her brow was furrowed, and she was concentrating hard in the harsh afternoon sunlight.

"Like it?" Jerome asked from behind her.

"It surprised me."

"It's one of my favorites," Jerome said. "It shows mood, contemplation and humanity. Anyone who looks at this wants to know what is so profound that you're giving it all your attention."

"Speaking of attention, I have something to show you."

Susan led him to a newly renovated room in the gallery. She stood to the side as he followed her in.

Jerome didn't speak. He stared from one wall to another, taking in the photos. Then he walked toward one wall and stood several feet from it.

"What do you think?" Susan asked.

"Are these yours?"

She heard the awe in his voice.

"They're mine," a voice behind them said.

Both Susan and Jerome turned around. Minette stood in the doorway, exactly where her father had paused a moment ago.

"Minette," Jerome said, with a smile on his face.

He moved toward his daughter and hugged her. Susan noticed the hug was a little awkward. Minette had agreed to see him. It was a first step.

"I'm sure you two need to talk," Susan said. "I'll

see you back at the apartment," she told Jerome. Then she signaled Minette as a reminder of her promise to listen and talk to her father with an open mind. Minette nodded.

Susan looked for a taxi, but as usual when she really wanted one, there was none available. She began walking and soon was standing across the street from the House of Thorn. She wanted to go inside. She wanted to see André again. She wanted to understand what his reasons were for ending their relationship.

Two days later she still hadn't heard from André. She also had not been in the store. She and Jerome talked a lot. Minette joined them a few times. They went to dinner together and talked about being in Italy together, about cameras and composing photos, about the upcoming show.

What Jerome and Minette talked about without Susan was their past. The two seemed to be getting better and better acquainted as the days went by. Right now they were out, leaving Susan alone in the apartment.

After an hour, Susan grabbed her camera and headed for someplace she had yet to visit in the city. She got on the first subway that came along and rode it to the end of the line. She got off at Forest Hills and wandered around the small town. It took her mind off everything except the beauty of the land, the century-old buildings and the stadium that was once the home of the US Open Tennis Championships.

It was a city about the past, even though the present ran through it with fast cars and boutiques. Susan thought of her own past. She'd made the decision to return to the United States. She could have gone back to Mountainview, but after Paris and Verona, she had wanted a place that was more anonymous, where no one would recognize her and she had the freedom to be herself.

Now she looked at where that had led her.

Chapter 9

Routine was routine, André thought as he made his way through the store. His heart was no longer in it. The House of Thorn had always been there for him. It was his rock, his anchor that made everything all right. So why had it deserted him? He no longer got the satisfaction he had in knowing the store was running like clockwork. It was, yet he almost wished for something to go wrong so he would have something to focus his mind on.

As it was, his focus was on a dark-haired beauty who'd wormed her way into his heart. Her reasons, however, were not true, and he'd classed her in the group with all the other gold diggers.

"André?"

He stopped at the sound of his name. He was in the furniture department, yet he had no memory of walking there.

"Jessica," he said.

"Did you get an invitation?"

Jessica always whispered in the store. André often thought it funny that she made everything sound like a conspiracy, when there was none. Susan had said she was speaking in her confidential voice so that customers wouldn't think she was allowing anyone else to overhear her.

"Invitation to what?"

"The photo show. The one that her friend from Italy is having?"

André knew exactly what she meant. He did have an invitation.

"I got one."

"But you're not going?" Jessica had asked a question, but she'd voiced it as a statement.

"I have another obligation."

"I see," Jessica said. "Not a problem."

In his mind, André was immediately transported back to his apartment. Those were the exact words Susan had used just before she'd walked out of his life. Just before he'd driven her out of his life. He couldn't go to that opening. He didn't even know why he had received an invitation.

Someone cleared his throat behind André. Both he and Jessica turned. A tall man with salt-and-pepper hair stood before them. André recognized him, but his attention was on Jessica.

"You must be Jessica," he said.

"May I help you?" she answered, thinking he was a potential customer. "Are you looking for something for your home?"

"Not exactly."

Jessica looked at André. "Excuse me, this is—"

"Jerome Marchand." André spoke the man's name. "I'm André Thorn."

"Good. I have you both here. I hope you can come to the show tonight."

"I got Susan's invitation. I wouldn't miss it," Jessica said, smiling as if the latest rock star had just introduced himself.

"I got an invite also, but I won't be able to come," André told him.

"That's why I'm here. I specifically invited you."

"The invitation…it's from you?" he asked in disbelief.

"I had it delivered. Susan doesn't know anything about it."

"I don't know what Susan has told you, but—"

"Nothing," Jerome interrupted. "Well, that's not totally true. She's told me how you met and that she worked in the furniture department, here in the store."

André looked around the furniture department. Jessica was called away by a customer, leaving the two of them alone.

"She did work here, but she quit a few weeks ago."

"I know. The invitation is for you. No strings."

"Will Susan be there?" André asked, but he was sure he already knew the answer. Susan had spoken of the art show and Jerome several times.

"She will," Jerome said.

"Thank you, but don't expect me."

"Think about it. If there is no reason for the two of you not to be in the same room, then there's no reason for a refusal."

But there was a reason, André thought. Rumpled sheets, the smell of the best sex he'd ever had and the stunned look on her face when he'd told her that date number four was it.

"Well," Jerome said, offering his hand in farewell. "I have to grab some souvenirs to take back with me. I'm sure there's a department that has all the New York slogans and memorabilia."

André shook his hand. "First floor, near the side entrance."

Jerome turned to the escalator. He waved at Jessica and kept André in view until the moving stairway was too far down for them to see each other.

He would not go, André told himself. He didn't need to continue seeing a gold digger. And he didn't know what Susan might say or do. Jerome could come and personally invite him to the program, but he shouldn't expect André to comply.

He would not go.

André was still telling himself that when he arrived home. He was restless, but he'd been that way since Susan had left. Tonight, however, his impatience seemed more pronounced. Several times, he went to get something to drink only to find nothing satisfying. He paced back and forth, passing the spot on the floor where he'd picked up the purple dress.

He would not go.

The invitation lay on his dresser; it was elegant. André fingered the heavy sparkling gold paper. It had a formal border with a shimmering pearl motif between the edge and a blocked ridge. It would make a brilliant statement for a wedding. An embossed panel framed the black raised lettering that was inviting him to attend the opening of the much-anticipated works of Jerome Marchand.

André had said he would not attend. And right up until he had showered, that had been his plan. The thought of seeing Susan again outweighed his objections. He was sure he could do this without any repercussions. They would be in a room filled with other people. If it was crowded enough, they may only get to see each other across a room. And if he was uncomfortable enough, he would be free to leave.

Yet the moment he stepped through the door of the gallery, he knew he wasn't free. By any form of the word, he was totally tied to Susan. Their eyes met across the room. Despite the crowds milling about, looking at the photos, he had a clear sight of her.

Thank God she wasn't wearing purple.

* * *

"What's he doing here?" Susan's stomach dropped three stories when André Thorn walked in through the gallery door.

"I invited him," Jerome said. He smiled at her, and with two wineglasses in his hands, he walked over to give one to André.

Susan felt rooted to the spot. Minette put her hand on Susan's shoulder and she nearly jumped out of her skin.

"Oh, Minette, I'm sorry. I..." She broke off, not knowing what to say.

"You didn't tell me he was better looking in person than in any of those online photos."

"Why would your father invite him?" she asked. "And not tell me?"

"He knew you wouldn't come if you knew he was going to be here."

Susan turned and looked at Minette. "You knew?"

"I delivered his invitation."

"Why?"

"Because you're in love with him," Minette said.

"I am not," Susan denied.

"Then talking to him won't be a hardship."

Susan didn't want to talk to him. He'd said enough in his apartment, nearly a week ago. He wasn't interested in date number five, and she wasn't one to run after a man who didn't want her. Suddenly she was hot. He'd said he wanted her, and he'd done a fine job of proving it throughout the night. But then the sun had risen, and the clear light of day had shone on them both.

André had made a decision, and Susan had not had an argument against it. Even if she'd had one, it wouldn't have made a difference. Susan had known that, and it was why she'd accepted his decision and had left.

"He's coming over," Minette whispered, dropping her head and taking a sip of the drink she held. "Gotta go. My father is calling me."

Jerome wasn't even looking in Minette's direction, but Susan was aware of what her friend was doing. Susan steeled herself to greet André. If she could have escaped, she would have gathered her things from the back room and slipped into the first taxi she could find.

But that was not to be.

"Hello," she said weakly. "I didn't expect to see you here."

"Neither did I. However, I received an invitation that was hard to refuse."

"Hard to refuse?"

"Jerome came to see me," he said.

Susan glanced at Jerome. He was speaking with other guests, looking like the ruler of his own kingdom. He was relaxed and confident, while she was edgy and nervous.

"Why?"

"To make sure I came tonight. I wasn't going to."

Susan looked up at him. He was as handsome as

ever. They stood in the middle of the gallery. People walked around them, but no one tried to join their conversation or stopped to say hello. Susan almost wished someone would.

"Because of me?" She purposely used the same phrase he'd begun a lifetime ago, when she had quit working at the House of Thorn.

"In part," he acknowledged.

"Well, I'm sure this room is large enough that we can navigate it without bumping into each other. Now, excuse me, I can see someone I need to talk to."

Getting the barb in didn't make her feel better, but what happened next did. As she turned, she bumped into a waiter carrying a tray of filled champagne flutes. She upturned the tray and the bubbly gold liquid pitched forward and dumped onto André.

Susan's eyes opened wide, along with her mouth, which she covered with her hand. The room quieted and all eyes turned to her. Susan looked around, took in the room as if in slow motion and then left the room as fast as her five-inch heels could carry her. Finding herself in the room with her photo hanging on the wall, she barely noticed it. Her stomach felt as if it had knots in it. She turned this way and that before remembering where the door was that held her purse and wrap. After finding it, she gathered it and slipped out a side door. She could explain everything to Jerome when he came in later, or she could throw her shoe at him for doing what he did.

At the moment, the shoe idea was winning.

The limousine Jerome had hired for the night and Susan had ridden to the gallery in was at the curb. She opened the door for herself, surprising the chauffeur, who was reading a book.

"Would you take me home, please?" she said. "You can come back and pick up Jerome and his daughter."

The chauffeur put his book down and prepared to drive. Before he'd fired the ignition, the car door opened and André jumped inside. He pressed the button for the privacy window and pulled Susan into his arms. She resisted.

The car had already begun to move.

"What are you doing?" She pushed him away and moved as close to the opposite side of the car as she could get.

"I saw you leaving."

"And you decided to follow me? Why?" she asked, with anger evident in her voice.

Susan was angry with herself. Her body had been as tight as a spring, and when André had pulled her to him, she'd nearly uncoiled. He smelled of the champagne she'd spilled on him. Where the strength came from to push him aside, she didn't know. Yet she had to keep her brain in gear and not let her heart defeat her.

"I know you don't understand what happened in my apartment."

"Yes, I do," she said.

André didn't say anything in answer. He opened

the privacy window and instructed the driver to take them to his address.

"No," she protested, as her hands wildly reached for the control, but André had already closed the window.

"Susan, please." He waited for her to stop fighting for the control and then said, "We need to talk."

"I heard that before."

"Okay, you're right. But I really need to talk to you."

"Would you like something to drink?" André asked when they'd reached his apartment.

"No, thank you." Susan wanted to keep control of her brain.

André decided to bring two glasses of water to the living room. He removed his jacket, which reeked of the champagne she'd spilled on him.

"Don't you want to go and clean up?" she suggested.

"If I did, it would give you the chance to leave. I will not hold you against your will, but I hope you will listen to what I have to say."

Susan took a seat on the edge of the sofa. She didn't want to sit back, since the sofa was so comfortable, she could sink into it and not be able to get up quickly, should the need arise.

André sat in a chair opposite her. Leaning forward, he steepled his fingers and then dropped them between his knees. "I hardly know where to start."

"The beginning is usually a good place." Sarcasm dripped from her lips.

André sighed, taking a long moment. Susan didn't think he was going to say anything.

"Her name was Gail."

Susan's interest was instantly peaked. She tried not to let André know.

"We met online—not on a dating site. She commented on a friend's message and so did I. She liked my message and I did the same for hers. This happened time and again, and finally she friended me and I did the same. We never set up a time or place to meet in person. We never even mentioned it in our messages."

"Then, how did you meet?" Susan asked when he appeared to fall into his own thoughts.

"It was at one of the many social functions I attend each year."

"Like the fashion show?" she asked. The show he'd taken her?

He nodded. "It was an electronics show. The House of Thorn was one of the sponsors, and they held a dinner for the major contributors. We met there."

Susan waited. So far he hadn't said anything startling.

"We dated for a while. We became engaged."

"You fell in love with her?"

He swallowed, as if relating the story hurt. "She started planning our wedding. Then she had to have the very best of everything. We began arguing over the cost of everything. One night I overheard her talking to a friend about our future together."

Susan tensed.

"She told her how she wasn't really in love with me, but I was her ticket to a better life, to a rich life. Those were her words."

"So you broke the engagement off."

He nodded.

She could see it hurt him dearly.

"I'm generally a good judge of character, but I totally misread her intentions."

"And you treat every new relationship the same way. Fourth date or less. Either way, you're out."

"Susan," he began. "I can't deny that. I met you and all the rules seemed to change."

He got up and moved to the sofa, where she sat. He wasn't next to her, but close enough that his presence seemed to reach out and touch her. Susan felt like shrinking back, but she refused to let him know he held any power over her.

"Change in what way?" Her voice sounded like a squeak.

"I want you in my life. I don't know where this will go, but I want to find out."

"You think I should agree to something like that? We've passed the fourth-date test and obviously I failed, or you wouldn't have thrown me out of this apartment."

"I didn't—"

"Are you comparing me to Gail? Is that why—"

"No," he interrupted her.

Susan stood up. "I won't agree to this. I've had bad relationships in the past. Who hasn't? But to agree with what you're suggesting is not part of my makeup."

She started for the door, but André cut her off.

"Stop," he said. "I may have said that wrong."

Susan stared at him. Every part of her body shouted at her to take him under whatever terms, but she couldn't. Her heart was already entangled. She wasn't sure if it was broken, but it could be, with only the slightest nudge.

"I think I'm falling in love with you."

All the breath and fight went out of Susan. She had the same numb feeling she'd had that morning in his kitchen, wearing her purple gown.

"You can't be serious," she said, speaking each word slowly and clearly.

André just stared at her. He *was* serious.

"What happens to me?" she asked. "When you decide you aren't really falling in love and that you want to go back to being the commitment-phobe you were in the past? Do I just pick up my purple gown and take a taxi back to my former life?"

"This is not going well," André said, more to himself than to Susan.

"It certainly isn't," she agreed.

"I know we can't begin again. Too much has

passed between us, so let me ask you a question," he said.

Susan said nothing. Her internal defenses went up, however.

"Do you have feelings for me?" André asked.

She glanced away, with her eyes going toward the bedroom, where they'd had mind-blowing sex.

"Beyond the sex." He paused. "Do you want to be with me?"

She didn't know how to answer that question. Her heart said yes, but her brain told her heartache would be waiting at the end of the road they were embarking on.

"I've just told you how I feel," André continued. "I know enough to believe that you have an attraction to me, but do you have any other feelings?"

Susan looked down, then back up. "I'd be lying if I said I didn't—and you'd know it."

Did he expel a held breath? If he did, it was gone in an instant.

"I need to ask you a question," André said.

"Go ahead."

"The purple dress."

She frowned. "The Valentino?"

He nodded. "Why did you rent it?"

Did this really have to do with a rented dress? "You told me about Gail. And I've heard enough rumors to know that she was a gold digger. And you think I am too."

He didn't deny it and that hurt Susan.

"I don't need or want your money. Not every woman looks at you and sees dollar signs. I rented the dress because I had nothing appropriate to wear. I looked for a dress to buy and found nothing that caught my eye until I saw that in the window of a Rent the Dress boutique. I'm sure you know them. There are ads all over television, and at least three locations in Manhattan."

"Why didn't you get a dress at the House of Thorn?"

"I didn't find one I wanted that fit." She wanted to make his eyes pop when he saw her. The dresses in the store could be pricey designer gowns, but nothing jumped off the rack and told her this was the dress. When she'd passed that rental shop, she had impulsively gone inside and found the Valentino. "You need not worry about my clothing. I am capable of supporting myself."

"Prove it," he challenged, taking a step closer to her. "Go out with me?"

"That won't prove anything," she said.

"It'll prove to me if my feelings are genuine or not, and if yours exist." He didn't hesitate with his answer.

"And if either one of us decides this isn't going anywhere, that there is no future, we end it immediately." She added a stipulation, not realizing she was already agreeing to his terms.

"No strings, no hard feelings," he said.

Susan was almost sure she would be the one to make the decision. Despite André's comments, she was still deceiving him.

He stepped toward her. "Should we seal this with a kiss?"

Susan's phone rang. Her heart sank. The anticipation of him kissing her forced new feelings to the surface of her heart. She fished the phone out of her purse and looked at the display. Minette's number appeared on the screen. She held the phone out for André to see the caller ID. After accepting the call, she lifted the phone to her ear.

"I'm fine," she said, without a greeting.

"Where are you?"

"I'm at André's."

"Are you sure you're all right?"

"I'm fine," Susan said again.

"Are you staying the night?" Susan could hear the smile in Minette's voice, which she'd lowered, as if she didn't want the people around her to hear the question.

Susan took a while to answer. Her eyes were on André, who could only hear one side of the conversation.

"Yes," she said and switched the phone off.

"Yes to me, or yes to her?" he asked. But he didn't give her time to answer. He kissed her quickly, and everything about the past few minutes was blotted out by the onslaught of emotional upheaval that invaded her like a body snatcher.

André knew where the kiss would lead. It was exactly where he wanted to go. The few days he hadn't seen her had been hell. André was falling in love. He had no doubt about it. Susan made his life worth living. He couldn't imagine being without her. He'd had a taste of life without her, and he didn't like it.

She slept next to him. André felt her warm, satiated body. They'd made love and he wanted her again. He wondered if it would always be like this. Lightly, he lifted a lock of her hair, played with it and dropped it onto the pillow, only to pull another lock and do the same.

He was in a predicament. With Gail, it had never been like this. Even when their engagement had ended, André had never felt as if he'd lost a part of his being. When Susan had walked out of his apartment, he'd felt as if she'd taken a piece of his heart with her and that he would never be whole again. He was sure that was why he had gone to the art show tonight. He had known she would be there, and while he'd told himself she wasn't whom he'd thought she was, he had gone anyway. He hadn't followed his own advice. He'd gotten dressed, just to see her.

And when he had, when he'd stood across the room from her, he'd known he was in love. How could he have just calmly walked away when he'd been shivering in reaction to her? Jerome had spoken to him, but he'd barely heard anything he'd said.

Now he had to talk to her. He had to convince her that they needed to be together. But André couldn't go all the way—at least not yet. He couldn't put a ring on her finger until he was sure of himself and sure of her.

She stirred and turned to face him. "You're still awake," she said in a drowsy voice.

"Go back to sleep," he said, drawing her close.

He ran his hands down her arms. He loved the smooth feel of her. She tucked her head under his chin and settled against him. He smelled the lilac shampoo. For the first time in his life, André knew he could be happy. There were kinks in their relationship, but they could work those out. He was sure of that. And he'd do whatever it took to straighten out those kinks.

Waking up in André's arms was a new experience for Susan. She took in the smell of him, like warm spice and sexy air. Taking a deep breath, she inhaled. His arms were around her, and their legs were entwined. It was as if sleep had joined them together, fitting them so it was hard to tell where one ended and the other began.

The feeling that went through her was powerful. After getting out of bed, she pulled on André's shirt and went to the kitchen to make coffee. If she said she was walking on air, it would be an understatement. She sang softly and the coffee maker brewed its single cup. Then she started one for André.

Susan didn't hear him come up behind her until she felt his arms wrapped around her. She leaned back, resting her head against his chest. He took her coffee cup and drank from it.

"I made one for you," she said.

"I like yours better."

They liked their coffee the same way—they both drank it with cream. He set her cup down, turned her around and pulled her into his arms.

"Aren't you going to the store today?" she whispered against him as he planted kisses over her face and neck.

"I'm thinking about it." He nibbled on her lower lip. "But there is something that is keeping me here, telling me to go back to bed."

"Really? Do you know what that is?"

His answer was to run his hands up her neck, briefly rest them on the rapidly beating pulse in her throat and then slide down to the soft flesh exposed by the open buttons of her shirt. With adept fingers, he undid the buttons on the shirt she wore. Susan's head fell back to give him access to her throat and to continue the feelings he produced in her with the touch of his hands. With her own hands, she pushed his robe aside to feel the dampened skin of his hair-roughened chest. The sensation of pleasure going through her body caused her to arch forward.

The naked desire shining in his eyes matched the emotion coursing through her body. He hesitated a moment, and she knew he was thinking of kissing her again. His eyes moved to her mouth, lingering there for long moments. She could feel his warm breath and smell the coffee as she moved closer to him. She felt, more than saw, him move. With his decision made, he gently cradled her face between his hands, then smiled slightly and, tilting her face, kissed her. Their touching ignited something. With an audible groan, he pulled her closer and deepened the kiss.

His mouth slid off hers, but he continued it along her jawline.

"I don't think I can work today," he said.

"Why not?"

"I'm going to be too weak," he said, with his voice already sounding gravelly.

With that, he slipped his arm inside the shirt, and once they were skin to skin, they forgot the routines of the day and went back to the bedroom.

Chapter 10

The smell of coffee and freshly baked bread filled her apartment when Susan stepped through the door. Both Minette and Jerome sat at the kitchen counter, smiling.

"Twice in one week," Jerome said.

"Stop it," Minette chastised him.

Susan ignored the fact that she was still in last night's clothes and poured herself a cup of coffee. "You baked?" she asked.

"Not me," Jerome said. "Minette brought these and we heated them."

Susan took one. They smelled heavenly, but then she hadn't had anything to eat since yesterday.

"You two look happy," Susan said. "What's going on?"

"I've made a decision." Jerome smiled.

Sunlight lit the room. Susan pulled one of the counter stools back and perched between father and daughter. Her black lace dress spilled down the sides. Both Minette and Jerome turned to look at her, wearing identical smiles.

"First, Minette is going to Italy with me."

"Wonderful!" Susan said. She would have clapped her hands, but she was holding a cup in one hand and a croissant in the other.

"We're going to close my apartment and studio," Jerome continued. "And I'm moving back here."

"Here, in New York?" Susan asked. She was thrilled. After setting the cup down, she hugged Jerome, her mentor and friend.

"We're not sure where I'm going to settle yet. Her apartment is too small for the two of us, and she needs an office. I need a studio."

"I couldn't be happier," Susan said. "Minette and I have become fast friends. And I've missed our talks and all the photo advice you've given me."

"It seems you've come into your own. I looked at some of the ones in your second bedroom," he said.

The second bedroom was a combination office/studio and guest room. Susan had moved her framed photos to one end of the room. They were in plain view and she had known he'd ask about them if they weren't available.

"And speaking of your photos," Minette chimed in. "The photo of you sold last night."

"Really?" She glanced from Minette to Jerome. Susan had learned not to get too close to a photo unless she didn't want to part with it. She liked the photo of herself, but she didn't have any regrets over having agreed to let it be put up for sale. Her photos of André that she'd taken on the street in front of the House of Thorn were too personal. Even if she had a show, she would never display or sell those photos.

"It went for a lot more than I thought it would," Jerome said.

"It's an original Jerome Marchand," Susan told him, as if he didn't already know. "I'm sure the buyer will let everyone know that."

"And how did your evening go?" Jerome asked. "After you dumped my show."

"I'm sorry about that, but I felt like I needed a little air."

"And did you get it?"

She smiled sheepishly. "Oxygen was plentiful."

"Can we take that to mean that the thorn that was bothering you has been removed?" Jerome asked.

"Well, he no longer believes I'm a gold digger, I think," she added.

"He doesn't know who you are?"

Susan glanced at Minette. She didn't know either, and the confused look on her face said as much.

"You haven't told him?" Jerome asked.

"Wait," Minette said. "What are you two talking about?"

"Please, let's drop this," Susan said. "He knows I'm Susan Dewhurst."

"No," Minette spoke. "You can't drop a comment like that and just let it go."

"Let's just say we've talked and we've decided to move on."

"So you're not going to tell me," Minette stated.

"Soon," Susan said.

Susan could tell Minette wasn't satisfied, but she wouldn't pursue it. Everyone had secrets. She was sure Minette had some too. For the time being, Susan's would remain safely hidden away. She would tell André. Jerome had intimated that she should have told him by now. She knew that was true.

The next time she saw him, she'd make sure he knew.

André hummed the same song he'd heard Susan singing a few days ago, as he walked through the store. He hummed often these days. Since he and Susan had decided to date, he found himself thinking of her all the time. The thoughts made him happy. He wanted to tell the world about her, but he settled for Jessica, who asked about her all the time, and his brothers, David and Blake. Christian and Carter had met her, but he hadn't said anything more to them since the ball. They may think she was just his date for the night. She was more than that.

A whole lot more.

"Hi, André," Jessica said as he reached her department. "Have you talked Susan into coming back yet?"

He smiled, shaking his head.

"I'm meeting her for lunch tomorrow. Maybe I can convince her how much she's needed here."

"Good luck with that," he said.

Since Jerome had arrived from Italy, she'd been practically living with André, and he liked it that way. She'd meet him for dinner after work, and they'd spend the night making love. Then they'd talk long into the night, holding each other until they fell asleep. André loved it. He wanted her with him all the time. He wanted to listen to her dreams and tell her his.

"Customer—gotta go," Jessica said.

André looked around, remembering when Susan had been there. He thought back to the night they had moved the beds and added the photos.

"Excuse me—who are you looking for?" André heard Jessica ask. He glanced back. She was talking to a customer and he recognized Jessica's customer-relations manner—interested, confident and smiling. He stood up straighter because he also remembered seeing the customer before.

"Marcia Atherton," the woman said. "She's from my hometown. I talked to her here about a month ago, when I was visiting. She works here. My job has sent me back here for a business conference, and I thought Marcia and I might have dinner or go to a show together."

Marcia, André thought. Had he heard her say Marcia before? André stepped closer. Jessica glanced at him.

"We don't have anyone here named Marcia," Jessica told her. "No one by that name has ever worked in this department, not as long as I've been here, but…" She paused. Using her hand, she invited André into the conversation. "This is our store president. Has anyone named Marcia ever worked in this department?"

"Not in this one," he said.

"That's odd," the woman said, questioning herself. "I know her whole family. We're from Montana."

"Mountainview, Montana?" André asked. He was almost afraid to say the words.

"Yes," she smiled broadly as if that bit of news was the key that opened the treasure chest.

"We had an employee from there, but I can't give you any information about her," Jessica said. She'd stepped in and helped André, who was trying to process the news. They only had one former employee from Mountainview, Montana.

"If you're a friend of the family, maybe you should reach out to them and get her phone number."

He heard Jessica speaking, but the sound seemed to come from a long distance away.

"Good idea," the woman said. "I'll give them a call."

She thanked them and pulled out her cell phone as she left the department. Marcia, André thought. Could that be Susan? Susan was from Mountainview, Montana.

Who was she? André suddenly had no idea who the woman he'd confessed his love to was. Had she been lying to him from the beginning? Marcia—the name repeated in his head. That was the name the woman had said before.

"André." Jessica's voice snapped him back to his surroundings. Both of them looked at the escalator, where the woman had gone. "Do you think she means Susan? Isn't that the place where Susan lived?"

He turned to her. "Susan is the only person I've ever met from Mountainview."

"How could she get a job here under an assumed name?"

André wondered that too. "I don't know, but I'm going to find out."

"Marcia Atherton."

André's voice boomed in the high-ceiling room of his apartment. Susan had arrived, as she usually did about this time. As she had lifted her camera-bag strap over her head and set it on the sofa table, André had called her by her real name. Her back had stiffened and she'd stopped in the act. A beat later—too long to say she didn't understand him—she turned to face him.

The blood had drained from her face, and her heart hammered in her chest. She was sure he could see the movement of it against her dress.

"Who is Marcia Atherton?" he asked.

"I can explain," she said, putting a hand up, as if to ward him off, even though he hadn't moved from the darkened area of the entrance. "How did you learn that name?"

"Does it matter? It's yours, isn't it?"

Susan didn't answer. She searched her brain for something to say, but the hard, cold anger in André's voice stifled her speech.

"It was mine," she said.

"Why change it and not tell me?"

"I planned to tell you, but—"

"But you conveniently forgot," André argued. "Why did you need to become someone else? Is it because you needed a new identity to cover something up?"

"I did, but not the way you're implying. I haven't done anything wrong or anything illegal," she said, defensively.

"You're a liar and who knows what else?"

Susan was shocked, dazed and angry.

"I can see you don't want to hear anything I have to say. You've already decided I'm a villain, and anything I tell you would be suspect or an out-and-out lie." She stopped and took a breath. "I had and still have a very good reason for what I did. I don't apologize for it."

"What is this reason?"

Susan didn't like the sarcasm, and she liked being accused of something even less.

"I told you once I wasn't a gold digger. That is the truth. But you don't want to believe it. How can we have anything based on trust if you—"

"Me!" He fumed. "I'm not the one who hasn't been honest, hasn't told the truth. You, however, have been lying to me since the day we met, and while you've had ample opportunities to come clean, you've chosen to continue this deception."

"You're right, I have. And long after I've gone, after I'm not even a memory in your accusing mind, I'll still have a good reason."

Susan grabbed her camera bag and headed for the door. André stood in her way. She stopped in front of him, waiting for him to move. He turned, giving her enough room to pass. She took one step and faltered. Then she went out the door and took care not to slam it, as she had wanted to do. She had wanted to hear the angry sound reverberate down the long hall. But it was the last thing she'd seen that had stopped her from doing so. André had bought her photo. She had seen the framed photo lying on the table where André always dropped his mail upon coming into the apartment.

She took several breaths as she waited for the elevator. On the street, she walked. The camera bag felt like a weight hanging from her neck, but she ignored it and continued walking until her heartbeat returned to normal and her breath wasn't coming in short pants. Susan looked at her life as a day late. She'd planned to tell André all about herself, confess that Susan Dewhurst wasn't the name she was born with, but it was her legal name. She was going to tell him about the money, about the need to keep under the radar because of shady characters who wanted to scam her out of her winnings.

He had to understand that those people existed and prayed on the ignorant and unsuspecting. Susan was a businesswoman, and she had known when the calls had started that any financial manager who called her wasn't someone she wanted to hire. A man of André's standing, someone who commanded his net worth, couldn't escape those kinds of people. But he had the advantage of family behind him. He'd grown up in a financially affluent environment. He'd probably had a financial advisor from birth.

She hadn't.

Susan slowly entered her apartment. She blew out a breath, and her shoulders dropped when she realized Jerome was out and the place was empty. He'd instantly know something was wrong, and she'd find herself pouring out the wrong story to him.

And after reviewing everything, she would know that André's anger was justified and he was right overall. She should have told him when they had begun to get serious about each other. Susan had been protecting herself from the world for so long, it was natural for her to keep her former identity a secret.

Susan Dewhurst was her legal identity. And no one should have to defend their legal identity.

Jerome had been out of the apartment most of the day and night. When he came in, Susan was already in bed. She wasn't asleep, but she didn't open her door to acknowledge him or have a long talk. She didn't want to let him know about the argument she'd had with André. She didn't want to show her wounds. André's distrust of her, even though she had deceived him, cut deeply.

In the morning, she knew Jerome needed to talk to his daughter. Susan gave them room. Leaving them in her apartment, she decided to go shopping. She hadn't been in the House of Thorn since she'd left, but she gravitated to their clothes. She knew she couldn't go there. André might be on the floor, and she wasn't sure that Jessica wouldn't call him if she saw Susan in the store.

She went to other stores. Yet after several hours of browsing and trying on one item after another, she returned with only a headache. Opening the door, she was prepared to call out and let them know she had returned, but the sound of laughter stopped her.

Things must have gone well if they were laughing. Susan entered and peered around the living room wall to the kitchen. Neither was sitting at the table between the two windows, which was strewn with empty espresso cups and the remnants of cheese, fruit, and bread.

Minette and Jerome were both in front of the stove, where several large pots were placed over an open flame.

"It needs more oregano," Minette said.

"It needs more salt," Jerome contradicted.

They laughed again.

Susan braced herself, hoping there were no telltale signs of her night of tossing and turning. "How's it going?" Susan asked, mustering as much joy as she could.

"Susan," Minette exclaimed. "Come here and taste this." She held up a spoon with a red sauce. "We're making spaghetti sauce and this needs more oregano."

"No, it doesn't," Jerome contradicted again.

"What's going on?" Susan asked.

"She's just like her mother." Jerome pointed to his daughter.

"They could never agree on the spaghetti sauce," Minette said.

Susan had to open her mouth, as Minette was prodding her with a spoon. She tasted the sauce. It was delicious.

"So, what does it need?" she asked.

"More salt," Jerome answered. "We had to start with one of your store-bought sauces and doctor it up. Now it just needs a little more salt."

Susan didn't say anything. She thought it was perfect the way it was, but both of her guests were looking to her to make a decision.

"I think it could use both," she said. "Not much of either—just a pinch."

"See, I told you." Jerome was the first to declare victory. He dumped a single shake of salt into the mixture. Minette followed with a few crushed oregano leaves. Jerome stirred and, a few minutes later, stated it was perfect.

He lowered the heat, covered the pot and put the spaghetti on. Minette pulled a sleeve of bread out and began cutting it for garlic bread.

"Can I help with anything?" Susan asked.

"We have it all under control." Jerome smiled. "You can sit down and we'll serve you."

"I can choose a bottle of wine," she said.

It wasn't long after that the table was loaded with spaghetti, meat sauce, salad, wine and bread. Jerome began the toasting, and soon they were all part of a celebration that had no attached holiday.

"I'm glad to see you two smiling," Susan said when they'd finished the meal. She sat back and enjoyed a second glass of wine. "You worked things out, right?" Her gaze swung from face to face.

"We did." Minette smiled at her dad. "I don't know if dad told you, but when he and Mom divorced, I stayed with Mom."

"I don't need to know this," Susan said. "It's

enough that you're friends and you're talking to each other."

They appeared to accept her comment. "How is your mom?" Jerome asked Minette.

"She's doing fine. I spoke with her yesterday. I told her you were here."

Jerome stiffened. Susan noticed it.

"What did she say to that?"

"Not much, although I think she still loves you."

"That's unlikely," Jerome said.

"She's never remarried."

"That could just mean I ruined her trust in men."

"Not always," Susan said. "We've all had our hearts broken a time or two, but we get over it."

Jerome was shaking his head as she spoke.

"You haven't remarried either, Dad. Why is that?"

Jerome bought himself some time by taking a slow drink of the sangria. "Your mom is the love of my life." He stated a fact. "It isn't that I haven't been in relationships, but none of them even came close to evoking the type of feeling I have for your mom. She's the love of my life. I guess I'm just cursed."

"Maybe not," Susan said. Both sets of eyes turned to her. "You can talk to her. Time has gone by. You're no longer the same person you were when you were married. She probably isn't either. Why don't you give her a call?"

"I'm sure I'm the last person she wants to hear from."

"I don't know," Minette said. "She bought one of your photos."

"What?"

"The phone purchase. That was Mom."

Jerome appeared to be speechless.

Susan had left her mark on André. He'd left the store and walked to the park across from the famous post office with the quote that millions of people recognized. He could call this a safe place. He'd never been here with Susan. At the store or his apartment, he couldn't look in any direction or speak to any employee who didn't tell him how her suggestions or her friendship had touched them. For someone with such a short employment record at the House of Thorn, she'd had a huge impact. He would applaud her for that, if it didn't hurt so much.

He'd spent part of the morning searching the internet for information on Susan—something he'd vowed not to do. But when the name Marcia Atherton from Mountainview, Montana, came up, André had to find out about her.

If she'd had a website for her business, it had been taken down. He found reviews related to framing, but clicking on them repeatedly returned the 404 error message. Even the newspaper account of the fire listed the name of the building's owner, but the name of the business owner had been withheld. Had she been burned? André rejected that. He'd been over every inch of Susan's body, and she had no scars.

At least no physical ones.

"They told me at the store I could find you here."

André didn't hear the voice at first. He was lost in his own world. He looked up as a shadow fell over him. Jerome stood there, with a small suitcase in his hand.

"Are you leaving?" André asked.

"Minette is meeting me at the airport."

André came off the table he was sitting on and offered his hand. "It was great meeting you, and I really enjoyed your show."

Jerome laughed at that. "You barely saw it. Your eyes were on Susan."

André looked away, then back. "They were," he said. But he didn't reveal that since that night, life had reached its height and then plummeted to the basement. He'd probably never see Susan again.

"I came to give you something."

Jerome handed him a piece of paper. He glanced at it, seeing a printed-out photo from a newspaper.

"What's this?" André asked.

"It will answer all your questions." That was all Jerome said. He picked up his suitcase and walked out of the park.

André sat back down and looked at the clipping. Photos in the papers were often grainy, making it hard to identify details. This photo was of someone in a Halloween costume. He read the caption, "Lottery winner arrives incognito." André frowned. What did this mean? He couldn't see who the winner was. The costume was of a life-size bunny. The only thing that came to mind was an old black-and-white film about a six-foot rabbit called Harvey.

André checked the entire piece of paper for more information. There was nothing else there—no date, no name, not even the newspaper that had printed it. After pulling out his phone, André used the scan feature to load the photo. Then, using an internet program, he searched for where the photo could be found.

When the *Mountainview Packet* came up as an option, he immediately clicked on it. Naturally, the photo wasn't there. The current issue of the newspaper appeared on the screen of his phone. He typed in the caption and the news story appeared. He read rapidly.

"Damn," he cursed as he stood up. Marcia Atherton was a fifteen-million-dollar lottery winner. When he clicked on images to see if there were any photos of her, pages of them came up. Most were from her high school days. A graduation photo with her family caught his attention, and he read the article associated with it. Perry Dewhurst was her stepfather's name, and he owned a small restaurant. Dewhurst. André read it again. He was in no doubt that Marcia Atherton and Susan Dewhurst were the same person.

André could kick himself. He'd accused her of being a gold digger when her net worth was impressive. He was part of a rich family, but she held her own. She wasn't after his money, just as she had said.

He couldn't go to her now. What would she think? He'd been an idiot. He'd thrown away the only woman he really loved. He wouldn't blame her if she never spoke to him again.

André stuffed the phone and paper into his pocket and started for the exit. He stopped short when he saw Susan. She had no camera hanging from her neck and no cell phone in her hand. She wasn't here for images. André's heart raced. Was she here to see him, to berate him for the things he'd said and thought about her.

They met in the middle of the path.

"My name was Marcia," she said. "I won the lottery in Montana. After that I was bombarded with letters and calls from phony financial managers and strangers asking for money."

"You don't have to explain," André said.

"I want to. I want you to know everything." She looked into his eyes. "To protect myself and my family, I had to change my name and leave the country. My stepfather adopted me. I took a new name and my old records were sealed. Then I went to Europe and stayed for a while. I became known there as Susan and began a new life there. Then I came back to New York and met you. I didn't know you, didn't know we'd have a relationship. That's why I didn't tell you my former name. And I was truly going to tell you that day, but you were so angry."

"How could you ever trust me?" André asked.

"I love you," she said.

André moved faster than he ever had. He hauled her into his arms and kissed her. He didn't care that they were in a park, with people milling around them. He only cared that the woman he loved was in his arms.

"I love you too," André said. His voice was unrecognizable to his own ears. "I want you with me forever. Marry me?"

"Are you sure?" she asked.

"I've never been more sure of anything in my life."

"I will," she said.

André kissed her again. He wanted her with him always. And he would never let her go.

* * * * *

Petra wrapped her arms around herself as she stood at the window in C's apartment peering out at the city's lights. Why had she made up an excuse to stay? Dessert? Psychologically, as her sister Desiree would say, she knew what dessert meant.

It meant that kiss had been too good to not wonder what more of the same would be like. C was delicious. She was undeniably attracted to him. She'd been curious about him at the bar. He'd made her laugh, and truthfully, when a man could make her laugh, that was 50 percent of the attraction right there. He was also intelligent, and now, after seeing where he lived and what he thought was important enough to be on his walls, she also felt he was good inside.

He returned wearing jeans and a T-shirt, his feet in a pair of slides. When he was standing before her, she looked down at his feet. He had neatly manicured nails on his immaculate toes.

She smiled. "Nice feet."

In fact, all of him was nice. Great pectorals and biceps were evident underneath that T-shirt, and his muscular thighs filled out those jeans quite well.

Janice Sims is the author of over thirty titles ranging from romance and romantic suspense to speculative fiction. She won an Emma Award for Favorite Heroine for her novel *Desert Heat.* She has also been nominated for a Career Achievement Award by *RT Book Reviews*, and her novel *Temptation's Song* was nominated for Best Kimani Romance Series in 2010 by *RT Book Reviews.* She lives in central Florida with her family.

Books by Janice Sims

Harlequin Kimani Romance

A Little Holiday Temptation
Escape with Me
This Winter Night
Safe in My Arms
Thief of My Heart
Unconditionally
Cherish My Heart

Visit the Author Profile page
at Harlequin.com for more titles.

CHERISH MY HEART

Janice Sims

This book is dedicated to Miss Pat Roberts, my favorite English teacher in high school. Miss Roberts always had a ready smile and knew how to hold her students' attention in class. She was the first adult to tell me I had a way with words. Thank you!

Acknowledgments

Thanks to my editor, Glenda Howard, and the rest of the staff at Harlequin who make sure the book you're reading is an enjoyable experience for you. I write the stories, but they fine-tune my work. I'm grateful to be working with such professionals.

Dear Reader,

Sometimes I feel like a matchmaker for the couples I write about. I saved Petra's story for last because I felt she would be a hard sell. Petra, as you know if you've read any of the other books in the Gaines Sisters series, doesn't believe in marriage. Therefore, what kind of man will it take to get her to change her mind? A magnificent man! Chance Youngblood fits the bill.

My next book, *His Christmas Gift*, will be in stores November 2019. The heroine is Chance's sister, Alia Joie Youngblood, who falls for a brilliant scientist, Adam Brathwaite. Their love story gets complicated when he's kidnapped by terrorists. Wait until you see how that's resolved! Look me up on Facebook to get updates on my work and feel free to write me the old-fashioned way at: PO Box 811, Mascotte, Florida 34753.

Blessings,

Janice

Chapter 1

It was midday in the jungle of the Democratic Republic of the Congo. It had just stopped raining, the sun was out again, and zoologist/anthropologist Petra Gaines lowered the hood of her water-repellent safari jacket and resumed filming two subjects that she had followed for the past six months: a mother chimpanzee and her male offspring. In her notes, Petra had named them Francesca and Joey. Sitting on a branch high up in the canopy, their fur sparkled in the sunlight, and seemed to have natural water-wicking capabilities. Mother and child appeared to have taken the downpour in stride.

On the other hand, Petra and her assistant, Paul Olomide, were thrilled the rain had stopped. It was difficult to record good footage in the middle of a rainstorm.

They communicated without speaking, using hand signals they'd developed over the years they'd been working together. Silence was necessary so as not to startle the subjects. Plus, nests of this size had male adults who patrolled the perimeter looking for interlopers who would be severely dealt with if found.

Petra didn't relish the thought of being the victim of a chimpanzee assault. They were a long way from a hospital.

She signaled to Paul to pull back. She was wrapping up the final shoot of the day. Six-month-old Joey began playfully bouncing on the branch supporting him and his mother. Francesca grabbed him, tossed him onto her back and leaped to an adjacent branch with Joey clinging to her neck. From there, Francesca made her way down to a banana tree just below the red cedar tree they had been perched in. She plucked a banana, tore it open with her strong teeth and gave it to Joey. Joey eagerly took it and munched on it with abandon, his enjoyment of the delicious treat apparent in his big brown eyes.

Petra caught it all on film and thought it a fitting ending to the many months she'd spent trailing this nest of chimpanzees. This was her life's work. She fervently believed that without these creatures, the forests would not thrive. They were important seed dispersers. In the jungle, sunlight, essential for growth, reached the forest floor only one to one and a half percent of the time. The great apes (which chimpanzees, along with gorillas and bonobos, were classified as) helped spread seeds simply by living in the forest, foraging from its trees. The seeds sprang up as new growth. And trees provided oxygen. To Petra it was a symbiotic relationship. The great apes did their part by helping to keep the forests alive and well, and people should in turn help keep them alive and well.

She and Paul quickly packed up what little equipment they had brought with them from camp and swiftly walked away from the nest. They didn't say anything to each other until they were well out of earshot of the chimpanzees.

"When do you think you'll be back?" Paul asked in his Congolese-inflected English. Born in the Congo, Paul was dark skinned, with brown eyes and a shaved head. He was medium sized and of medium height and wore a khaki cap, shirt, slacks and hiking boots, his normal attire when going into the jungle.

"I'm not sure," Petra said. "I have a meeting with the research organization that funds my work when I get back to the States. I'll stay in touch. You're graduating from college soon and have that wonderful job offer. You've learned everything you need to from me." Petra, African American, was petite with golden-brown skin and long wavy black hair that normally fell down her back but was now in a twist underneath her wide brim khaki hat. Her clothing was similar to Paul's, except she wore a safari jacket and she reeked of eucalyptus oil, a natural insect repellent.

She knew Paul considered her a role model, and sometimes that turned into hero worship. But the fact was, Paul had a brilliant mind and lacked only self-confidence. He was twenty-two and about to graduate from The Catholic University of Kinshasa with a degree in anthropology. His goal was to save the great ape population in his country. In Petra's eyes, he was a noble man.

"I don't know," said Paul. "One can always learn something new."

Petra loved his Congolese accent. When they'd first started working together, she'd insisted that he speak French, the official language in the Congo, with her because she needed to practice her college-learned French. But soon they were speaking only English together because he wanted to practice his English. He'd offered to teach her Lingala, a Bantu language spoken in the northwestern portion of the Democratic Republic of the Congo, but she'd politely turned him down. French was difficult enough.

The lush jungle was thick with trees and plants, wet and glistening, and the air was redolent with smells of the many species of flowers and herbs and broad-leafed trees like the African oak, red cedar and mahogany, some of them growing to forty feet above the ground. Sounds of birds singing and the screech of apes were all around them. The jungle made Petra think of being in a huge cathedral with the tallest ceiling in the world. Looking up made her feel close to heaven.

"We may not be the same when you get back," Paul lamented. He often talked about politics and the state of his country. The Democratic Republic of the Congo had been in tumult for many years with infighting. If one regime didn't like another, the argument often ended in bloodshed. Over ten million people had been killed in the past twenty years. It was a dangerous place to live. Petra was constantly amazed by the optimism of the people of the Congo. They were positive even in light of the chaos around them. They'd had to rebuild time and time again, yet their spirits were not broken. They looked forward to a better future. She felt the people of the Congo deserved so much more from their leaders.

She spoke with optimism now. "Everything will be all right, Paul." She gestured to their surroundings. "You live in paradise!"

"It would be, if not for certain serpents," Paul said with a smile. His brown eyes were lit with laughter. He grinned, showing perfect white teeth in his good-looking face. "You must come to dinner tonight. Noella told me not to tell you, but we're giving you a going-away party. So act surprised."

Petra laughed delightedly. "You two are so sweet. Still on your honeymoon and inviting someone into your love nest. That's so generous," she teased.

Paul blushed. "Just you and a few colleagues from the university."

"I'll be there," Petra said with a smile.

"Poulet à la Moambé. I could eat this every day if I could get it," Petra said happily as she took the last bite of the delicious chicken in a moambe sauce over rice. The dish was spicy and made with cassava leaves, peanuts, hot pepper sauce, chicken, bananas and palm nuts. She swallowed and washed it down with a local dark beer.

Noella Olomide, a beautiful, petite twenty-one-year-old woman with reddish-brown skin, black dreadlocks that fell to her waist and dark brown eyes, smiled broadly at Petra. "I'll write down the recipe so you can."

"One of these days I'm going to take the time to learn to cook," Petra said.

The eight people around the table all groaned at hearing that statement, knowing she had no interest in learning to cook. Which made Petra laugh.

"It's not my fault that Kinshasa has so many Nganda restaurants. What do you want me to do, put all those hardworking women out of work?" She often frequented the Nganda restaurants, street restaurants around the capital city of Kinshasa which were mostly set up by women who earned a living by selling cuisine inspired by recipes from all over the Congo.

"I'm sure they're going to miss you when you're

gone," Paul said sympathetically. But she could tell he was laughing at her, too.

"All right, all right," Petra said, when she had her own laughter under control. "I'm probably never going to learn how to cook. No wonder I'm still single at thirty-three. Some people are born to be geniuses in the kitchen, and others are born to enjoy their efforts. That's me! I'm always happy to wash dishes, though."

She stood and raised her glass. "A toast to our hosts. Thank you for a sublime meal and for the loving spirit you two possess in abundance. I'm going to miss you."

Everyone raised their glasses in response, smiles on their faces, eyes twinkling with good humor.

"To our hosts," they all said, and drank deeply from their glasses of beer.

She looked around the table at the people she worked with at the university where she taught a course in anthropology. Most of them were native Congolese, but there was also a Lebanese gentleman and a woman from China in their group. Kinshasa was a multicultural city.

"I'm going to miss all of you," she said sincerely and felt she might cry.

Then Dr. Koffi Botende, the head of the anthropology department at the university, saved her by standing up and saying, "If I had known you were going to be such a thorn in my side, I never would have hired you."

The others at the table gasped in astonishment. Dr. Botende was usually such a kind, patient man. He sternly regarded Petra, his bushy white eyebrows raised in consternation. His white afro was also bushy, and he reminded Petra of a black Albert Einstein. She could not look at him without smiling.

Which she was doing now. "I know you love me," she said confidently. "Even if I am a pain in the ass."

Dr. Botende let out a loud guffaw and hugged Petra. "I love you like a daughter. And I will miss you, *ma petite*. Although, I think you'll be a lot safer in America where you won't run into any armed poachers."

"It was only one time," Petra said in her defense. "And it ended well."

"With a prosecution," Paul said.

"Yes," Dr. Botende said softly as he released her and sat back down. "But did you have to engage in a fistfight?" he asked exasperatedly.

"He was trying to kidnap Joey!" Petra cried. "They steal babies because they're easier to transport. None of them want to tussle with a full-grown ape. They would get killed. No, they sneak around and snatch the babies!"

"That guy got what was coming to him," Noella said defiantly, rising in protest.

Petra smiled at her feminist friend. "Yes, and he won't be out of jail for three years."

"A year and a half with good behavior," Dr. Botende cautioned. "Jails are crowded, and the authorities release prisoners back into society as soon as possible. The state doesn't want to pay for their upkeep. You've made an enemy, my dear. Not only did you interfere with his thievery, you beat him up in front of his friends. His pride won't let him forget that. You keep your eyes open when you go back into the jungle."

Petra nodded in agreement. "Those are wise words, and I intend to take your advice."

She wasn't giving him lip service. She knew how dangerous the incident had been. Her opinion on poaching was that it was a horrible practice. No animal should be killed or stolen from its natural habitat for food or money. On the other hand, many Congolese were living below the poverty level, and some poached in order to feed their families. It wasn't a cut-and-dried situation.

She only knew it was her job to protect her subjects. And she would defend them by revealing their beauty, intelligence and their usefulness to the world through her work.

Petra flew economy from Kinshasa to New York City, trying to sleep as much as possible. The flight took nearly nineteen hours, and when the plane landed, after going through the airport's strict time-consuming protocol subjected to anyone who was entering the US from a country where diseases like Ebola were reported, she went straight to the Manhattan hotel where she'd reserved a room.

It was a little after two in the afternoon, and the first thing she did upon entering her room was begin peeling off her clothes so she could take a nice long soak in the tub. She didn't feel sleepy when she got into the tub of sudsy warm water, but after toweling off and slipping into the plush robe provided by the hotel, she suddenly felt so tired she could barely hold her eyes open.

She turned the covers back on the fresh-smelling bed and lay down in the robe, only her feet beneath the covers. Propped up on pillows, she relaxed against the headboard and closed her eyes.

Her body seemed to be floating on a cloud as she sank into the cool, heavenly scented sheets. Sleep claimed her. The next thing she knew, her cell phone was ringing. She'd placed it on the nightstand beside the bed earlier, and she turned to read the display now. It was Susie Greer from the Bitty Berensen Primate Conservancy, with whom she had a meeting the next day.

She yawned and then answered, "Hi, Susie."

Susie sighed. "Oh, I'm sorry. I woke you, didn't I? You must be exhausted after that long flight."

Petra smiled. Apparently she sounded sleepy.

She sat up further in bed and swung her legs off the side, then glanced at the time on her cell phone: five fifteen. She'd slept almost three hours. "No, no, it's all right. I need to get up and find something to eat, anyway. Has the meeting been rescheduled?"

"No, it's not that. I wanted to talk with you about

something before you got here tomorrow." She cleared her throat. "Petra, there's no easy way to say this. The conservancy is running out of money and things look bleak unless we can find investors. We've managed to raise some funds, but what we need is the backing of a company, or private individual, who is as devoted to saving the lives of primates as we are. We think we've found someone. His name is Chance Youngblood, and he's the CEO of Youngblood Media. They're a billion-dollar company that's involved in television, the internet and publishing. Mr. Youngblood will be at the meeting tomorrow, and we need you to give your usual brilliant report on your progress in the Congo. You know, when you show us footage and talk about your research. Nothing extra. I'm only calling to give you a heads-up because I didn't want you to be surprised to see someone else at the meeting tomorrow. So no worries, all right? Just be you. Okay?"

Petra stood up and began pacing the floor. From the nervous inflection in Susie's voice, and her attempt to downplay Petra's part in it, she sensed tomorrow's meeting was not going to be routine. "You don't sound calm, Susie. How important is Mr. Youngblood's support to the conservancy?"

"I'm not going to pretend with you, Petra. It's *very* important."

"What happened, Susie?" Petra asked. "Are donations down? Did someone do something creative with the books? We've known one another for nearly ten years. You can be frank with me."

Susie took a deep breath and let it out in a rush. "Jon is under investigation for misuse of funds, Petra."

Petra's mind was racing. Jon Berensen was the founder of the conservancy. He'd formed it in honor of his mother, Bitty Berensen, an American zoologist who had studied mountain chimpanzees in the Congo for thirty years before her untimely death from a fall in the mountains.

Six years ago, he'd generously offered to finance Petra's research in the jungles of the Congo because he said she reminded him of his mother. They were both American zoologists devoted to preventing primates from becoming endangered species. Also, Petra's training and education were impressive. He felt it was almost as if she were carrying on his mother's work.

"I would never suspect Jon of something like that," Petra emphatically told Susie. "Never!"

"I don't, either," Susie whispered, as if she were afraid of being overheard. "I think Kent did it."

Kent Marshall was the conservancy's accountant. Petra sighed. Not another accountant cooking the books. She shook her head. What was she supposed to do now? The company was in dire straits. She'd been friends with Susie for nearly ten years. They'd met in college. Susie had introduced her to Jon because Petra had been a big fan of Bitty Berensen. It had been an honor to meet her son. She just couldn't believe Jon would embezzle money from the conservancy.

She sat back down on the bed, feeling hopeless. Was she supposed to run the other way when her friends were in trouble?

Or stand by them and try to help save the conservancy? She would have to put on one hell of a show tomorrow to sway Mr. Chance Youngblood to invest in a company that may have a crook at its helm. And the conservancy would have to be transparent with him in order to get his help. She couldn't imagine an intelligent businessman putting his money on a losing horse.

Susie said, "Petra? Are you still there?"

"Yes, I'm here," Petra said tiredly.

"I know I'm asking a lot of you, and that's the reason I told you the whole truth. You would do that for me." She paused. "You don't have to assure me that you're going to be there tomorrow. Think about it and call me back, if you like."

Petra couldn't stand the hopeless note in her friend's voice.

Susie must be under tremendous pressure. She must feel like her world was collapsing. She'd devoted her life to the conservancy, to the detriment of her personal life. She was around the same age as Petra, and had never been married, either.

"Don't worry, Susie. I'll be there tomorrow, with bells on."

"Thank you, Petra! And I'm sure Jon will be found innocent. He has to be. I can't believe he would bring shame on his mother's name. He loved her too much."

"I don't believe it, either," Petra assured her. "Now, I'd better go find something to eat. See you in the morning."

"Yes, see you soon," Susie said softly.

You certainly made me want a drink, too, Petra thought after she ended the call.

Chapter 2

"What makes you think you deserve a hundred thousand per episode?" Chance Youngblood asked Drea Jackson, one of the stars of the network's most popular reality shows, *'Round the Way Girls*. It was based in Brooklyn, New York, and followed the lives of five women trying to make it as actresses in New York City.

He supposed it was true that Drea was the most reactionary, loud and boisterous member of the cast, and because of that, she received a great deal of media attention and had avid fans on social media, but that didn't mean she deserved twice as much as the rest of the cast received. Frankly, he thought the twenty-one-year-old was out of her mind. And way too egotistical, to say nothing of believing the hype about her that made the rounds on the internet.

No doubt she was beautiful. She sat pouting now, her full red lips announcing to the world, *Look at me, I'm gorgeous; therefore you should reward me with your rapt attention. And don't forget money. After all, beautiful women deserve to live in the lap of luxury!*

"You can't deny that I bring in the viewers," she said, pointing at him with her forefinger, the nail of which was painted to look like a black-and-silver dagger encrusted with diamonds. The nail looked as sharp as a dagger, too.

"Drea," Chance said calmly, "I only let you in my office out of respect for the work you've done on the show for the past three years. *'Round the Way Girls* is doing well. But it's due to a concerted effort of all of the cast members, not just one. Your pay is commensurate with how much revenue the show brings in. When the show earns more, you'll earn more. We can revisit your request next year. Now, please go. And remember, your agent is the one who discusses this sort of thing with the company. Not you. You're the talent. He or she is your representative."

Chance could tell she was furious by the Clint Eastwood–like squint trained on him. Her well-endowed chest heaved as she rose from the chair in front of him. He hoped she wasn't going to make a scene because he wasn't averse to calling security. He would not lay one hand on her. Not with the climate the entertainment industry operated in these days. He wasn't going to be accused of sexually harassing anyone.

He sat quite still. Their eyes were locked. She appeared to be trying to make him change his mind by just the intensity of her stare. He almost laughed, because this was beginning to feel like one of those classic shoot-outs in the middle of the street in a Western. Would she draw first, or would he?

She let out an exaggerated sigh and turned toward the door. "It was worth a try," she said nonchalantly.

"No harm in trying," he said, his tone casual. He watched as she opened the door and quietly let herself out.

It was only then that he sighed with relief. Young people were so entitled these days. As if everybody owed them something. What had happened to working hard and being patient while earning your rewards? No. Everything had to happen in an instant. They were so eager to be stars and live like ballers. She was lucky she hadn't gone into his father's office back in the day with her grievances. His father would have tossed her out and told her to come back when she had a valid reason for receiving a raise in pay. She would have been lucky to not have been fired on the spot.

He chuckled softly because his thoughts had reminded him of his father. And he wasn't even thirty-one yet. Was responsibility turning him into an old man already? He'd been CEO of the company for only two years, since his father had retired. He'd assumed the position would go to one of his older siblings: Alia or Brock. But Alia wanted time to concentrate on her painting and chose to have minimum participation in managing the company, and Brock preferred finance and the nitty gritty of actual numbers involved in running a billion-dollar multimedia company. He was the numbers man. Chance was therefore the reasonable choice to lead the company and be the face of Youngblood Media to the world. He was the idea man, with his finger on the pulse of America—or more accurately, what type of entertainment the world craved.

He got to work at seven every morning and didn't leave until he felt he'd put in a full day's work, and that was usually after the office staff had cleared out. He worked hard, and he played hard.

Tonight, when he took the elevator down to the ground floor, there was only the senior security guard at the front desk.

"Good evening, Mr. Youngblood," was his friendly greeting. "Another late night, huh?"

"Unfortunately," Chance said with a smile. "Have a good evening, Mr. Robinson."

"You, as well," said Walter Robinson, an African American gentleman in his early sixties. He'd been with the company for over thirty years. Chance had known him from childhood and could remember all the jokes Mr. Robinson had told him when he was a kid. His parents had always taught him to respect his elders, and even as an adult, he had never referred to

Mr. Robinson by his first name, Walter. And even though he'd told Mr. Robinson on numerous occasions to call him Chance, Mr. Robinson preferred to call him Mr. Youngblood.

Chance left the Manhattan offices of Youngblood Media and turned right. He was within walking distance of his apartment. He enjoyed walking to work every morning, people watching as he strolled down the street. New York had its share of characters, and he'd encountered all sorts on his walks around the city. But basically, he believed New York City was like any other city in the world where people were pursuing their dreams. Everyone just wanted a safe place to live while making a decent living and fostering lasting personal relationships. Your basic recipe for happiness, as far as he was concerned.

He joined the throng of people getting off work and winding their way to subway stations, buses, personal cars or hired cars. He was heading to his favorite bar for a drink—an establishment which wasn't one of those trendy places where young professionals met and commiserated with each other. It was a quiet, rather old-fashioned bar in a luxury hotel not far from his apartment. He'd discovered it by chance one night when he was walking home.

The place had the ambience of a 1930s' speakeasy. It was dimly lit, with a huge U-shaped, highly polished oak bar, behind which were bottles of spirits lined up on shelves with a mirrored background. The bartender—at least the one he encountered every time he frequented the place—was a big muscular bald guy with tattoos on both arms. In a luxury hotel bar. The whole thing felt incongruous to Chance, which somehow made the experience richer. What Chance liked most about the bar was that it was usually practically empty. He could sit and enjoy his drink without being approached by anyone.

It was half past six before Petra walked out of her hotel and went in search of a restaurant, preferably a casual one because she was dressed in jeans, a pullover shirt and hiking boots, plus the ever-present safari jacket, which came with a zip-in faux fur liner. It was chilly tonight, and she needed the extra warmth.

She finally decided on a diner not far from a luxury hotel she'd always wanted to tour on Fifth Avenue. She figured the diner served good food because there was a line out the door and the crowd was uncomplaining. If the food wasn't worth waiting for, she suspected they'd be much fussier. Or wouldn't be there at all.

Once she got in and her plate was set before her, she knew she'd been right because the aroma was mouthwatering. One bite of the mac and cheese and they had a customer for life. Somebody's Southern momma had created this recipe. She smiled appreciatively, and the guy sitting next to her (the tables were quite close together) grinned at her.

"This must be your first time here," he said conversationally. He looked around forty, was tall and dark haired. Cute in an academic kind of way. Oxford shirt and conservative haircut. His eyes were dark blue.

"It is," she confirmed.

"But it won't be your last, I hope," he replied, eyes on her mouth, she noticed. She felt self-conscious because her mouth was presently occupied.

"I'm afraid it might," she said frankly. "I'm only in town for a couple days."

"What a shame. Well, I hope you have a good visit," he said as he rose and dropped a tip onto the tabletop. "Enjoy your evening."

"You, too," Petra said, smiling at him.

She enjoyed the rest of the mac and cheese, baked chicken and garden salad in peace. Or as much peace as being in a packed diner could provide. She was comfortable in crowds or in solitude. People interested her, so she found them very entertaining, and got along with people from all walks of life.

What had made her slightly uncomfortable in the presence of the academic type was the notion that he might start flirting with her. She was out of practice with the opposite sex.

Since she'd been dumped by her last boyfriend (fiancé, if she was going to be technical), Gareth Graham, a British scientist, adventurer and now TV personality, she had avoided all emotional entanglements with men. When he'd been offered the opportunity to star in his own show she had been happy for him, until she learned he felt he needed a new beginning. That new beginning hadn't included her. The last she'd heard about him, he was dating a well-known actress.

Was she bitter? Yes and no. Yes, because she'd loved him and apparently he hadn't loved her. No, because bitterness only hurt the one who was bitter by lessening your own happiness. The person you were bitter about contentedly went on with his life while you were stewing in your own juices. Completely unfair. If she were going to be bitter then, by God, he would feel the effects of that bitterness, if she were actively trying to exact revenge for his maltreatment of her. Which she wasn't.

Gareth Graham was in the past. He didn't matter anymore. However, the experience had made her cautious and not an advocate of marriage. Gareth had asked her to marry him. Another thing he hadn't been sincere about.

She'd thrown the engagement ring in his face. Okay, maybe she *was* a little bitter.

Now, she told herself, she was going to concentrate on her career and avoid relationships. What were men good for, anyway?

Not that she was an inveterate man hater. She had many male friends, like Paul Olomide and Dr. Botende, but there was nothing sexual between them. Sex was where the trouble came in.

Or maybe not the sex, because women got something out of that even if it was only the physical release. It was the men who pretended they liked you, even loved you, in order to get to the good part, the sex. Perhaps they thought they had to lie to get you to have sex with them. She wasn't that gullible. But the pain that was sure to come when you allowed your tender heart to open up to someone, and then that someone trampled on it? That was unforgiveable.

She believed if a woman was interested in making love to a man, she should do so. With no expected declarations of love afterward. That was honest. She had stipulations, though. No married men, or men involved with someone else. Here's where it got tricky—if the deal wasn't based on truth. There were so many liars out there. Gareth had lied. Could she depend on the next male she found attractive and worthy of sharing her body with to not be a liar, too? She had no idea. She hadn't tested her theory yet.

She sighed. She'd finished her meal, left a good tip for her waitress and now made her way to the cash register by the exit. This was such an unassuming place to have such delicious food. But then some of her best meals in Kinshasa had been prepared by unlicensed chefs just trying to make ends meet.

On the street again, she walked for several blocks, enjoying the sights, window shopping and people watching until she ended up on Fifth Avenue in front of the hotel she'd always been curious about. The place seemed to take up an entire city block. She glanced up at the golden angel statue beside a gentleman on a horse out front.

She felt a bit intimidated as she stepped beneath

the awning with flags flying above it. But the door-man merely gave her a friendly nod hello and held the door open for her to enter.

Once she was in the lobby she tried not to stare at the elegant trappings of one of New York City's five-star hotels. When she was a little girl, she'd read the Eloise books. She almost expected Eloise herself to skip down the stairs. But no, only posh people were in the lobby, going about their business. No one gave her a second look, for which she was grateful. She wasn't exactly dressed for these digs in her jeans and safari jacket.

She continued walking and stopped suddenly when she noticed they had a shop devoted entirely to Eloise, the fictional little girl who, in the children's books, had lived in this hotel.

Some rich little girl could pretend she was Eloise and take back home with her all sorts of Eloise memorabilia. Ah, to be a child again. Petra beat a hasty retreat before she was tempted to buy something.

She discreetly looked around for a bar. She was determined to have a drink here. A place this size probably had more than one bar on the premises.

She kept her gawking to a minimum. There was so much to see. They had everything anyone could imagine wanting. There were even shops where you could buy clothing if you happened to have forgotten a cocktail dress when you'd packed for your stay.

Finally, she found a bar that looked like a throw-back to the thirties. Upon entering the darkened watering hole, she noticed the bartender looked like he could pick her up and toss her across the room, he was so big. He smiled when she sat down, though, and asked her what her poison was.

Other patrons were sitting around the bar, whose mirrored walls, behind the shelves of every conceivable alcoholic beverage you could think of, reflected their images back at them.

"Whiskey, neat," said Petra, returning his smile.

He poured her whiskey into a glass and placed it in front of her.

"Thank you," said Petra.

She picked it up, admired its color for a moment and then tossed it back. She didn't drink whiskey because she liked the taste. She drank it for its effects.

The bartender smiled as if he approved of her manner of drinking. But he didn't ask her if she wanted another drink. He simply continued polishing glasses as he'd been doing when she'd walked up to the bar.

Petra felt the warmth of the drink as it hit her stomach and began inching its way into her bloodstream.

Her cell phone buzzed while she was sitting there and she looked down at the display. It was her sister Lauren sending her more photos of Colton Jr., or C.J. as everyone was calling him. Petra smiled at his adorable image. She looked forward to finally holding him in her arms when she got to Raleigh, North Carolina. She gave a contented sigh. She missed her family.

She sent a quick text thanking Lauren for the photos and telling her she was still in New York City and would be in Raleigh as soon as possible. She and her sisters were planning an anniversary party for their parents. She was part of the surprise because her parents had no idea she was back in the States.

I can't wait to kiss my nephew's chipmunk cheeks. He's adorable, she wrote. It's about time one of you made me an aunt!

It's going to be your turn soon, Lauren texted back.

Nah, not me. I'll be the kooky aunt who gives weird presents, she countered. And she couldn't help laughing out loud at the thought of that.

As he entered the bar, Chance heard the delightful sound of a woman's laughter. His gaze followed the sound and discovered the owner of that laugh, an exotic-looking, brown-skinned woman with the most beautiful head of hair he'd ever seen. It was dark and wavy and fell almost to her waist. She couldn't be more than five-four, he judged, and was wearing the least seductive outfit he'd ever seen on a woman. But then, he was used to women who went to bars to ensnare a man. And this woman wasn't showing any skin.

Curiosity made him sit down on the stool next to her. The bartender zeroed in on him. "Welcome back," he said in his friendly manner. "What's your poison tonight?"

"A Scotch on the rocks," Chance said. "Thank you."

The bartender moved away to prepare his drink, and the woman beside him was looking intently at her cell phone and smiling with pleasure. *Must be a man she's texting*, Chance thought.

On closer inspection he noticed she had dimples, a cute nose, long lashes, a full mouth—the lower lip a bit poutier than the top—and that her fingers were slender and she didn't wear nail polish. Her nails were neatly trimmed. As she typed on the keypad of her cell phone, she bit her bottom lip.

She let out a soft sigh suddenly and put her phone into the pocket of her jacket. When she did, Chance got a whiff of eucalyptus. It reminded him of that cold medicine his mother used to rub on his chest when he was a kid. A strange perfume for a woman to be wearing, sure, but it wasn't unpleasant.

What's with men staring at me today? Petra wondered. This guy probably thought she hadn't noticed him boring a hole in her with his eyes. She'd seen him out of the corner of her eye, and had decided to see just how long he was going to stare at her without saying anything.

When it went on for two more minutes, she turned on her stool and looked him straight in the eyes. Her breath caught in her throat. She'd been prepared to dislike him on sight, but good Lord, the man was stunning! And here she sat in her jungle togs!

The bartender came back and set a drink in front of the guy. He murmured his thanks, but he didn't break eye contact with her. "May I buy you a drink?" he asked her, and he smiled. It was a smile that melted her core. It made crinkles appear at the corners of his cinnamon-colored eyes and made his already luscious lips ten times sexier. It was lust at first sight.

She found herself accepting his offer even though one drink was usually her limit.

The bartender was just waiting for his cue, obviously, because as soon as she uttered, "That's so kind of you," to Gorgeous Guy, he asked, "Whiskey, neat again?"

She gave a curt nod. "Yes, thank you," and he turned away to get her drink.

"Are you enjoying your stay here?" Gorgeous Guy asked conversationally.

From his expensive attire to the Rolex on his wrist, she was pretty certain he could afford to stay here, but how was she going to state the obvious?

"Um, actually, I had dinner near here, saw the hotel, which I'd always wanted a look inside of, and came in for a tour. All I can afford here is the drink I just had." And if that put him off, so be it. He was probably out of her league, anyway.

He laughed shortly. "To be honest, I'm just here for a drink, too. I live near here and pass this hotel on my way to work every day."

So he lived in this very highly priced part of the city. When she'd worked at the Central Park Zoo, in her early days as a zoologist, she'd had to take several subway lines to Midtown Manhattan from her Brooklyn neighborhood. Now, she was positive he was out of her league.

"How about you?" he asked as the bartender set her drink in front of her.

"I'm just passing through," Petra said. She smiled at him. "I've been out of the country for a while and I'm only in town for a meeting with the company I work for. Then I'm heading south to visit family."

"Born and raised in the South?" he asked.

"My dad was a general in the army. I was born in Germany, but raised in Raleigh, North Carolina."

"Mother German?" he asked.

She laughed shortly and gestured to her hair. "Oh, you mean this? No, my mother is half Cherokee and half African American. I guess I got the hair gene from my Native American grandmother. I don't know. Maybe some of my African ancestors had lots of hair."

"Well, it's beautiful. *You're* beautiful." His tone was intimate, and the sound of his baritone voice sent shivers down her spine. No one had told her she was beautiful since Gareth, and chances were, he hadn't meant it.

"Thank you," she said shyly. She didn't know why she was flushing from embarrassment. This wasn't the first time a man had tried to pick her up. It was the first time she was seriously thinking of letting herself be picked up, though.

He might be the one to help her prove her theory.

He smiled and glanced at her drink, still sitting untouched in front of her. "You're not going to drink that?"

"The thing is," she told him, "I'm not much of a drinker and I've already had one. I only accepted it because I wanted to stay and talk with you."

"Then, please, don't drink it," he said. "I want you to be able to hold up your end of the conversation."

She laughed at that. "So do I," she said as she boldly appraised his features. He had a cleft chin in his square-jawed face, and his skin was the color of a fine dark chocolate, which contrasted sharply with those cinnamon-colored eyes of his. His hair was dark brown, natural and cut close to his well-shaped head. He had beautifully formed ears that neither stuck out nor were too large. Everything about him screamed masculinity. Big hands, large feet, a broad chest and muscles straining against the sleeve of his suit every time he brought his glass to his mouth. His height was just right. He was nearly six feet tall, she guessed. She didn't like it when a guy was a whole foot taller than she was. Sure, some guys liked to think it was perfect if they could pick their women up and handle them as if they weighed next to nothing, but she didn't like being manhandled, no matter how adorable a guy thought she was in all her petite glory.

He caught her looking him over and smiled knowingly. She didn't mind getting caught. After making sure he wasn't wearing a wedding ring, she'd decided he was the one to test her theory on. But he had to make the first move. She wasn't going to be the aggressor here.

His eyes drifted down to her feet. "I'm curious," he said. "Why the hiking boots?"

"Like I said, I've been out of the country for a while. And where I've been, the boots were a wise footwear choice. I haven't had a chance to go shopping yet."

"Then you do like women's clothes?" He said this with a twinkle in his eyes. Otherwise, she might have been offended.

"Would you still be sitting here if you thought I wasn't all woman?"

He chuckled. "You've got me there. I think any woman who can look sexy in that outfit is all woman."

"What about you? Do you dress like that every day?"

"I'm a businessman. I dress accordingly. But do I love it? No. I like the effect it has on people. When you dress like this they know you're serious about what you do. However, it's a pleasure to get out of this getup every evening when I get home and slip into some sweats and a T-shirt. Why am I telling you all this?" He looked chagrined.

"Because that's what you do with anonymous people," Petra said softly. "People you meet in bars or on the train. You'd be surprised by some of the things people have told me without even knowing my name."

"Speaking of which—" he began.

She cut him off. "Please don't tell me your name. Nine times out of ten, you and I may never see each other again. I'm out of here sometime tomorrow or the next day, and I doubt you're in Raleigh much, are you?"

"I've never been to Raleigh," he admitted.

"Then let's go with the first letter of our names, shall we?" she suggested. She offered him her hand. He took it. "I'm P."

After she'd said that, she frowned. "On second thought I'd prefer using the first three letters of my name. Call me Pet."

"I'm C," he said. He looked deeply into her eyes after releasing her hand. "You're doing something to me, Pet. I don't know exactly what it is about you, but I would really like to get to know you better."

"Maybe it's because you want to see if my hair is real," she joked. "Or if I have a good body underneath these layers of man-like clothing?"

"That could be it," he said, grinning. "Or maybe I see in you a kindred spirit, and I would be remiss if I didn't throw caution to the wind and get to know you better while I have the chance."

"A once-in-a-lifetime opportunity?" she asked.

"Yes," he said emphatically. "And if you're willing, I'd say let's get out of here and go someplace more private. Someplace where I can, perhaps, see your ankles. A hundred years ago, I hear, men were quite turned on by women's ankles. I think your look would have been very suitable back then."

She gazed at him for several moments before saying, "All right."

She got up and gestured to the bartender, preparing to pay for her drink. But C told her, "I've got it," and gave the bartender a bill that covered the drink and also included a generous tip, judging by the delighted expression on the bartender's face.

C offered her his arm in a gentlemanly fashion. She took it and they walked out of the bar together.

Petra smiled nervously up at him as they walked through the hotel. "Where are we going?"

"My apartment is only a few blocks away," he said.

She thought it was better to go to his place than to her hotel room. But honestly, having never gone to someone's apartment with them after a drink in a bar before, she didn't know what the proper etiquette was, or if you could call it proper at all.

"Do you do this often?" she asked.

"I've never done it before," he told her, and the expression on his face looked completely innocent.

"You're a man and you've never picked up a woman in a bar before? How old are you?" She sounded skeptical.

"You're a woman and you've never been picked up in a bar before?" he asked with a smug smile.

She laughed. "No, and I'm beginning to think *this* time is a mistake!"

"I'll be thirty-one next month," he said.

"I'm two years older than you," she said accusingly, as if he'd had something to do with their age difference.

"It worked for Denzel and Pauletta Washington," he joked. Which made her laugh.

She peered up at him. He was a good conversationalist and quick witted. Even if her experiment failed tonight, at the very least, she would be entertained.

Chapter 3

As Chance unlocked the door of his apartment, he wondered what kinds of fool his brother and sister would call him when they found out he'd brought a stranger home with him. And they would definitely find out because they were his confidants, as he was theirs.

This was so unlike him. Yeah, he might enjoy risky sports like mountain climbing and motocross, but when it came to women, he was careful. Extremely careful after two relationships—count 'em, two—that had ended when the women had revealed themselves as gold diggers.

He allowed Pet to precede him into the foyer, and then he closed the door and locked it. He shrugged out of his overcoat and hung it in the closet. He watched as Pet looked around her, a huge grin on her face. "You have a lovely place, C," she said as she let him take her jacket and hang it next to his coat in the closet. She set her shoulder bag on the foyer table.

The apartment had been professionally decorated to his specifications. He wasn't emotionally invested in it. It was simply a place to lay his head, to entertain in when the mood hit him.

He did like the sheer size of the apartment, though. And the tall, wide windows that let in a lot of light. The views were spectacular. It was on the twentieth floor, and he had a bird's-eye view of the city.

Now, though, he just wanted to look at Pet. She stood there with her hands on her shapely hips, admiring the place, but with a total lack of covetousness in her eyes. He'd become accustomed to that avaricious manner of calculating how much everything cost. She seemed to like what she saw, but wasn't ultimately interested in acquiring it for herself.

She glanced down at the highly polished hardwood floor. "This must be a beast to keep up," she said. "You should pay your housekeeper double to do these." She spun around. "This is a big place. You're not married, are you?"

Once again, she looked him straight in the eyes. He supposed a woman couldn't be too careful.

"No, I'm not married. I'm not involved with anyone. And I'm healthy. I practice safe sex whenever I have sex, and I'm not into bondage or any kind of freaky acts depicted in romantic movies. I'm just a grown man who's a little lonely and wants to make love to you because I suspect you're lonely, too."

Her beautiful, full-lipped mouth twitched in a half smile. Her eyes smoldered. He must have said something she liked because she walked up to him and rose up on the tips of her toes and kissed him.

He didn't know what he had expected when his mouth finally covered hers, but this spark of electricity that shot through him when her body collided with his and her sweet mouth met his threw his equilibrium off. He felt lightheaded and his libido, already strong at this point, increased by leaps and bounds.

Her arms went around his neck and he automatically grasped her about the waist. She felt firm, yet soft, and she smelled wonderful, as if she'd just gotten out of the tub. His hands came up her back and rested in her silky hair, and he was cognizant enough to want to put his hands on her scalp, just to see if that hair was real. He knew it was foolish, but he had to know. Sure enough, that was her scalp with no extensions protruding from it.

She broke off the kiss when he did that and laughed. She was adorable when she laughed. He felt a tenderness toward her when she smirked and asked, "Satisfied?"

"Yes," he said. "Is there anything on me you'd like to authenticate?"

"That's a foolish question," she said, and reached up to tug at his tie. "Shouldn't you be getting out of that suit and into something more comfortable?"

With that, she turned her back to him and walked farther into the apartment, as if she owned the place. She strode over to his wall of photos. He didn't have anything connected to work on his walls, just personal shots of friends and family. And photographic memories of his various excursions. There were pictures of him and fellow climbers in the Himalayas. Riding a bike in the Sonoran Desert. Skydiving in Namibia.

She stopped in front of his family photos and he could have sworn she was about to cry as she looked at a photo of him with his parents and his siblings.

He put an arm about her shoulders. "What's the matter, Pet?"

She turned and her eyes were misty. "You seem like such a sweet guy. Those are your relatives, aren't they? You all look so much alike."

"Yes, they're my parents and my brother and sister. You miss your family, huh?"

"I do, but that's not why I feel sad," she told him. She breathed deeply and with her exhale, blurted out, "You're an experiment, C. I'm using you to prove something to myself."

Then she told him about her former fiancé and how he'd broken her heart, and her resolve to never trust another man with her heart. And tonight was her chance to prove to herself that she could be as detached as any male when it came to sex. But he doubted very much that she was of that ilk. She had a tender heart and was failing miserably.

Smiling, he looked into her eyes and said, "Pet, it has been my pleasure just to talk with you and hold you in my arms tonight. If you want to, I'll call you a cab and you can go home right now. I am certainly man enough to know when to call it quits. Or, if you don't have anywhere else to be for the next few hours, we could hang out here. I haven't had dinner yet and I have plenty of food in the fridge. I could whip us up something to eat."

Her eyes brightened. "I've had dinner, but I haven't had dessert yet."

He was surprised at how much pleasure those words gave him. He didn't want this night to end yet. "All right, then. I'll go change and we'll reconvene in the kitchen."

With that, he let go of her and went to his bedroom to change into something more comfortable, looking back twice to make sure she was still there. He feared that she was going to disappear in his absence.

Petra wrapped her arms around herself as she stood at the window in C's apartment peering out at the city's lights. Why had she made up an excuse to stay? Dessert? Psychologically, as her sister Desiree would say, she knew what dessert meant.

It meant that kiss had been too good to not wonder what more of the same would be like. C was delicious. She was undeniably attracted to him. She'd been curious about him at the bar. He'd made her laugh, and truthfully, when a man could make her laugh that was 50 percent of the attraction right there. He was also intelligent, and now, after seeing where he lived and what he thought was important enough to be on his walls, she also felt he was good inside.

He returned wearing jeans and a T-shirt, his feet in a pair of slides. When he was standing before her, she looked down at his feet. He had neatly manicured nails on his immaculate toes.

She smiled. "Nice feet."

In fact, all of him was nice. Great pectorals and biceps were evident underneath that T-shirt, and his muscular thighs filled out those jeans quite well.

She followed him to the kitchen and sat on a stool at the big center island while he opened the refrigerator and began pulling out sandwich makings: lettuce, tomatoes, pickles, mustard and slices of roast beef, turkey and ham. He was obviously not a mayo man, and the mustard was spicy.

As he built a sandwich, he grinned at her. "What do you want for dessert? I've got four kinds of ice cream. Chocolate chunk, French vanilla, Ben & Jerry's Chunky Monkey and strawberry."

"Chunky Monkey?" she said, laughing softly. "If you only knew!"

He looked puzzled and she didn't enlighten him. "You like ice cream," was all she said.

"Love it," he said. He piled items on top of wheat

bread until the sandwich was a good two inches high. Then he cut it in half with a butcher's knife, transferred it to a plate and put everything back in the fridge except the bread, which he put in a bread box in the adjacent pantry.

After doing that, he got two bowls from the cabinet above the sink, took an ice cream scoop and two teaspoons from the utensil drawer and lastly pulled cartons of ice cream out of the freezer and set them on the island's countertop.

He looked at her. "Come on, let's go to the living room and watch a movie while these melt a bit."

He grabbed a bottle of water from the refrigerator. "Would you like some?"

"Yes, thanks," she answered, and he handed her a bottle of spring water.

They moved to the living room area, where the inviting seating arrangement was positioned around the big screen TV.

Petra sat on the couch and got comfortable. C sat down and placed his plate and bottle of water on the coffee table in front of him, then he picked up a huge remote control, the likes of which Petra had not seen in her years in the Congo, and proceeded to pull up names of movies on the big screen. Petra wasn't familiar with any of them.

"What do you want to see? Action adventure, drama, comedy?" C asked. He bit into his sandwich and chewed while she made up her mind.

"Let's try a drama," she said. She felt as though

she had been living in the Dark Ages. As he scrolled down the list, she still didn't recognize any of the film titles. "I give up," she said. "You pick something."

He finished chewing a bite of his sandwich and looked at her. "Where have you been living that you don't know any of these movies?" he asked curiously.

It wasn't that she was unaware of what was going on in the world of entertainment. She simply had little interest in movies or television. Instead she read books. She watched the news. She had intelligent conversations with her colleagues. Yet she was woefully inept about social media. She used her cell phone for communication and research. Google was her friend. Facebook was not. She had never sent a Tweet in her life.

"I've been living in a country where many homes don't even have a TV," she told him.

This bit of information apparently made him so sympathetic to her plight that he got up, went to her, pulled her into his arms and hugged her tightly. "Ah, Pet, I just want to hold you like this all night long."

She had no objection to that, and relaxed in his arms for a moment, but then, in her most authoritative voice, told him, "That sounds good, but you need to finish your sandwich, find us a movie—nothing gory, please—and then give me that ice cream you promised me."

He laughed shortly and sat back down. She did, too. A couple of minutes later, the movie *Creed* starring Michael B. Jordan and Sylvester Stallone was playing on the big screen TV.

Petra watched with rapt attention. She was a sports fan and found boxing fascinating. She had some martial arts training in her background. Her father, forward-thinking parent that he was, had made sure all five of his daughters had enrolled in judo classes at a young age. Judo was good for girls because it was a sport that didn't depend on size and bulk. A small person could use their size to their advantage against someone larger. Being supple, strong and intelligent was sufficient. She had earned her black belt by the time she was eighteen. She liked to visit certain dojos in various cities, and she practiced on her own whenever time permitted.

C must have thought her intense interest in the film was due to Michael B. Jordan's physique, because he looked at her after finishing his sandwich and said, "Don't get attached. He's even younger than I am."

"But he's so cute," Petra said playfully.

C stood up and reached for her hand. "Come on, let's get some ice cream into you so you can cool off."

In the kitchen, Petra used the scoop to put a bit of French vanilla and chocolate chunk ice cream into her bowl. "What would you like?" she asked C. Their eyes met.

C looked at her with such unbridled passion that she knew he wasn't interested in ice cream. "I'll just lick whatever you're having off your lips," he said.

Petra took that challenge. She tasted some of the French vanilla, then she went to him and kissed him.

She moaned with pleasure as the kiss deepened. She realized that she didn't want this sensation to stop. Her body needed this. She needed this. She was not going to regret it in the morning, either. She was simply going to let herself enjoy being with C.

She must have looked drunk with desire as C peered into her eyes and said breathlessly, "Does this mean you've decided to stay, my Pet?"

It was the 'my Pet' that slayed her. She was ripe for the plucking, and there was no turning back. "I'm yours," she said.

He picked her up, and she wrapped her legs around his hips. And they were kissing again, even more urgently than before. Then she thought about the ice cream that would melt on the counter while they were heating up the sheets in his bedroom and cried, "Put the ice cream back in the freezer first!"

C laughed uproariously. "Girl, you're going to drive me crazy!" But he set her down and put the ice cream back in the freezer. In Kinshasa, people didn't waste food.

He picked her back up and carried her to his bedroom, with her clinging to him all the way.

Chance was more sexually excited than he'd been in a long time, and he didn't know if it was because he was doing something he'd never done before, or if he was simply very attracted to Pet.

Or both. Probably both.

Once they were in the bedroom, he set her down at the foot of the king-size bed and they raced each other getting out of their clothes. She neatly folded her things and placed them on the back of the chair that stood at the entrance of the walk-in closet. He was down to his briefs by the time she'd walked across the room, and she turned around wearing nothing but matching bra and panties.

Her body was perfect, as far as he was concerned. She was fit and slightly muscular, her legs and thighs showing delineated muscles due to physical exercise. Whatever she did to look like that, it was definitely working for her. Her arms and belly also were femininely muscular, pleasing but not bulky. Her skin was a uniform golden-brown color. Perhaps she had tan lines when her underwear was off. He'd wait to see.

She reached back as if she were about to twist her hair up and out of the way, but he cried, "Don't change a thing."

Her arms fell to her sides and she smiled as she walked toward him. "It's all right with me if you don't mind hair all over you. I've been told it can get in the way."

"Whoever told you that is a fool," he said as he went and pulled her into his arms.

Warm naked skin touched warm naked skin, and the sensation made him sigh with pleasure. He felt her tremble slightly in his arms, and he wondered if he frightened her or if this whole situation was making her nervous. "There's still time to back out of this," he gently told her.

She met his gaze and tilted her head back, and her exquisite neck seemed to beckon him to kiss it, so he did. Again he felt a slight tremble in her. But when he looked into her eyes, he saw desire and determination in them.

"I hope you have a good supply of condoms," she said, smiling.

"I aim to please," he said with confidence.

After that, she licked her lips. The small act suddenly struck him as highly seductive, and he could no longer wait. She must have sensed his urgency, or felt the subtle change in his body, because she ran her hands down the sides of his body, ending at his butt, and pressed him against her crotch. His engorged penis grew even harder. She let out a soft sigh and pulled down his briefs, her eyes never leaving his.

She removed his arms from about her with slow deliberation and took a step backward, unfastening her bra as she did so.

Her breasts were full, but not large. They were enough to fill his big hands, and they were firm and round and natural. The nipples were darker than her skin color, and they were erect. He began to salivate at the thought of taking their plumpness into his mouth.

He finished taking off his briefs and tossed them onto the floor behind him. He eagerly stepped toward her, but she put a hand out. He froze. She peeled off her panties and his heart thumped excitedly at the sight of her womanhood. The hair covering her vagina was the same color as the hair on her head. She was natural from head to toe. His penis must have grown another inch or two at the sight of her.

"Now?" he asked patiently. At least he hoped he sounded patient. He didn't feel patient at all.

She smiled and walked into his embrace. Adam and Eve, he thought. I feel like Adam holding Eve. This is how man and woman are supposed to come together. Naturally.

They kissed, hands touching, massaging erogenous zones that he didn't even know he had until he'd met this marvelous woman.

Now he knew what people meant when they said their toes curled.

All of him was curling in excitement. Tingling might be a more descriptive word. He wished he could just shut down his analytical mind and simply enjoy the physical experience, the here and the now, but all he could think was that maybe this was going to be the last time he saw her and he'd better make it good.

So he slowed down as he backed her toward the bed, and when she sat down and scooted farther onto it, he gently picked her up and set her on top of him with his back propped up on a pile of pillows. He then reached into the top drawer of the nightstand, got a plastic-wrapped condom out, tore it open and rolled it onto his rock-hard penis. He looked into her eyes and she responded by rising up, positioning his penis at the entrance of her vagina and slowly impaling herself on it. It felt so good, it took all of his willpower not to come. She was tight and hot, and the utter look of pleasure on her beautiful face was almost his undoing.

She bent and kissed him, and the pleasure heightened even more. Their thrusts were slow, languid, the kind you wanted to last forever but even though you knew it was futile, you still sent up fervent prayers for longevity anyway.

He closed his eyes, relishing the level of synchronicity they shared. But then he opened them again because he didn't want to miss anything. He would have the visual memories of her in his mind forever. Logically, he knew this was a one-night stand, but emotionally, it didn't feel like one.

After several wonderful, extremely sensual minutes, Pet's thrusts sped up. Her nipples were more swollen and he couldn't resist them any longer. He rose up on his elbows and gently took one of them in his mouth. Pet moaned loudly. "Oh, God, that feels so good."

The feeling was mutual. He gave the other nipple equal time. She began panting. He enjoyed twirling his tongue around the areola. He licked the berry-like nipple with the tip of his tongue. She groaned as though her pleasure was coming to a peak and she was trying to hold it off.

Her thrusts sped up. He grasped her firm bottom

and held on, letting her ride him, concentrating only on giving her pleasure. When she screamed, he knew he'd hit her sweet spot. She collapsed on top of him, and the fact that she'd orgasmed on top of him, her body convulsing with the release, sent more blood rushing to his already hard penis.

He gently rolled her onto her back and smiled at her. "Open up for me, my Pet," he growled.

Pet smiled seductively. "C, you say such romantic things."

She looked so beautiful with her hair splayed out on the pillows, her face flushed, penny-colored eyes looking at him with passionate intensity. He couldn't have been more aroused.

He intended to give her something to remember him by. And she surprised him by matching him thrust for thrust. It was as if his sexual readiness empowered her. But then, women, wonderful creatures that they were, didn't need to rest between orgasms. They could have multiple orgasms to a man's puny one during lovemaking. The bed was getting a workout tonight.

When he came, he didn't collapse on top of her, but lay on his side and pulled her close to spoon her. "I was right," he said softly in her ear. "You're all woman."

She laughed softly. "And you're quite a man, C."

She sounded sleepy. He wondered what her day had been like.

He wanted to know which country she'd recently

flown in from. When she talked about herself, it was never with specifics. He supposed that was because she figured they'd never see each other again after tonight and didn't want to set herself up for more disappointment. When she'd told him about the guy she was engaged to and how he'd broken up with her so coldly after he'd gotten a lucrative job offer, she hadn't mentioned names, but the description of the guy had rung some bells in his mind.

He didn't want to think about it right now. He just wanted to hold Pet. He could worry about that tomorrow.

A few minutes later, after he heard her sleeping soundly, he got up, went to the bathroom and cleaned himself up. Then he got back in bed. Pet snuggled closer to him in her sleep. He switched off the light on the nightstand and gave a little sigh of contentment. Soon, he was asleep.

Chapter 4

Just so you know, the experiment failed, Petra wrote in the note she left for C the following morning. *I want to see you again. But I can't be presumptuous and think the feeling is mutual. We both know how this thing works, right?*

After she left C's apartment, she went back to her hotel, showered, dressed for her meeting with the conservancy and made it to their Manhattan offices with five minutes to spare.

The good thing about her night with C was that her mind was so preoccupied with memories of them together, she didn't have time to be nervous about her presentation.

She was shown to Susie's office after she checked

in at the reception desk. Susie opened her door and pulled her inside. Petra set her shoulder bag and big satchel with her laptop and digital recordings in it on the floor, then Susie hugged her tightly.

Susie was tall and blond with big brown eyes. She was dressed conservatively in a navy slack suit and a white blouse with matching navy pumps. Petra was wearing the only item of clothing she had with her that was suitable for a business meeting: a beige cotton scoop-necked dress, whose hem fell about two inches above her knees. It fitted her figure as though it were made expressly for her. A pair of brown pumps were on her feet, and she'd put her hair in a ponytail. She'd kept her makeup to a minimum.

"You look wonderful," Susie exclaimed. "The jungle suits you."

Petra laughed. "Yes, I suppose it does."

Breaking off the hug, she looked up at her friend. "You look great, too. I see you let your hair grow."

Susie fluffed her blond tresses, which were shoulder length now, and glanced at her watch. "We'd better get to the conference room. I had them set up the TV and video player like last time so you can show the footage on the TV screen. Shall we go?"

"Sure," Petra said, removing her jacket and hanging it on the coat tree in Susie's office. She also left her shoulder bag in the office, needing only the satchel.

When they walked into the conference room, the first person Petra noticed was Jon Berensen sitting at the head of the long conference table, dressed in a gray pinstripe suit, still looking as distinguished as he always looked except for the dark rings under his eyes. A man in his late sixties, he was tall and had a head full of wavy iron gray hair. His skin was tanned because he was an outdoorsman. An only child, he'd grown up in Africa while his mother pursued her career.

Jon got up, grinning. "Petra! It's wonderful to see you again." Jon walked toward her, his arms outstretched.

Petra went into his arms and they hugged tightly. "It's wonderful to see you, too, Jon. How're you holding up?"

Jon released her to get a better look at her. "Susie told you, then?"

"Yes, I'm so sorry you're going through this."

His expression was grave as he looked down into her upturned face. "I dropped the ball, my dear. I wasn't taking care of business as I should have been."

"But can you really take the blame when someone deceives you?" she asked plaintively. "Someone you've trusted for years?"

Jon was not ready to shirk his responsibilities, though. "I still should have known better."

There was a knock on the conference room door, and Susie went to answer it.

Petra turned her gaze toward the entrance, and the moment she saw who was joining them, her jaw dropped. It was C. Her C from last night.

C spotted her and frowned, apparently confused as to why she would be there. He was dressed in another one of his tailored business suits, this one in dark blue, with a long-sleeve white shirt, red tie and gold cufflinks. The man was a throwback to a more resplendent age when it came to dressing. Her heartbeat sped up. What fresh hell was this?

They stared at each other. She couldn't speak now if her life depended on it.

"Petra, may I introduce you to a potential partner in the conservancy, Chance Youngblood? Chance is the CEO of Youngblood Media—they're an entertainment company. He's going to sit in on your presentation today. And Chance, this is Dr. Petra Gaines, who is both a zoologist and an anthropologist, as well as the author of a couple of books on the subjects. We have gladly been supporting her work in the Congo these past six years."

Chance was smiling benignly, as if his emotions were fully under control. But Petra knew that couldn't be the case because she was, frankly, freaking out inside.

Their eyes met as she stepped forward and offered her hand. "Mr. Youngblood," she managed, her voice soft. "It's a pleasure."

"Pet," he said equally softly as he shook her hand. "I mean, Petra. What a lovely name."

"Thank you," Petra said. He released her hand. She took a deep breath to avoid passing out. Then, "I like your name, too."

Susie interrupted them by saying, "Petra, now that Mr. Youngblood is here, we can get started. Do you need help with the equipment?"

Grateful for the interruption, Petra smiled at her. "No, thank you. I can handle it." She smiled at Chance again. He winked at her, and for some reason his playfulness calmed her down a bit. "All right, then," she said, turning away to grab her satchel and walk over to the TV, which was sitting on a mobile stand with a shelf below it that housed the digital video player. All she had to do was put the digitized video cartridge in the player and press Play.

She began by showing them footage of her first encounter with the nest of chimpanzees she'd been studying for the past two years. She told them how deforestation had reduced the size of their habitat and poaching had also decreased their populations. She told them how the presence of wild preserves like the one in which she did her research in the Congo influenced natives living near it to stop eating bush meat. They began to see the primates as more than a food source, but as sentient beings.

Lastly, she showed them footage of Francesca and Joey, explaining that she'd been observing Francesca before Joey's birth and what a loving, protective mother Francesca had become since Joey's birth.

Upon seeing Joey, Susie cried, "He's adorable!"

To which Chance replied, "Yes, but they are dangerous when they grow up, aren't they? They're very strong and can be aggressive."

Petra smiled at him. "They *are* very strong and protective of their nests. That's why I'm always careful."

She wasn't sure that he was showing concern

for her when he'd made that statement, but it had warmed her heart, nonetheless.

After the presentation was over, the four of them sat down at the conference table.

"Well," Jon said, turning to Chance, "what do you think of our Petra?"

Chance appeared totally in control. His emotions hadn't shown on his face since that initial frown when he'd walked into the conference room. He sat there looking cool and collected in his impeccable business suit, while Petra's heart rate quickened, and perspiration gathered on her forehead.

What if he thought she had stalked him? What if he thought running into him in that bar had been calculated on her part? A way to manipulate him, coerce him into supporting the conservancy?

But how could he think that? She had already been in the bar when he sat down next to her. She let out a deep sigh, and she could have sworn he'd heard her from the other side of the conference table.

"I think Dr. Gaines is delightful," Chance said at last, giving her an enigmatic smile. If she were inclined to think badly of him, she could have taken that statement negatively. As in, he had found her delightful in his bed last night.

"I totally agree with that," Jon said, beaming. "I'm glad you think so, too."

"In fact," Chance continued, "I think the network can build a show around you and your work, Dr. Gaines. Something along the lines of the type of shows Bear Grylls does, but less risky and dangerous, of course. Set in the Congo. A show like that could provide jobs for locals, like Paul Olomide, the assistant you spoke so highly of. And I think we should do a book, too, since you're a writer, as a tie-in to the show. I believe a show like that would be beneficial for the African American community. Little girls will see a woman who looks like them doing something worthwhile in the world, protecting the environment for future generations. Showing how we all should take care of each other. If the primates become extinct, we become extinct."

Petra was amazed by the words coming out of his mouth. He had the charm and exuberance of P. T. Barnum, and it had been said of that promoter that he could convince anyone of anything.

It made her a little afraid, how persuasive he sounded. All of this felt surreal. Turned out the man she'd made love to last night was none other than the conservancy's golden goose: the man who they were hoping would save them.

How was she supposed to react to that? She'd done her part. She'd given an excellent talk without fainting from the stress of the situation. Now she needed to get out of there, and soon.

Chance wondered what he had said to cause that deer-caught-in-headlights expression on Petra's face. Her face softened after a few seconds and she smiled again. "You're very kind to think I could carry a show like you describe, but I'm a scientist, not an entertainer."

"You're wrong," Chance said. "You're very entertaining. I couldn't keep my eyes off you while you were talking about your work. Plus, you have charisma. You are nice to look at, and the way you express yourself is very appealing. You're a natural."

Petra laughed. "You've just met me!"

Chance smirked and then immediately regretted it, because he didn't want her thinking that their encounter last night had anything to do with what was happening right now.

"I apologize," he said. That was strictly between him and her, and he hoped she got his meaning. "Knowing what entertains people is my business, Dr. Gaines. When I say I believe you would be a natural, I know what I'm talking about."

"Do you mean a reality show?" Petra asked, her tone horrified.

"What?" Chance asked. "Are you a television purist? Someone who looks down her nose at reality shows?"

He didn't want to think Petra could be so close-minded. After all, in the space of an hour he had gone from confused by her actions after he'd found her gone from his bed that morning, to sympathetic when he'd read her note, to hopeful when he'd walked into the conference room and found her there. For a split second, after seeing her, he had thought someone had been pulling a cruel joke on him. But then he'd seen how floored she'd been upon seeing him again, and he'd instantly known there had been no subterfuge on her part. She was genuinely surprised to see him again. At that instance, he hoped only that the part she'd written in her note to him about wanting to see him again was true. Because he definitely wanted to see her again.

"I wouldn't call myself either an opponent of reality shows or a proponent," Petra said. "I rarely watch TV."

Then it dawned on him why she'd been stumped about what to watch last night. And the ice cream thing. Living in a part of Africa where the locals probably scrabbled to put food on the table had made her loath to waste food. He was suddenly ashamed of his tendency to not even give a second thought to such things.

"Take your time and think about it," he said. "You don't need to give me your decision right now."

"I think it's a wonderful idea, Petra," Jon said. "Imagine how many more people you'll reach with that kind of platform? I know you're a serious scientist. Like my mother, you love the field work, but the world is different than it was in her day. The world communicates differently. News travels faster thanks to the internet. Ideas travel faster. You are a positive image. You put your heart, your passion into your work. That will translate well through the medium of television."

Petra's eyes met Chance's. She was looking at him

as if she didn't know him. He suspected her mind was still reeling from the number the universe had pulled on them. If this wasn't some cosmic joke, he didn't know what was. What were the odds of their meeting last night and then ending up in this conference room together? Astronomical, no doubt.

"Thank you," she said. "I'll think about it. It's just so unlike anything I ever thought I'd do."

He smiled. "That's understandable." He stood. "Well, Jon, I think you and I should have that private talk you mentioned earlier."

Jon gave a decisive nod in his direction. Chance already knew what Jon wanted to talk about in private. He'd had the company investigated and knew there were questions about Jon's trustworthiness. He wouldn't be there if he believed Jon Berensen was stealing from the conservancy. He was a thorough man, though, and wanted to hear the explanation from Jon himself.

Susie pulled Petra aside and whispered something in her ear, then Susie said, "All right, gentlemen, Petra and I will give you some privacy."

Petra and Chance's eyes met across the conference table. He saw indecision in hers, and curiosity. He couldn't wait to get her alone and talk, but first he had to settle some business with Jon.

He hoped she saw the reluctance to see her go in his eyes as she backed away and went to gather her belongings. It was with regret that he watched her and Susie leave the conference room.

He and Jon sat back down and regarded each other with sober expressions on their faces.

"I guess you've heard the rumors already," Jon began. "Your being a savvy businessman and all. It isn't true. When the conservancy's accountant disappeared we knew who the culprit was, but it's been a real challenge tracking him down and trying to recover what he stole. I don't know how long it's going to take to finally rectify the situation."

"Sometimes you never get answers," Chance said. "But you have to try to save your reputation. Your organization has been transparent for years, Jon. That's one of the reasons you have such loyal supporters. I know this. But yes, you need to take a hard look at how this happened and make sure it doesn't happen again. If you're not having any luck tracking him down, I know a guy who's very good at that sort of thing."

"It's been a long time since we had a girls' night out," Susie was saying as Petra collected her shoulder bag and made sure she'd put everything back into her satchel. "Do you have plans for tonight?"

"I'm sorry, Susie, but I can't. We'll do it next time I'm in town, I promise!"

Susie looked so hopeful, Petra hated to tell her no, but she'd already made up her mind that she was getting the next flight out to Raleigh, North Carolina. She had to put some distance between herself and Chance Youngblood. During the last few minutes in the conference room with him, her body had felt like a magnet to his steel. She'd felt herself involuntarily drawn to him, wanting to touch him. Even after he'd shown his true colors and let a smug, egotistical part of himself show when he'd given her that knowing look after she'd exclaimed, *You don't even know me!*

Know you? his expression had seemed to say. *I know you in the Biblical sense.*

They hugged goodbye and Petra left. She felt bad for turning down a night out with Susie, because she intuited that Susie could use some fun in her life right now with the fate of her career unknown, but she promised herself she would phone Susie later and have a long conversation with her. It didn't take the place of being there, but it might comfort her.

As for leaving Mr. Chance Youngblood high and dry for the second time in less than four hours, she had no guilty feelings.

Had she known he was the CEO of a successful entertainment company last night, she would have run the other way. She'd already dealt with one egotistical rich guy. Gareth had been born with a platinum spoon in his mouth. Enough was never enough for him. The prospect of getting even richer had been impossible for him to resist. Did rich men care about anything except getting richer?

Already, Chance Youngblood was making plans to change her life. To perhaps mold her into one of his reality stars. What did she know about reality shows? Her sisters complained that all the women in reality shows did was pursue material possessions, complain about the men in their lives, worry about their weight, put their bodies on display, keep the drama high with made-up arguments and use offensive language. That couldn't possibly be what he had in mind for her?

To be fair, she hadn't heard exactly what he had in mind. However, putting a few states between them was still a good idea. Thinking in his presence was difficult to do, what with her strong attraction to him. What was up with that, anyway? She was such a wuss. He was supposed to be an experiment, a piece of man candy that she would use and toss away. But no, she had ended up wanting more, as she'd written in that note. Another bad idea. Now he knew exactly how she felt about him. That had probably been a big boost to his ego. Especially after they'd been thrown together again by fate or whatever was moving pieces around on the chessboard of life up there.

Three hours later she was on a plane listening to the music of Beninese singer Angélique Kidjo through her earbuds, trying to suspend time.

As soon as Jon and Chance finished discussing the terms of their new partnership, Chance went in search of Petra. Susie, looking flustered, told him that Petra had been in a hurry and had rushed out soon after they'd left him and Jon in the conference room. So Chance asked her for Petra's cell phone number.

Susie appeared indecisive about giving it to him. He guessed it was because she didn't want to give him Petra's number without her express permission. But he told her he wanted to try to reassure Petra about her misgivings pertaining to reality shows, so Susie gave him the number. He'd gambled that Susie would want to help the conservancy, and Petra's agreeing to do the show would benefit the conservancy.

Armed with the number, he punched in the digits on the way out of the conservancy's offices. On the street, he listened to Petra's voice when her phone went into message mode.

He put his phone in his inside coat pocket without leaving a message, and hailed a cab. Why would she run out on him for the second time in one day? Especially when fate had so generously thrown them together again. He'd taken it as a good sign.

As he got into the cab and gave the cabbie his office address, his phone beeped in his pocket.

It was a text message from Petra. Please give me a couple of days to put in perspective what's happening between us. Don't you think it's weird?

He texted back, No, I think it's wonderful.

She sent a frowning emoji. Susie texted me to expect this.

Yes, she gave me your number. Only because I told her I was going to try to convince you that a reality show can be a good thing, he countered. Don't hold it against her.

You're very sneaky, she texted.

I'll go to any lengths to see you again.

I'm packing to go home. I managed to get a seat on a plane leaving soon.

He noted she didn't tell him how soon. Was she afraid he'd rush to the airport to prevent her leaving?

He sat back on the seat in the cab with a resigned sigh. How long will you be gone?

I don't know.

Can't we talk about this? Texting is so impersonal.

Your voice does things to me a text doesn't.

Fair enough. Then, I'll be silent for two days. After that, all bets are off.

Okay, she agreed. Bye for now.

Bye. He reluctantly put away his phone.

Two days later, his plane was landing in Raleigh, North Carolina. He rented a car and checked into a hotel, then sat down on the bed in the hotel room and calmly texted Petra. Where R U?

A few seconds later, she texted, Y do U want 2 know?

Must talk 2 U face 2 face.

I'll be back in NY in 2 weeks.

I can't wait that long.

U have 2.

Y did U run away?

Because I didn't want 2 face U, isn't that obvious?

Just tell me where U R.

She took longer to respond this time, but she finally named the luxury hotel in downtown Raleigh where she was. Then added, sarcastically he imagined, R U satisfied?

He smiled, imagining how annoyed she was with his persistency. Not yet, but soon.

Chapter 5

Across town, Petra was sitting in an alcove in the lobby of the hotel where her parents' thirty-fifth anniversary party was being held, waiting for her cue to put in an appearance. For the last couple of days she'd caught up with her sisters' lives while hiding from her parents. Although now she'd been informed that the surprise party the girls had planned was no longer a surprise. Their mother, the nosiest woman in the South, had gotten the secret out of someone. Once again, the sisters' plan to surprise their mother had been foiled.

It irked Petra because Virginia was going to brag about her detecting prowess for yet another year. However, the girls had one more card up their collective sleeves: Their parents didn't know Petra was home. She was their secret weapon.

She was wearing a beautiful African-print caftan in gold and black, with a matching head wrap and sexy golden-hued strappy sandals. Her only jewelry was a pair of gold hoop earrings that she'd bought from a talented artisan in Ghana on her first trip to Africa. She didn't own much jewelry, and these were special to her.

About half an hour later, after she'd joined the party, and she and her sisters finally succeeded in pulling one over on their mother, she discovered she'd somehow lost one of her earrings somewhere in the hotel. So she was forced to retrace her steps in hopes of locating the missing earring.

She was in the lobby once again, in the alcove where she'd been sitting earlier, when she found the piece of jewelry between the cushion and the back of the chair she'd sat in. Earring in hand, she turned to follow the corridor to the bank of elevators and return to the party when a familiar voice from behind her said, "There you are."

She momentarily closed her eyes and uttered a prayer that Chance Youngblood wasn't standing behind her. But when she opened her eyes, there he was, with an irritated expression on his handsome face. In spite of his being the last person on earth she wanted to see at that moment, she wound up thinking how fine he looked in those jeans, light blue pullover shirt and black motorcycle boots. The man exuded masculinity.

She must have stood there a little too long, with how sexy she found him written all over her face, because he suddenly laughed.

"We have unfinished business, Dr. Gaines," he said in his deep baritone.

"What? How?" she sputtered and backed up, nearly tripping over a big square coffee table.

He quickly moved forward and prevented her from falling. "I was already in Raleigh when I phoned you," he explained. "But I didn't know where you were staying. In New York, you only told me you were going to see relatives in Raleigh."

"I can't believe you're here!"

He removed his hand from her shoulder and calmly walked around the coffee table and sat down on the white leather couch, making himself comfortable. He looked up at her. "I'm not a man to be trifled with. You owe me an explanation."

Now he'd pissed her off. She sat down across from him, and being careful to keep her voice low, said, "I don't owe you anything. We didn't make any promises to each other. It was just sex."

"Oh, I see, you make it a habit of having sex with any convenient male you run into?"

"No, of course not!" Petra hissed. "I've never done anything like that in my entire life!"

His eyebrows rose. "Then I guess that makes me special," he said sarcastically.

"You know," Petra said with equal sarcasm, "most guys would be happy to be let off the hook. Instead *you* travel all the way here to get into an argument with me in the lobby of a Raleigh hotel."

"I'm not most men," Chance said. He got to his feet, his gaze on hers. "Look, can we go somewhere and talk about this? I have a car waiting."

"I can't go anywhere right now," Petra said irritably as she rose, too. Sitting while he towered over her made her feel like a child who was being reprimanded by a parent. "I'm attending a family gathering. I'd have to go back into the ballroom and let one of my sisters know I'm leaving."

"No problem," the stubborn man said. "I'll stay right here until you get back."

Petra was so angry at his putting her on the spot like this, she wanted to slug him. Looking at him, so strong, so solid, he was clearly determined to be an immovable force tonight.

She was momentarily stumped as to what to do next. Finally, she blew an exasperated breath between her full lips and exclaimed, "All right! You might as well come with me. My sisters would never forgive me if they found out you were here and they didn't get a chance to meet you."

He gave her a smug smile. "You told them about me, huh?"

"Don't look so pleased," Petra said as they began walking toward the elevators. "I told them you were a one-night stand."

"But a memorable one-night stand," he wagered.
"Don't make me change my mind," Petra warned.

Chance knew he would never be able to remember all of the names of the people Petra introduced him to that night. When he and Petra got to the ballroom, the crowd was doing a line dance, which they joined. The music was loud and the dancers were hilariously bad, just like the dancers at his family's gatherings. Petra and her sisters were lined up next to each other, and he could see they were in sync and had probably practiced dancing together a lot over the years. They were talented and beautiful and fun loving, and he was grateful to see that side of Petra. She was the tiniest of the sisters and, if he were reading them well, the bossiest. They followed her lead. As for the guys the sisters were matched up with, they were all tall, good-looking men who were clearly in love with the Gaines sisters.

After the upbeat line dance, a slow song started playing and Chance got to hold Petra in his arms. Their first dance as a couple was wonderful. She was gazing into his eyes as though their altercation was forgotten and she'd forgiven him for following her to Raleigh, which he instinctually felt wasn't the case. He knew she was still unsure of what to make of his behavior because she was stiff when she went into his arms. A minute or so later, though, she seemed more relaxed and gazed up at him. And he finally got to talk with her in private, the music providing a good buffer.

"Have you and Jon come to a decision about the conservancy?" she asked.

"We have," he acknowledged. "You will, no doubt, be apprised of the details soon, but I can tell you that I've signed on to support the conservancy's projects worldwide until its financial problems are solved. In the meantime, Jon is incorporating safeguards to ensure the problem doesn't raise its troublesome head again."

"So, it was the accountant?" Petra asked.

Chance grinned. "He was found in Switzerland and was persuaded to return to the US and face the music."

"Persuaded or forced?"

"There might have been a few strong-arm tactics used," he said as he bent his head and inhaled her heady fragrance. "You know, when I woke up and found you gone, I was very disappointed."

She smiled. "Disappointed and angry? Or disappointed and resigned to it?"

He gave her a deadpan look. "What do *you* think? You left me that heartbreaking note..."

"Heartbreaking?" she cried in hushed tones. "Is that what you think of me? That I'm a sad, lonely woman who finds comfort in the arms of unsuspecting men and leaves heartbreaking notes on their pillows?"

Chance laughed. "Did I say that? I didn't say that.

I don't think you're sad. I think you've been hurt and you're afraid I'll turn out to be like your last boy… um, fiancé."

She cocked her head and eyed him suspiciously. "You know who he is, don't you?"

Chance paused before answering because he was taken aback by her intuitiveness. They'd known each other for only three days, and she was already reading him like a book. Yes, the truth was, once he'd learned her identity, he had done some digging. Earlier, when she'd told him about her former fiancé, he'd thought her description sounded like someone he knew.

A Google search turned up British millionaire and adventurer Gareth Graham, who was host of a popular British reality show about his travels to exotic locales. He'd found a few photos of Gareth Graham with Petra on his arm at social events, but for the most part, she seemed to avoid the spotlight. Later photos of Gareth showed him with a well-known American actress on his arm. There were plenty of those online. The actress and Gareth both seemed to enjoy the attention.

"I don't know where his brain was, letting you go," he told Petra.

Tears sat in her beautiful eyes, and he cursed himself for having caused them. Why couldn't he keep his big mouth shut?

He pulled her to his chest, and she didn't resist when he hugged her tightly. "Oh, Pet, I'm sorry. I just thought you'd prefer me to be honest with you. Yes, I looked him up because, God help me, I wanted to know everything about you, and you were running away from me."

"I was not running away from you," she denied, looking up at him again. "I was trying to get my head on straight. The emotions I felt for you the morning after we'd been together were overwhelming. Believing I'd never see you again, I wrote exactly how I felt."

"I felt the same way," he said softly. "That's what I was going to tell you the next morning—that I didn't consider what we had a one-night stand. What does it matter how we met and how soon we made love? What matters is where this goes. And that depends on you and me. We can make it whatever we want. I swear to you, if you're having misgivings about how quickly we went to bed together, it'll be our secret. Well, you told your sisters, but that doesn't count. And I told my brother and sister."

"You what?" she nearly shouted.

He smiled warmly. "So we're equal now. Your sisters know, and my siblings know. They're named Brock and Alia, by the way. You're going to love them. Alia's the oldest and then Brock. I came last."

Her eyes were filled with wonder. "A, B and C?"

He chuckled. "You got that far faster than most people. My parents are weird that way."

"Did they get your sister's name from a character in *Dune*, the novel by Frank Herbert?"

"How'd you guess?"

She laughed. "I'm a fan of his—of science fiction, in general."

"Mom's going to get a kick out of you," he told her. "That's one of her favorite books. She loves Octavia E. Butler, too."

"What are your parents' names?"

"James and Debra," he answered. "Mom said she and Dad have such common names that she wanted to make sure their children had more unique monikers."

Petra nodded as though that made perfect sense. "Okay, you know about my heartbreak. Who broke your heart?"

"The first time was when I was in college," he began. "I fell in love with a girl who was in my economics class."

"Two nerds in love?" she asked with a playful expression in her eyes.

"Yes, it's one of the sweetest kinds," he said. "The two of you have so much in common, plus there's the fact that neither of you have had much experience in love and you learn everything together."

Petra smiled wistfully. "I understand all too well."

Chance wondered if she had thought, while she and Gareth were together, that because they were both zoologists their bond would last forever. And then he'd left her.

"But when we graduated and I went to work for my family's company and started at the bottom, she told me she couldn't live on my salary. She'd met someone whose rich parents weren't of the mind that their sons had to earn a living, but were rewarded with millions of dollars upon graduation. Did it break my heart? Yes, but not for long. I was too busy working. My dad was a hard taskmaster. He didn't believe in coddling his children. He didn't think he was doing us any favors by handing us everything. He figured we'd be more grateful if we earned everything we got. And he was right. But turns out, I didn't learn from my first serious relationship because I later fell in love with another woman who pretended to love me for me and not what I could give her, but she couldn't keep up the act well enough.

"I found out she only wanted me for the money when she was caught cheating on me and tried to convince me that it was partly my fault because I was working too much. I'd driven her into another man's arms."

"She sounds like a talented manipulator and a narcissist," Petra said sympathetically.

"Yes, she was," Chance said.

"You haven't been in a serious relationship since?" Petra asked, her eyes on his.

"I've become kind of wary since then," he admitted. "And am I the only man you've been involved with since Gareth?"

She nodded with a smile on her lips and with a

happier expression in her lovely eyes than a few minutes ago when he'd made her cry.

"I think I like you, Chance Youngblood." She looked so delectable he wanted to kiss her, but restrained himself.

He grinned. "That's good, because I like you a lot, Pet."

Petra was jittery inside as Chance held her. What was happening here? She wanted so much to simply let go and enjoy the moment, but deep down she didn't believe in fairytales, and this felt like a fantasy. One of those wonderfully vivid dreams that you woke up from and wished it had lasted longer.

She'd done some digging, too. Her sisters knew who he was as soon as she mentioned his name. They kept up with social media and pop culture and watched television, unlike Petra who wasn't on Facebook and rarely turned on a TV. She was aware, now, that his family had been in publishing first. His grandfather published a newspaper for many years in Harlem. They had then branched out to magazines and books. They still published magazines and books, but were no longer in the newspaper business since newspapers were struggling to survive in the twenty-first century. They had grown in the seventies and started an African American television network. Today, Youngblood Media's empire included publishing, broadcasting and the internet.

His family was worth billions. What in the world did he want with an unsophisticated scientist who couldn't even fake glamour? She figured that's why Gareth had dropped her. She no longer fit in his world. He now had a woman who obviously thrived in that environment. She, on the other hand, belonged in the jungle.

She gazed up into Chance's handsome face. He smelled wonderful, and his body was so hard. Memories of their lovemaking and how he'd been able to anticipate all her needs triggered her body's response to his nearness. She was tempted to drag him off somewhere and rip his clothes off.

But that wouldn't be wise. Everything was up in the air. She hadn't expected to see him again. Now that she had, she didn't know how to proceed. Sure, he'd said they could choose to take their relationship anywhere they wanted to. How did you come back from sleeping with someone the very night you met them, though? Did couples actually form lasting relationships after one-night stands? She knew Lauren and Colton had made love the very first night they met, but that had been different. Even though the two of them hadn't actually ever met, they were aware of each other. Lauren knew Colton's parents well. Colton and Lauren's ex-husband had been business rivals. And Colton had seen Lauren before, when she'd been married to her ex, and had admired her from a distance.

What happened to them that night at her snowed-in cabin had been spontaneous and was also an act of comfort on both their parts. She helped him when he was grieving his father. He helped her when she was getting over a bad divorce. Now they were married with a baby. That was a happily-ever-after scenario.

With her and Chance, it had been nothing but lust. She could admit that. What else could it have been? She'd known nothing about him. He had known nothing about her. Could you build something worthwhile from a beginning like that?

He was looking at her as if she was the most beautiful woman in the world. Apparently, he believed they could.

What the heck, she thought. *He's here and he's hot. I'm going to kiss him, at least.* So she kissed him—right there in the ballroom while couples danced around them.

He smiled at her afterward and asked, "Does that mean you're going to give us a chance?"

"No, that means you're adorable and hard to resist. We need to think about this for a while longer. Is it even advisable to be involved with someone you work with?" she asked sensibly. "You *are* here to persuade me, aren't you? I'm not sure I want to do one of those shows. I hear really negative things about them."

He laughed. "It's not as if it's going to be a reality show like the *Housewives*," he tried to reassure her. "The show will be more like the *Planet Earth* programs on BBC. You'll narrate, talk about your work, we'll see the animals in their natural habitat and showcase the people of the Congo. For the most part, African Americans don't know much about their homeland. Genetically, most of us come from several countries in Africa, not just one. I had a DNA test done and found out my ancestors came from Ivory Coast/Ghana, Cameroon/Congo, Nigeria, Senegal, Mali, South Africa and Benin-Togo. To say nothing of Great Britain and other parts of Europe."

"The legacy of slavery," Petra said sympathetically.

"Yes, that vile practice," Chance said. "But wherever we came from later on, we're all Africans. That's where mankind originated, after all."

"Yes," she agreed, smiling at him and wanting to kiss him again. Nothing turned her on more than an intelligent man.

He hugged her a little tighter. "You will consider doing the show, won't you?"

She nodded slowly. "Yes, if it'll benefit the primates and the people of the Congo. The people, not the government."

Chance looked at her with a serious expression. "Yes, I know about the government. If we're going to set the show there we'll have to deal with them. We'll see what happens when we make the proposal to them, and hope for the best. The first season depends on how much footage you have already. We may be able to do the first season using just your footage, which you had a permit to shoot, right?"

"Yes, of course, I did. You sound like you've given it some thought," Petra said, knowing she shouldn't be surprised. He did this sort of thing for a living, after all.

As if he'd read her thoughts, he said, "It's what I do."

Chapter 6

Petra went back downstairs to the lobby with Chance to say goodbye to him. She could see the disappointment in his incredible cinnamon-colored eyes when she hugged him and said, "I appreciate the romantic gesture of your coming all the way down here to see me, but I need more time to figure out what to do about you."

"You make me sound like a problem you need to solve," he said softly. Even the vibrato of his voice turned her on.

They stood near the bank of elevators, out of the path of other hotel guests and personnel, their eyes locked. His hand was gently rubbing the back of her arm, his touch igniting little fires of desire in her erogenous zones.

"If you're a problem to be solved, you're a wonderful problem that I don't mind having and will take great pleasure in finding a way to make you make sense."

He gave her an askance look. "Maybe you think too much, Dr. Gaines, and should just go with your gut feelings."

"That's what I did when I slept with you."

"Wait a minute. Are you saying that was a bad thing?"

"No, I'm saying I'd like to see how you feel about me a few weeks from now. I don't know much about producing television shows, but I'm pretty sure it'll take a while to get a show like the one you're proposing off the ground. Call me and let me know when you want me back in New York City, and I'll come. In the meantime, I'll stay here and get to know my nephew."

He grinned. "There's a new addition to the family?"

"Yes, you met Lauren and Colton. They have a toddler. He's my first nephew and I already adore him."

He sighed as he gazed into her eyes. "I love kids. All right, you stay and spoil your nephew. I'll try to behave like the mature man I am and wait for you." He frowned. "You're not still running scared, are you? The odds are looking in my favor?"

"No, and yes," she answered. "I'm not going to

run from my feelings, and the odds are very much in your favor."

His grin got wider, and he bent down and kissed her cheek. "I'll dream of you every night until we're together again," he whispered in her ear.

Petra pulled him down and kissed his mouth. His soft lips parted and their tongues sensually danced around each other, slowly and powerfully arousing her to the point where all she wanted to do was press her body closer to his. How could this sensation be anything but good for her? Still, she had the strength to break off the connection and release him. He was so much more than a guy she'd slept with. If she wanted more from him, and for him, she needed to step away and use logic instead of falling headlong into animal passion every time she was near him.

After their lips parted, they looked at each other. He was smiling, and there was an amused light in his eyes. "That'll hold me until I see you again," he said, and turned and walked away.

Petra stood and watched him until he walked through the hotel's front entrance, his muscular form poetry in motion.

"Damn, I'm probably going to regret sending him away like that," she said under her breath.

Chance's ego was a little bruised when Petra didn't jump into his arms and willingly go to his hotel with him and make passionate love to him, but he was man enough to accept her verdict with an understanding heart. This was a new experience for him, too, and he felt that letting a bit of time pass before they saw each other again was a good thing.

He would go home. He'd go home and put things in motion for the reality show he wanted to build around her. He hadn't been this excited about a project in a long time. And it wasn't because he was attracted to Petra. It was because it was a brilliant idea.

When was the last time he'd seen a person of color talking about the African jungle on film? The most a lot of people knew about the jungle was from the Tarzan books and movies. Yes, some people watched nature shows that featured African wildlife, but how many times had the hosts been black? You might see African guides or African rangers who worked on game reserves. But you never saw black people in authority discussing their own country and their efforts to save animals that were, and always had been, part of the African landscape. He was excited to become the first producer of such a program.

As for Petra and whether or not they would continue to see one another, he felt positive that what they had already shared had been so wonderful, they would be fools not to take it further. Petra Gaines didn't strike him as a fool. And neither was he.

When he got back to his hotel room that night, he phoned his sister, Alia, who lived in Harlem in a building she'd purchased and turned into an artist's sanctuary, as she called it. She lived on the top floor in a loft and rented apartments in the building to fellow artists. He suspected her rates were very reasonable because most of them were struggling. But that was his kindhearted big sister. She would never admit to it, but he knew she'd bought that building in Harlem in order to show respect for their grandparents' legacy.

Both Nero and Angelique Youngblood were gone now, but in their heyday, they were pillars of Harlem society. Nero's newspaper was so successful he was able to provide jobs for the community. Even today journalism scholarships were given to students in his name. Angelique was a businesswoman in her own right. An artist, like her granddaughter after her, she opened the first art gallery in Harlem, which was still alive and doing well today. Angelique's daughter-in-law, Debra, a successful sculptress, was its curator. Therefore, Alia was a third-generation artist in the Youngblood family.

Alia answered the phone with her usual enthusiastic "Speak to me!"

Chance heard music in the background. Alia liked to listen to music when she was painting. Tonight it was Aretha Franklin's voice soaring to "I Never Loved a Man the Way I Love You."

"I know you're not having man trouble," he joked.

Alia laughed. "No, just giving the queen her props tonight while I'm painting a portrait of her."

"A commission?"

"Nah, it's part of my *Women of Strength* series," Alia told him. "You remember. I've been working on it for a while now. Women from all walks of life who inspire us to be better human beings."

Of course Chance remembered. He was just a little spacey right now. Alia had started that series about two years ago after her husband, Adam, a physicist, had gone missing while on a secret government mission in the Middle East. They still didn't know whether Adam was alive or dead. For a while there, he had wondered if Alia would survive the grief. He and Brock had moved in with her for over a month just to keep an eye on her. It was during that time she'd begun painting her *Women of Strength* series, starting with a portrait of Harriet Tubman.

The series, he suspected, had been cathartic for her. She'd grown stronger since then and was her former cheerful self.

"How many portraits do you have in the series now?" he asked.

"Twenty," she said. "This will be the last one. Twenty-one to represent the twenty-first century." She laughed suddenly. "Stop procrastinating, Chance. What happened with Petra?"

Chance groaned, then laughed too. "I never could get away with anything with you. Okay, it isn't hopeless, but let's just say I was underwhelmed by my reception."

"You mean she didn't drop everything and run into your arms and be ravished by you?" Alia asked, laughter evident in her tone.

"Not only that," Chance informed her, not at all

fazed by her sarcasm, "she now needs time to think about what to do about us after the one-night stand didn't turn out the way one-night stands are supposed to—with the two parties never seeing each other again, thereby saving them from embarrassment."

"That's life," Alia replied, still laughing. "It's always embarrassing you."

"Now we're supposed to not see each other for a while so we can determine if the attraction was just physical or if there's something more to it."

"I take it you already know the answer to that," his sister astutely observed.

"It's physical, all right," Chance allowed. "But I believe I may have met my match in every other way, too."

"Then be patient and do the work, my brother," Alia said. "Anything worth having is worth working for. Tread carefully, though. Developing a show around a woman you're interested in may prove to be tricky. You've never been subjected to rumors before because you've never been involved with anyone who worked for you. You should probably be very discreet. Although, from what you've told me about Petra, she isn't an attention seeker. Seems like she would prefer to stay out of the limelight."

"Yeah, I totally agree," Chance said. "And I can't see Petra disagreeing with that reasoning. She's really kind of shy, for all her accomplishments."

"I can't wait to meet her," Alia said happily. "I

haven't heard you sound so excited about anyone in a long time."

"That's because I haven't been," Chance said. "I was turning into a workaholic."

"When has any Youngblood looked down on working hard?" Alia jokingly asked.

"Never," Chance replied. "As far as we're concerned, it's a virtue."

"Exactly," Alia said. "Now, I'd better get back to work. This may be an all-nighter."

"Good night, then," Chance said. "To you and The Queen of Soul."

"Don't worry about it," Alia reiterated.

Chance knew what she was referring to—he tended to dwell on things instead of allowing himself to float on life's currents and seeing where they led him. Alia wanted him to loosen up.

"I'll try not to worry," he promised.

"Give her space. She'll be happy to see you when she's ready," Alia said, sounding so centered and calm. Everything he wasn't. That's why he'd called her, to calm himself down.

What if Petra decided after all that getting more involved with him while working on a project that was important to the survival of the conservancy, perhaps to the chimpanzees of the Congo and to her career was a bad idea?

"Look," he said. "You have been through a lot more than I have. If Petra decides that I'm not worth the risk, then I'll get over it. But I'm a man of my word, and the show goes on."

"That's my baby brother!" Alia said triumphantly.

Her enthusiasm put a wide smile on his face. "Good night, sis," he said.

"Good night," she replied softly. "I love you."

"I love you more," he replied, and they hung up.

Petra loved being home again. She spent a lot of time with her sisters, Desiree, Lauren and Meghan, who lived in Raleigh. Mina lived farther away, near the Great Smoky Mountains. Desiree took her on a shopping spree, replenishing her wardrobe. She was staying with her parents in the house she'd grown up in, and the memories of her and her sisters getting ready for school in the morning, of dressing for special occasions like the prom or Easter services, and the fun they had together made her grateful to be a part of such a loving family.

Her favorite spot at her parents' house was the back deck, where she would prop her feet up on a chair while she sat in another, pondering her life and where it was going. Her mother went to work early in the morning and her dad, now retired, went to the golf course almost as early as her mom left for work. He was part of a foursome of retired military men who golfed and drank and generally goofed off. That's how he described it, anyway.

While they were out during the day, Petra would go visit Lauren, who was working from home. A sought-after architect, Lauren found that after she went off maternity leave, there were plenty of clients waiting to hire her to design their dream homes or businesses. While Lauren worked in her office, Petra spent time with her nephew, C.J., who, at eighteen months old, was very active. He was toddling all over the place and Petra had fun keeping up with him.

One afternoon, she had him cracking up over a rousing game of don't-step-on-the-car, a game he'd made up which had her operating the remote to try to keep a remote-controlled red SUV from being stepped on by C.J. He was a rambunctious little boy who delighted in trying to destroy his toys.

Lauren came into the playroom when they were in the middle of the game, and Petra looked up at her guiltily. "Am I being a bad aunt by letting him do this?"

Lauren laughed. "Girl, please, he has been trying to crush that car underfoot ever since his Auntie Meghan gave it to him. He's just being C.J. Momma warned me about little boys, as if she has any experience raising them."

Petra laughed as she wrestled C.J. into her arms and kissed his pudgy brown cheek. "I love his energy."

"You're going to be a great mom someday," Lauren said, settling down in a chair and sighing wearily. "Are you thinking more about it since you've been bonding with C.J.?"

"Of course," Petra answered as she kneeled on

the floor hugging a squirming C.J. She let go of him and he went and grabbed the toy car, plopped down on the floor and began intently examining the car's undercarriage.

"I've always wanted children, but I just don't think it'll ever happen for me."

"Why not?" Lauren asked.

"Because I don't think I'll ever trust a man enough to want to have a child with him. And even though I talk a good game about women being independent of men, I don't want to have a child who won't have a father in his or her life. Fathers are as important as mothers in a child's life."

"Petra," Lauren said seriously. "The only thing keeping you from realizing your dreams is you."

Petra met her sister's eyes. Eyes quite like her own. Big and honey-colored. Lauren's experience with love had mirrored her own, too, in some respects. Her former husband had cheated on her. Then he'd lied about it and had tried to hang on to her when she'd wanted a divorce. She'd had to fight for her freedom from the narcissistic creep. But she'd not only fought, she'd won.

Lauren got down on the floor with her and reached out to grasp her hand. "I know you're getting ready to go to New York and start a new phase of your life. Promise me that when you get there, you'll live in the moment and try to appreciate the love that a certain male might want to give you. With love, you sometimes have to risk getting hurt. But when it works, it's really worth the risk. If you keep running from love, it'll never catch you, and that's a fact! Be brave, sis."

Petra squeezed her sister's hand reassuringly. "I promise to give it my best shot."

"That's good enough," Lauren said positively. "You've always achieved anything you set your heart on."

Chance was exhausted when he got home from work Friday night. Tired and lonely. More lonely than tired, really. The tiredness he could cope with. It was the loneliness that ate at him and made him feel as if his life were incomplete. He supposed everyone felt this way at some time in their lives, as if no matter what they did, happiness was always out of reach.

As he exchanged his business attire for a comfortable pair of well-worn jeans and a short-sleeve gray T-shirt, and slipped his feet into a pair of slides, he wondered what his playboy brother was doing tonight. He probably had another beautiful woman to wine and dine and then make love to. Brock was not cruel in his pursuit of women, but he was fully committed to it and sometimes left a trail of broken hearts in his wake. Chance believed his brother immersed himself in beautiful women to avoid feeling lonely. Brock stayed so busy that his loneliness never caught up with him.

Chance couldn't live like that. He didn't have the time or the inclination. To him, loneliness was worth it if the reward was true love in the end.

He went to the kitchen to warm the Thai take-out he'd picked up on the way home, and as soon as he popped the food in the microwave to nuke it, his cell phone rang.

He'd left it on the counter next to the take-out bags, and he glanced down at the display now. Petra. His heart thumped excitedly. They'd been talking regularly since they'd parted in Raleigh about a month ago. Sometimes they would use Skype to chat for an hour or more. The excitement never lessened when he spoke with her, though.

"Pet! How are you?"

"I'm good," she said sultrily. "How are you?"

"Missing you," he said.

"Are you alone?" she asked teasingly.

"Yes, are you?"

"Yes. Would you like some company?" Her tone was getting sexier.

"Are you jerking me around?"

"I would never do that. Open your door."

Chance hurried to the door and looked through the peephole. For a moment, he thought his eyes were deceiving him. But sure enough, Petra stood on the other side of his door wearing a cheeky smile. He couldn't get the door open fast enough.

Petra was so nervous, she was prancing in place waiting for the door to open. Against her better judgment, she'd gotten on a plane and come here, hoping Chance had missed her as much as she'd missed him.

She hadn't waited for his promised call after he'd done all the preliminaries on the show. She wasn't here because of the show. She was here for him. Yes, their phone conversations and Skype sessions made her feel as though she would be welcomed. But the proof would be what kind of expression he wore on his face when they saw each other again.

So it was with great anticipation that she met his eyes when he opened the door and, thankfully, saw the sheer joy on his face. She dropped her shoulder bag and carry-on bag and suitcase (she had extra luggage due to Desiree's generous shopping spree) onto the foyer floor and flew into his arms.

Chance laughed and picked her up—something she could get used to—and spun around with her. She clung to him, inhaling the heady male scent of him and reveling in the warm, hard feel of his body against hers.

"Pet," he murmured against her neck, in turns kissing her and nuzzling her there. "God, I missed you so much."

His honesty and lack of guile bewitched her. He wasn't afraid to be vulnerable, and that touched her. "I missed you, too!" she said and turned her head to kiss his mouth.

She kissed him deeply and with all the pent-up desire she'd saved up for this moment. There had been so many times when they were apart that she imagined kissing him, touching him, making love to him. In the midst of their passionate clench, he loosened his grip on her and she slid down his body until her feet were touching the floor and he was bending down in order to avoid breaking off the kiss. When they came up for air, he was smiling contentedly, his gorgeous eyes filled with tender amusement. "Why didn't you tell me you were coming? I would have picked you up at the airport," he said.

"And ruin my surprise?" she asked. "Turnabout is fair play."

He laughed. "You got me back."

"Actually, that never crossed my mind until this moment. I had to come up with some reason why I'm just showing up on your doorstep."

"Babe," he said, looking serious, "you don't need a reason. You're welcome in my home anytime." He glanced over her shoulder and noticed the door was still open, and walked over and secured it.

Turning back around to her, he grinned. "I see you still have your carry-on bag with you. Does that mean you came straight here from the airport?"

"It does," she confirmed.

"Did you make reservations anywhere?"

"Nah, I figured NYC had at least one room available somewhere," she said nonchalantly.

"Sure," he said. "And it's right back there." He pointed in the direction of his bedroom.

Petra laughed shortly. She walked up to him and placed both hands on his muscular chest. "I didn't come to seduce you."

"My sweet Pet," he said, his arms going around

her. "You did that the moment you showed up." He began pulling her jacket off.

Their eyes met and held. "I want to take a shower," she said.

"With me," he replied. His frank, sensuous stare made her weak in the knees.

"Of course."

The bathroom was sleek and modern with a floating vanity, subway tiles in the glassed-in shower, which had plenty of room for the two of them, and beautiful marble mosaic floors.

After shedding her clothes, Petra piled her hair up and put a clip on it to keep it out of the way, then she joined Chance in the shower.

His gaze roamed over her with lascivious delight, which made her feel ironically shy on one hand, and deliciously wanton on the other. She found herself comparing Chance's open admiration to Gareth's manner of looking at her. As if he were entitled and he took her presence in his life, and in his bed, for granted. Why hadn't she paid more attention when she'd been with him?

Chance made her feel as though she were the prize, and he was the lucky winner. That was the difference.

Chance was glad he'd had nonslip tile put in the shower. He'd never dreamed he'd be making love to a Bohemian beauty like Petra in here, though. The woman was a goddess. She was taking his thrusts with gusto, her firm, wet, brown body responding to the demands of his. Her moans of pleasure fed his enthusiasm and sexual potency. The more she gasped, the more he wanted to give her something to gasp about.

Her back was against the shower wall, her legs wrapped around him while he held her firmly and thrust deeply. She was looking at him with her pleasure reflected in her eyes; her lips, a little swollen from feverish kisses, were delectable. He'd never known a more responsive lover.

Their coupling became so explosive at one point, he thought the condom might break. So he slowed down, and that was when she screamed as an orgasm ripped through her. He felt it the moment she came, her vaginal walls pulsating, loosening, tightening and quivering. He came a few seconds later. He held her in his arms, her legs still firmly wrapped around him. Their breaths came in short intervals then stretched out until they were breathing normally. Still, he held her as warm water from the shower head fell on their bodies.

At last, she gave a languid sigh and said, "I love the way you make love to me."

He smiled as he loosened his grip on her and let her slide down his body until her feet were on the shower floor. It was the best compliment she could have given him, seeing as how he felt the same way about her. "Ditto," he said.

She gazed up at him as they stood with their arms wrapped around each other in the shower.

"Sam Wheat in *Ghost*."

He laughed. "You do know something about movies."

"The old ones," she said. "It's the newer ones that stump me."

"It'll be my pleasure to introduce you to some newer ones, then," he said softly. "We'll begin with what I think is the best film in the last ten years, *12 Years a Slave*, directed by Steve McQueen. It won the Academy Award for Best Picture in 2014. It's based on an 1853 memoir by Solomon Northrup who was a violinist and a free man of color with a wife and children living in Saratoga, New York but was abducted and forced to become a slave. It stars Chiwetel Ejiofor, Michael Fassbender and Lupita Nyong'o, among others. It's intense, passionate and you won't be able to take your eyes from the screen."

She smiled appreciatively up at him. "Sounds wonderful."

He couldn't help thinking that he could describe their relationship in the same way: intense and passionate.

Chapter 7

"It's sweet of you to want me here. But Susie's invited me to stay with her until I find a place. Her parents gave her their house in Queens when they retired to Florida. I think she's a little lonely, and it'll be fun catching up with her," Petra said while they devoured the sweet and spicy Thai chicken later on. He looked relaxed across from her as they sat on stools in the kitchen at the island. He'd gotten a bottle of white wine from the refrigerator and filled their glasses before sitting down.

His hair was still damp from the shower. Hers was, too, and was curlier now as opposed to its usual wavy when it was dry. She'd taken the clip out and let her hair fall down her back. She was wearing his robe. He had pulled his jeans and gray T-shirt back on.

He smiled at her and said, "Okay, now for the hard question. What made you change your mind and decide to come back to me?"

She laughed shortly. "My sisters wouldn't let up on me. If one wasn't encouraging me to be brave and risk my heart, another one was." She looked straight into his eyes. "You know about Gareth. Before Gareth, my focus was entirely on my career. I started college at 16 on a full scholarship. My mother's an educator, so she knew where to find grants and scholarships for hardworking students. And I was motivated. I knew what I wanted to be at an early age. I wanted to be an advocate for animals. Protect them. I earned doctorates in zoology and anthropology back-to-back. That takes a lot of work and you don't really have time for a personal life. Gareth was the first man I ever loved. He was also the only man I ever made love to."

"You mean I'm your second lover?" he asked softly. She had a feeling he was trying his best not to gawk at her after that revelation. That endeared him to her even more.

"You are," she confirmed.

"That puts a lot of pressure on me," he joked. He peered deeply into her eyes. "I'll try my best not to disappoint you."

She laughed delightedly. "You goofball!"

He just smiled at her, crinkles showing at the corners of his eyes and his beautiful mouth looking so tempting.

She carried on more seriously. "You called it right when you came to Raleigh. I *was* running away from you because I was afraid you were like Gareth, a spoiled rich boy. But I came to my senses and realized you're nothing like him. You're really mature and hardworking and from all indications, someone who loves his family. All things I want in a man."

He grasped her hand, brought it up to his mouth and kissed her fingers. "And you're smart and caring and devoted to your loved ones. That's what I want in a woman."

His gaze held hers. "And it doesn't hurt that you come in a smoking hot package!"

She snatched her hand from his and playfully slapped his face. "You animal!"

"Damn right I am," he said, apparently unashamed. He got up and pulled her into his arms. "I want you again."

"A girl could starve around here," she joked as she accepted his very passionate kiss, which led to a short sprint to the bedroom where they made love in the bed this time.

The next morning, Chance awoke and almost experienced déjà vu when he felt Petra's side of the bed and found her gone. But then he heard water running in the adjacent bathroom, and he let out the breath he'd been holding. Petra had not run out on him again.

It was Saturday, and he could think of many things they could do together today—and not all of them involved making love. But he had to admit, that was at the top of his list.

He was sitting up in bed, naked with the sheet covering him from the waist down when Petra strode into the bedroom wearing his robe. She had obviously combed her hair, which was no longer in its "wild woman" style that he loved so much. It now fell down her back in tame waves. She smiled at him, her golden-hued eyes sparkling with pent-up laughter. "Good morning, C. Did you sleep well?"

She bounced onto the bed beside him and kissed his cheek. He hoped the relief of still having her there didn't show on his face. It wouldn't be good for her to decipher that he'd grown so attached to her already, this early in their relationship. It would make him seem needy. Or would it? God, he was rusty. Out of practice at relationships. He felt like that nerdy boy he used to be in high school and college, just hoping that some girl liked him enough to allow him to hold her hand.

"I slept like a log," he told her. "I had the best sleep aid last night—making love to the most beautiful woman in the world."

She grinned and got up on her knees. "I know I'm not, but I'm glad you think so."

He pulled her into his arms. Their faces rubbed,

and he hoped his stubble didn't scratch her lovely skin too badly. She showed no signs of being turned off by a day-old beard. Quite to the contrary, she seemed to enjoy it. "Pet, you are the most natural beauty I've ever met. Look at you now. Eight o'clock in the morning and you're glowing without any makeup on at all."

"I'm not wearing any because I never took the time to learn how to apply it correctly," she said softly. She peered into his eyes, her own shy. "I may be a disappointment as a reality star for your network, C. Someone will have to take me in hand and teach me how to wear makeup, dress appropriately, smile for the camera. I'm not star material."

"The hell you aren't," Chance scoffed, kissing her forehead. "You're a brilliant scientist. You think fast on your feet, you're physically imposing..."

"At five-three?" she asked incredulously.

"You exude physical strength and good health. It's how you carry yourself. I could spend all day just watching you move."

"That's probably because of the judo," she said. "I've been training since I was seven. I earned a black belt at eighteen. Which reminds me. I've got to phone Yoshi and set up a time to visit his dojo. He's who I practiced with when I lived here."

Chance smiled at her, his admiration no doubt shining in his eyes. "That just turns me on."

"Oh, yeah?" she teased as she leaped from the bed and ran out of the room. "If you can catch me, I might help you with that morning problem you have."

She had obviously felt his erection he'd covered with the top sheet. That girl could move when she wanted to. He threw the sheet off and gave chase.

Petra moved into Susie's guest room in her house in Flushing, a neighborhood in Queens, New York. When she arrived on Sunday, the day after she'd gotten back to the city, Susie met her at the door of the two-story home with a warm smile.

"Welcome back," she said, hugging Petra and pulling her inside at the same time.

Petra had set her bags on the portico before ringing the bell. "That's right, I came here once for a pool party when we were in college. Your parents were so nice to me."

Susie was wearing yoga pants and a loose-fitting blouse over them. She was barefoot. Her blond hair was pulled back in a smooth chignon. Petra looked into her eyes. "Thanks so much for asking me to room with you. I promise not to overstay my welcome."

Susie laughed as she helped Petra bring her bags into the house. She shut and locked the door after they'd put the bags on the foyer floor, and turned to regard Petra. "There are four bedrooms and three baths in this place. I walk around here listening to my voice echo most days. I'm happy you're here."

She picked up Petra's heaviest bag. "Let me show you to your room. I gave you the one with its own bathroom and sitting area. I think you'll be comfortable in there."

Petra gathered her other things and followed Susie upstairs. As she walked, she noticed that the house looked about the same as when she'd visited years ago. The furnishings were of good quality, but out-of-date.

Susie peered behind her. "How was your flight? How're your sisters? Four sisters! I wish I had *one*."

"My flight was uneventful, thank God. I don't really like flying. My sisters are all doing great. Give me a minute and I'll show you pictures of my parents' anniversary party and my nephew, of course. I took dozens of photos of him."

Susie stopped at the second door on the left and opened it to a large bedroom whose two big windows allowed plenty of sunshine in. Petra decided she'd call it the green room because the walls were a pale green, and the queen-size bed was covered with a green print comforter set. The floor was hardwood, and she could tell it had recently been polished.

She set her bags on the bed, took the suitcase from Susie and set that on the bed too, then hugged Susie again. "I love it!"

Susie grinned, and to Petra's surprise, tears sat in her eyes. "I'm so glad someone could enjoy this place before I sold it."

"You're selling?" Petra asked, and she shoved the bags aside on the bed so she and Susie could sit on the edge.

Susie was obviously upset about her decision to sell her parents' house, and she wanted to help in any way she could. "What's wrong?"

Susie sniffed and wiped her tears away with the back of her hand. "My parents left me the house as a gift to do with as I please. That's how they put it. I could live in it and decorate it to my taste. Which, honestly, I just don't have the money to do. According to the real estate agent I spoke with about selling it, this property is worth a lot. But I'm having guilty feelings because selling it is my only option. Property taxes are so high. I'm afraid that eventually, I won't be able to pay them, and then I could lose the house anyway. I grew up here, so it also has sentimental value. I'm a mess!"

Petra just listened and stroked her friend's back. She mentally calculated property taxes for a house of this value. No wonder Susie had looked so stressed-out when they'd met again at the conservancy's offices.

"Are you sure you want to sell it?" she asked softly.

Susie looked her in the eyes. "Yes, I've talked to my parents and they say they have no emotional attachment to this place. They're happy in West Palm Beach. I'm the only child, so there's no one to give me problems about selling. The one problem I do have is that the Realtor says to get full price, I'm going to need to spruce up the place. And I don't know where to begin."

"Now you're in *my* territory," Petra happily told her. "The one thing I'm good at is cleaning things up and organizing. And when it comes to painting, minor repairs and decorating, I'm your girl! I can't cook to save my life, but everything else in a house is my domain."

"Really?" Susie asked, eyes wide with astonishment.

"Really," Petra stated confidently. "And another thing—I insist on paying rent while I'm here."

"No," Susie said emphatically. "I'm not going to charge you rent!"

Petra smiled. "You just said you couldn't afford the property taxes on this place. Are you going to refuse money that could help pay for repairs? Be reasonable, Suze."

"I'll think about it," Susie said. She smiled at Petra. "You haven't called me Suze since college."

"Get used to it," Petra told her. "We're living together again."

Susie laughed and got to her feet. "What do you want to do today? It's still early. Do you want to take a drive around Flushing to see the sights?"

Petra laughed, too, as she rose and walked over to one of the windows and looked out at the neighborhood. The houses were all well maintained in this neighborhood. There were trees and sidewalks populated with neighbors walking their dogs and children on bikes or skateboards, all wearing helmets to protect themselves.

"It's May," she said speculatively. "When does it get warm enough to use that pool we swam in all those years ago?"

"Probably next month," Susie said, coming to stand beside her at the window. "Last summer the temperature got in the nineties."

"Does it get rainy here in the summer?" Petra asked.

"Yes, lately it's rained a lot in July and August," Susie said.

"Then we should get any painting done on the outside before July," Petra said. She'd been living in a part of the world where it rained often, and she knew how precipitation could disrupt your plans.

Susie looked at her with wonder. "You're serious about helping me fix up the house, aren't you?"

"I am," Petra said. "I'm looking forward to it. I'm about to embark on a stressful time in my life. I don't know what I'm getting myself into with this reality show thing, and physical work has always kept me centered. So, yes, let's agree that we're going to turn this house into a showplace. Buyers will be bidding against each other to own it."

Susie threw her arms around Petra's neck. "You haven't changed a bit. You're still willing to stick your neck out for a friend."

Petra chuckled. "Let's start making a list of things that need to be done around here, then make a list of the supplies we're going to need. After that, you and I will go to Home Depot."

"Home Depot?" Susie cried. "I've never set foot in a Home Depot in my life!"

"There's a first time for everything," Petra said.

Chance knew that the only reason Brock insisted on coming to the first business meeting with Petra following her signing the contract with the company was in order to meet her. Petra had been in New York for two weeks now, and preparations for the show, such as hiring the writers, the director, videographer and others, had taken a while, but everything was set now.

The videographer, Arianna Davis, had told him that the footage Petra had taken was extraordinary. She believed that with Petra's narration, coupled with the footage, they'd be able to tell a compelling story about her experiences among the chimpanzees of the Congo.

They had gotten permission from the Democratic Republic of the Congo to use the footage. Brock had said the fee was substantial, but not prohibitive. Brock was one for the bottom line, and Chance knew that if Brock considered a fee to be not prohibitive, he had gotten a good deal.

He and Brock were in his office now, waiting for Petra's arrival. After Petra got there and Brock got a good look at her, he knew his brother would make some excuse and leave. After which, Chance would escort Petra to the conference room where key people who were going to work on her show were waiting to do some brainstorming with her and share her input on the direction the show was to take.

Chance's office was nontraditional. It was a large, elegantly appointed space with highly polished hardwood floors, a leather couch and two Queen Anne chairs, both brown, and floor-to-ceiling windows overlooking Central Park. But it also had a foosball table in one corner and a vintage full-size Pac-Man arcade game standing in another corner of the office. Playing the games helped him to relax and focus his mind.

Both he and Brock were dressed for business: Brock in a dark gray suit and him in a navy one. Brock was four inches taller but less broad shouldered than he was. He was devoted to keeping in shape. Brock was, too, but enjoyed running more than weight lifting. The brothers used to work out together to keep each other motivated. But Brock soon found gym work boring and preferred running in the park to sweating it out in the gym. Chance did both.

Brock was checking something on his cell phone when Chance cleared his throat and said, "You know, you don't really need to be here if you have somewhere else to be."

Brock peered up at him, his dark brown eyes laser sharp as always. "You want to keep her to yourself for a while longer, huh?"

"I don't know what you mean," Chance said casually. He kept his eyes trained on his brother, though. If he looked away, Brock would take that as a sign of agreement with him. That he was, indeed, attempting to prevent his brother from meeting the woman he was interested in.

He and Brock had a history of disagreeing where women were concerned. Brock considered himself a connoisseur of women. Therefore, he believed his baby brother should take his opinions to heart and act on his superior advice. Chance thought it was best to ignore his brother's advice on women. If Brock knew women so well, why was he always trading one for another? Happiness to Chance involved one woman, one special woman with whom he could spend the rest of his life. Brock, on the other hand, was never satisfied.

There was a knock on the office door. Chance rose and went to open it. He grinned when he saw Petra standing there in a beautiful soft brown sleeveless dress, brown pumps on her feet and a new purse, not a shoulder bag, in her right hand. Her hair was in soft waves, parted in the middle and hanging down her back, and because she was standing with her back to a window through which sunlight streamed into the hallway, there were golden-brown highlights in her hair. Her eyes sparkled. He hadn't seen her in forty-eight hours and had been counting the minutes until he'd see her again. And now his big brother was there to assess her, and quite frankly, that fact irritated him. He would not let Brock size her up like a filly at an auction.

She stepped inside the office, and Chance saw the

surprise on her face when she spotted Brock standing in front of his desk. Brock had stood up, no doubt, expecting Chance to introduce him to Petra. Chance froze for a moment so Brock took the opportunity to introduce himself.

He grinned at Petra. On his handsome mug, a grin, for most women, was a prelude to sex. Brock had the chiseled features females found to be extremely sexy. Brock reeked of confidence too, which often had the effect of a powerful aphrodisiac on women.

He moved closer to Petra and bent his head toward her in an intimate manner, then he said in his suave baritone, "Dr. Gaines, I presume."

Petra chuckled. "Oh, I get it, that's a play on words of *Dr. Livingstone, I presume.* You must be Brock," she said. She offered her hand. "It's a pleasure to meet you. Chance speaks very highly of you."

Brock seemed taken aback. Chance couldn't figure out if it was because Petra had said he spoke highly of him, or because she didn't appear to be affected by his charm.

In fact, after shaking his hand, Petra walked over to Chance and planted a kiss on his cheek, and whispered for his ears only, "Hello, handsome."

Chance pulled her into his arms and squeezed her tightly. Then he turned with her and said to Brock, "This woman is going to be the next sensation around here."

Brock smiled warmly. "I think she's already a sensation around here." Then he picked up his briefcase and strode toward the door. He turned when he got to the door and said to Petra, "I should get back to work. But I hope to see you again soon, Petra, in a more social setting. I can see why my brother talks of little else except you these days."

"Thank you, Brock," Petra said with an equally warm smile on her face.

After Brock left, closing the door behind him, Chance pulled Petra into his arms and looked deeply in her eyes. "That's the first time I've ever known him to be at a loss for words."

"That was a loss for words?" Petra asked, looking confused.

"Yes," he said. "Brock usually flirts outrageously when I introduce him to women I'm dating. He calls it testing the waters to see if they'll be totally loyal to his baby brother."

"So he's the litmus test?" she asked, smiling skeptically, it seemed to him. "I think he might be a little full of himself."

Chance laughed. That was putting it mildly. "Yes, that may be true, but deep down, he's a good guy. Just unable to see that women are to be cherished and are not interchangeable. I have faith that he'll change one day."

Petra smiled up at him. "Did he like me?"

"Oh, yeah, he liked you a lot," Chance told her. "He liked you so much, he had nothing to say."

She laughed. "I do hope that you're telling me

the truth and not trying to stroke my ego. It's okay if your brother doesn't think I'm good enough for his baby brother. I know how siblings can be. My sisters are like warriors when it comes to protecting each other. If anyone harmed a hair on my head, they'd be on that person in an instant! And I think that's a good thing, C. You should be close to your siblings."

He held her tight, inhaling the wonderful scent of her hair, something with coconut in it. "I wouldn't lie to you. He left here totally confused as to why he liked you so much. He'll tell me all about it later." He looked into her eyes. "Now, let's get to your first brainstorming session."

They began walking to the door, arms around each other's waists. "I'm nervous," she told him.

"Don't be, Pet," he said. "I don't want to give you a big head or anything. I'm sure you're not going to turn into a diva, but the fact is, you're the star of the show. You have no reason to be nervous."

She grinned at him. "Nice pep talk. Too bad it didn't work. Still nervous."

During the following weeks, Petra spent hours working with the videographer in a viewing room where her footage was shown on a screen and she was tasked with providing commentary. She realized that if she had been speaking while filming her subjects she would not, now, have to explain what had been happening while she'd recorded the action on the screen. However, in the field, she was obliged to be quiet. She would never have been able to get such good footage had she been talking throughout the filming. The chimpanzees would not have stuck around to be subjects. Or worse, she and Paul would have been discovered by aggressive males who would have severely dealt with them.

Looking back at early footage, she got emotional because of how far she had come. With tears falling as she watched, she realized that by documenting the lives of the Congo chimpanzees, she had been able to reinforce the hypothesis that other researchers before her had put forth that the chimpanzees were forced to move deeper into the jungle to avoid human contact. And their populations were adversely affected by deforestation and poaching. Especially the violence of poaching, which reduced these noble creatures to meat or condemned them to slavery when they were sold to humans for their amusement, snatched away from their families for the rest of their lives.

Arianna, the videographer, an African American woman in her fifties who was sitting beside her in the viewing room, saw the tears on her face and offered her a tissue. “Slavery,” she said softly. “With humans or primates, it’s atrocious either way.”

Petra looked at her and smiled. “Yes, it is.” It was nice to have such a sensitive person working on the project.

It was at that moment that she saw the usefulness of a television show to illustrate to viewers the importance of caring for animals and, ultimately, for each other.

"It's going to be a good show," Arianna said. "I'm proud to be a part of it."

"I'm glad you think so," Petra said. She hoped and prayed that the show would garner interest and devoted followers, but she was still new to all of this and didn't know what to expect. "I'm keeping my fingers crossed."

Following long hours working on making the footage as coherent as possible and worrying if she was doing a good job, it was with relief that she went back home to Raleigh for a happy occasion: the wedding of Desiree and Decker. She had a glorious time communing with her sisters again, complaining about the pink bridesmaid dresses they had to wear, but was so pleased that Desiree was a vision in her wedding gown, which Desiree had dubbed "a white rose blushing," which meant pale pink.

Now it seemed that all of her sisters were either married or in love. Even her baby sister, Meghan, was in love with Jake's, her sister Mina's husband, twin brother, Leo. Was there the possibility that two of her sisters were going to be wed to twins? And what were the odds of one of her sisters giving birth to twins? Petra was happily anticipating Meghan and Leo's wedding announcement.

With all of her sisters paired up, her subconscious must have concluded that it was her turn to find love because she started having dreams about her own wedding. The dreams were in Technicolor and very detailed. She saw images of herself and her mom and sisters choosing her wedding dress. There was a scene with her and a faceless fiancé at their engagement party. She and her father, Alphonse, walking down the aisle with the sweet music of violins wafting in the air. She even saw the gold-and-diamond rings she and her groom exchanged while taking their vows. However, none of the dreams allowed her to see the face of her future husband.

"That's because the man who is going to marry you doesn't exist!" she cried out one morning after abruptly waking up from one of those annoying dreams.

Chapter 8

"I think it's time you met the parents," Chance said one Sunday morning as he and Petra made breakfast. He'd insisted on teaching her what cooking skills he possessed, and she was a willing student.

It was a beautiful June morning. The sun was bright and the sounds of traffic below could barely be heard from his twentieth-floor apartment. They were both dressed in robes. He'd bought her a matching robe since she had a habit of commandeering his whenever she slept over.

She looked up at him in surprise and nearly dropped the brown egg she was about to crack into a bowl to make scrambled eggs.

Before she could speak, he said, "It won't be anything formal. Just a meal at my parents' house in Harlem. You and me, my parents, Brock and his date, whomever that may be, and Alia. Alia isn't dating anyone."

"How should I dress?"

"Any of the dresses you wear to the office would be perfect," he told her casually.

She broke eye contact and returned to her eggs. "All right. Date and time?"

"Next Friday night," he replied. "I'll pick you up at seven."

"I live in Flushing now," she reminded him. "Funny, the only thing I used to know about Flushing came from Fran Drescher on *The Nanny*. I'll take the train to Harlem."

"No way," he said. "I'll pick you up."

She smiled at him as she added a pinch of red pepper flakes to the egg mixture in the bowl. "Okay, but I can't spend the night on Friday because Susie and I are doing some painting on Saturday. But I'll be free for our Saturday night date, as usual."

He hoped the disappointment didn't show on his face at that bit of news. He knew she was helping Susie renovate her house so that she could sell it for a good price, but any time she spent with Susie was time not spent with him.

He smiled, though, and said, "I'll try to be a good boyfriend and share you with your friends. I'll even help you paint."

She went over to him and stood on tiptoe to plant a

kiss on his mouth. "That's sweet of you. We're almost finished. She's going to let the Realtor start showing the house in August. In the meantime, I think my agent has found me an apartment in Harlem."

"Harlem?" he asked. "Why Harlem? I thought you might find something closer to me. Or even move in with me."

"I like Harlem," she said patiently. She reached out and grasped both of his biceps, her hold firm. "You and I can't live together. Didn't you tell me you thought we should be discreet about our relationship?"

"I hate feeling as though I'm hiding. I want the whole world to know how happy you make me."

Her smile broadened, and her eyes were alight with joy. "You make me happy, too. But we're attending the gala for the series launch in December together, so everyone will know then."

He hugged her tightly. "Besides our families, only Susie knows, so I guess we're good until December. By then, it'll be clear that you earned your spot on the network because you're highly qualified, not because you're sleeping with the CEO."

"We've done everything the hard way, haven't we?" she murmured against his chest. "Sleeping together before we knew each other and having an inappropriate employer/employee relationship." She looked up at him, her expression skeptical. "Do you suppose we can do things in a more traditional manner from now on?"

"Like what?" he asked, smiling.

"Like when your parents ask how we met, you'll say something like I saw her on the subway and had to say something."

He chuckled. "I can't tell them the subway story because I rarely take the subway. I'm just going to say we met at the meeting with the conservancy. If we hadn't met a few hours earlier, that would have been how we met."

She smiled at him, obviously satisfied.

He released her. "Now, let's finish cooking breakfast. I'm ravenous."

"I'm hungry, too," she said with a sultry smile and a naughty twinge in her big brown eyes.

And that was all it took for his libido to go into overdrive.

He turned the stove off and swept her into his arms.

"I've lost five pounds since meeting you," she complained as he carried her into the bedroom, but she was laughing, and he knew she was as game for some morning loving as he was.

The following Friday, Petra was enjoying the view as Chance drove them to his parents' brownstone in Harlem. She'd read that Harlem, in its heyday, used to be the mecca of blacks who moved to New York for opportunities they couldn't find down South. Not just for American blacks, though. Senegalese also made up a small part of Harlem, as did Hispanics, who occupied Spanish Harlem.

Harlem was a place of dreams, and the people who came there contributed to its unique culture. During the Harlem Renaissance many famous artists, politicians and businessmen lived in row houses in the Sugar Hill neighborhood of Harlem. And many Harlem neighborhoods boasted beautiful brownstones and tree-lined streets. Today, gentrification had put its stamp on the community. It was more racially mixed than ever.

Chance's parents' home was a three-story brownstone in Sugar Hill. They parked at the curb in front of the house and got out. Chance placed his hand on her lower back as he walked with her to the front steps.

She paused a moment to admire what must have been turn-of-the-century architecture. "How old is it?" she asked, her voice awe filled.

"It was built around 1910, I believe," Chance said. "My grandfather bought it in 1950. The family has renovated it several times since then. Mom jokes that there's always construction going on in order to keep it from falling down on our heads."

"And they're called brownstones because of the kind of stone that was used in construction more than a hundred years ago, right?"

"That's right. I looked it up once. Brownstone refers to a townhouse that's covered in brown sandstone that comes from the Triassic-Jurassic age."

"How did you remember that?" Petra asked, gazing at him with admiration.

"I'm weird that way," was his reply.

They walked up the steps and he rang the bell. "I have a key, but Mom likes to greet guests, so I let her have her fun."

Petra smiled at that. A son who indulged his mother. That was so sweet.

They didn't have to wait long. In less than two minutes, the door was unlocked and a lovely petite woman with reddish-brown skin, silver hair which she wore short and curly, and eyes the same shade as Chance's cinnamon-colored ones answered the door with a broad smile on her elfin-like face. She was about the same height as Petra and wore a simple black scoop-necked silk dress, black suede pumps with two-inch heels and silver drop earrings.

Petra's dress was quite similar except it was rust-colored, the soft material falling down her fit body and clinging in all the right places. She also wore pumps in leather that were the same shade as her dress. Her hair was in a casual upswept style.

"Hello!" Debra Youngblood cried. She reached out and grasped Petra by the arm. Her hand was warm and soft. Smiling, she looked into Petra's eyes. "Come in, dear, come in. Welcome to our home."

Petra stepped inside, Chance right behind her. She took in the resplendent stairs in front of her. It appeared that the Youngblood family had tried to save as much of the house's historic features as possible because the staircase was an intricately carved marvel. She guessed it was made of cherrywood, and some artisan had carved images of grapevines into it.

"Thank you, Mrs. Youngblood," she breathed. "You have a beautiful home."

Debra looked pleased. "I'm glad you like it. Would you like a tour?"

Chance took that moment to clear his throat and say, "Hi, Mom, how are you?"

Debra laughed. "Sorry, baby." She hugged him briefly and kind of shoved him in the direction of another room in the house. Petra smiled at that. It showed that Debra Youngblood could be playful, suggesting, not too subtly either, that she wanted to talk with her without her son present.

Chance took the hint and said, "I'll go see what Dad's up to."

"He and Brock are talking sports, as usual," Debra said drolly. She smiled at Petra. "This way, my dear, we can do the tour thing later. Alia and I are preparing dinner in the kitchen."

Petra walked alongside her. "Oh, good. I'm beginning to like learning how to cook."

Debra laughed. "It *is* a learned skill. Cooking used to be a necessary skill that some elevated to an art form. Therefore, more people learned to do it from their youth. Nowadays, women are having to be the breadwinners and the homemakers. It's a lot of work. I don't know how some of them do it. Plus, families are going in so many directions, it's difficult to get everyone at the dinner table at the same time. Prepackaged foods are popular, as is takeout from fast food restaurants. No wonder we're fatter than we've ever been."

Petra laughed with her. She liked Chance's mother already.

In the kitchen, they stepped into a modern wonder consisting of a high ceiling, a beautiful timber floor, a waterfall granite island, pendant lighting, white cabinets and brushed stainless steel appliances, including double ovens. Standing at the farmhouse sink was a tall, fit woman dressed in black slacks and a white pleated tunic, her feet in black boots. She turned when Petra and Debra entered the kitchen, and flashed Petra a white-toothed smile.

"Hey, Petra, I've been dying to meet you!"

Petra was hugged enthusiastically, and when the woman released her, she knew she must be Chance's sister because looking up into her face was like seeing Chance in female form. She had Chance's cleft in the chin, his cinnamon-colored eyes and his exact shade of dark brown hair. Her genetic mixture was, however, unmistakably feminine, whereas his was ultramasculine. When she'd met Brock, she had noted no real resemblance between him and Chance.

"Oh my God, you and Chance could be twins!"

Alia laughed heartily. "That's not the first time I've heard that. Yes, my baby brother and I look quite a bit alike. I'm the female version of him, and he's the male version of me. Genes did a number on us."

Debra chuckled. "In other words, they look a lot like their father, and Brock looks a lot like me."

She went and grabbed a couple of aprons from a drawer near the farmhouse sink. "For you, my dear. What are you comfortable doing, making salad or grilling steaks?"

"Better put me on the salad," Petra said. "I've never grilled a steak before."

"Done," said Debra.

Petra breathed a sigh of relief as she washed her hands at the sink and tied the apron around her waist. In the past few weeks she'd become adept at making salads, and she felt she could do a good job preparing the salad for tonight's meal.

"So, tell me all about where you lived in Africa," Alia said as the three of them went about preparing the meal. Alia was seasoning the steaks, her mother was at the gas range getting the grill ready for the steaks and Petra was getting vegetables from the crisper in the refrigerator.

"I lived in Kinshasa," she said. "That's the capital of the Democratic Republic of the Congo. It's the biggest city in the Congo, and it's a mixture of rich and poor. Some parts of it will remind you of South Florida with congested freeways and palm tree–lined roads. The weather's like Florida, too, hot and muggy because it rains a lot."

She continued describing Kinshasa to Alia as she choose two kinds of lettuce, cherry tomatoes, cucumbers, bell peppers, Vidalia onions, snow peas in their pods, carrots and radishes. There was also a pint of fresh strawberries in the refrigerator, which she grabbed.

"There's a great divide between the rich and the poor in Kinshasa," she said. "There are few rich and a lot of poor people. The country is constantly thrown into chaos by so many civil wars that many people never get the chance to get back on their feet. Corrupt government officials make it worse by catering to rich businessmen who want to rape the country of its natural resources. It's like they're selling out their country to get rich while most of the people suffer."

Alia and Debra were both shaking their heads sadly. "There's so much of that going on in the world," Alia said.

Finished choosing the ingredients for the salad, Petra set them on the counter beside the sink. She saw that someone had already placed a big salad bowl on the counter along with a salad spinner. She recognized the salad spinner because she'd seen one demonstrated on YouTube, but she'd never actually used one.

"Africa never catches a break," Debra said. "But in spite of it all, many African countries are progressing, establishing democratic governments and championing human rights."

"Oh, the people themselves are wonderful," Petra wholeheartedly agreed. "It's the politicians who're greedy and corrupt."

Alia walked over and handed her mother the platter of steaks she'd seasoned. "Chance says you were there for years," she said softly.

"Six years in total," Petra said. "So I got to know the people pretty well." She washed the vegetables under running water and placed them in a colander to drain before tearing the lettuce into pieces and putting it into the salad spinner.

"They're so hopeful for a better future, in spite of everything they've been through."

"Yes, that's a hallmark of the human spirit, isn't it?" said Debra. "We endure. We have to. There is no alternative. We have to keep going."

Alia, obviously the prankster in the family, sidled up next to Petra now that she was finished with her task and said, her eyes sparkling with humor, "Is it true you've got a black belt in judo? Could you beat up Chance if you wanted to?"

Debra laughed. "Alia, quit being nosy." But she turned her gaze on Petra too, and asked, "Do you?"

Petra laughed as she kept pressing the button on the spinner that propelled the spinning action. "I do have a black belt in judo. Dad made sure all his girls took lessons. But I'm out of practice, so I don't know if I could beat Chance in hand-to-hand combat. And I hope I never have to attempt it."

"Good answer," Debra said, giggling. "Now, Alia, help Petra with the salad."

Alia immediately did her mother's bidding, going to get a vegetable peeler out of a drawer and starting to peel a couple of carrots. "I have to tell you," she said for Petra's ears only, "Chance is one happy guy since he met you. I couldn't be happier for you two, and I hope you and I will be friends."

Petra met her eyes and smiled gratefully. "I'd like that. Chance talks about you a lot. He really adores you."

"The feeling's mutual," Alia said. "We've always been close. Speaking of which, he says you have four sisters. Wow, your cup runneth over! I always wished I had a sister. Sometimes having brothers was frustrating. They just don't think the same way a female does. Their behavior can be confusing."

"If you're talking about males versus females," Debra said from her position in front of the grill, "you couldn't be more on the money. Males and females don't think alike. You'd just as well get used to it."

"They believe they're logical," Alia said as she scrapped the skin off the carrots. "But actually they're illogical."

"They think they're unemotional compared to the emotional creatures females are supposed to be," Debra said. "But let an emergency happen, and they fall apart while we unemotionally handle it. Although we might fall apart later."

"But I wouldn't trade them for the world," Petra said, thinking of Chance.

"Amen!" said Debra and Alia in unison.

Chance's father, James, wanted to know where Petra was the moment Chance joined him and Brock in the library. His father looked askance at his youngest child, while Chance thought he detected a smirk on Brock's face.

"Mom stole her right out from under me," Chance joked. He was happy his mother seemed to take an instant liking to Petra. But who wouldn't? Petra was a sweet person.

"Let's hope that's not a portent of the future," Brock said.

Chance cocked a disapproving eyebrow at his brother, but didn't rise to the occasion. Sometimes Brock liked nothing better than to get into a battle of wits.

His father stood six foot tall, and like his youngest son, he had dark brown skin that was like smooth dark chocolate. He had wrinkles around his eyes, but otherwise his age was indeterminate at a glance. His hair was still mostly black with a little gray at the temples. Brock was more reddish-brown skinned like their mother.

"Still in the honeymoon phase?" Brock asked about his and Petra's relationship.

Chance mixed himself a drink while he ignored his brother. "How've you been, Dad? Still trying to figure out what you're going to do now that you've been retired for two years?"

It was a running joke among the family. James had officially retired, but hadn't yet figured out what to do with his retirement. Debra wanted to move someplace tropical. But James was so used to Harlem that he thought he'd go crazy with boredom anywhere in the world where the seasons rarely changed and the pulse of the community was slow and steady. He'd grown up on action.

James had risen when Chance had come into the room. He sat back down and picked up his drink. Whiskey, Chance guessed. His dad took a sip, gave an audible "Ah," and then regarded Chance with sober eyes. "Retirement is for the birds. I'd rather be working. Your mother looks at this time as an opportunity to get closer as a couple. She's got me going to classes with her. We're doing something called hot yoga for couples. I don't want to do yoga, let alone *hot* yoga. It just dehydrates me and I have to drink a couple beers before I feel right again. Your mother thinks it's sexy."

Chance couldn't help laughing. "It does nothing for you, huh?"

James smiled. "Your mother doesn't need hot yoga to be sexy. That woman's still got it. I don't know if I'm still man enough to handle it, though."

Both he and Brock laughed this time. Their father had always been frank on the subject of sex, although never explicit about his relationship with their mother. He promoted respect for women. He urged his sons to choose women who not only turned them on sexually, but intellectually. Someone they could be friends with as well as lovers. That was the sort of relationship he had with their mother.

"You and Petra, son," James said, looking expectantly at Chance. "Do you think she's the one?"

Brock made a choking sound, his eyes filled with pent-up laughter.

"What's wrong with you?" Chance asked, unable to keep the anger out of his voice.

Their father was watching both of them with a confused expression on his face.

Chance didn't want to get into an argument in front of his father, so he put his drink down and gestured to Brock to follow him. "A word, please, brother."

Brock hunched his shoulders as if he had no idea what this was all about and followed Chance out of the room.

Chance walked all the way down the hall to the foyer where he hoped his and Brock's voices would be unheard in the kitchen or the library. He kept his voice low, just in case.

Looking Brock in the eyes, he hissed, "What the hell is up with you? Making these snide remarks whenever Petra is mentioned? If you have something to say, say it to my face!"

Brock took a deep breath and let it out as if the effort to explain something to his little brother that he should be smart enough to already know was a huge burden. "She was a one-night stand and you're already introducing her to the family as though she were someone you're thinking of marrying one day."

"Listen, and listen well," Chance said. "I realize you have never treated a one-night stand as anything but what it was to you, but I'm not like you. Petra and I don't believe how we met should have any effect on what we have now. I respect her. I believe she's my equal in every way. Are we clear on that? Because even though you're my brother and I love you, if you ever make her feel as if she isn't good enough, I swear I'll knock your teeth down your throat and enjoy it!"

Brock laughed, but Chance suspected it was bravado on his brother's part. "I'm just trying to save you some heartache," Brock said. "She'll hurt you in the end."

Chance shook his head. He felt sorry for Brock. Maybe that was why he could never connect with one woman. He was afraid of getting hurt.

"I'm not afraid of getting hurt. I've been hurt before and survived. I'm also not afraid of taking a risk on love. Haven't you noticed how cold and unfeeling this world is without it? Or do you equate love with sex, and think all the sex you have is good enough?"

Brock frowned. "You're not the only one who's been in love," he stated coldly, eyes narrowed.

Chance was stunned. "You never mentioned it."

"She was a one-night stand," Brock said. "Someone I used to work with. Afterward she never spoke to me again."

Chance nodded, finally understanding his big brother. "So that's why you think what Petra and I have is going to fail."

"It's been my experience," Brock said, seeming to take no pleasure in the statement.

Chance impulsively hugged his brother. “I’m sorry you got hurt. But please, don’t treat Petra badly because you think she might hurt me. She might also be my perfect match.”

Brock shrugged out of his embrace. He was never one to show emotions or be demonstrative. “Okay,” he said gruffly. “Fact is, I like Petra.”

“I knew you did when you met her,” Chance said confidently.

“I’ll keep my fingers crossed for you,” Brock joked.

“And I’ll keep my fingers crossed for you,” Chance returned.

Chapter 9

"Dinner's ready, you two," James called, walking toward Chance and Brock in the foyer. He looked from one son to the other. "Everything all right?"

Chance smiled at his father. "Yes, Dad, Brock and I just had to get something straight between us. No worries."

His father's brows rose in confusion. Taking his gaze off Chance, he turned to Brock.

Brock cleared his throat. "Yeah, Dad, it's nothing for you to worry about. We're cool."

His father still didn't look convinced to Chance, but turned on his heels anyway and led them to the kitchen where the family had their informal meals. Their father tended to stay out of squabbles between his children, allowing them to figure it out for themselves unless things got too complicated, in which case he'd step in and try to help resolve the issue.

In the kitchen, Chance's eyes immediately sought out Petra, who was looking quite in her element, smiling at something his mother was saying. When she heard him and his father and brother enter the room, her eyes zeroed in on him and she smiled, which went straight to his heart. Alia came over and hugged him. "I like her!" she whispered in his ear. "I hope you can keep up with her. She's a fireball!"

And his father went straight over to Petra, whom his mother was still, it seemed to him, keeping close to her side, greedy woman. He and Alia strode over to them, too. Brock, he noticed, had sat down at the table, which was laden with what looked like a feast, and was already putting salad on his plate.

"Petra," his mother said, "this is Chance's father, James. James, this is Dr. Petra Gaines, zoologist, anthropologist, soon-to-be reality show star and our chief salad maker."

Petra laughed delightedly. "It's a pleasure to meet you, Mr. Youngblood," she said, eyes lowering from a tinge of embarrassment. He knew that look all too well.

His father was beaming. He was like his mother and Alia, a hugger, and he gave her a friendly bear hug.

Petra was still laughing when his dad released her and said, "I'm happy to meet you, Petra." Then his father looked at his mother and back at Petra. "You remind me of another beautiful lady I know."

Chance didn't know if his father was referring to the fact that Petra and his mother were both petite women, or if he was comparing their lust for life. Petra's adventurous spirit did remind him of his mother's.

"All right!" Brock called from the dinner table, "Shall we get this show on the road? My stomach's beginning to think my throat's been cut."

Their mother gave him a withering glance, and Brock visibly gulped and cried, "Just kidding, Mom!"

Everyone else laughed and joined him at the table. After a short prayer of thanks by James, they enjoyed a meal of grilled steaks, garden salad, stir-fried green beans, dinner rolls and fresh peach upside-down cake with whipped cream.

The family caught up on each other's lives as they always did at these meals. Chance was happy that his parents were focusing on Alia tonight more than on him. She was gearing up for a one-woman show at an art gallery in Manhattan soon.

"I'm ready," she assured everyone. "All of the paintings are finished, and psychologically, the fear of discovery that I'm a talentless hack has subsided. So I'm looking forward to the public's reaction to my work, positive or negative."

"How can it be negative?" her mother asked reasonably. "You're a wonderful painter, baby. Just wonderful!"

"I'd love to see your work," Petra said, smiling at Alia.

"You already have," Debra said proudly. "Practically all of the paintings on the walls of this house are by our Alia."

There was a huge painting of Lady Day, Billie Holiday, with a white gardenia in her hair on the wall directly in front of where they sat at the dinner table. Petra looked at the painting with an awestruck expression on her lovely face.

"You painted that?" she asked Alia. "It's beautiful!"

He was surprised by his sister's reaction to his mother's and Petra's praise. She began silently weeping. Petra, sitting beside her, offered her first the cloth napkin from her lap. And then her shoulder for his sister to cry on.

"It's just stress," Alia told them, her voice muffled behind the napkin. "I'm all right."

"Sure you are, baby," James said comfortingly. "But it's a proud day for us. Your grandmother would be so happy to see you following in your mother's and her footsteps."

It was a very emotionally satisfying evening for Chance, seeing his family and Petra bonding.

In July, Petra got a phone call from Meghan telling her she and Leo Wolfe were engaged.

Petra was in her new apartment in Harlem, having recently awakened. The one-bedroom apartment in a walk-up building near 125th Street was in great shape and had plenty of room for her needs. She liked the details in it, like a coffered ceiling in the bedroom and wainscoting in the living room. There was also an original fireplace in the dining area. Plus, the kitchen had recently been updated and had sufficient cabinetry for storage, counter space and new appliances.

"Meghan, when did this happen?" she cried, hoping she didn't sound as shocked as she was. Her baby sister was going to marry Jake's twin brother.

Calm down, girl, she told herself, *and listen to Meghan.*

"He asked me on our trip to San Francisco," Meghan told her, sounding breathlessly, deliriously happy. As a big sister, that sound was both music to Petra's ears and a reason to cringe. She was happy Meghan was ecstatic. On the other hand, she was losing another sister to a man. The bond they had would change somehow. Subtly, but it would still change, because the devotion they had for one another would now have to be shared.

So she got straight to the point. "Then he's as good a man as you suspected him to be?"

"Oh, yes." Meghan sighed. "He's the best man I've ever known. I love him so much."

"Then that's all I need to know," Petra said. "When's the wedding? In a year? Two?"

Meghan laughed. "I'm not going to wait that long. Mina's having her baby in August, so Leo and

I are planning to be married in October to give her a chance to recover."

"That's only three months away! What's the rush? Are you pregnant?"

Meghan laughed again. "Listen, now that we're engaged, Leo says we can be open and honest with our families."

Then Meghan went on to tell her that Leo was sterile, and on top of that had lived with what he thought was a congenital heart defect. In spite of his challenges he'd proved to be strong and loyal and capable of deep love and affection. The two of them, Meghan told her, after going through the fire of a tempestuous relationship, had forged an unbreakable bond. After Meghan was finished, Petra let out a long sigh. "You both deserve your happiness. I don't know what to say, Meghan. You two are a perfect match."

"I couldn't agree more," Meghan said, her tone rife with emotion.

"How is Mom taking it?" Petra asked cautiously. Their mother, Virginia, who was known to try to control their lives, could be a loud opponent if she didn't agree with the direction their lives were going. On the other hand, she could be their biggest cheerleader when she thought they were headed in the right direction.

"She loves him," Meghan told her. Then she filled Petra in on the plans for the wedding, including the date and the venue.

"I'll be there," Petra promised.

"Are you bringing Chance?" Meghan asked expectantly.

"I'm pretty sure I can persuade him to be my plus one," Petra said confidently.

"Oh, it's like that, huh?" Meghan teased.

"Let's just say he has restored my faith in men," Petra said.

"Hallelujah!" was her baby sister's reaction.

Petra laughed. "Yes, praise God. Only He could have worked a miracle like that in my life."

Two weeks later, Petra, with Chance along for support, flew to Kinshasa to tape an introduction which would run during the opening credits. They had finally agreed upon *Primates of the Congo* for the show's title. While they were in the Congo, they would also tape a few vignettes to be used in promos for the show.

She had phoned Paul ahead of time, and he and Noella were excited that he was to be given the opportunity to be a part of the show. Chance had also told her Paul would be a cast member of the second season, if the show was picked up for an additional season, which they were all hoping would be the case.

They would start shooting before daylight. The director, Zakes Moreno, wanted to be able to catch the sunrise as they motored to the jungle in a convoy that numbered eight Range Rovers filled with crew and camera equipment. Petra and Paul were asked to simply do what they did every day, and Zakes and his crew would film them.

Petra dressed once more in her jungle togs of khaki slacks, safari jacket, perspiration-wicking shirt, and comfortable hiking boots. Her floppy khaki hat was on her head, hair tucked underneath.

This morning, looking around her just before she and the others piled into the Range Rover they were to ride in, she saw most of the crew were outfitted similarly. They had obviously taken her advice about jungle apparel that she'd related to Zakes after she'd heard they were coming here.

Chance stood next to her and Paul, looking alert and interested in everything around him. "This is amazing," he said, head tilted back to look up at the purple sky. The sun was just peeking over the horizon.

Zakes yelled, "Everybody load up! Got my shots. I want to be in the jungle when the sun rises."

"Break a leg," Chance joked, squeezing Petra's shoulder reassuringly. She was sure he would have kissed her for luck if they weren't being discreet in front of the crew. He was not riding in her Range Rover. It was only her in the passenger seat, Paul, who was driving as he usually did, and Zakes with a lone cameraman in the back seat.

"Thanks, I think," Petra joked.

They climbed into the Range Rover, and soon the convoy was following Paul as he drove. She and Paul kept up an easy conversation all the way to the reserve, trying to ignore the fact that they weren't alone in the vehicle.

Once there, she and Paul began their trek into the jungle.

The sun had risen by then, and Zakes seemed happy that his cameramen were getting wonderful footage of the surrounding sights of the game reserve as the convoy entered it, as well as the vast forest when they disembarked and began following the damp, verdant trail that led into the jungle.

The crew was quiet, as Petra had asked them to be while they walked, but the jungle was not. Around them the voices of birds, primates and other animals could be heard as jungle creatures awakened to another day. A five-foot-long green garden snake slithered in their path, and several of the crew screamed in fright. "It's harmless. It's just doing what it does. It's more frightened of you," Petra told them.

"I doubt that!" one of the men said shamelessly.

They walked on, encountering insects, chittering birds and monkeys leaping from branch to branch in trees above their heads. Petra felt relaxed, and although she was alert and watched her step, she felt sheer joy at being in the jungle again.

She and Paul led the way with Chance and Zakes behind them, Zakes telling the cameramen what he wanted captured on film. Two hours into their trek, Petra spotted chimpanzee dung, so she knew they were near a nest. She took her binoculars from her bag and after motioning for the others to stand still, she surveyed the area. Sure enough, she saw several chimpanzees in the branches of a tree about fifty yards away. "This is close enough," she whispered to Zakes. "Your cameramen can zoom in on them, right?"

"Yes, of course," Zakes whispered back, smiling. She could tell he was thrilled by the prospect of filming the chimpanzees in their natural habitat.

Zakes began directing his cameramen to film from all sides of the tree the chimpanzees were perched in. After only a few minutes, he gave them the "cut" signal, and they all began their trek back to the reserve.

After they returned to the Range Rovers, there was a sort of celebration. Cans of beer were passed around and everyone toasted to a successful shoot.

Petra playfully clicked cans with Chance and smiled up at him. "Still think what I do is going to be a hit with the American audience?"

He grinned at her. "If we can capture what I felt walking through the jungle—the fear, the feeling of awe at witnessing nature firsthand—I think we'll have a hit on our hands."

Petra shook her head at his enthusiasm. She was beginning to believe everything he said. Was it just wishful thinking because she truly wanted the show to be a success? Not for her as much as for Paul and the people of the Congo and, especially, for the chimpanzees? Or was she falling in love with this complicated, caring and wholly too appealing man? She felt it might be love. And that scared her.

Zakes, who had been looking at footage on a digital recorder, laughed suddenly. He walked over to Petra and showed her the footage one of his cameramen had taken of a young male chimpanzee prancing upright on a branch as though he were a tightrope walker.

She immediately recognized Joey, the youngster who belonged to Francesca. She burst out laughing. "That's Joey," she said. "He's growing so fast!"

Of course, everyone had to look at the footage. They were so enthralled by it that Joey on his tightrope became the opening of the show.

After returning to New York, Petra went home alone one weekend in late August to see Mina and her newborn daughter, Journey. She went to Cherokee, North Carolina after spending the night in Raleigh with her parents, and when she got to the lodge where Mina and Jake lived in one of the cabins dotting the property, she was pleased to see her grandfather, Benjamin Beck, whom they all called Grandpa Beck, there. And if Grandpa Beck was there, her step-grandmother, Mabel was somewhere nearby. The couple was inseparable. They were usually off seeing the country in their high-end Winnebago.

Grandpa Beck was the first person she saw when she pulled up to the lodge and got out of the rental car. He was up on a ladder polishing the big double doors of the lodge that were hand-carved to look like a totem pole.

Her first thought was to admonish him for being on a ladder at over eighty years old, but she quickly quelled that foolish thought. She would have been admonished herself for saying such an outrageous thing to her still spry grandfather. Benjamin Beck didn't suffer fools gladly.

So she walked up to him on the ladder and quietly, so as not to startle him, said, "Good morning, Mr. Beck. How are you?" She'd tried to disguise her voice.

Her grandfather, a trim, wiry man with dark brown skin and solid white, naturally wavy hair that fell to the middle of his back, and which he wore in a ponytail tied back with a strip of leather, stopped polishing the door and peered down at her.

"Petra Gaines, if you don't quit that nonsense I'm going to get down off this ladder and give you what for!"

Petra quaked in her boots. "I wouldn't want that to happen."

He climbed down and gave her a hug. He was around four inches taller than she was. He was not an imposing man with his slight build, but to her he was a giant among men. "I missed you, girl," he said, smiling, the skin around his eyes crinkling.

"I missed you, too," she said and kissed his weathered cheek.

"Where is everyone?"

"Oh, Mabel's somewhere inside the lodge. Probably in the kitchen, knowing her. Mina and Jake are in their cabin, and the baby, who turned out to be a girl but I love her anyway, is with her parents. No doubt that's who you really came to see."

Petra laughed at his allusion to Mina and Jake's daughter being disappointingly female. Grandpa Beck had been campaigning for another boy following the birth of Lauren and Colton's son, C.J. He said females already outnumbered the males in the family.

"I'm heading over to Mina and Jake's place," she told him. She began walking in the direction of the outlying cabins.

A few minutes later, she was knocking on Mina's door.

Jake answered with baby Journey in his arms, bundled in a pink blanket. He smiled. "Petra! Why didn't you tell us you were coming?"

"It wouldn't have been a surprise if I'd done that," Petra said, stepping across the threshold and dropping her shoulder bag onto the foyer table. She moved closer and looked into the pink-and-brown scrunched-up face of her niece. "She's adorable," she cried. She peered at Jake. "She doesn't look a thing like you."

Jake laughed. "Thank God for that. I'm glad she's a mini Mina."

Mina slowly came into the room wearing her bathrobe and slippers and rubbing sleep from her eyes. Her natural hair was in braids down her back. When she saw Petra, she ran and hugged her tightly. "I just spoke to you earlier this morning, and now you're here? Why you little—"

"Language," Petra said, laughing. "You've got to set an example for Journey."

Mina laughed. "Now you know I don't use profanity. I was going to call you a sneak. Getting information from me to make sure we were going to be here when you arrived!"

"Yes, well, I didn't want to show up and you were gone somewhere," Petra said, looking around the cabin. "Let me go wash up so I can hold my niece."

She went to the guest bathroom, just past the foyer, and washed her hands. When she returned, Jake placed Journey in her arms and she gazed at her niece, her heart full and her eyes watering. She sniffed and tilted her head back, blinking. "Allergies," she murmured for Mina and Jake's benefit.

"Liar," Mina said, smiling at her.

When Petra got back to New York, Chance was waiting for her at the airport. He had gotten there over an hour earlier and had been impatiently anticipating seeing her again. He logically knew it had been only two days, yet it seemed much longer.

She had invited him to go with her, but he'd had to handle some business that needed his attention. Now he stood in the waiting area, looking in the direction of the passenger boarding bridge, his heartbeat accelerating because he'd just heard the announcement that passengers would soon be disembarking.

Passengers began entering the terminal, and he craned his neck trying to spot Petra. When he saw her, looking sexy-chic in her jeans, white T-shirt and black leather boots with four-inch heels, and holding that carry-on bag, her hair in a high ponytail, he smiled. He was grateful for her tendency to travel light because they would be able to get out of there as soon as possible and go back to his place.

He saw her looking around for him and called, "Pet!"

She flashed him a toothy smile and cried, "Babe!"

It did something to his insides when she called him that. It made him feel as though she were claiming him as her own. It was caring as well as blatantly sexual, in his opinion. But that was possibly because she cooed the word quite a lot when they were making love. He got a little hot under the collar every time she called him babe.

They met in the middle of the waiting area, and she put her carry-on bag down and hitched her shoulder bag farther up as he grabbed her in a warm hug that made her moan.

Then they kissed. She kissed him with gusto, no holding back for his queen. When she kissed him, she electrified him and made him feel emotions he didn't even know he possessed, the strength of which intensified as the kiss deepened. He'd read somewhere that your lips' sensitivity sent signals to the brain, which caused the brain to release chemicals that made the act pleasurable. In which case, his brain was working overtime because Petra was the best kisser he'd ever known.

When they came up for air, she looked at him with starry eyes. "I feel like we've been apart forever! Am I crazy?"

"If you are, so am I," he told her, and kissed her again.

Chapter 10

Chance wanted this night to be special. He'd had his assistant make reservations for him and Petra at Le Bernardin for dinner, and he'd personally visited his family's favorite jewelry store, Van Cleef & Arpels, in preparation for their Saturday night date. He told Petra to dress up because they were going to splurge tonight. When he got to her apartment and she opened the door, he saw she had taken his advice to heart and was wearing a beautiful red ruffled-back, off-the-shoulder knee-length cocktail dress with black strappy sandals that made her lovely legs even sexier. She held a matching black clutch in her hand, as well as a black pashmina to put around her shoulders should the temperature drop. Although it was August, he knew Petra, having lived in a temperate climate for years, got cold easily.

"You're a vision," he breathed, leaning in to briefly kiss her lips. After they parted, he stepped back to admire her further.

She smiled and stood on tiptoe to kiss his clean-shaven cheek. "And you're making me want to stay home," she said huskily.

He smiled, reached into his pocket and retrieved a jewelry box. Opening it, he presented the contents for her viewing pleasure. It was a Sweet Alhambra pendant, exclusive to Van Cleef & Arpels, made of white gold and studded with diamonds. Alhambra jewelry was supposed to be a symbol of luck. He hoped it brought him good luck tonight, because this was only a fraction of what he had planned.

She peered down at the necklace, and he could guess what was going through her frugal mind. She raised her gaze to his and said, "It's gorgeous! But it's much too expensive a gift. I know that jewelry store, and they don't sell trinkets."

He gave her a mock stern stare. "Listen to me, woman. If you're going to be with me, you're going to have to get used to expensive gifts."

She started to protest again, and he bent and kissed her objections away. When he raised his head this time, she simply took the necklace from the jewelry box and put it on. She gingerly fastened it around her neck, fingers slightly trembling, and walked over to the mirror on the foyer wall near the front door.

He stood behind her, admiring her reflection in the mirror. Her hair hung in waves about her shoulders. He knew jewelry and expensive clothing were not high on her priority list, but sometimes you just had to spoil the one you loved.

"You look amazing," he said softly. "Please, just accept it as a token of my affection."

He'd come up behind her and put his arms around her waist. She turned in his embrace until they were facing one another. Their eyes met. "Thank you," she said. "I'll cherish it."

"And I'll cherish your heart," he said. "Always!"

She smiled, and this time it seemed her smile encompassed her whole being. The reticence he'd sensed in her at accepting an expensive gift was replaced by the promise of everlasting love. That's what was important to her. It was refreshing for him to know a woman like her.

They briefly kissed again, and then she collected her clutch and pashmina and they were on their way.

Over dinner, he said, "Pet, we've known each other for over six months now, and I think you know how I feel about you. I know you think we got off on the wrong foot, but I never held that opinion. I believe meeting you was the luckiest day of my life. It was kismet. How else can you explain the fact that we met again after spending the night together when we both figured we'd never see each other again?"

She was watching him with quiet intensity. All night, in fact, she'd been gazing at him with tender affection. It excited him that she might be open to what he was about to ask her. He'd been skeptical for a while because he knew she valued her independence, and she had also told him she'd been averse to marriage ever since Gareth Graham had broken their engagement. She had also, however, told him that she realized she shouldn't lump every other male on earth in Gareth's category. There was hope for him.

"You're adorable when you're nervous," she said.

Around them in the three-Michelin-star restaurant, diners were holding intimate conversations, their voices muted and the tinkling of silverware on fine china as they consumed sumptuous meals a kind of musical accompaniment to the elegant atmosphere.

"Yes, I'm nervous," he admitted. "Because I adore you, Petra. I can't imagine my life without you." He paused. Walking toward their table was someone he never dreamed of running into, anywhere, anytime.

Yet there he was, making a beeline for him and Petra.

Petra's eyes widened, undoubtedly having noticed the stricken expression on his face. "What is it?" She turned her head to glance in the direction he was looking.

She half rose out of her seat in apparent panic when she saw who was approaching their table. She turned back around and looked pleadingly at him. But all he could do was give her an encouraging smile. They were either going to get up and leave, causing a scene with a quick departure, or they would stay and see what Gareth Graham wanted.

He reached over and grasped her hand. "We can go if you want to, Pet. Whatever you decide, I'm here for you."

She squeezed his hand until it hurt. She was clearly not looking forward to this encounter. Neither was he.

Petra's body reacted negatively to seeing Gareth Graham again. Her stomach muscles contracted painfully and her heartbeat accelerated in a fight or flight response. Flight was winning right now.

Gareth was grinning, his perfect teeth showing in his obnoxiously handsome face. He was still in perfect shape, something he worked hard at. You couldn't be a world-renowned adventurer with a beer gut. He was impeccably dressed in what was undoubtedly one of his Savile Row suits. He was as suave as James Bond and, worst of all, he knew it.

He smiled at her as he stopped beside their table. "Petra Gaines, as I live and breathe!" he said in his proper British accent. "I was shocked to see you walk into the restaurant on the arm of Chance Youngblood." He smiled in Chance's direction, and Chance narrowed his eyes at him, his ruggedly handsome face a mask of barely contained loathing. But to her amazement, he rose and offered Gareth his hand to shake.

"Mr. Graham," Chance said with a nod of acknowledgment.

Gareth shook it with enthusiasm. "Yes indeed, Mr. Youngblood, it's a pleasure to meet you. I've heard good things about your company." He switched his gaze back to Petra. "I never thought our Dr. Gaines would be associated with your network, though. You're into entertainment for the masses, and she's more eclectic in her tastes. However did you two meet?"

"First of all, let me make this perfectly clear," Chance said in steely tones. "You are here only because Petra hasn't indicated that she wants you gone yet. So watch your manners."

Gareth trained his dark blue eyes on Chance. "Of course. I'm a gentleman, after all."

"That's debatable," Petra said at last. She took a deep breath. "What possessed you to come over here? You could have ignored me and I would have never known you were here."

Chance sat back down, and she reached over and grasped his hand for emotional support.

"It's been two years," Gareth said. "I figured you would be over it. I'm in town on a press junket. And when I heard about your new show and happened to see you here tonight, I thought I'd come over and offer my congratulations."

He politely asked the couple at the next table if the extra chair at their table was taken. When they said no, he pulled it up to Petra and Chance's table and sat down.

He regarded Petra with a hint of humor in his keen eyes. "I was a fool. I can say it now. An arrogant fool. But I've paid for my arrogance. Haven't you heard? Danica left me for someone else."

"I don't keep up with gossip," Petra said. "At any rate, what do you want from me, sympathy?"

"No, I don't deserve your sympathy," Gareth said. His soulful eyes, eyes she used to endlessly gaze into, begged her to understand. "I just wanted you to know I'm sorry for how I treated you. I debated whether or not to come over here, and some sense of chivalry made me get up and do this. I was a cad and you deserved so much more. Accept my apology, or not. That's how I feel. It may not do you any good, but I'll know I tried to make amends, and I'll sleep better at night."

"Okay, you've had your say, you can go now. Sweet dreams," Petra told him, looking down at her and Chance's clasped hands. Chance was probably under the impression she was allowing Gareth to speak because she needed to get closure, but that wasn't the case. She was doing it to confirm that she was over him. She had been convinced the relationship was a thing of the past, but how her spirit, what she was inside, would react when she saw him again, *if* she ever saw him again, was something she hadn't been sure of. Now, sitting less than two feet across from him, she knew that part of her that had belonged to Gareth Graham was free. The butterflies in her stomach were gone, and her heart beat with a healthy rhythm. It had been shock that had made her react so violently to his sudden appearance.

She met Gareth's eyes. "You know what? You did me a favor by coming over. Now I know, without any doubt whatsoever, that I'm free to wish you well. There is no more acrimony. I don't hate you, Gareth. So if what you're looking for is my forgiveness, you have it. Go, and be happy!"

Gareth looked stunned. She knew him well enough to recognize when he was stumped for words. What his agenda had been when he'd decided to confront her, she couldn't be sure. However, he was most certainly surprised by her attitude.

He rose a bit shakily, she thought, then took a deep breath and, looking down at Chance, said, "Thank you for being so understanding when I came over here. I realize it was presumptuous of me." He gazed into Petra's eyes. "'She walks in beauty, like the night of cloudless climes and starry skies; And all that's best of dark and bright meet in her aspect and her eyes.'"

Chance rose menacingly at that point, and through clenched teeth said, "Man, I was patient with you, but if you don't leave now, you're going to wish you had. Quoting Lord Byron to my lady right in front of me? Get lost!"

Gareth looked at Petra.

"You heard my man," she said, smiling. "Get lost, Gareth."

Gareth walked off, adjusting his tie no doubt because his throat was full of the crow that he'd been forced to eat. He had obviously thought he could come over there and disrupt their romantic evening. Well, he hadn't. Petra gave a little sigh of satisfaction. That had actually felt good.

Chance sat down, and she reclaimed his hand and brought it to her mouth and kissed his palm. "Thank you," she said, looking deeply in his eyes. "For not letting that escalate into a slugfest, and for being there for me, no matter what."

"You had to do it your way, my Pet," he said reasonably.

Petra pressed his hand to her cheek and asked sweetly, "Now, what were you about to say before we were so rudely interrupted?"

Chance was still angry over the colossal nerve of Gareth Graham! What could he have possibly hoped to gain by showing up out of the blue like that? But perhaps it hadn't been out of the blue at all. No, come to think of it, the odds of his coincidentally being in the same restaurant as he and Petra, when New York City had thousands of restaurants, were astronomically low.

Focus, Chance told himself. Petra held his hand firmly in hers. He knew she'd just asked him a question but his mind was elsewhere, trying to figure out what had just happened.

For one thing, Graham had stolen his thunder. He'd been so hyped up to propose to Petra tonight. He'd planned everything down to the last detail, and now he felt like if he proposed, some of the impact, the chance of it being a highly memorable occasion, would be lessened somehow.

Petra must have sensed his mood because she squeezed his hand and said, "Don't let him ruin our evening, babe."

He took a deep breath, rose, bent down and kissed her lips. He didn't care who was watching. When he sat back down across from her, she was beaming. Her smile, which reflected her essence, helped dispel the rancorous emotions that were seething inside of him. To hell with Gareth Graham!

He got up again and got down on one knee beside Petra, grasped her hand in his and looked into her eyes. Retrieving the engagement ring he'd hidden in his inside coat pocket, he brought it out and presented it to her. "Petra, Pet, will you marry me?"

She gasped in surprise, then she stared into his eyes for what seemed an interminable length of time to him, and finally she cried, "Yes, yes, Chance, I'll marry you!"

Relieved she'd said yes, Chance had the presence of mind to put the ring on her ring finger before getting up and pulling her into his arms and kissing her soundly.

Until that moment Chance had been unaware that he and Petra had become the center of attention in the busy restaurant, but now, everyone around them applauded and cheered them on.

When he raised his head and peered into her upturned face, she was grinning happily. "I love you so much!"

It was the first time she'd told him she loved him, although she'd shown it in so many ways. The knowledge that she loved him made him want to protect her, support her in every possible way, to always be her shelter, whether it was storming or not. His mind was in a tumult. He unashamedly felt like bawling, but suppressed the feeling, though his voice was full when he told her, "I will love you till my dying breath."

"Champagne, Mr. Youngblood." Their waiter interrupted their celebration with a big grin on his face. "Compliments of the management."

He held two tall glasses of sparkling champagne aloft on a serving tray. Chance and Petra took the glasses, thanked the waiter, saluted the other diners as their way of saying they appreciated their kind encouragement and drank deeply.

Afterward, he and Petra sat back down at their table, the rest of the diners resumed their own conversations and all was quiet again.

However, he and Petra would not have cared what was going on around them because they had eyes only for each other at that moment.

"Where do you want to have the wedding?" Chance asked, his gaze taking in the rosy hue of her lips, now even fuller after several passionate kisses tonight. "Here or in your hometown? Does your family have a tradition of your sisters getting married at a certain venue?"

"No," she said. "My sisters have all been married at different places. Where do *you* want to get married?"

"It would be my pleasure to marry you anyplace in the world you want," he said.

She laughed. "Does your family have a tradition?"

"My mother and father and his parents were all married at Abyssinian Baptist Church in Harlem. Alia had a destination wedding in the Bahamas because that was where Adam, her husband, was from, and many of his relatives couldn't afford the trip to New York for a wedding."

"I don't know," Petra said, sounding wistful. She glanced down at the diamond solitaire on her finger. "I kind of feel like I'm dreaming right now." She looked into his eyes. "All I know right now is I'm drunk with happiness." And then she whispered, "And I very much want to make love to you."

Their waiter happened to be close by, and Chance called out to him, "Check, please!"

Primates of the Congo was in postproduction, work having concluded the first season of the show.

It was mid-September, and Chance's sister, Alia's, one-woman art show was tonight.

The art gallery in Manhattan where the show was to be held was only blocks from Chance's apartment, so Petra and Chance were going to walk to the event.

It was Friday night, and since Petra was no longer working on the show she had plenty of time at her disposal. She'd practically moved in to Chance's place since the show went into postproduction. She was soaking in his tub right now.

These days her time was split between working out with Yoshi at his dojo, jogging in the park, redecorating her apartment and having lunch with her friends like Susie, or Alia and Debra. She also kept in touch with Paul and Noella, who had recently told her they were expecting. And her sisters were texting on a daily basis, keeping her updated about the family. She was busy, but happy to be busy.

She and Chance had told only their families about their engagement. They were saving telling the media until after the show's premiere. And thankfully, she hadn't seen or heard from Gareth since that night in Le Bernardin. Chance hadn't brought him up, for which she was grateful.

She relaxed further in the bubbly warmth of her bath, her head on a tub pillow and eyes closed. She couldn't believe how much her life had changed in the past seven months. It wasn't the prospect of actually being on television that was the biggest surprise. It was the fact that she was in love. Her!

She was the staunch believer in singlehood. She'd admonished every single one of her sisters not to get married, sometimes just before the wedding. Her sisters now laughed at her. But then they had never taken her seriously. They knew she was speaking from the perspective of a wounded bear: she'd been hurt and was fighting back by being ferocious. Chance, with his optimism, his confidence and firm belief that they belonged together, had changed her. She wished all women all over the world could have a Chance in their lives. Someone who supported them, no matter what. Someone who was able to quell their fears and make them laugh. Someone who was a thoughtful, passionate lover, who cared about their pleasure.

She smiled to herself. This generosity of spirit must be proof that she was in love.

Chance knocked on the door. "Pet, are you going to stay in that tub until you turn into a raisin?"

When she wanted a solo soak in the tub, he felt deprived because he wasn't in it with her. But a girl needed some alone time.

She did miss him, though. "Get in here!" she called.

He didn't have to be asked twice. He strode into the bathroom doffing his clothing as he came, which didn't take long because he was wearing only sweats and a T-shirt.

She enjoyed the view. Sometimes she felt unusually blessed to be able to watch the play of muscles in his chest, arms, legs, stomach, buttocks—all incredibly toned and entirely impossible to resist touching.

He got into the tub, raising the water level so much that suds spilled onto the tile. She smoothly slid her body on top of his. They'd done this before, so she knew there would be no intercourse in the tub. They never made love without using condoms. They'd agreed that they wouldn't bring a child into the world until after marriage.

His hands were squeezing her firm buttocks, and they lay crotch to crotch. His penis was hard and getting harder. She smiled sultrily and kissed him. The kiss was a substitute for sex. He was a master of French kissing, never too deep, always gentle and sensual. A slow burn. Pleasure was heightened in stages, each leaving her panting for more. A man who could kiss well was worth his weight in gold.

His penis was right at the opening of her vagina, and she thought it best to break off the kiss before they got carried away. "Let's move this to the bedroom," she said softly, her mouth on the corner of his.

But Chance simply turned his head and devoured her mouth once more. She melted, her core throbbing fiercely. All she wanted was him inside of her, fulfilling her, claiming everything she wanted to give him.

He was the one to break off the kiss this time and said with a deep groan, "Get up, girl, or we'll end up making twins."

She slowly got up off him. She stepped from the tub and he got out too. She grabbed a towel from the shelf and gave him one. Standing in the warm bathroom, they toweled each other semidry, just enough not to soak the bed they'd be falling on seconds from now.

The bed didn't even creak as Chance fell backward onto it and Petra landed on top of him. Laughing, he opened the nightstand's drawer and withdrew a condom in its package. Petra took it from him, tore it open and efficiently rolled it onto his engorged member. She was quite adept at it. "What's so funny?" she asked.

"Nothing's funny," Chance told her. "I'm just so damn happy, I can't stop laughing."

Petra raised herself up, and when she went back down, it was onto his penis. She pressed down until the full length of him was inside of her. She couldn't help sighing with pleasure. "Is there such a thing as too much sex?" she asked. "Because I've never had so much sex before. Will we wear each other out?"

Chance laughed, his eyes dancing. "Let's give it a try, shall we?"

"Okay," Petra said, riding him enthusiastically. "I'm always up for a challenge."

Chance just smiled at her.

They were almost late getting to the art gallery.

Chapter 11

"Petra, don't you look beautiful!" Susie cried, walking up to Petra at the gallery with a tall, handsome Scandinavian-looking guy in tow. Petra smiled warmly at Susie and hugged her briefly. "So do you!" she said enthusiastically. She had invited Susie to the showing but hadn't been sure she would attend.

Susie had sold her house five days after it'd gone on the market in August, collecting way over the asking price. She now had no financial problems, except learning how to carefully manage her portfolio. Petra was so proud of her.

Susie had cut her thick shiny blond hair and now wore a sophisticated bob. "Petra, this is Ian Iverson. Ian, this is my friend, Dr. Petra Gaines."

Petra smiled up at Ian. "It's a pleasure, Ian."

"The pleasure's all mine," Ian said in a friendly manner, returning her smile. "Susie told me you two have been friends for a long time."

"Since college," Petra said, wondering where Chance was. He and Alia had gone off somewhere when they'd gotten there half an hour ago. There must be a problem.

"And we don't want to say how long ago that was," Susie joked, and they all laughed.

"How long have you two known each other?" Petra asked.

"Susie and I were raised in the same neighborhood," Ian said.

"We knew each other when we were younger, but lost touch when we went to college." Susie picked up the story. "Ian moved back to take care of his ill mother three months ago, and we met again."

"Just when she was getting ready to move out of the neighborhood," Ian said, laughing softly. He looked adoringly at Susie. "I almost missed my opportunity."

Susie blushed a lovely shade of pink. "But we didn't," she said, taking his hand and peering lovingly into his eyes. Then she must have remembered she and Ian weren't alone and abruptly asked Petra, "Where's the artist? I've been admiring her work and wanted to tell her how talented I think she is."

Petra could only shrug and say, "She's definitely

here somewhere, but I haven't seen her in a few minutes."

Then she spotted Chance coming toward them from the back of the huge gallery. He had to make his way through a crowd of over two hundred people standing around chatting, eating hors d'oeuvres and drinking champagne off trays carried by uniformed waitstaff. He had a grim expression on his face, which sent her Spidey sense spinning off into the stratosphere.

Susie saw him, too, and said, "Oh, there's Chance. He probably knows where his sister is."

Petra thought it was a good idea to head Chance off at the pass, before he got to them. "Excuse me," she said to Susie and Ian. "I'll go see."

When she reached Chance, he took her by the upper arms, his facial expression still quite serious, and said, "Petra, Alia is very upset." He held her gaze. "I told you Alia was once married?"

"Yes, his name was Adam, and he was kidnapped two years ago," Petra murmured.

"Well, soon after we got here, Alia received a phone call, and the man who was calling told her he was Adam. He said he and his team had been rescued and were being debriefed in Washington, DC. She's really shaken up."

"Oh, my God!" Petra cried. "Was the call real?"

"She says the caller sounded like Adam, but she was so traumatized that she can't be sure. He did know certain things that Adam would know, like how they met, her birthdate and so forth. Anyway, Mom and Dad and I tried to persuade her to go home, but she insists on going on with the show. Whether that was Adam or not, she says her life must go on. It's the attitude she adopted after she thought he was lost to her forever. I don't know, Pet. I think my sister may be losing it."

He sounded so anguished that she pulled him into her arms and held him tightly. "We'll see her through this. She managed to survive his being missing. If it's really Adam, it's a good thing. But, imagine what he must have gone through all these months Alia didn't know whether he was alive or dead."

Chance's eyes were haunted. "I didn't think about that. He's not going to be the Adam she knew and loved. At any rate, Alia wants to go to DC as soon as possible, and I'm going to arrange it. The company plane will fly us there after her showing."

"That girl's brave," Petra said with admiration. Then she added, "I'm going with her."

Chance nodded in agreement. "She'd like that."

Shortly after Chance had told her what was going on, the museum's curator, a compact middle-aged gentleman dressed in a gray pinstriped, double-breasted suit with a bald head and huge rectangle-shaped black-framed glasses, stepped onto a dais, bent toward the mic on the lectern and cleared his throat to get the crowd's attention. "It is with great pleasure that I introduce an artist who will one day, I am certain, be considered one of New York's iconic visionary painters. Her exhibition, *Women of Strength*, encompasses women from all backgrounds, from Ruth Bader Ginsberg to Aretha Franklin. Her work is both emotional and intense. It is transcendent and will resonate in the minds and hearts of those of us who are fortunate enough to view it. She is truly an artist to watch, and we are proud to exhibit her work in our gallery. Ladies and gentlemen—Alia Youngblood Braithwaite!"

Tears formed in Petra's eyes as she watched Alia step onto the dais and shake the curator's hand. She looked calm and collected, and radiated confidence in an African-print dress and her long hair in braids. She smiled and said, "Thank you, Charles. That was lovely. And thank you all for coming. Art has always been a part of my life. My mother gave me my first set of watercolors when I was three. I made a real mess on the dining room table."

People laughed, warming up to her easy charm. She continued, "Luckily, I've improved since then. What inspired my collection, *Women of Strength*, begins with a sweet love story. I met a wonderful man and was swept off my feet. We got married, and less than a year later, he went to the Middle East to work on a project for the government and wound up getting kidnapped. The government couldn't tell me if he was dead or alive. My gut feeling was that he was dead because if there were any possible way to make it back home to me, Adam would find it."

Stunned silence followed this. She smiled. "After

he died, something inside of me died, too. I couldn't eat, I couldn't sleep and I definitely couldn't paint. I cursed God. Don't worry about Him, He can take it. He takes so much abuse from us humans who tend to blame Him for everything!"

More laughter, but it was soft and hesitant. Petra was standing with Chance, his parents, Brock, Susie and Ian. Everyone was watching Alia with rapt attention.

"Then one night I woke from a very vivid dream about Adam. In it, he said, 'Alia, what the hell do you think you're doing? I died. You didn't! Get out of that bed and go paint. You're stronger than you think you are.'

"When I woke, I didn't hesitate, I went straight to my studio and started painting a portrait of Harriet Tubman from memory. I'd seen so many portraits of her in the past that I knew every contour of that brave woman's face. I worked until dawn, and when the sun rose that morning, I had the beginning of my collection. I thought I'd choose twenty-one women, representing the twenty-first century, who epitomized the strength and resiliency of all women." She gestured to the paintings on the walls of the gallery around them. "And there you have it. I hope you see something that touches you and inspires you, or at the very least reminds you of a strong woman in your life. Thank you."

Private plane or not, Petra knew a flight plan had to be filed and various other items needed to be checked off the list before the company plane could take off for Washington, DC. So it wasn't until the wee hours of the morning that Chance, Petra and his family boarded the plane, and they were in the air a few minutes later.

The plane had a full crew, Chance told her: a pilot, copilot and a flight attendant. The Gulfstream extended range jet seated sixteen, so there was plenty of room. The engines were very loud when they boarded, but inside the noise was muted.

Having never been on a private plane before, Petra wasn't prepared for how luxurious the interior was, with big comfortable seats that converted into sleeping surfaces.

She sat with Alia in the back of the plane while Chance and Brock and their parents were in the front, discussing something that they obviously didn't want to concern Alia with.

Alia had her eyes closed, but she was not asleep because she started talking a few minutes after they sat down. "They're discussing the situation," she informed Petra. "They're figuring out how best to support me. I know you and Chance are in love and you're planning to marry him, but you need to know that you're marrying into a family of troubleshooters. He's the best of the lot. When a problem arises, he's the one they send in to solve it. That huddle you see them in? It's their strategy session. When they come back here, they will have decided what to do when we get to DC. If Adam is Adam, they'll know how to proceed. If Adam is being detained longer than he should be, my father, who's a lawyer, will know exactly what to do to get him back home. If he's not well, he'll get medical attention. God, I hope he wasn't tortured or anything. I keep seeing images of him as a prisoner of war, starved and beaten."

Petra held on to her hand. "Tell me about Adam. What did he do? Was he an artist like you?"

Alia opened her eyes and smiled at her. "Believe it or not, Adam was a physicist. He was doing post-graduate work in quantum physics and how the brain perceives consciousness. He believed consciousness creates reality. That we create our own reality. What's amazing is he came from a very impoverished family in the Bahamas, won scholarships to come here and went to school for ten years on those scholarships. He was that brilliant. He was weird—weirdly brilliant. Besides being smart, though, he was loving and generous."

"He sounds wonderful," Petra said.

"He was wonderful," Alia said softly, smiling at Petra.

"He *is* wonderful," Petra said firmly, smiling back.

"He *is* wonderful," Alia repeated, with more confidence.

When they landed at Washington Dulles International Airport in Loudon, VA, a driver in a large black SUV met them in front of the terminal. By that time, Chance had ascertained the steps they needed to take in order to extricate Adam, if he indeed was Adam, from the predicament he was in. Adam was a naturalized American citizen, so he had certain rights under the US Constitution. Still it made Chance nervous that his brother-in-law was being debriefed at the Pentagon.

First, they had a drive ahead of them because the Pentagon was located outside of Washington, DC in Arlington, across the Potomac River. The last time Chance had been in Washington, DC, it had been to attend President Barack Obama's second inauguration along with the rest of his family. Those circumstances were much more pleasant than these. Just the thought of Adam, a gentle giant, being interrogated at the Pentagon gave him a sick feeling in the pit of his stomach.

Once in the car, Chance, who was riding in the passenger seat next to the driver, turned around to direct a question to Alia, who was in the back with the others. "Alia, I know you said you wanted to go directly to the Pentagon, but are you sure? You haven't had much sleep."

Alia, whose eyes had dark circles around them but still held a determined aspect, nodded. "I won't be able to sleep until I see Adam," she said.

"All right," said Chance, knowing it was useless to argue with her. "Please take us to the Pentagon," he instructed the driver, a young African American man in a traditional chauffeur's uniform, including the cap.

"Yes, Mr. Youngblood," he answered. "That's a forty-one-minute drive from here."

"Thank you," Chance said, and fastened his seat belt.

Under different circumstances, Petra would be enjoying the view out of the window of the moving car. It was a beautiful sunny, cloudless day in Virginia. She was always happy to be back on Southern soil. A Southern girl through and through, she loved the greenery in this part of the country. The slower pace, as compared to New York City. The general friendliness of the people.

However, the atmosphere in the car was tense. No one was talking. She had a crazy urge to tell a joke, anything to relieve the oppressive silence. But she didn't because everyone had their own way of coping with a crisis. Chance's family was so different from her own. With the Gaineses, right about now, someone would be making the others laugh out loud. She remembered Meghan telling her about when she'd gone to the hospital to be with Lauren when she delivered C.J. Lauren was in pain and still laughing. Her family could be in the middle of a major argument, then someone would make a hysterical comment and everyone would crack up. Gaineses had even been known to laugh at a funeral.

Suddenly, Brock's stomach growled so loudly,

everyone heard it. "Look," he said, "I haven't had a proper meal since yesterday. I'm a growing boy."

"You're a growing boy with a tapeworm, obviously," said Debra. "You ate on the plane with the rest of us."

"Those snacks don't even qualify as food," was Brock's opinion on that subject. "What do you have in your shoulder bag, Mom?"

Debra rolled her eyes at him. Petra's interest was piqued. What was Brock referring to?

Alia smiled. "I could swear I smell cinnamon and other spices."

Debra sighed. She reached into her voluminous bag and withdrew a large Hefty bag filled with homemade oatmeal cookies. She handed the bag to Alia. "I couldn't sleep while we were waiting for the plane to be ready, so I made Adam's favorite cookies."

Alia, who was sitting between her mother and Petra, handed the bag to Petra then hugged her mother. "You're so sweet."

Brock cleared his throat. "Can I have one of those?"

Alia laughed. "Why not? I think everybody could use a cookie right now."

So Petra opened the bag and handed it around. Soon, all that could be heard in the car were the sounds of delicious oatmeal cookies being consumed by everyone, including the driver, who didn't hesitate when he was offered one of the treats.

Petra decided the Youngbloods had more in common with her family than she'd originally thought.

* * *

At the Pentagon, Chance and the rest of his party were ushered into the office of Colonel Edward Butler, the officer who was in charge of debriefing Adam. Colonel Butler appeared to be in his mid-forties and possessed a calm demeanor. His assistant brought in more chairs so everyone could be seated, and when they were, he sat down behind his desk and regarded them with a solemn expression.

Chance made the introductions, after which Colonel Butler took a deep breath and started talking, his accent undeniably Southern. "I thought it best to warn you that Dr. Braithwaite may not look quite the same as when you saw him last. When we found him, he was malnourished and in a very unkempt state. The people who kidnapped him are considered, shall we say, rather unorthodox in their beliefs and practices. I won't get into the political ramifications of their actions. That's not my province. The government wants you to know we never gave up on rescuing Dr. Braithwaite and we regret it took so long to accomplish our goals. I'm sure Dr. Braithwaite will fill you in on how he survived all these months. It truly is a harrowing tale, and he's lucky to be alive."

"Since he's been here with us, Dr. Braithwaite has been allowed to bathe and shave and get some much-needed sleep. He's been seen by a physician who says he's healthy except for malnutrition. And I'm sure you'll understand that he may have some psychological issues to deal with due to his experience with his captors."

Chance felt chills running up his spine. He feared the future for Alia and Adam would be bleak and filled with uncertainty and pain. They had both already been through enough.

Colonel Butler paused in his recitation of the events leading up to their presence there. He sat behind his desk and looked at each of them in turn. Then he said, "All right. If you're ready, I'll take you to Dr. Braithwaite."

Chance looked to Alia for confirmation. She nodded, and he said, "We're ready."

They followed Colonel Butler down a long corridor, Alia flanked by her parents directly behind Colonel Butler and Brock behind them, with Chance bringing up the rear beside Petra. He took the opportunity to reach for her hand and bend close to her. "How're you holding up, Pet?" he asked softly.

She smiled up at him, and as always, her smile gave him life.

"Don't worry about me," she said equally softly. She brought his hand up and kissed the back of it. "Everything is going to be okay."

For a moment, his anxieties were lifted by that positive affirmation. But as soon as Colonel Butler opened the door of the room where Adam was waiting, they all came rushing back.

Adam, who used to be a big muscular guy with a penchant for order in all things, from his surroundings to his appearance to his very thought system, looked like a man who had never known what peace and security were. He was still tall, of course. But due to major weight loss, he was haggard, and his eyes appeared more deep set than they used to be. His eyes were always the first indication of what Adam was thinking. Before he would open his mouth, you would know what kind of mood he was in. He was a sociable, gregarious guy who was somewhat of a nerd due to his genius IQ, but a total people person. He was the kind of person you loved to be around because you never knew what kind of earth-shattering notions would come out of his mouth.

Dressed in a T-shirt, sweatpants and a pair of athletic shoes which, Chance was sure, were items the authorities had scraped up for him to wear after they'd rescued him, Adam was a shell of his former self.

Then Adam seemed to focus in on them. Everyone except Alia had stopped in their tracks upon entering the room. She was the only one who kept moving toward Adam. She didn't run to him and throw herself into his arms, though. She approached him slowly and without saying a word. She let him raise his eyes to hers. When they'd entered the room behind Colonel Butler, Adam had looked up, but his gaze had appeared unfocused, as if he were looking but not seeing. Chance noticed the instant Adam really focused and recognized Alia walking toward him. The spark of hope flashed in his eyes and he cried, "Alia Joie!" He always called Alia by her first and middle names. He said Joie could not be left out because it meant joy. And that's what Alia was to him. She was his joy.

Alia ran into his arms then. "Oh, my God, Adam. Adam, I thought I'd lost you forever!"

Both she and Adam were crying as they hugged and kissed each other's faces repeatedly.

Chance held Petra in his arms. She was weeping, too. He had to fight back tears himself. His parents were in a huddle with Brock, and they were crying. Their tears were ones of happiness and relief. Adam was alive.

Chapter 12

"We still haven't decided when and where we're going to get married," Chance reminded Petra on a Monday morning in late October. They were in her apartment in Harlem, sitting at the island in the kitchen. Her building wasn't far from Alia's building or his parents' brownstone. Earlier he'd protested when she'd told him she was moving to Harlem. Now he was glad she was in Harlem. He was spending more time here lately to be closer to his family and his fiancée. With Adam's return, he simply wanted to be nearby if he was needed.

However, Adam seemed to be recovering nicely. Physically, he'd put on weight and looked a hundred percent healthier than he had when they'd seen him at the Pentagon. Adam had also decided to talk with a therapist about his experience with his kidnappers, and Alia had told Chance that the appointments were going well.

Meanwhile, he vowed to concentrate on him and Petra. Last night they had gotten back to New York after spending the last two days in Raleigh, where they'd helped to celebrate the marriage of Meghan to Leo. The first night, Friday, he and Petra had split up, with Petra joining her sisters and friends for a night on the town. He had gone to the bachelor party Jake had thrown for Leo. There, he'd gotten to know all of the men, Jake, Leo, Colton and Decker, who were either married to or preparing to marry one of the Gaines sisters. They all had one thing in common: they were strong men. He suspected a man had to be sure of himself if he were to live the rest of his life with one of the sisters. The women were all accomplished, something he attributed to their parents.

Their mother, Virginia, struck him as very strong willed. She must have been an important influence on her daughters. Their father, Alphonse, had also, by all indications, set a fine example for his daughters. Petra told him how their father always said they could do and be anything they wanted to. The sky was the limit. He also touted physical fitness, she'd said, inculcating in them the desire to be the best they could be.

Chance and Petra ran together most mornings, and she was as good an athlete as he was, if not better. He had been running for years and enjoyed weight training. But martial arts were beyond his abilities. She was more of a well-rounded athlete than he was.

Petra was doing something on her laptop this morning. She'd finished eating breakfast and was typing rapidly. Oh, yeah, the book. How could he have forgotten she was writing a book about her experiences in the Congo? The book was supposed to be a tie-in to the show. They would release it after the show's debut in December.

She was wearing her robe (he was in his, too), her hair in disarray, and for some reason, she had a pencil dangling between her teeth. What she was doing with a pencil in this day and age, he couldn't fathom. Eventually, every form of writing would be done electronically and be paperless, let alone pencil-less. He smiled at her quirkiness.

She looked up at him, her big brown eyes wide with curiosity. "What?" she asked innocently as she took the pencil from between her teeth and placed it on the island's countertop. "What was that you said about the wedding?"

"It's time we set a date," he said. "I want to be married to you sooner rather than later. Or are you trying to get out of it altogether?"

She met his eyes over her laptop. "I'm not trying to get out of anything. I'd marry you tomorrow."

"Convenient, isn't it, that you can't arrange a wedding in twenty-four hours."

"You could if you went to Vegas," she countered smartly.

It was like the sky opened and revealed Nirvana to him. "I know you're just being your adorable sarcastic self," he said. "But Vegas sounds good to me."

Petra pushed her laptop aside and gave him her undivided attention. "Tell me you're joking!"

He grinned, and that must have convinced her of his sincerity more than words could ever say because she got up and complacently went into his open arms as he sat on his stool at the island. He kissed the side of her neck, enjoying the scent of her skin and hair. "Who says we can't get married twice? Once in Vegas, and then another ceremony for family and friends. What's important is the marriage, not the wedding."

"I totally agree," she said. She paused a long moment before looking him in the eyes and saying, "We haven't even talked about the legal stuff."

"Oh, you mean a prenuptial agreement? I'm not marrying you for your money." He laughed shortly.

"Laugh if you want to," Petra said seriously. "But we both know that's the first thing people are going to say, that I'm marrying you for money. You're worth a whole lot more than I am."

"You're invaluable to me," was his reply, pulling her in for a squeeze. "I know how you feel about wealth, Pet. You think it corrupts people who don't have their heads on straight. Remember when we first met? You were afraid I was like Graham—a spoiled rich boy. You found out differently. Money hasn't transformed me, or my family, into elitist snobs. We're as human as anyone else. We're generous, caring people. You know because you've spent time with us. You won't just be getting me when you marry me. You'll be getting my family because I'll always be close to them. They are my heart. Now, you are number one on my list. So, will you marry me and forget about the money? And if you *do* turn out to be a gold digger and take me for everything I have, I can always earn more money."

She playfully punched him in the arm. He figured he deserved it.

"This weekend?" he asked hopefully.

She didn't answer, but instead began loosening the belt of her robe. He smiled.

He was still smiling when their mouths met.

Petra wondered what had lit a fire under Chance. After he had talked her into getting married in Las Vegas, he arranged everything. He decided on a chapel on South Sixth Street, and Chance, of course, chose the most expensive package offered by the chapel, which included a limousine picking them up at their hotel, music during the service and digital photos of the wedding, plus a wedding DVD, flowers for both of them and a candle-lit ceremony.

She wore a white Ralph Lauren lace sheath dress, the hem of which fell just above her knees, and a pair of high-heeled sandals, her hair parted in the middle and falling about her shoulders. Chance wore a suit in cobalt blue with a white shirt, tie and black dress shoes.

They were in a playful mood all day. Every experience they shared was a laughing matter. It was the first day on the job for the limo driver, and he had trouble figuring out the limo's GPS so they got lost twice before getting to the chapel. When they got there, everyone was so nice to them. But the minister kept calling Petra "Peetra."

The minister's mispronouncing her name aside, though, the ceremony was touching. She and Chance held hands, and when the minister asked them if they'd prepared their own vows, they told him they had. Chance then looked into her eyes and said, "Pet, from the moment I saw you, I knew you were unique. I'd never met a woman so unconcerned with her outward appearance. And your coat smelled like that stuff Mom used to rub on my chest when I got a cold as a kid. But when you smiled at me, I was smitten. And when you started talking, I knew I was a goner. I could spend the rest of my life talking to you about anything and everything and never get tired of it. I'll always love you. Even when I'm ninety and can't lift you anymore. I want your face to be the last thing I see when I leave this earth. And when I get to heaven, I'll start searching for a house for us to live in once you join me up there."

He wasn't even halfway through what he had to say before Petra started crying. She wept silent tears as she said her own vows: "You should have known me just a year ago. I boasted to my sisters that marriage was good for men but horrible for women. I told them that marriage was outdated and women had outgrown it. But the fact was, I was hurting from a bad relationship and had adopted that attitude to avoid getting hurt again. Then I met you and your joie de vivre, your ability to make me laugh at myself and your knack for always having a comeback whenever I pointed out why we shouldn't be together won me over. I'm yours. My heart belongs to you, and I hope we live forever because forever isn't long enough to spend with you."

When the minister pronounced them husband and wife and told Chance he could kiss his bride, they tasted each other's tears as they kissed.

After the wedding, upon returning to their hotel room, Chance insisted on carrying her over the threshold. He joked about her being a bit heavier than usual, but she felt great, although, her breasts were a bit tender. That could be attributed to rough lovemaking, though. Chance was the most passionate lover she'd ever had. Plus, the frequency with which they made love was unprecedented for her. Chance cared about her pleasure more than his own and always made sure she was satisfied.

After he set her down in the middle of the room, he kissed her before saying, "I've got something for you."

She glanced at their gold wedding bands on their fingers. "I've already got everything I need," she said.

"Humor me," he insisted. He kissed the top of her head then went into the closet where they'd stored their carry-on bags on the top shelf.

While he was in there, Petra took her shoes off and wiggled her toes in the plush carpeting as she waited on him.

Returning from the closet, Chance handed her a white bag that had come from a pharmacy, judging by the logo on it. She assumed it was a package of condoms. But upon opening it, she saw that the cardboard box inside was a home pregnancy kit.

"Is this some kind of a joke?" she asked.

He stood there, stunningly handsome in his cobalt blue suit, his eyes dancing with humor. "I wouldn't joke about something this life changing."

Suddenly weak in the legs, she sat down on the bed. He seriously thought she was pregnant.

"Do you know something I don't? Because it seems to me I should be the first to know whether or not I'm expecting a baby. It *is* my body, after all!"

Chance came and sat beside her on the bed, his gaze seeking hers, and when their eyes met he said, "I'm not certain I know something you don't. But I do know your body, Pet. For months I've made a thorough study of it, from the top of your head to the tips of your toes. I know how you feel when you're in the throes of passion. I know how you feel when you're relaxed as opposed to tense. It was about two weeks ago that I noticed you weren't enjoying it as much—"

"You're talking about my breasts," Petra said.

"They have been kind of tender, but I figured it was just my hormones acting up."

Now that she thought about it, she'd been so content, she probably hadn't been paying as close attention to her body as she should have. She'd been feeling powerful in her sexuality, as if nothing could touch her. However, she was an adult and should know that there were consequences to sexual intercourse, and one of the biggest was pregnancy. Could she be pregnant?

She got up. "I'd better go pee on a stick."

Chance got up to follow her. She spun around. "Where're you going?"

"I'm going with you."

"No, you're not."

"But we're married. I've seen you naked."

Petra laughed. "There are some things that should remain a mystery between a man and a woman."

Chance laughed. "Are you getting moody on me already? And you're probably only three months pregnant."

"Stop making predictions, Nostradamus!" she cried, laughing so hard there were tears in her eyes. She went into the bathroom, shut the door in his face and locked it, imagining him standing outside the door, his arms akimbo, laughing at her.

In the bathroom, she sat down on the edge of the bathtub and read the instructions on the box. After peeing on the digital test strip, she cleaned herself, avoiding looking at the digital display all the while.

She opened the door and strode out of the bathroom, carrying her dress over her left arm and the test strip in her right hand.

She handed it to Chance. "You read it," she said as she walked to the closet to hang up her dress. "But wait until I get back."

"You're making me crazy," Chance complained.

She came back to him and took a deep breath. "All right. What does it say?"

He looked down at the test strip. "A big, fat yes!" Chance exclaimed happily, then picked her up and spun her around with abandon.

Petra laughed along with him. "My mother is going to have a heart attack! She always said, 'You'd better not bring a baby in this house until you're married!'"

"You *are* married," Chance said, crowing with delight.

Petra couldn't contain her merriment. To think that in the space of less than a year after meeting Chance, she'd broken every rule she'd made for herself: she'd fallen in love, gotten married in a chapel in Las Vegas and found out she was pregnant!

She peered into his face, finally realizing what her selfless new husband had done. "You wanted to get married quickly because you suspected I was pregnant, and I'd told you I definitely didn't want to have children until we were married."

He nodded. "I was covering all my bases, Pet."

She slowly slid down his muscular body until her

feet hit the floor. Looking up at him, she said, "We're going to be parents. Have you contemplated what that means?"

"It means our lives will change for all the right reasons. Kids are worth the sacrifice. And I promise you, I'm going to be a hands-on dad. I'll change diapers, get up in the middle of the night, take him or her to school when the time comes, be a soccer dad. You name it, I'll be there for you and our child."

"I know you will," Petra said. She gave him a worried look. "How should we tell our folks?"

"Let's discuss that some other time," her handsome husband said with a mischievous glimmer in his beautiful golden-brown eyes. "We're on our honeymoon."

Chapter 13

"Chance! Chance Youngblood! Over here!" screamed a man with a video camera as he rushed toward Chance and Petra the next morning as they were leaving the hotel to go to the airport.

Chance barely had time to put himself between the man and Petra before the guy shoved a handheld video camera in his face and demanded, "Is it true that you and Petra Gaines were married in a chapel here in Las Vegas yesterday?"

Chance knew he probably looked menacing on camera, because anger was the initial emotion he felt at this intrusion. Petra was clutching his arm as she kept her face turned away from the odious man and his camera.

"No comment," Chance said decisively. He saw that their hired car was waiting at the curb. He recognized the driver from yesterday standing beside the car.

"Why Vegas?" asked the guy, an average-size African American in his early twenties with dreadlocks and wearing jeans, a black T-shirt with the logo of a well-known gossip show etched on it and black Reeboks.

Chance and Petra kept walking toward the car waiting in front of the hotel, but the reporter was impeding their progress in an attempt to get him to make a comment. Chance made it a habit of not commenting whenever he encountered the paparazzi. He supposed he and Petra were lucky they weren't being bombarded by more reporters from gossip shows. Someone from the chapel had probably recognized him and dropped a dime on him for profit. No matter how careful you were, if they wanted to dig up information about you, there were ways to do it. It came with the territory. But he knew Petra must be feeling violated, so he did his best to protect her from being exposed.

Finally, they were at the car and the driver, knowing the drill, put himself between them and the reporter as he held the door open for them. Chance helped Petra into the back seat, then he climbed in after her, the reporter still recording. "Help a brother out," the guy pleaded. "You're CEO of the biggest network that caters to black folks, and they want to know if you and Ms. Gaines are married, and if so, why you chose to do it in Vegas. Couldn't you give her the wedding of her dreams if she's the woman you love?"

Chance turned his back on the reporter, and continued to block the guy's view of Petra. The driver got into the car and pulled away from the curb. "I'm sorry about that, Mr. Youngblood," he said with sincerity.

"It's not your fault," Chance told the driver. Although it might be, he thought suspiciously. Anyone could have told that reporter where to find him and Petra.

Concerned about Petra's state of mind, he held her close to his side. "It could have been worse," he whispered. "Hopefully, we won't run into more of them at the airport."

They were flying commercial. He didn't use the company jet except for emergencies, like when they had to get to Adam quickly, or specifically for business. Trips for pleasure were done the regular way, just like everyone else.

She looked at him with sober eyes. "Is that what I have to expect by being on TV?"

"They're annoying," Chance told her. "However, most of them know their boundaries. If you don't speak to them, they move on to something more salacious. The good news is, those promos for the show are reaching an audience. He knew who you were."

"Lucky me," Petra said sarcastically.

He coaxed her to relax and sit back on the car seat. She laid her head on his shoulder. "I haven't even told my sisters we were going to elope. They're going to freak out when they see that online. Do they even check their facts before broadcasting gossip all over the internet?"

"That's another reason I don't talk to them," Chance told her. "No matter what you say, they're going to say what they want to. When you're in the public domain, they can say what they want, with the exception of slanderous comments that they can be sued for. They know how far to go. And Youngblood Media has many lawyers on retainer who're always happy to get litigious if the need arises."

He placed his hand on her stomach. "How're you feeling today?"

"I'm great," she said softly, looking deep into his eyes. Leaning toward his ear, she whispered, "I think marriage agrees with me."

"Me, too," he said, and kissed her gently on the mouth.

They were not accosted at Las Vegas International Airport; however, when they got off the plane at JFK, there were several reporters waiting to hopefully interview them. Petra guessed the reporter who failed to get a comment in Las Vegas had alerted NYC colleagues, because these reporters were from the same gossip show.

Chance made sure a car was waiting to take them

to Harlem, and once they were through the reporters, they got in it and the driver sped off.

"I see the news has spread," Chance said to her once they were alone. "You probably should phone your family and let them know what to expect. I'll phone mine."

Petra didn't look forward to phoning her parents, but she knew it was the right thing to do. She would prefer to tell her sisters she had eloped. They wouldn't be judgmental. They would be happy for her and congratulate her. Her mother, on the other hand, would want to know why she'd chosen to elope. Didn't she know that parents dreamed of being present when their children got married? Didn't she know that parents, especially if they had daughters, considered it a rite of passage to symbolically give their daughter away to the man of her choice?

She dialed her mother's cell phone number. When her mom answered, Petra said, "Hi, Momma. How're you and Dad?"

"Congratulations," was the first word out of her mother's mouth. "I was just online, and guess what popped up in the entertainment section of my home page?"

Petra frowned, which caused Chance to frown too. She placed her hand over the cell phone and said, "She knows."

He gave her a sympathetic look. Petra spoke into the receiver. "Exactly what did you hear?"

"That you and Chance got married in Las Vegas!"

her mother almost shouted. "Some woman who was also waiting to get married was interviewed. She said she would recognize Chance anywhere, but she didn't know who the pretty lady he was marrying was."

"Excuse me a minute, Momma." She related what her mother had said to Chance. "Mystery solved about who called the gossipmongers."

To her mother, she said, "I hope you're sitting down, Momma."

"Give me a second," said her mother. "All right, I'm sitting."

"It's true, we got married yesterday. And more good news—I'm expecting." She waited on pins and needles for her mother's reaction.

Her mother screamed. Petra held the phone away from her ear. Then she heard her father's calm voice. "Petra," said her dad, "we're happy for you, darlin'. Your mother is unable to speak right now. She's too busy dancing around the room, actin' a fool. That's a good sign. Put Chance on the phone."

Petra did her father's bidding. Chance smiled as he held the phone to his ear. "Mr. Gaines?"

Petra cried, "Put it on speaker!"

Chance did and then held the phone away from his ear. "I'm here, Mr. Gaines," he prompted her father.

"Chance," said Alphonse Gaines. "Welcome to the family. I know you two didn't do things the way most of us deem is the proper way, but the results are the same and we couldn't be happier for you and Petra.

Virginia and I were already on the way to becoming parents when we married, too. So you're not alone."

Petra could have died from shock then and there. That meant Lauren had been a bun in the oven when her parents tied the knot.

She could hear her mother in the background calling her dad a blabbermouth. She laughed softly.

"Thank you, Mr. Gaines," said Chance. "I'm honored to be a part of the family."

"Take care of my little girl," Alphonse said.

"I will, sir," Chance promised. "With all of my heart, I will!"

"That's good enough," Alphonse intoned. "Goodbye, now. Your mother-in-law is about to kill me."

"Good luck, sir," said Chance.

"I'll need it," Alphonse replied, just before hanging up.

Chuckling, Chance handed Petra's cell phone back to her. "I really love your parents."

Petra gave a contented sigh. After that conversation, she loved her parents more than ever.

Their revelation about their shotgun wedding, though, weighed on her conscience. She phoned Lauren.

"I was getting ready to call you," Lauren said without saying hello. "Then Momma and Daddy phoned me and told me I was on the way when they got married. Obviously it's something that upsets Mom, but hey, these things happen."

Petra breathed a sigh of relief that she was saved

from having to tell Lauren. She went on to tell Lauren why their parents had phoned her and spilled the beans.

Lauren laughed. "Oh, Dad let it slip. I wouldn't want to be in his shoes!"

Both of them laughed at that. Then Petra said, "You heard about me and Chance, too, then?"

"That you're married? I heard that on TMZ. Chance did a good job of keeping your face off that video, by the way. This is so bizarre. We tell each other everything. But regardless, I do want to say congratulations, and I love you!"

"I love you, too," Petra said. "And I'm sorry I didn't tell you all we were planning to elope. Chance and I kept it to ourselves. But I am telling you now that we're expecting. I guess Mom and Dad were leaving that up to me to tell you. I just got off the phone with them."

Screaming in someone's ear obviously was a trait passed down by Virginia because Lauren also screamed shrilly in her ear. "Didn't I tell you that you would be next?"

"Yes, you did," Petra said, remembering that day she'd been playing with C.J. and Lauren had walked in to try her hand at making her give Chance a try instead of running from love.

"You let yourself get caught, sis," Lauren said, laughing.

Petra smiled into Chance's eyes. He seemed to be enjoying her end of the conversation. "Yeah, I let myself be caught and I couldn't be happier. Okay, sis, love you. I'm going to phone the other girls now. Give my nephew a kiss for me."

"Will do," Lauren said warmly.

After she'd hung up, Petra smiled at Chance. "Now I see why people post news on Facebook. Informing everybody takes time."

"My turn. I'll phone Mom. Dad loses his phone too often," Chance responded, dialing a number on his cell phone. He cleared his throat before speaking: "Mom, I guess you've heard."

Unlike Petra's mother and sister, Chance was greeted with laughter instead of screaming from his mother. He put his hand over the phone and whispered to Petra, "She can't stop laughing."

He put the phone on speaker. Petra's eyes lit up when she heard his mother's tinkling laughter. "I thought you were going to hit that guy when he said you could have given Petra a dream wedding instead of going to Vegas. And have you two seen the story on TMZ online? The headline is, Youngblood Media CEO Gets Jungle Fever." She laughed some more. "The good news is, this is great publicity for the show. Now, to the important point here, son. You are not going to cheat me and our joint families out of a wedding. For this little stunt, you owe us a church wedding."

"Mom, that's not why I phoned," Chance interrupted her. "Well, yes, I phoned to tell you we got married yesterday, but that's not all. Petra and I are expecting a baby." He waited expectantly for a scream this time, and his mother didn't disappoint him.

She shouted, "James! James! Our baby is going to be a father! Petra is pregnant!"

His father was on the line in two seconds flat. He was laughing hysterically, too. "Good God," he said once he had his laughter under control. "Our first grandchild. You've made us so proud, my boy, so proud! Debra, go crack open the champagne. We're toasting to the newlyweds and expectant parents!"

He heard his mother giggling in the background, and then the sounds of her going through cabinets in the kitchen where the two of them had apparently been when he'd phoned.

Soon, there was the distinct sound of a cork being pulled from a champagne bottle, followed by the drink being poured into flutes, no doubt—his mother had a habit of always matching the appropriate glass with the appropriate beverage.

"To you and Petra!" his father said. Chance heard the tinkling of glasses being touched together, then he imagined his parents drinking from their flutes.

His mother came back to the phone. "Son," she said just before she burped loudly. "Son, tell my new daughter we love her dearly. Tell her we're so happy she came into our lives!"

Chance was staring into Petra's eyes when his

mother said that. Petra was smiling widely. "I love you, too, Mom!" she said into the phone.

Chance heard his mother burst into tears.

"Son," his father said, "I'm going to say goodbye. Your mother needs me."

"Talk to you later, Dad," Chance said, and hung up. He smiled at Petra. "I would say they're happy."

A few weeks later, Chance had moved in to Petra's apartment and given up his place. He proposed buying property farther south, but she made an argument for living in Harlem. There were several brownstones available in the Sugar Hill neighborhood where his parents lived, and when the baby came, they would probably be grateful family was so close by.

Since he'd agreed with her, they were temporarily living in her apartment until they bought and renovated a brownstone in Sugar Hill, which Chance estimated would take them about six months, or more. Just in time to bring the baby home from the hospital.

In the meantime, they began planning a combined party to celebrate both their marriage and the arrival of their child. Three months after their baby's birth, they would have a party in their Harlem brownstone, inviting family and friends. This, Petra believed would satisfy their families' desire for a traditional wedding, plus welcome a new family member simultaneously.

It was early December and Petra, who was seeing a doctor on a regular basis now and learned that at the time she found out she was pregnant she was already three months along, was following her doctor's advice and eating well, exercising moderately and finding her bliss.

Dr. Chrissie DuBois, an African American in her midthirties, was a yoga enthusiast and believed in meditation among other things. She told Petra a mother's state of mind was as important as what she put into her body while carrying her child. Petra didn't know if she believed in meditation, but she did believe in prayer and decided there wasn't that much difference between the two practices. So she started adding a bit of meditation to her prayer in the mornings.

This helped keep her calm when she was obliged to go on television and promote the show on the major networks, not just Youngblood Media's network. She did all the major morning shows in early December, and afterward, Youngblood Media's publicist, Elaine Shaw, told her the interviews had gone viral on YouTube. "You made social consciousness look desirable," she said over the phone one morning as Petra was getting ready to go to downtown Manhattan for a CBS Morning News interview. "Adults are saying you're bringing back the Good Samaritan principle, where it says we should look out for our fellow man, and kids think the chimpanzees are cute and want to emulate you."

"I just hope it moves them to action," Petra told her. Chance had made Jon Berensen a coproducer on the show, and the conservancy's 800 number would be displayed after each show, telling viewers if they wanted to help the chimpanzees, they could phone that number.

"We'll know soon," Elaine said. "The debut is next week."

She didn't need to remind Petra. She was terrified. The company had planned a red-carpet event at a theater on Broadway. They were pulling out all the stops. They'd invited key people in New York City who worked in television, film or on the stage.

She and Chance had not given any interviews about their marriage or the fact that they were expecting a baby. However, on the night of the gala, everyone would see them together as a couple. Also, she had a baby bump, so they would know she was expecting, too. It was all nerve-racking, but she tried to take it with a grain of salt. This was her life now, and she would rise to the occasion.

Chapter 14

"Wow," Chance breathed, admiring Petra in her beautiful white Oscar de la Renta gown. It was an off-the-shoulder creation with a neckline just plunging enough to give him a glimpse of her magnificent breasts. Lately, they'd been even more magnificent, as far as he was concerned. She was wearing the Van Cleef & Arpels necklace he'd given her plus her engagement ring as her only jewelry. The hem of the gown fell just above her ankles, which was perfect for displaying those sexy sandals she was wearing.

"What do you think?" she asked him as they stood in the foyer of the Harlem apartment, preparing to go downstairs and get into the limousine waiting for them.

Her hair was combed back from her forehead in a smooth, straight ebony cascade down her back. Speaking of her back, he walked around her, admiring her in the dress from all angles. It fell like molten silk over her shapely bottom.

He stopped in front of her and said, "What do I think? I think I'm a hell of a lucky guy to be coming home with you tonight, that's what I think."

She laughed and reached up to straighten his red bow tie. He was wearing a Tom Ford black tuxedo, the jacket in crushed velvet with satin lapels. The wool slacks were flat-front, and his slip-on, highly shined black leather dress shoes were also by Tom Ford.

"Are you at all nervous?" she asked, peering into his eyes.

"Maybe a little," he said with a roguish grin. "Nights like this come with the territory, but they're the least enjoyable part of my job. I get a thrill out of creating something. What I've enjoyed most about the process of building a show around your life is getting to know you, Pet. And see you do your thing. That turns me on. That gives me satisfaction. You've done so well, from start to finish. Even when you doubted yourself, you gave it your best shot. I'm so proud of you."

Her eyes were twinkling with delight. "And I'm proud of you," she said. "I'm so blessed to call you my husband."

Chance felt close to tears, so he sprang into action

and ushered his beautiful wife out the door. "Look at the time! We should be going."

Petra looked at him with those intelligent eyes of hers. He knew she had his number, but she was letting him slide this time. "Okay, okay," she said, grabbing her clutch and pashmina off the foyer table.

Chance was pleased to see a sizable crowd at the theater, most of them snapping photos with their cell phones of the celebrities arriving. Some of the notables were even stopping to sign autographs.

As for the professional photographers, anyone getting out of their car to approach the theater was in danger of being blinded by the abundance of flashes coming from cameras.

On the red carpet, where sections had been roped off to provide an easy path into the theater for invited guests and to keep possibly dangerous fans at a safe distance, he and Petra were stopped every few feet by reporters wanting to ask questions.

For this occasion, Chance and Petra were prepared to answer any reasonable questions.

After Chance had already answered several, a female reporter stepped up to them and said, "Good evening, Mr. Youngblood, Ms. Gaines. Charlayne Williams here for Channel 13."

"Good evening," Chance said.

"What do you hope to accomplish with a show that focuses on African wildlife when our African American men are being shot down in the streets?" she asked.

Chance could have answered the question, but he chose to defer to Petra. He smiled at her. "Darling, would you care to field that question?"

"I'd love to," Petra said with a warm smile directed at the reporter.

"Ms. Williams, the show isn't just about African wildlife. It's about chimpanzees who are, genetically speaking, as close to a match with us humans as any living thing on earth. These are intelligent creatures who are threatened with extinction. Creatures who do their part every day to help keep us alive by spreading seeds in the jungle that grow into trees, which provide oxygen for every human being on this planet. We hope to educate, elevate and inspire youths about the symbiotic relationship we have with every living organism on this earth. If we step up and get involved, our young people will know that we care enough about them to offer alternatives to the streets. We hope the show will remind people that, on planet Earth, we're all in this together."

The reporter looked genuinely impressed. "Thank you, Ms. Gaines, and enjoy your night."

"Thank you!" said Petra enthusiastically.

And Chance escorted his wife inside the theater, his chest puffed up with pride.

In the theater, seats had been reserved for special guests, which included his family, Petra's family and close friends.

He and Petra sat down in the front row along with his parents and her parents. Behind them were all of

Petra's sisters and their husbands, Alia and Adam, and Brock with a date. Chance didn't know his date because Brock hadn't yet brought her to any family get-togethers. Jon Berensen was there as well. Next to him sat Susie with her boyfriend, Ian.

Soon after they were seated, the lights were doused and the film began on the big screen. The dramatic theme music rose to a crescendo and then lowered into the background so Petra's voice, as the narrator, could be heard. "Welcome to the Democratic Republic of the Congo, a country in Central Africa which has a population of over seventy-five million people and a total area of over nine hundred thousand square miles. It's a country of contrasts. The Democratic Republic of the Congo has had political unrest since, well, forever. King Leopold the Second of Belgium, who ruled from 1865 to 1909, exploited the Congo for every natural resource within its borders, especially natural rubber. He basically used the Congolese as slave labor to cut down rubber trees on Belgian rubber plantations and process them, and if they didn't cooperate he had his soldiers cut off their hands. But these were only some of the atrocities committed against the Congolese people."

Chance was riveted. Not only was Petra a pleasure to watch, her sincerity made what she said have an urgent quality to it. He looked around him. The audience was captivated. He had a gut feeling the show was going to do very well in the ratings.

He observed Petra's face in the glare of the light

reflected off the screen. She had a pained expression on her face, as though she wasn't quite certain she liked what she saw on the screen. He thought she judged herself much too harshly. He reached over and grasped her hand. She held on to him tightly.

After the film concluded, the audience rose as one and gave it a standing ovation. The lights came up and a podium was brought onto the stage. Several workers quickly set the stage for the question-and-answer session that was to follow shortly thereafter.

Sitting on the chairs onstage would be the director, videographer, writers and the theme song's composer, as well as he and Petra.

During the question-and-answer session, he was happy the audience was fired up and genuinely interested in the show. That made the experience much more enjoyable.

The moderator was a host from one of the network's game shows, Rick Walsh, a tall, handsome, thirty-something African American who was impeccably dressed and great at loosening up an audience.

At first the questions were specifically about the content of the show and its origins. The audience wanted to know who had thought of the show's concept, and Chance was happy to tell them that he'd dreamed up the idea after meeting Petra at the offices of the Bitty Berensen Primate Conservancy. A woman stood up and said, "I remember Bitty Berensen. I used to love watching her TV specials back in the day."

On a whim, Chance stood up and said, "Then you're in luck, because we're honored tonight by the presence of that great lady's son, Jon Berensen. Jon, won't you stand up!"

Jon, looking pleasantly surprised, rose from his seat and playfully saluted the woman who had mentioned his mother. He was handsome and debonair, and with that rugged look of an outdoorsman. The lady, who was middle-aged and quite attractive herself, blushed and joked, "Gee, you could be Tarzan's stunt double!"

"I'll take that compliment, madam, in the good intent it was given," Jon said gallantly. "And thank you for remembering my mother so fondly." Then both he and the woman sat down.

"Jon is a coproducer with the show," Chance informed the audience. "Petra did research for the Bitty Berensen Primate Conservancy for years, and it was through them that we met."

He saw no reason to bring up why he had been at the meeting that day: to help solve the conservancy's financial problems. Jon had recently told him there had been a resurgence in donations and the conservancy was back on steady legs. He was happy for him.

Another woman stood, and Chance saw that it was the same reporter from Channel 13 whose question Petra had answered earlier that evening on the red carpet. "I noticed something interesting," she said. "You and Ms. Gaines are wearing matching wedding bands—nice engagement ring, by the way—and you arrived together tonight. A while ago there was a rumor that you and she had eloped to Las Vegas. Is there any truth to that rumor, Mr. Youngblood?"

Chance and Petra had discussed the possibility that the subject of their marital status might come up tonight, and they'd agreed that if it did, they would come out of hiding to the world. Therefore, he turned and gestured to Petra to join him. She rose and they held hands as he announced, "Petra and I were indeed married in Las Vegas several weeks ago. But if any network is going to get the exclusive story, it'll be ours!"

There was thunderous applause. Everyone, apparently, enjoyed a good love story. People stood up, and one woman down front started dancing in the aisle. It was Virginia Gaines, Petra's mother. "I have a question for you," she said after the applause had subsided. "When's the wedding ceremony for the family and friends? Getting married in Vegas is good and fine, but what about tradition?"

Chance turned to Petra and said, "Sweetheart, you haven't told your mother about our plan to have a big party for friends and family at the beginning of the year?"

Petra smiled at her mother. "The party's in February, Mom."

"All right, then," said Virginia, satisfied. She went and sat down beside Alphonse in the front row.

Everyone in the theater, possibly surprised by the

fact that the woman with the dance moves in the front row turned out to be Petra's mother, responded with another round of raucous laughter, and Chance took that opportunity to bend and kiss his wife on the lips. The photographers in the audience couldn't resist capturing the moment on film. The evening had been a resounding success!

A week later, the show debuted on the network on Sunday night. The next morning, Chance told Petra that they'd gotten the lion's share of viewers in their time slot. Over seventeen million people had tuned in, which he said was a phenomenal number for a show of its kind. He told her that his hope was that the numbers would stay the same or increase with subsequent episodes. The network had ordered eight episodes for the first season, but if the show was a success, the network would bump that up to twelve.

All that television jargon kind of went over her head, but she could see by the excited glimmer in his eyes that he was pleased with the numbers.

They were sitting across from each other having breakfast in the kitchen. He was scheduled to go in to work later because they were going to check on the renovations on the brownstone this morning. Work on the four-bedroom, three-bath townhouse was supposed to last three months, tops. She thought that estimate a bit optimistic, but Chance was of the mind that if he kept an eye on the contractors they would get the work done in that time. Petra had suggested he let her handle the contractors since she was versed in their language. She reminded him that she and Susie had renovated Susie's house with very little help from males. Also, she was currently not working on anything except the tie-in book for *Primates of the Congo*, and she was nearly finished writing it.

"You have enough to think about with work," she said, looking at him with concern.

"Are you sure it won't stress you out?" he asked. "We don't want the baby's health to be compromised."

"If it gets stressful, I'll step back," she promised.

He seemed to be turning it over in his mind and then, reluctantly she believed, said, "All right. But I hate putting that burden entirely on you."

Three months later, the house was still not done. Petra approved of the quality of work; however, workers sometimes showed up late or not at all, and the contractor didn't seem able to curtail their lackadaisical attitude. Finally, one day she got to the townhouse early enough to catch the contractor alone before the workmen started straggling in and confronted him.

By this time, she was six months pregnant and had quite the baby bump. "Jack," she said to him the moment she came through the front door of the brownstone. He was measuring one of the big windows in the great room when she walked in. He turned around to face her.

Jack O'Hara was a big burly man in his late thirties with green eyes and thick dark brown hair. His eyes lit up when he saw her. Petra got the feeling he was partial to pregnant women because the bigger she got, the more solicitous he got. He didn't want her on her feet too long, he worried if she didn't wear a face mask when they were painting and so forth. She was careful also, so she appreciated his thoughtfulness.

But today, she meant business. "Jack, I've got to ask you a question and I hope you'll be completely honest with me."

Bushy eyebrows rose questioningly. "Sure, Petra, what is it?"

"I try not to be underfoot when you guys are working, but I've noticed that your people don't seem to be on a tight schedule, and we're behind here." She put her hand on her belly. "This little guy will be coming soon, and we'd like to be moved in and prepared for him. You do understand my concern."

"Yes, I do, and I'm behind these guys every day to show up and do the work."

"The work's not shoddy," Petra said. "And I appreciate your making sure that when the work's done, it's done well. My complaint is how slow the progress is. I've noticed some people show up hours after work has begun."

Jack nodded, a hangdog expression on his face. "I know what you're referring to, Petra, and I'm working on it."

Then it occurred to her the reason why Jack was

having problems with some of his men. "Jack, do you have relatives working for you, and they know you won't fire them so they're taking advantage of your kindness?"

Jack's mouth hung open in shock. "How did you know?"

Petra smiled. "I have relatives, too."

"One's my brother, the lazy bum. He's always been jealous of my success. I'd fire him, but if I fire him, our mom will have a fit."

"You don't have to fire him," Petra said, eyes narrowed, but with a smile on her lips. "Do you think he resents you so much that, out of spite, he'd let you lose this job?"

Jack considered the question. "No, I don't think he resents me that much. That means no food in his mouth, too."

"Okay," Petra said. "I'll tell them I need this house done by say, the end of the month?"

"Yeah, we should be able to get it done perfectly for you by then if no one slacks off," Jack said.

"Good. When they all get here this morning, I'll tell them that if the job isn't done by the end of the month, I'm firing your company because I don't have time for this. And you know pregnant women don't play."

Jack chuckled. "No ma'am. And I apologize for the hassle."

When the six men on Jack's payroll got there, Petra laid down the law.

It worked, because three weeks later the house was done according to her and Chance's specifications.

The show's ratings continued to steadily climb and her belly continued to grow. Checkups with Dr. DuBois were all good. Her baby was developing nicely. She and Chance didn't want to know the sex of the baby until she or he was born, so Dr. DuBois had kept the ultrasound results a secret. The only thing she and Chance cared about was that the baby was healthy. Although Petra had a sneaking suspicion the baby was a boy, while Chance kept talking about how great it would be if they had a girl who looked just like her.

They moved into the brownstone the very next day after the workers left. Chance hired a company that treated their belongings as if they were museum quality treasures, so there was not one dish broken during the move. Then he hired a full contingent of domestic workers to unpack boxes and arrange the furniture according to Petra's keen decorative style. He didn't want her lifting a finger, let alone a heavy box.

After they were in the house, all Petra had to do was go into nesting mode and await the arrival of their baby.

Chapter 15

From the first episode to the eighth, *Primates of the Congo* earned excellent ratings and Petra became a sought-after guest on late-night and early morning talk shows. After the book was published, she had a book signing at an independent New York City bookstore, where the profits from the sales would go to helping the homeless and people with HIV/AIDS. Petra had suggested that particular bookstore, Chance guessed, because she was thinking the sales of the books at that venue would benefit the people they served, plus the conservancy would get something out of it since those reading the book would learn about the conservancy's efforts to save the primates and hopefully be inspired to donate to it.

He thought his wife was brilliant. He also thought that, at nine months pregnant, she should be slowing down. However, Petra's energy level seemed to have increased after the first trimester. She was no longer nauseated, and except for her back aching a little, she showed no signs of discomfort. But then, she was the type of person who rarely complained.

On the day of the book signing, he insisted on going with her, although she assured him that if he'd prefer to go to work, she already had an entourage: his sister, his mother and Susie were all going to be there to support her.

He stood in the huge walk-in closet that morning watching her try to smooth a snug-fitting tunic over her big belly. She was wearing leggings that looked like jeans but were obviously made of some stretchy material because there was no way she was going to get into regular jeans in her condition. He smiled when she turned sideways to see how her silhouette looked in her outfit. She grinned. "I look like a python that swallowed a goat."

He laughed because, on the contrary, he thought she looked delectable. Her skin glowed. Her hair was still as thick and lustrous as ever. She was wearing it natural now. No more using a flat iron to straighten it as she sometimes had in the past. It was curly and wild, the way he liked it. As for her body, she turned him on more and more each day. He couldn't stop touching her, and he knew he made a nuisance of himself, especially in bed, while she was trying to sleep. Her temperature would climb during the night and she'd throw the covers off, when all he wanted to do was hold her in his arms. At those times she would prefer some space so the air currents could flow between their bodies, thereby keeping her cool, while he preferred no air whatsoever between his body and hers.

Now, after laughing at her comment, he told her, "You're beautiful and you know it!"

She looked at him with a deadpan expression. "No amount of sweet talk is going to get me back in that bed with you. I've got to be out of here in ten minutes."

"I know, I'm going with you," he said.

"My people will be arriving with a driver very soon," she informed him. "I don't know if there's room enough in the car for you."

"When did the husband become dispensable around here?" he asked, following her from the closet to the bedroom.

"When the husband wasn't part of the plan in the beginning," Petra said calmly. "Come outside if you want, and we'll see if we can fit you in."

Sure enough, when they walked out of the brownstone there, waiting at the curb, was a late model Mercedes Benz GLS SUV. He recognized the model. He knew there was room for him because it could seat seven adults. He peered inside. His mother, sister and Susie were sitting in the back, in the third row. Behind the wheel was a professional driver whom he didn't recognize, but the person in the passenger seat beside him was his father.

"What is this, a conspiracy?" he said loudly as Petra climbed into the second row of seating and slid over so he could get in, too.

"Boy, just get in," his mother said, laughing. "We thought you had to work today."

"Good morning, Chance," called Alia and Susie.

"Good morning, ladies," he returned the greeting. Then, "Dad, how did they rope you into this?"

"I'm no dummy," said his father. "When I get the chance to spend the day with four, count 'em four, beautiful ladies, I get on board."

To which his mother said, "I didn't marry no dummy!"

"I didn't, either," Petra whispered as she kissed his cheek. "Thanks for coming, babe."

That made him feel indispensable.

When they got to the bookstore in the SoHo neighborhood of Manhattan, Petra realized they'd done well by hiring a car and driver. There was very little parking near the bookstore on the cobblestone street. Once there, she and her entourage got out and the driver left to find a parking space.

To her surprise, there was already a crowd waiting on the sidewalk outside the store. They made their way to the door to go inside and were met by the bookstore manager, a very nice middle-aged woman with brown hair and eyes. Genuine warmth emanated from her as she greeted them when they got inside. The space had high ceilings and hardwood floors. The bookstore was a combination bookstore/café, and the aroma of coffee was in the air. "Welcome!" she said excitedly, looking at Petra. "I'm Peggy and you're Dr. Gaines-Youngblood. I read your book and I loved it. Actually, I enjoyed all three of your books. You've led a fascinating life."

Petra smiled at her. "Thank you so much!" Then she introduced Chance and everyone else.

Peggy led them through the store's customers to the back of the building, where a large table with a comfortable-looking straight-backed chair with a thick cushion was set up for Petra to sit on and sign books. Someone had put a banner up that read: Welcome, Dr. Petra Gaines-Youngblood!

"This is nice," Petra said appreciatively.

"I hope you'll be comfortable," Peggy told her, her eyes on Petra's stomach.

"Oh, I'm sure I will be," said Petra with a winning smile.

"All right, then," Peggy said. "Can I get you some water, a cup of tea, anything before we get started?" She glanced at Petra's party. "And can I get anyone something to drink?"

Petra and everyone else politely declined her offer, after which Peggy signaled her assistant waiting nearby. Petra guessed it was the assistant's cue to usher those who wanted to meet Petra and buy a book to start lining up, because shortly afterward she was busy signing books. Peggy and her assistant kept the line moving briskly.

Petra noticed Chance, his parents, Alia and Susie were sharing a table a few feet away in the café section of the bookstore. She looked up occasionally and smiled in their direction while she chatted with the bookstore's customers and signed their books. She hadn't done much in the way of promotions for her previous books, so this was quite the experience for her.

An hour after getting there, she must have already signed over a hundred books and the line was still out the door. She'd agreed to sign for two hours and was determined to last that long. With the baby pressing against her bladder, she made frequent trips to the bathroom these days and would have to take a bathroom break soon.

Suddenly, she felt the baby shift. In fact, she not only felt it, but saw the imprint of her baby inside of her on her stomach when the baby moved. A customer waiting to get his book signed also noticed it.

He smiled. "Looks like someone is changing position."

"This little guy likes to dance," she joked.

Petra managed to smile at him, but she was a little concerned. She'd been having twinges all morning. Not pain, exactly, but instances where the baby would move, her belly would grow tight and then relax. Dr. DuBois had told her about Braxton Hicks contractions, or false labor. She hadn't been unduly concerned when she'd started having them before dawn. She hadn't even mentioned them to Chance. He tended to panic when there was something wrong with her health. She stubbed her toe not too long ago, and he'd wanted to take her to the emergency room for an X-ray. He'd totally overreacted.

She continued to sign books, enjoying meeting the customers, a diverse group who were from all kinds of backgrounds. Peggy and her assistant supported her by handing her the books and keeping the customers moving along. Peggy also showed concern for her energy level by offering refreshments from time to time.

Peggy leaned toward her now and asked, "How're you doing? I didn't know what to expect when you offered to come here and sign. I hope we don't run out of books!"

"How many left outside?" Petra asked. She estimated there were fifty people waiting inside the store.

"The line outside is nearly a block long," Peggy said almost apologetically.

Petra suppressed a tired sigh. She was actually getting fatigued. Maybe it was dehydration. She hadn't been sipping from her water bottle because she was trying to stave off a trip to the bathroom. She drank some water and continued signing.

Half an hour later, she had to go to the bathroom. Rising, she asked Peggy, "Where's the restroom?"

"You can use the one in my office," Peggy said gently. "Follow me."

It was, fortunately, a short walk, because as soon as Petra got to the small, very clean restroom, her water broke. Peggy had gotten only two feet away from the bathroom door before Petra called, "Peggy, please go get my husband, Chance! I think I'm going to have this baby any minute."

She cursed her habit of ignoring pain and being stoic. She should have known those weren't Braxton Hicks contractions she'd been having all morning, but real contractions. She was going to deliver her baby in a bookstore.

She tried not to panic as she heard Peggy screaming, not at all trying to disguise her own panic. "Chance! Chance! Petra's having the baby, come quick!"

Chance was on his feet and racing in the direction of Peggy's voice as soon as he heard the word *baby*. His mind, although gripped by panic at the thought of what might transpire in the next few minutes, also told him it was imperative for him to stay calm.

Peggy was frantically waving him forward. "This way!"

Out of the corner of his eye, Chance registered that everyone at the table where he'd been sitting was following him. So when he got to Peggy and she pointed in the direction of her small office, he wasn't surprised to have several people go into the office with him. He found Petra sitting on the toilet, holding her stomach. Her face was twisted in pain, but she laughed anyway when she looked up at him. "Today's our baby's birthday."

He went to her and kneeled in front of her, not caring that he was kneeling in some kind of liquid. "Can we make it to the car?" he asked hopefully.

She winced and shook her head. "I don't think so. My water broke and the contractions are coming on top of each other. I misread my symptoms, sweetie. I thought the contractions I was having were false ones. They've been coming and going for hours."

Chance made a decision. "Okay, darling." He rose and helped her off the toilet. Her leggings were soaked. He helped her out of them and her panties. The tunic she was wearing was long enough to give her some modicum of modesty.

Behind him, his mother asked, "What can we do, son?"

"Call 911," he said. "Petra's having the baby now."

Peggy, standing in the doorway to her office, said, "I'll go see if there's a medical professional in the store."

She left, and Chance's mom got on her cell and dialed 911.

Chance picked Petra up and carried her to the small leather couch in front of the desk in the office. He gently laid her down.

Peggy returned with an African American woman with silver hair wearing a pair of scrubs. "I'm Alice

Montgomery. I'm a nurse," she said when she saw the tableau opening up before her. "I just got off from work and came by here to meet Dr. Gaines-Youngblood."

"Thank God," Chance said.

Alice got to work ordering everyone around her to clear out of the room except for Chance. When the room was empty except for the three of them, she told Chance, "I want you behind her on the couch, supporting her back."

Chance got into position. In the meantime, Petra was moaning slightly, but otherwise quiet. Her eyes were keenly watching the woman who was there to help her, though. "Just tell me what to do," she told Alice. Chance knew she was concentrating on doing everything right.

Alice took a careful perusal between Petra's splayed legs and said, "This kid isn't wasting any time. The head's crowning."

She looked straight into Petra's eyes. "I know you want to push and you're going to in a minute, but I need you to try not to push too hard. Push, but gently. Do you understand?"

Petra took a shuddering breath and slowly released it. "Yes, I understand."

"Okay, then, here we go," said Alice with a smile, and she bent to the task. "Push, Dr. Gaines-Youngblood, push!"

"Call me, Petra," Petra said as she pushed. "I feel like we're already intimate friends."

Alice laughed, but her concentration was unswerving. Chance held Petra underneath the arms as she lay against his chest. He hoped he provided the stability she needed. He hoped she knew how much he was praying she and their baby would come through this with flying colors. He'd never known this kind of fear. But in spite of the fear, he felt fortunate to be there because this was a moment he'd never forget, and they were going through it together.

The next thing he knew, Petra fell back against him as though she no longer possessed any muscle control. Then the baby was crying and Alice was cradling the baby in her two hands while simultaneously looking the baby over.

"It's a boy!" she cried joyfully. "And he's a big one."

The baby was covered in mucus and blood, with the umbilical cord dangling. Alice laid the baby on Petra's stomach and Petra enveloped the child in her arms. Chance took his jacket off, covered his wife and child with it and kissed both Petra's head and his son's.

"I love you, Pet. I love you so much. You and our son."

"I love you, too," Petra said, gently cradling her son in her arms. "What are we going to call him?"

"We never could settle on a name," Chance said. "No juniors in the family. How about Benjamin Alphonse James, after your grandfather and both our dads?"

"That's a lot of name for such a small guy," Petra joked. "But I like it."

She regarded Alice, who had taken a step back to allow the family their privacy. "Thank you, Alice. We're grateful for your help."

Alice smiled at her. "I'm honored," she said. "I'm a fan."

Petra laughed softly. "I'm very appreciative. You've got to come to our get-together in February, Alice. You'll be our honored guest."

Petra and Chance hosted the family get-together at their brownstone in Harlem in February. They had a nondenominational minister perform their wedding ceremony, with Chance holding Benji in his arms. Both their families were there, as well as some of their closest friends, including Paul and Noella Olomide from Kinshasa. Paul had secured a spot on the show for season two. All of the male relatives they'd named Benji after were present: her dad, Alphonse; his dad James; and her Grandpa Benjamin Beck, there with her step-grandmother, Mabel. Grandpa Beck was particularly pleased there was another male child in the family.

Petra found out that Alice Montgomery was a widow with four children who, although she was a respected, hardworking RN, couldn't afford repairs that her house in Queens sorely needed. Chance insisted on paying to have it fully renovated. They invited Alice and all of her children to the party. Her children were among the many children of family and friends who attended.

At the get-together, they also found out Meghan and Leo had been approved to adopt a three-year-old boy, and shortly after getting the good news, Meghan had learned she was pregnant. The fertility specialist who'd treated Leo had been right when she'd told him twenty-five to thirty-five percent of couples who were dealing with his type of infertility would eventually have children. Now they would have two children to love. Petra marveled at the way the universe worked. She knew that Meghan and Leo had feared they would never be blessed with a child.

Besides that, Desiree and Decker were also expecting. Petra imagined her mother would be dancing in the aisle for quite a while.

She was so happy with her little family, she might try a few steps herself.

She and Chance stood together looking over the people they loved having a good time in their home. Chance still held Benji in his arms. He loved looking after their son.

"You know, Pet," he said, peering into her upturned face. "This never would have happened if I hadn't picked you up in that bar."

"Who picked up whom?" was Petra's reply to that.

* * * * *

Soulful and sensual romance featuring multicultural characters.

Look for brand-new Kimani stories in special 2-in-1 volumes.

Available September 3, 2019

Forever Mine* & *Falling for the Beauty Queen
by Donna Hill and Carolyn Hector

Spark of Desire* & *All for You
by Sheryl Lister and Elle Wright

The CEO's Dilemma* & *Undeniable Passion
by Lindsay Evans and Kayla Perrin

Then Came You* & *Written with Love
by Kianna Alexandra and Joy Avery

www.Harlequin.com

KPST0719

SPECIAL EXCERPT FROM

Rita feels an instant connection to homegrown hunk Keith Burke. A hot fling with the sweet-talking Realtor could be just what she needs. Until an unexpected arrival shatters the fragile bond between Rita and Keith...and their trust in a future together.

Read on for a sneak peek at
Undeniable Passion,
the next exciting installment in the Burkes of Sheridan Falls series by Kayla Perrin!

As Rita watched Keith carry her two large suitcases from the trunk, she couldn't help thinking that he was seriously attractive. He was the kind of guy she could enjoy gazing at. Like someone on a safari checking out the wild animals, she could watch him and not get bored.

However, she knew that wouldn't be wise. Keith wasn't a man on display. And he was the kind of man that she knew would be risky to get close to. If she had him pegged right, he had an easy way with the ladies, and how many times had Rita seen women fall for guys like that during vulnerable times? She knew her heart was especially weak after her breakup with Rashad a few months ago and the reality that their wedding would have been just weeks away. The fact that her mother was getting married on top of that only made her heart more fragile.

Vulnerable women looking for a way to forget or ease their pain often brought on more heartbreak. Rita read about it in the various stories sent to her for her magazine, *Unlock Your Power*. The magazine was a voice for women who'd endured devastating situations but were picking up the pieces of their lives. Sharing their stories was a way to help ease their pain and let others in similar situations know that they weren't alone.

So Rita definitely knew better than to think of men as a distraction. She could look at Keith or any other man and leave it at that. It was a matter of choice, wasn't it? Knowing the risks and behaving accordingly.

The first rule of guarding your heart was to not get involved on any level. Keith was simply a man who wanted to help her out—a good guy doing the courteous thing. No need to let herself think that there might be more motives to his actions.

Keith exited the bedroom, where he had brought her two big suitcases.

"I know it's a lot, but considering I might be here for a while..." Her voice trailed off. "Speaking of which, are there laundry facilities?"

"Excellent question. Forgot to mention that. There is a stacked washer and dryer in the cupboard in the kitchen. You'll see it."

"Perfect, thank you."

Keith headed to the door again, and Rita said, "I can get the rest."

"You don't have too much more. I'll get the big box I saw in the back seat. Plus, wasn't there a case of water?"

"Yes, but—" Rita stopped when her phone rang. She pulled it out from the back pocket of her jeans and glanced at the screen. It was her best friend, Maeve.

Keith jogged down the steps, and Rita swiped to answer the call. "Hey."

"How's it going?" Maeve asked without preamble.

"Good. I got here okay."

"You said something about a mishap," Maeve said, concern in her voice.

"Yeah, but… It's not really a big deal. It was a small fender bender, but the situation's been resolved."

"Someone hit you?" Maeve asked.

"Actually, I hit someone."

"What?"

"I was distracted for a second when I was pulling up to the coffee shop. And…it was barely a touch. No real damage."

"Did you leave a note for the owner?"

"Actually, he was in the car," Rita said as she watched Keith make his way back up the steps with the box of food items. "There was just a bit of paint transfer." He gave her a little smile as he passed her, and Rita smiled back. Then she stepped outside the unit to continue her call. "I offered to pay. He refused. Everything's good."

"Okay, that's great to hear. Just make sure you follow up. You don't want the guy to start claiming back pains tomorrow."

"I doubt that's going to happen. Something tells me that people in small towns like this are honest, not opportunistic. And from the sense I got from the guy…I highly doubt he would do that."

"All right, if you're sure, then I trust your judgment."

"I am sure," Rita said. She didn't bother to tell her that the very man whose car she'd hit was currently helping her move in.

Don't miss Undeniable Passion
by Kayla Perrin, available September 2019
wherever Harlequin® Kimani Romance™
books and ebooks are sold.

KPEXP0719

Love Harlequin romance?

DISCOVER.

Be the first to find out about promotions, news and exclusive content!

Facebook.com/HarlequinBooks

Twitter.com/HarlequinBooks

Instagram.com/HarlequinBooks

Pinterest.com/HarlequinBooks

ReaderService.com

EXPLORE.

Sign up for the Harlequin e-newsletter and download a free book from any series at **TryHarlequin.com.**

CONNECT.

Join our Harlequin community to share your thoughts and connect with other romance readers!
Facebook.com/groups/HarlequinConnection

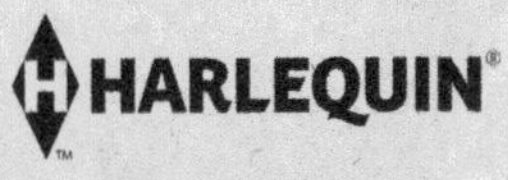

ROMANCE WHEN
YOU NEED IT

HSOCIAL2018